THEY WERE SPECIAL,
SET APART BY THEIR MARVELOUS GIFTS—
AND THEIR SHATTERING SECRETS. . . .

———

Cinnamon
She lives in the shadows.

Ice
She hides behind a wall of silence.

Rose
She is a stranger in a strange world.

Honey
She must hold on to her dreams—
or they will slip away forever. . . .

V.C.ANDREWS®

Shooting Stars

Together in one marvelous collection,
here is the bestselling miniseries
featuring four truly unforgettable heroines.

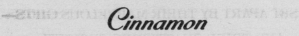

Cinnamon

It wasn't just hard to believe that I was on my way to visit my mother in a mental clinic . . . it was painful and actually very frightening. I could feel the trembling start in my legs and slowly vibrate up into my spine. The building looked so white in the afternoon sun, the reflection made me reach for my sunglasses. The moment I saw my image in the car window, a whole new persona came over me. I brushed back my hair, took a deep breath, and moved forward like an actress about to step on a stage. It felt good, liberating. Pretending was like wearing a mask, and when I wore a mask, no one could see how terrible and how frightened I felt inside.

Ice

I was smart enough to realize the school psychologist had a theory that I was trying to remain invisible because my mother didn't want to be a mother, and my existence reminded her she was. I had stood by quietly many times when I was much younger and wished I was invisible, especially when Mama told new friends I wasn't really her child. She'd lie and say I was her sister's child, and she was just keeping me for a few years. . . .

Rose

Near midnight, I saw the car headlights pulling into our driveway. *Daddy,* I thought. *Finally.* But when I stepped up to the window, I saw it wasn't Daddy. It was a police car with the emblem on the side identifying it as a Georgia State Police vehicle. Two officers stepped out, put on their hats, and walked toward our front door. For a moment, I couldn't move; I couldn't breathe. . . .

Honey

As we started away, Grandad Lester came out of nowhere onto the driveway and stood in the wash of Chandler's car headlights. His gray hair looked like it was on fire, his eyes blazing at us. Chandler hit the brake pedal and I gasped. Suddenly, Grandad raised his hand and I saw he was holding his sacred old Bible. He held it up like some potential victim of a vampire would hold up a cross in a horror movie, and then he disappeared into the shadows. I choked back my tears. I was filled with a mixture of anger and fear. . . .

V.C. Andrews® Books

Published by POCKET BOOKS

V.C. ANDREWS®

Shooting Stars

POCKET BOOKS
New York   London   Toronto   Sydney   Singapore

Following the death of Virginia Andrews, the Andrews family worked with a carefully selected writer to organize and complete Virginia Andrews' stories and to create additional novels, of which this is one, inspired by her storytelling genius.

 POCKET BOOKS, a division of Simon & Schuster, Inc.
1230 Avenue of the Americas, New York, NY 10020

Cinnamon copyright © 2001 by the Vanda General Partnership
Ice copyright © 2001 by the Vanda General Partnership
Rose copyright © 2001 by the Vanda General Partnership
Honey copyright © 2001 by the Vanda General Partnership

These titles were previously published individually by Pocket Books

ISBN: 0-7434-4902-9

First Pocket Books paperback printing December 2002

10 9 8 7 6 5 4 3 2 1

V.C. ANDREWS and VIRGINIA ANDREWS are registered trademarks of the Vanda General Partnership.

POCKET and colophon are registered trademarks of Simon & Schuster, Inc.

For information regarding special discounts for bulk purchases, please contact Simon & Schuster Special Sales at 1-800-456-6798 or business@simonandschuster.com

Cover design by Jim Lebbad
Front cover illustration by Lisa Falkenstern

Printed in the U.S.A.

Contents

—m—

Contents

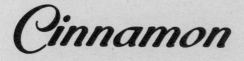

Cinnamon

Prologue

—⁓—

"Cinnamon Carlson."

I was just as surprised as everyone else to hear Miss Hamilton call out my name. Edith Booth, the student hall monitor and everyone's candidate for this year's Miss Goody Two-shoes, had just interrupted our English literature class. She had opened the door and tapped her perfect little steps across the hardwood floor while walking with flawless posture. Her shoulders were pulled back firmly, and an invisible book was on top of her clump of dull brown hair, hair that everyone knew her mother trimmed unevenly at the base of her neck and around her ears.

She had looked in my direction as soon as she had entered the classroom and then handed Miss Hamilton the note from the principal's office as if it were a speeding ticket or an eviction notice. I wanted to crack an egg over that smug, arrogant little smile she had pasted on her face.

3

Miss Hamilton's face was already flushed with crimson frustration at the interruption. She had just gotten into the flow of Desdemona's pathetic defense right before Othello was about to smother her to death with a pillow. Even some of the zombies in class, as Clarence Baron and I liked to refer to them, were glued to her performance. What could you expect? It was practically the only live theater some of them had ever experienced.

After having once made a futile effort to become an actress, Miss Hamilton had fallen back into a teaching career like someone who had tried to ski professionally and quickly found herself on her rear end gliding down into mediocrity. She spent the rest of her young adult life gazing wistfully at the skiers who went gracefully beyond her. Now, in the role of the school's drama coach, she dreams of being the inspiration, the greatest influence on the next Meryl Streep or Jodie Foster. Lately, she's been eyeing me, urging me to try out for the school play, which was something Mommy thought I should do as well because of the role-playing she and I often perform in the attic of our house.

"You're so good at it, Cinnamon," she would tell me. "Someday, you'll be a wonderful actress."

You have to be a wonderful actress or actor to survive in this world, I thought. Controlling your face, your voice, your posture and most of all being able to invent reasons and excuses to answer questions are the real skills of self-defense. To me, especially lately, going out in the world with honesty on your lips was the same as going out naked.

I looked up when I heard the door open and Miss Hamilton pause. While she had been reciting her

Desdemona, I had kept my eyes glued to the top of my desk. Her over-the-top histrionics was embarrassing to watch, and I really liked *Othello*. Listening to Miss Hamilton read it was similar to being forced to observe someone ruin a good recipe for crème brûlée. Everyone who hadn't eaten the dessert before would think this was it, this terrible tasting stuff was it? They would never ask for it again.

I knew instinctively that Desdemona at this point in the play should still not believe it was possible Othello would kill her. Her voice should ring with disbelief, innocence, love and faith. Why didn't Miss Hamilton know that, or if she did, why couldn't she express it?

How many times had Shakespeare spun in his grave?

I liked Miss Hamilton, probably more than any of my other teachers, but I was never good at overlooking faults. I always flip over the brightest coin and look at the tarnish.

"Your grandmother is waiting for you at Mr. Kaplan's office," Miss Hamilton said.

I looked back at Clarence Baron who was practically the only one my age with whom I communicated these days. I hesitated to call him my boyfriend. We hadn't crossed that line yet and I was still not sure at the time if we ever would. That wasn't because I thought he was unattractive. Quite the contrary. He had an interesting face with dark, lonely eyes that revealed not only his sensitivity but also his intelligence. He kept his chocolate brown hair long and unruly, full of wild curls. I knew he thought it made him resemble Ludwig van Beethoven, not that Clarence had any interest in composing music. He just enjoyed classical music and knew more about it than anyone else I knew.

He was slim, almost too thin for his six feet one inch height, but I liked his angular jaw and nearly perfect nose over a strong full mouth. I've overheard girls often commenting about him, always saying things like "Too bad he's so weird. He's sexy."

I knew why they thought he was weird. He admitted that he couldn't help doing what he called his rituals. For example, Clarence was in the last seat in the first row. It was a very important thing for him to take the same seat in all of his classes, if he could. I suppose it was really compulsion. Another ritual was never leaving a building on an odd step. He counted his steps toward the exit and always made sure he walked out on an even number. I've often seen him stop and go back just to be sure. He also eats everything on his dinner plate from left to right, no matter what it is, and he's right-handed! He even manages to do it with pasta. I don't ask him why he does these strange things anymore. If I did, he would just say, "It feels right," or he would shrug and say, "I don't know why, Cinnamon. I just do it."

Clarence raised his heavy, dark brown eyebrows into question marks and I sucked in my breath and shook my head.

I had no idea why my grandmother was coming to take me out of school, but I did have fears boiling under the surface of my confusion.

Two days ago, Mommy had suffered her second miscarriage. After the first miscarriage eight years ago, she and Daddy seemed to have given up on having another child. I even harbored the belief that they had stopped having sex. Rarely did I see them express any passion toward each other, especially after Grandmother Beverly had moved in with us. A peck on the cheek, a quick embrace or a brush of hands was generally all I witnessed, not that I spied on my parents or anything. It was just an observation of something that had settled into their lives and mine, seeping through our days like a cold, steady rain.

So I was just as surprised as my grandmother when one day a little more than six months ago, Mommy made the announcement at dinner.

After swallowing a piece of bread, she released a deep sigh and said, "Well, I'm pregnant again."

Grandmother Beverly, who had moved in with us shortly after Grandfather Carlson had died, dropped her fork on the plate, nearly breaking the dish. She turned and looked at my father as if he had betrayed some trust, some agreement in blood they had signed.

"At her age?" she asked him. "She's going to have another child now?" She turned to my mother, who had always had the ability to ignore Grandmother Beverly, to seem not to hear her or see her whenever she wanted, even if she was sitting or standing right in front of her. She could go as deaf and as stony as a marble statue. Of course, that made Grandmother Beverly even angrier.

"You're forty-two years old, Amber. What are you thinking?" she snapped with her same old authority.

Grandmother Beverly has never hesitated to express her opinions or make her demands. My grandfather had been a meek, gentle man whose strongest criticism or chastisement of her was a shaking of his head and only twice at that. He went left to right, left to right and stopped with a shrug and that was always the extent of his resistence. No arguments, no pouts, no rants or raves or anything added. Once, when I tried to describe him to Clarence, I dryly said, "Think of him as Poland after Hitler's invasion."

It was not difficult for me to think of Grandmother Beverly as a ruthless dictator.

"What I'm thinking," Mommy replied slowly to Grandmother Beverly's question, "is that I'll give birth to a healthy child. Besides, it's not so uncommon these days for a woman my age to give birth. I recently read where a woman in her fifties got pregnant. And not as a surrogate mother either," she quickly added.

Grandmother Beverly's eyes darkened and narrowed with disapproval. She picked up her fork and returned to her methodical eating, gazing furiously at my father who busied himself with cutting his steak. After that, silence boomed in our ears as loudly as Beethoven's Fifth Symphony.

However, silence was no sign of surrender when it came to my grandmother. She never missed an opportunity to express her disapproval. All through Mommy's months of pregnancy, Grandmother Beverly nagged and nipped at her like a yapping poodle. As soon as Mommy started to show, Grandmother's complaints intensified.

"A woman your age walking around in maternity clothes," she barked. "What a sight you must make. You even have some strands of gray in your hair, and now you have to watch what you eat more than ever. Women at your age gain weight more easily. You'll end up looking like my sister Lucille who popped children out like a rabbit and ended up resembling a baby elephant. Her hips grew so big, she once got stuck in a chair," Grandmother emphasized, looking at me and nodding.

Whenever she couldn't get a reaction from Mommy, she would try directing herself at me as if I were a translator who would explain what she had said.

"Aunt Lucille has only three children, doesn't she?" I asked.

"That's too many," Grandmother Beverly replied so quickly anyone would have thought she and I had rehearsed the dialogue. "Children are expensive and difficult nowadays. They make you years older than you are in short order. They need, need, need. When I was a child, the word *want* did not exist. My mouth was stuffed with 'please' and 'thank you' and 'no sir' and 'yes ma'am' and that was that. I can't even imagine my father's reaction to my asking him for a new dress or a car or money to waste on silly jewelry. Why if he was alive today and saw some of those . . . I don't know what you call them . . . walking around with rings in their noses and in their belly buttons, he'd think the world had come to an end and rightly so."

"Well, they'll be only two children in this house," I said and looked at Mommy. She was trying hard not to pay attention, but Grandmother Beverly was wearing her down, her snipping words coming at her from every direction like a pack of hyenas. By now Mommy was full of aches and pains and too pale, I thought.

And then she suffered the miscarriage. She started to hemorrhage one night and had to be rushed to the hospital. I woke to the sounds of her screams and panic. Daddy wouldn't let me go along. He came home alone hours and hours later and announced she had lost the baby.

Grandmother Beverly felt no guilt or sorrow. Her reaction was to claim it was Nature's way of saying no to something that shouldn't have been begun in the first place. When they brought Mommy home the day after, Mommy couldn't bear to look at her. She didn't look at anyone very much for that matter, not even me. Her eyes were distant, her sorrow shutting her up tightly, a prisoner in her own body.

Now I trembled inside imagining the possible reasons for my grandmother's very unexpected arrival at school. Quickly closing my copy of *Othello* and my notebook, I gathered all of my things and rose. I knew everyone in the class was watching me, their eyes loyally following my every gesture, but most of my life I've felt people's eyes on me. It doesn't bother me anymore. In fact, it probably never did or at least never as much as it should. That indifference, or that dramatic *fourth wall*, as Miss Hamilton likes to call it, was always up, always between me and the rest of the world whenever I wanted it to be. In that sense I'm really like Mommy, although I must say, Daddy can be deaf and dumb at the drop of a nasty word, too. He certainly was that way more often around Grandmother Beverly these days.

I know that people, including some of my teachers and especially my grandmother, would say I deliberately attract attention because of the way I dress and behave. My auburn hair is thick and long, down to my shoulder blades. I won't cut it any shorter than that and barely trim my bangs. Sometimes, strands fall over my eyes or over one eye and I leave them there, looking out at the world, my teachers, other students, everything and everyone through a sheer, rust-tinted curtain. I know it unnerves some people and especially drives Grandmother Beverly to the point where her pallid face takes on crimson blotches at the crests of her bony cheeks.

"Cut your hair or at least have the decency to brush it back neatly. I can't tell if you're looking at me or what when I speak to you," she often carped. One criticism led to another. She was a spider weaving its web. "And don't you have anything cheerful to wear to school?"

Like Mommy, I favor dark colors. I'm always dressed in black or dark blue, often dark gray, and I put on a translucent white lipstick and black nail polish. I darken my eyebrows and wear too much eyeshadow, and I keep out of the sun, not only because I know it damages your skin, but I like having a light complexion. My skin is so transparent, I can see tiny blue veins in my temples, and I think about my blood moving through these tiny wires to my heart and my brain.

At the moment, my heart felt as though it had been put on pause.

Edith Booth waited for me at the classroom door. She was performing her role as hall monitor, which meant she would escort me out and to the principal's office like some military parade guard. She pressed her thin, crooked lips together and pulled her head up, tightening her neck and her chin. She held the door open, but as I walked through it, I reached back, seized the knob and pulled it hard out of her hands, slamming it behind me.

I could hear the class roar at the sight of her staring into the shut door, her jaw probably dropped, her perfect posture definitely ruined. I heard her fumbling with the knob and then come charging out, flustered, rushing to catch up with me, her heels clicking like an explosion of small firecrackers on the tile corridor floor.

"That wasn't very nice," she said.

I turned and glared at her.

Everyone who knows us and who has seen our house thinks the spirits inside the house will eventually drive us all mad. They think it's haunted. They call it "The Addams Family House." The outside is so dark and it

does have this foreboding presence. I actually believe
Daddy is ashamed of his house. Grandmother Beverly
certainly didn't want him to buy it, but that was one time
Mommy won out over her when it came to having Daddy
decide something. Mommy was determined.

It's a grand Second Empire Victorian house about ten
miles northwest of Tarrytown, New York. The original
owner was a former Civil War officer who had served
under General Grant. His name was Jonathan Demerest
and he had five children, two boys and three girls. Both his
wife Carolyne and his youngest son Abraham died of
smallpox less than a year apart. Their graves, as well as
Jonathan's, are on our property, up on a knoll from where
you could once see miles and miles in any direction. At
least that's what Mommy claimed. She said when they
first moved into the house, the forest wasn't anywhere as
grown as it is today; of course, there weren't all those
houses in one development after another peppering the
face of the landscape like pimples.

"It was a peaceful place, a wonderful place to be
buried," she told me. "It still is, actually. Maybe I should
be buried here, too," she added and I cried because I was
only nine at the time and I didn't want to hear about such
a thing as my own mother's death.

"We all die, Cinnamon," she said with that soft,
loving smile that could always bring my marching heart
back to a slow walk. She would touch my cheek so gently,
her fingers feeling like a warm caressing breeze, and she
would smile a smile full of candlelight, warm, mesmeriz-
ing. "It's not that bad when our time comes. We just move
on," she said looking out at the world below us as if she
already had one foot in the grave. "We just move on to
somewhere quieter. That's all."

"Quieter? How could it be any quieter than this?" I wondered aloud.

"It's quieter inside you," she replied. I didn't understand what that meant for years, but now I do.

I really do.

Anyway, Mommy told me she had fallen in love with our house before she had fallen in love with Daddy, and she got him to buy it after only a year of marriage.

The house appears larger than it really is because it was built on a hill and looms over the roads and homes below us. It has three stories with a cupola that looks like a great hiding place for a monster or a ghost. Some of the kids think I crawl up into it every night and send spells and curses down on unwary travelers below. Whenever I hear these kinds of things about myself, I laugh, toss back my hair and say what Mommy told me Katharine Hepburn once said about publicity: "I don't care what they say about me, as long as it isn't true."

Very few people understand what that means. They think it's just more proof of my weirdness. They don't understand that when people invade your life and uncover the truth about you, they expose things you want to keep private, keep personal so you can keep your self-respect. It's why we lock our doors and close our windows and pull down our shades, especially in my house.

I don't care what impression my house makes on people. I love it as much as Mommy does. Second Empire houses have what are known as mansard roofs, which are roofs having two slopes on all sides with the lower slope steeper than the upper one. The house itself is square, and it has elaborate decorative iron cresting above the upper cornice. The front of the house has paired entry doors with glass in the top half and a half-dozen steps leading up and under the one-story porch. All of the windows are paired. The downstairs ones are all hooded. Mommy loves talking about it, lecturing about the architecture to anyone who will listen.

Grandmother Beverly thought it was a dreadful place to live, even though she readily moved in with us. Mommy said it was Grandmother Beverly's sole idea to move in, despite Daddy's telling me and everyone else that he asked her to move in with us since we had so much room and there was no reason for a woman of her age to have to live alone.

"No reason," Mommy told me, "except to give us peace of mind."

Anyway people often look at me as if they expect that any day now—because we live in the eerie looking, supposedly haunted house—I'll become a raving lunatic and maybe even try to hurt myself. Even when some of my teachers talk to me, I notice they stand a foot or so farther away from me than they stand away from their other students. All I have to do sometimes is stare at someone the way I was staring at Edith Booth and I can see him or her suddenly become overwhelmed with small terrors. The truth is, I've begun to enjoy it. It gives me a sense of power.

"What?" I snapped at her.

She stepped back.

"Mr. Kaplan . . . wants you . . . right away," she stuttered.

"Then stop interrupting me," I ordered. I locked my eyes onto hers and the color fled her cheeks.

She remained a few feet behind me all the way to the principal's office where I found Grandmother Beverly sitting anxiously on the small, imitation leather settee.

She was rubbing her fingers in her palm as if she were trying to sand down some imaginary calluses, something she often did when she was very nervous.

The moment I entered the outer office, she rose to her full five feet four inches of height. Grandfather Carlson had been six feet two inches tall, but he always looked diminished in her presence, and Daddy never seems his full six feet next to her either. Her shadow shrinks people.

"Stature comes from your demeanor, your self-confidence," Mommy once told me when we talked about Grandmother Beverly. "You've got to give the devil her due for that."

Mommy was practically the only person I knew who wasn't intimidated by her, but she wasn't strong enough to do constant battle with her, not with what I've come to think of as the Trojan Horse in our home, my own father. He could be strong in so many ways, but when it came to facing down his own mother, he became a little boy again.

For instance, Grandmother Beverly was as critical of the inside of our house as she was of the outside. She hated Mommy's taste in decorations, furniture, curtains, flooring, even lighting and bathroom fixtures. From the moment she moved in, she seemed determined to slowly change it all. She would point out the smallest imperfection, a tiny stain in a chair, a tear in a rug, and advised Daddy to have it replaced. Once he agreed to that, she went forward to choose what the replacement would be, as if Mommy wasn't even there.

One day a chair would be supplanted or a rug, and when Mommy complained that what Grandmother Beverly had chosen didn't mesh with our decor, Daddy would plead and moan and promise that after this or that there would be no more changes. Of course, there always were.

It was easy to see why I compared Grandmother's march through our house and lives to Hitler's march through Europe. Daddy was our own little Chamberlain promising "Peace for our time," if we just made one more compromise. Then we would be a happy little family again.

That's something we would never be again.

But I didn't know how definite that prophecy was until I went home from school with Grandmother Beverly.

1

Darkness Descends

"What's wrong? Why have you come for me?" I asked her.

Once I had arrived, she had simply started out of the principal's office and begun her stomp through the corridor to the exit for the parking lot. As usual she expected me to trail along like some obedient puppy.

She continued to walk, ignoring my questions. She always fixed herself on her purpose or destination as if she were a guided missile. Getting her to pause, turn or stop required the secret abort code only her own private demon knew and was reluctant to relinquish or reveal. You just had to wait her out, calm yourself down and be patient as difficult as that was. Grandmother Beverly could spread droplets of poison frustration on everyone around her like a lawn sprinkler.

But this was different. She had ripped me out of school and sent my head spinning. I would not be denied.

"Grandmother?"

"Just let's get out of here," she said sharply, not looking at me. She lowered her voice and added, "I don't want anyone hearing about this, if I can help it."

My heart was racing now, galloping alongside my unbridled imagination.

"Your foolish father," she muttered. "I warned him. No one can say I didn't warn him."

We passed through the doors and headed toward her vintage Mercedes sedan.

"Grandmother," I cried, planting my feet firmly in the parking lot. "I'm not taking another step until you tell me exactly what is going on."

She paused finally and turned to me, hoisting those small shoulders like a cobra preparing for a deadly strike.

"Your mother has gone mad and you're the only one who can talk to her. I certainly can't. Of course, I can't reach your father," she said, "and there's no time to wait for him anyway. I don't want to call an ambulance if I can help it."

"Ambulance?"

"You know how one thing leads to another and in this community there's enough gossip about this family as it is," she continued. "Maybe you can get her to stop."

"Stop what?"

"I can't even begin to describe it," she said, wagging her head as if her hair had been soaked. "Let's just get home," she insisted and hurried to get into the car. Now that she had sharpened my curiosity and raised the level of my anxiety like mercury in a thermometer, I rushed to get in as well.

Once I was seated, my head bowed with the panic I felt.

"I must tell you," she continued after starting the

engine and pulling away from the school parking lot, "I have always felt your mother was unbalanced. She had tendencies I spotted from the first moment I set eyes on her. I warned Taylor about her minutes after he had brought her around for me and your grandfather to meet her.

"She was coming to see us for the first time, but she wore no makeup, draped herself in what looked to be little more than a black sheet, kept her hair miles too long like you do and had enough gloom in her eyes to please a dozen undertakers. She could have worked constantly as a professional mourner. I could count on my fingers how many times I've seen a smile on that face, and even if she did smile at me, it was the smile of a madwoman, her eyes glittering like little knives, her wry lips squirming back and into the corners of her cheeks like worms in pain. How many times have I asked myself what he could possibly have seen in such a woman?"

I had heard a similar lecture before.

"Maybe he was in love, Grandmother."

"Love," she spat as if the word put a bitter taste in her mouth. "How could he be in love with her?"

She glanced at me and then put her eyes back on the road. She was a good driver for someone in her early seventies, I thought, but then again, she was good at everything she did. Failure wasn't in her personal vocabulary.

"Your mother was certainly never what I would call beautiful. I'm not saying she doesn't have pleasing features, because she does, but she does nothing to enhance them. In fact, what she does is diminish them just like you do with that silly makeup you wear.

"Of course, it didn't help that she had the personality of a pallbearer. Believe me," she said, "that takes the

light from your eyes, the glow from your smile. It's no
wonder to me that she never made any friends. Who
wants to listen to the music she likes or read those poems
about loss and death and insanity? She has no social
graces, doesn't care about nice clothes or jewelry. She
was never interested in your father's work or helped him
meet business associates."

"Then what do you think it was, Grandmother," I
asked dryly, "a magic spell?"

"You think you're being facetious, I know, but let me
tell you that woman can cast spells of sorts. I'll tell you
what it was," she said, after a short pause, never wanting
to admit to not knowing something. "She was probably
his first love affair. Men, foolish men, often mistake sex-
ual pleasure for love. Sex is like good food. You can eat it
with anyone, Cinnamon. Remember that," she ordered.

"Then what's love?" I asked her.

"Love is commitment, responsibility, dedication. It
requires maturity."

"Sounds boring," I said. "If that's love, I'll take good
food."

She opened her mouth wide and glared at me, shaking
her head.

"You'd better be careful of your thoughts," she
admonished. "Insanity can be inherited, you know. The
genes from our side of the family just might not be
enough."

I wanted to laugh at her, but I kept thinking about
what awaited me and how it might make her right.

No one could tell anything about the inhabitants of
our home by simply driving up, especially this time of
the day. The front faced east so that all morning the win-

dows were turned into glittering slabs, impenetrable
crystals, twisting, turning and reflecting the sunlight. In
fact, if it wasn't a day for the gardeners, and today
wasn't, there was a look of abandonment about the place.
Our cars were always left in the rear, out of sight. Two
tall weeping willows on the northeast end painted long
shadows over one side of the structure, adding to the
sense of desertion.

There was a swing under a maple tree to the right on
the west side. I noticed it was going back and forth,
which made me smile. Anyone looking at it would be
convinced there was a ghost sitting on it. I imagined one
myself, one of the Demerest girls, smiling.

Fall had just lifted its head and begun to blow the
cooler winds over the landscape, waving a magical hand
to change the greens into yellows, browns and oranges.
The grass, however, seemed happier, waking to heavier
dews every morning. It was a deeper green. I loved the
aroma of freshly cut lawns, the freshness traveled into
my brain and washed away the cobwebs and shadows
from my darker thoughts.

As Grandmother Beverly turned up the drive, she
finally revealed the situation in detail.

"I was in the living room, watching a good Cary Grant
movie, when I heard her humming in the hallway. What is
she doing downstairs? I wondered. The doctor had specifically told her that if she was going home, she was to
remain in bed, resting, getting stronger. I offered to be her
nurse, to march up and down those stairs as many times as
need be, so she couldn't use that as any excuse.

"But your mother never listens to wiser voices. She
hears only what she wants to hear. Secret voices out of
the shadows," she muttered.

"Anyway, I went to the family room doorway. At first, I didn't see her. Then I heard her talking to her plants."

She paused, smirked and shook her head.

Mommy often spoke aloud to her plants as if they were her little children. She said when she was sad, which was far too often, the leaves were limp and dreary, but when she was happy, they were crisp and alive.

Anyway, I didn't think much of that.

"She's always talking to flowers, Grandmother. Many people do that."

"Naked?"

"What?"

"She was standing there in the hallway, watering those plants naked, and she was using a bed pan to water them," she said, her voice rising. "Who even knows if it was water?"

I felt the blood drain a bit from my face and looked at the house as we started around back.

"But that wasn't the horror of it, Cinnamon. 'What are you doing, Amber?' I asked, and she turned slowly toward me, a crazed smile on her face."

Grandmother stopped the car and turned to me before shutting off the engine.

"Over her stomach, with a stick of red lipstick, she had drawn the outline of a baby, a fetus!" she cried with a grimace. "I screamed, 'Oh, my God!' I nearly fainted at the sight, but she continued to smile at me and then went back to watering the plants, humming and watering.

"So, I got into the car and went for you."

I swallowed back the rock that had risen into my throat and got out of the car. All I could think of was Ophelia's mad scene in *Hamlet*. With my head down, my feet feeling like they had turned into marshmallows, I charged toward the rear entrance and quickly went inside, through the rear entryway and down the corridor to the stairway, gazing in each room to be sure Mommy wasn't downstairs.

Then I pounded up the stairs and paused when I reached the top. I could hear her humming and talking to herself. It was coming from the room that had been set up to be the nursery. Slowly, I approached it and looked in. It was just as Grandmother Beverly had described: Mommy was naked, the imaginary baby crudely drawn over her stomach in her apple red lipstick.

She was folding and unfolding the same little blanket at the side of the bassinet.

"Mommy," I said.

She stopped humming and looked at me.

"Cinnamon, you're home. Good. I was having labor pains this morning. It won't be long now," she said.

"Labor pains? But Mommy—"

"It's expected, I know, but it's still very difficult, Cinnamon. Most wonderful things are difficult," she muttered, "and worth the pain," she added with a new smile.

How could she have forgotten she had just had a miscarriage? It was so sad, so tragic, I thought, and then: Maybe that's why she's forgotten. She doesn't want to remember. She and I have done so much pretending in this house. This comes easily to her.

"Mommy, you've got to return to bed."

"I will as soon as I do this. I want everything to be ready when we come home with little Sacha," she said, gazing around the nursery.

"Come back to bed, Mommy," I said, moving to her. I gently took her by the elbow. She smiled at me and put the blanket in the bassinet.

"My grown-up little lady, taking care of me. You're going to be such a big help with Sacha, I know. I'm as happy for you as I am for Daddy and me," she said. "Did you know I always wished I had a sister, especially a little sister who would look up to me for everything?

"Sacha's going to idolize you, Cinnamon. She'll want to do everything you do just the way you do it, I'm sure. You mustn't be short with her or impatient," she warned, her face full of concern. "Always remember she's just a little girl who doesn't understand. Explain things; make sure you and she always talk and never hide anything from each other. A sister can be your best friend in the whole world, even more than your mother. I'm sure mine would have been."

She started out with me, but she didn't stop talking.

"It's all right for her to be a better friend to you than I am. I'll never be jealous of the two of you, honey. I realize you will have more in common with her than you will with me. You don't ever have to worry about that."

"Please get into bed, Mommy," I said when we entered the master bedroom.

Mommy and Daddy had a king-size, oak four-post bed with an oversized headboard on which two roses with their stems crossed were embossed. Mommy loved roses. The comforter and the pillow cases had a pattern of red roses, which made the room cheerful. When they were younger and more affectionate toward each other, I used to think of their bed as a bed that promised its inhabitants magical love, a bed that filled their heads with wonderful dreams when they slept afterward, both of them, smiling, contented, warm and secure, those four posts like powerful arms protecting them against any of the evil spirits that sought to invade their contentment.

I pulled back the comforter and she got into the bed, slowly lowering her head to the pillow. She was still smiling.

"I want you to help take care of her right from the start, honey. You'll be her second mother, just as Agatha Demerest was a second mother to her younger brothers and sisters," she said. "Remember?"

Mommy was referring to a story she and I had actually created during one of our earliest visits to the attic.

When I was a little more than fourteen, she decided one day that we should explore the house. She had been up in the attic before, of course, and told me that shortly after she and Daddy had moved into the house, she had discovered an old hickory chest with hinges so rusted, they fell off when she lifted the lid. The chest was filled with things that went back to the 1800s. She had been especially intrigued by the Demerest family pictures. Most were faded so badly you could barely make out the faces, but some of them were still in quite good condition.

Daddy, who works on Wall Street and puts a monetary value on everything in sight, decided that much of the stuff could be sold. He took things like the Union army uniform, old newspapers, a pair of spurs and a pistol holster to New York to be valued and later placed in a consignment store, but Mommy wouldn't let him take the pictures.

"I told him family pictures don't belong in stores and certainly don't belong on the walls of strangers. These pictures should never leave this house and they never will," she vowed to me.

She and I would look at the women and the men and try to imagine what they must have been like, whether they were sad or happy people, whether they suffered or not. We did our role-playing and I would assume the persona of one of the women in a picture. Mommy would often be Jonathan Demerest, speaking in a deep voice. That was when we came up with the story of Agatha Demerest having to take on the role of mother when her mother died of smallpox.

But Mommy was talking about it now as if it were historical fact and we had no concrete information upon which to base our assumptions, except for the dates carved in a couple of tombstones.

"Okay, Mommy," I said. I was thinking about washing the lipstick drawing off her stomach, but I was afraid even to mention it.

I have to try to get in touch with Daddy, I thought.

"Oh," Mommy suddenly cried. "Oh, oh, oh, Cinnamon, it's happening again!" She clutched her stomach. "It's getting worse. I'm going into labor. You'd better call the doctor, call an ambulance, call your father," she cried.

She released a chilling scream that shook my very bones.

"Hurry!"

I didn't know what to do. I ran from the room. Grandmother Beverly was already at the top of the stairway.

"What is it?" she asked, her hand on her breast, her face whiter than ever.

"She thinks she's in labor. I think she really is in pain!"

"Oh dear, dear. We'll have to call the doctor. I was hoping you could calm her down, get her to sleep and be sane," she said. Another scream from Mommy spun her around and sent her fleeing down the stairway.

Mommy continued to moan.

I glanced at my watch. Daddy had to be at his desk. Why did Grandmother Beverly say before that she certainly couldn't reach him? He should be easy to reach.

I rushed to my room and tapped out the number for his office quickly. It rang and rang until his secretary finally picked up and announced his company.

"I need to speak to my father immediately," I practically screamed.

Mommy was crying out even louder now, her shouts of pain echoing down the hallway and through the house.

"He's not here at the moment," the secretary said.

"But he has to be. The market is still open."

"I'm sorry," she said.

"Where is he?"

"He didn't leave a number," she said.

"It's an emergency," I continued.

"Let me see if he answers his page," she relented. Why hadn't she said that first? I wondered. I held on, my heart pounding a drum in my ears.

"I'm sorry," she said. "He's not responding."

"Keep trying and if you get him, tell him my mother is being taken to the hospital."

"The hospital? Oh, dear. Oh," she said. "Yes, I'll keep trying."

I hung up just as Grandmother Beverly came up the stairs, looking more her age.

"The doctor has called the ambulance," she said. She swallowed and continued. "It's no use. She has to return to the hospital. When I told him what she had done, he said he'd have her brought to the mental ward."

"Mental ward?"

"Of course. Look at her behavior. That's exactly

where she belongs," she added with that damnable look of self-satisfaction I hated so much.

She put her hands over her ears, but Mommy's heart-wrenching scream drove Grandmother Beverly back down the stairs to wait.

I was hoping it would drive her out of our lives.

2

~~~

Escape to Dreams

Apparently, Daddy's secretary was unable to reach him before the ambulance arrived. I returned to Mommy's bedroom and held her hand while she went through her imaginary labor pains. I guess I shouldn't say imaginary. The doctor would emphasize later that she actually felt the pain.

"Psychosomatic pain is not contrived," he explained to Daddy when Daddy and I met with him in the corridor of the hospital. "The patient feels it; it's just caused by something psychological as compared to something physical." He looked at me and added, "We shouldn't get angry at her."

"I'm not angry at her," I snapped back at him. "I'm upset."

I almost added, I'm frightened, too, but he got me so angry I didn't want to confide in him.

Afterward, Daddy and I sat in the hospital cafeteria having a cup of coffee. Daddy said he hadn't had a chance to eat anything so he nibbled on a Danish pastry.

"When my secretary reached me, I was on my way home," he told me. "I stopped at the train station and called and Grandmother answered and told me what was happening so I came back as quickly as I could and took a cab here. Lucky Grandmother was still in the house."

"It wasn't luck. Grandmother didn't want to come along. I drove myself and followed the ambulance. I'm sure she was afraid she might be seen by one of her society friends," I muttered.

"That's not fair, Cinnamon. Your grandmother was never very good in hospitals. It makes her sick."

"So? What better place to be sick if you have to be sick?" I countered.

One thing Daddy wouldn't ever get from me was sympathy for Grandmother Beverly. I never saw her shed a real tear, not even at Grandfather Carlson's funeral, although I have seen her cry at sad scenes in her favorite old movies. She has a lock on the television set in the family room, fixing it on her old-time movie channel. She complains incessantly about today's movies, television, music and books, calling it all depraved and claiming the most degenerate minds are responsible.

Occasionally, I would sit and watch an old movie with her. Some of them are very good, like *Rebecca*. I especially liked the scene where the evil housekeeper, Mrs. Danvers, tries to talk the second Mrs. de Winter into jumping to her death. The first time I saw it, I thought she was going to do it. Mrs. Danvers made it sound so inviting, I felt like jumping.

After I saw the movie, I began to think of Grandmother Beverly as our own Mrs. Danvers trying to talk Mommy into jumping off a cliff or at least helping drive her off the cliff of sanity into the bog of madness, where she now resided.

"That's not funny, Cinnamon," Daddy said. "Some people have less tolerance for unpleasant things."

"Grandmother Beverly? Weaker than other women? Please, Daddy," I said.

He blinked and nibbled on his Danish, quickly falling back to his relaxed demeanor. Daddy has a quiet elegance and charm. He is truly a handsome man with rich dark brown hair and the most striking hazel eyes I have seen on any man. He has those long eyelashes, too, and a perfect nose and firm mouth. He's almost square-jawed with high cheek bones and a forehead that's just wide enough to make him look very intelligent. He's an impeccable dresser and never goes any longer than three weeks without having his hair trimmed.

I understood why Mommy once told me he was the most attractive man who had ever looked at her twice. When she did speak about the early romantic days between them, she emphasized his solid, even-tempered sensibility and how she had come to rely on him to keep her from going too far in one direction or another. Whatever happened to that? I wondered. It was almost as if he had abandoned ship.

"Your mother could be here a while," he said. "Or, she could be moved to a more comfortable place, a place that specializes in her problems."

"You mean a nut house?"

"No, a clinic," he corrected sharply.

I looked away. Tears didn't come into my eyes often, but when they did, I held them over my pupils tightly, battling to keep them locked behind my lids. I took deep breaths.

"We've got to be strong," Daddy said. "For her."

I looked at him. He was checking the time and looking toward the doorway.

"I haven't even learned about today's market results. I hopped on the train as quickly as I could," he muttered.

"Where were you, Daddy? Why weren't you in your office? I thought you have to be there to call your clients while the market is open."

"Sometimes, I go to visit a big account," he explained. "It's good politics. I have an assistant who does a good job covering for me."

"How come you didn't leave a telephone number where you could be reached?"

"I just forgot," he said. "I left too quickly."

Lying is an art form, I thought. Good lying, that is. It requires almost the same techniques, skills and energy that good acting requires. When you tell lies, you step out of yourself for a while. You become another version of yourself and yet, you have to do it so that the listener believes it's still you talking because he or she has come to trust you, have faith in you. I like making up stories, exaggerating, changing the truth a little—or maybe a little more than a little—sometimes just to see how much I can get away with. It's all in how you hold your head, keep your eyes fixed on the listener and how much sincerity you can squeeze into the small places around the lie.

Maybe Daddy was a bad liar in person because he did most of his lying over the phone. He didn't have to be face-to-face with his customers. He could quote statistics, talk in generalities, blame his mistakes on other people, other businesses or agencies than his own. It's much easier to sound convincing when you talk to an ear and not a pair of eyes.

I knew Daddy was lying, but I didn't know why. It never occurred to me what the reason might be. Maybe I was spending a little too much time in my make-believe world.

"We'd better head home," he said. "You've got schoolwork to do, I'm sure, and there is really nothing else we can do here tonight."

"I want to go see her one more time," I said.

"You might only disturb her more."

"I might help her be comfortable in an uncomfortable place," I countered.

I could hold my gaze on Daddy so firmly that he would be the first to look away. Mommy taught me how to do that. You actually think of something else, but keep your eyes fixed on the subject.

"All right, but make it quick," he said. "I'm going to make a few phone calls."

He left and I went back upstairs. Mommy had been given a sedative to help her sleep, but she was still moaning and turning her head. I took her hand in mine and spoke softly to her.

"Mommy, it's me. Don't you feel a little better now?"

"Baby . . . born too soon," she muttered.

"What?"

"Little Sacha." She opened her eyes and looked up at me. Then she smiled.

"Cinnamon! How is she?" she asked. "What have they told you?"

I shook my head.

Now she believes she has given birth, I thought, but to a premature baby.

"I know she'll be all right. I know it. She's in the pre-natal intensive care unit, but premature babies can do fine. You tell me how she's doing, all right? Tell me," she insisted, squeezing my hand tightly.

If I told her the truth, I thought she'd come apart right before my eyes, her hand crumbling in mine like a dry fall leaf.

"She's doing fine, Mommy. She's getting bigger every moment."

She smiled.

"I knew it. I knew she would. How wonderful. How beautiful. She is beautiful, too, isn't she, Cinnamon? As beautiful as you were when you were born. I'm right? Aren't I?" she asked with a desperation that nearly took my breath away.

"Yes, Mommy, she's beautiful."

"I knew she would be. You've got a little sister. How wonderful. Wonderful," she said relaxing, her eyes closing and staying closed. Her breathing became regular. At least she was relaxed and at ease for a while.

See, I told myself, you can lie better than anyone you know.

Sometimes, that comes in very handy.

Maybe you will be a successful actress, after all.

Daddy and I rode back in silence, mine growing out of the soil of sadness and fear. Daddy looked like he was in deep thought, probably worrying about a stock he had recommended today. Lately, I felt that my father was a guest in his own house, and when he looked at me, he was surprised to discover he had a daughter. It's almost as if he thinks he's having a dream. His whole life—my mother and I, all of it—is just a passing illusion. He would blink hard and we would be gone, I thought. I almost wished it were true.

"How's school?" he asked suddenly. It was as if the question had been stored for months in a cupboard in his brain and he had just stumbled upon it.

"School?"

"Yes, how are you doing in your classes these days?"

"Fine, Daddy. I've been on the honor roll every quarter," I reminded him.

"Oh, right, right. Well, that's good, Cinnamon. You want to get yourself into a fine college like my alma mater, NYU. It's important." He looked at me quickly. "I hope this unfortunate situation won't have a detrimental effect on your school grades. I know it can," he said. "You've just got to be strong and take care of business, consider priorities."

"Mommy's wellbeing is my priority," I said dryly. I wanted to add, as it should be yours, but I kept my lips pressed together as if I were afraid my tongue would run off on its own and say all the things I had been thinking for months and months. Thoughts, words, screams, all were stored in my mouth, waiting to pop out like bees whose hive had been disturbed and sting Daddy in places he couldn't reach. That way, he'd wake up to what had been happening all this last year or so since Grandmother Beverly had moved into our home and invaded our lives.

He should have woken the moment we entered the house. Grandmother Beverly had been busy all day, ever since the ambulance had come to take Mommy to the hospital. The first thing I noticed was that Mommy's favorite two works of art, the pictures she had bought in New Orleans when she and Daddy and I had gone there for a short vacation, were gone from the wall in the hallway. They were both watercolors of swamps with the Spanish moss draping from the trees. In one a toothpick-legged

Cajun home was depicted in great detail, shrimp drying on a rock, animal skins hung over a porch railing, and a woman working on the porch weaving a rug. In the other picture, a young couple were in a canoe, poling into the mist. They looked romantic, but in a deeply sad way.

Grandmother Beverly always complained that the pictures were too depressing to be art. She said they were more like someone's nightmares and certainly not the first thing with which to greet a visitor to our home.

"Where are Mommy's pictures?" I demanded as soon as Grandmother Beverly stepped out of the family room.

"How is she now?" she asked my father instead of responding to me.

He shook his head.

"They've given her a sedative, but the doctor wants to treat her for deep depression. If she doesn't snap out of it soon, he's recommending more serious therapy, the sort that takes place in a mental clinic," he replied.

"Exactly what I expected would happen someday. You had to be blind not to see this coming, Taylor."

My father didn't agree or disagree. He kept his head slightly bowed, looking like an ashamed young boy confronting his mother.

"Where are Mommy's pictures?" I repeated. She finally turned to me.

"I thought there was enough gloom and doom in this house today. I'm trying to cheer things up."

"Mommy wants those pictures on the wall," I cried. I looked at Daddy. "Make her put them back."

"We'll put up something more pleasant," Grandmother Beverly continued. "I'll buy brighter pictures. We've got to lighten up this hallway. It needs stronger lighting, the walls should be painted a lighter color and I think this entryway rug is worn to a thread. Good riddance to it."

"It is not. What are you talking about? Daddy!" I moaned. "Tell her!"

"I'm so tired," he said. "It's all been quite a shock and right after losing the baby." He shook his head.

"Of course. You're exhausted, Taylor. Come have a nice cup of tea. I made your favorite biscuits," she added, "and there's some of that jam you love, the kind that tastes homemade. I bought it for you yesterday."

"Yes, that would be good," he said. He glanced at me. "Don't worry about this stuff now, Cinnamon. It's not what's important at the moment."

Grandmother Beverly smiled at me.

"Would you like something, dear?"

Mommy hated her in the kitchen. Until she had suffered the miscarriage, Mommy had not permitted her to make a single dinner for us, even though she claimed she knew all of Daddy's favorite meals. I knew Mommy's resistence wasn't born out of any great desire to be a cook. She warned me from the start that Grandmother Beverly wasn't just moving into the house.

"That woman can't live in a home without taking over," Mommy assured me. "It's not in her nature to be second in any sense. She'll take over and replace me everywhere except in bed, and sometimes," Mommy said her eyes small, "I even fear that."

Of course, she was exaggerating.

That's what I tell myself even though it gave me a different kind of nightmare.

"I'm not hungry," I told Grandmother Beverly, glared furiously once more at Daddy and ran up the stairs to my room, slamming the door behind me.

I was fuming so hot and heavy, I was sure smoke was pouring out of my ears.

The ringing of my phone snapped me out of my seething rage. I took a deep breath and lifted the receiver.

"Hello."

"Cinnamon, what happened?" Clarence asked.

"My mother had to be taken to the hospital," I replied. He was the only one who knew Mommy had suffered a miscarriage. "She's had a nervous breakdown because of what happened."

"Oh, I'm sorry," he said. "Is there anything I can do for you?"

"Yes, call the Mafia and get a hit man over here pronto to save me from my grandmother," I replied.

He laughed, but the sort of short laugh that indicated he knew it really wasn't funny.

"You were all the buzz at school."

"I'm glad the airheads had something to talk about."

"I could see Miss Hamilton was upset for you. You coming to school tomorrow?"

"I'm not staying here, that's for sure," I said.

"What are you going to tell people?" he asked.

"I'll come up with something."

"Let me know so I can be part of it," he said. I knew what he meant. He and I enjoyed making up stories and telling them together, verifying what the other had said, shocking other students whenever we could.

"Meet me at my locker in the morning before home-room," I told him. He promised he would and hung up.

I fell back spread-eagled on my bed and looked up at the eggshell white ceiling. Sometimes, when I stared into the white void long enough, I'd see the faces of the young women who once lived in this house. It was as if their spirits had been trapped in the walls and I was the only one with whom they could communicate.

My memories of Mommy and me up in the attic returned. They brought tears to my eyes. I wondered if even now, sedated in that hospital room, she was afraid or just sad. Deep inside herself, despite her temporary madness, she must know she has had the miscarriage. Can you get so you could really lie to yourself as well as you could lie to others, actually believing your own fabrications? And is that madness or is it the simplest way to escape the turmoil and unhappiness that sometimes storms around you?

I need inspiration, I thought. I would die before telling anyone the truth. There was only one place to go for it. While Daddy sat below in the kitchen, numbly watching Grandmother Beverly weave a web of control around him, I went up to the attic to conspire with my spirits and my own resourceful imagination.

Mommy told me that when I was only four, I had an imaginary friend. I don't remember, but I've learned it is a very common thing for a child to do: create his or her own companion. Maybe it's just as hard to be alone when you're very young as it is to be alone when you're very old, I thought. Old people imagine friends, too.

There's something about growing up, about being in society and mixing with real people that restricts your imaginative powers. If you say something that seems like fantasy, people laugh at you or make you feel self-conscious about it, so you smother your make-believe and drive the creative thoughts down into the grave, bury them in the cemetery of originality, and work harder at being like everyone else, safe, unremarkable, just some more wallpaper. It takes courage to revive your imagination and risk the ridicule. In an ironic sense, it takes a brave soul to contrive exaggerations, fantasies, elaborate and eloquent lies.

I flipped the switch and the dark attic became illuminated, but not so brightly as to drive away the small shadows and brighten the dark corners. Neither Mommy nor I wanted it that well lit anyway. Some darkness is comforting, warm, inviting. Mommy used to say it felt protective.

"Most people are afraid of the dark," she said. "They'll never trespass on our privacy."

There was some old furniture up here, dusty and worn. If Grandmother Beverly ever made the trek up the second set of narrow stairs and opened the attic door, she would gasp and vow instantly to have it immediately cleaned out. None of it had any real value anymore. That was true, but there were other kinds of value than monetary value. For Mommy and me this small, dusty room had always been cozy, inviting, comfortable.

Dust particles spun in the beam of the light, glistening like particles of diamonds. It had been a while since Mommy and I were up here. When we were coming up here more frequently, we did do some cleaning, washing down the two windows and sills, vacuuming and some polishing. We wanted it to maintain its special charm, but we wanted it to be clean enough to inhabit as well.

If there were rodents up here, they were excellent at keeping themselves invisible. We never found any droppings and the worst thing we did discover were spiders. Mommy thought we should leave some of the webs untouched. They weren't poisonous spiders. She called them nature's housekeepers who kept any other insects in check.

There were some areas of dampness, places where rain had seeped through or in between cracks. We would burn incense to drive away any musty odors or sometimes spray some flower-scented air freshener.

I went directly to our incense burner and lit a stick. Then I opened the window so the tiny smoke would spiral in that direction.

Mommy and I always felt the attic had been someone's hideaway at one time or another. On the floor there had been a brown oval rug, worn through in many spots and very faded; why would anyone have put a rug up here if it wasn't a place for some sort of retreat or privacy.

"Maybe the children used it as a playhouse," Mommy suggested, "or maybe Carolyne Demerest had a lover and brought him up here for romantic trysts," she pondered, her eyes widening with excitement.

We both decided that was more fun and elaborated on the story.

Carolyne Demerest had fallen in love with the young groundskeeper.

"Who was a closet poet, leaving the poems tacked to a special tree."

"And she fell in love with him through his words!"

"Just like Elizabeth and Robert Browning," I added.

"Exactly, and the first time they met up here . . ."

"It was snowing. The window was glazed and she sat in this old rocker wrapped in a heavy shawl she had made herself."

"He fell to her feet and held them against his cheeks and said . . ."

"I have dreamed all my life of this moment."

We both laughed and laughed. What fun it was. I

could almost hear her laughter now and feel her hugging me. We were like sisters, truly. I was the sister she had wanted, and her daughter and best friend forever and ever.

Mommy, I cried looking at the empty rocking chair.

I sat there on the small settee and wondered what she was dreaming in her deep sleep, what were the images and the words. What could hold her so firmly and keep her from wanting to see and be with me so much that she couldn't overcome her mental problems?

Surely, I'll wake up tomorrow morning to the sound of commotion, lots of footsteps, doors opening and closing, a car horn and some cries of delight. I'll rise from my bed and look down at our driveway where I will see a car stop and Mommy step out, looking like her old self, strong, full of energy, joyous at the sight of her beloved old home. She would be cured and the first words out of her lips would be, "Where's Cinnamon? Where's my little girl?"

Mommy, I would cry inside, Mommy.

And I would practically fly out of my room, descending the stairway so quickly that I couldn't remember my feet touching a step, and then I'd go charging out the front door and into her awaiting arms.

She would hold me and kiss me and say, "Don't worry, sweetheart. I'm back.

"All will be well again," she would promise.

She and I would enter the house and she would look up at the wall and demand to know where her two works of art were.

"Who dared take them off the wall?"

Daddy would hurry to the basement—or wherever they had been hidden—and he would rush to get them up.

"Sorry," he would say. "I just wasn't paying attention to these things."

"Well, now that I'm home, see that you do," Mommy would tell him.

And Grandmother Beverly would pop like a bubble and be gone along with all the other demons that haunted our home.

We could change the channel on the television set. We could play our music and light our candles and talk to the lonely dead spirits.

And never be afraid of the darkness.

3

—w—

Playing the Part

I fell asleep in my chair, dreaming about the love story Mommy and I had created in the attic. It wasn't what I had intended to do, but it almost didn't matter that I didn't come up with a story to tell the Nosy Parkers in school. I decided to simply ignore their curiosity and hope they would stop gaping at me, but Grandmother Beverly was right about gossip, especially about gossip concerning us. It had its own life, its own momentum. People act like they don't want anything to do with you, but as soon as they can learn something about you, they seize it and then take great pleasure in spreading the news, especially if it's bad news. It didn't take too long, less than forty-eight hours, actually.

Classes at my school might as well have been interrupted and an announcement delivered over the public-address system that went something like, "Attention, attention. Two days ago Cinnamon Carlson's mother had a mental breakdown."

That was how fast the news about my family spread. Reactions of my teachers went from aloofness to pity to looks that said, "It's not surprising to me."

The only teacher who did show sympathy and concern was Miss Hamilton. When the bell rang to end class, she asked me to stay a moment. She waited for the rest of the class to leave and then she turned to me, giving me her best long face and saddest eyes and asked how I was doing.

"I'm fine," I told her.

"I want you to know you can come to me anytime, Cinnamon. Please don't hesitate," she said as if we both suffered from the same disease. Well, she lived alone and, these days, I felt alone; maybe loneliness is a disease, but everyone has his or her own way of curing it, I thought. If she knew some of the things I did, like talk to the dead Carolyne and her son Abraham at their grave sites, she might not be so anxious to have me try out for one of her plays.

I nodded, kept my eyes down, and left as quickly as I could. Clarence was waiting for me in the hallway.

"What was that all about?"

"Act One, Scene Two," I said.

"What?"

"Nothing. Forget it. I'm hungry," I said and marched off to the cafeteria.

Clarence had to sit near a window and preferably one on his left side. If there wasn't a seat free that satisfied him, he would eat outside at the bench tables we used in the early fall or spring, no matter how cold it was. Fortunately, today, a day with a dreary overcast sky and a constant northerly wind, there were free seats at a table right below a window. He rushed to it and put down his books to claim the place. I followed and put my books beside his before going into the lunch line.

Sometimes, I brought my lunch, which usually consisted of a container of yogurt and an apple, but with all the commotion at home, I had not had time to buy any yogurt and Grandmother Beverly certainly hadn't bought any for me. She didn't consider it to be proper food. She called it novelty food or, if anything, a dessert. It did no good to read the description of nutrients on the side of the cup.

Today, I thought I would just have some soup and a platter of chicken salad. When I glanced to the right, I saw the heads of other students practically touching temple to temple as they gazed my way and cackled. In moments, I expected to see eggs rolling under the table.

I got my food as quickly as I could and returned to our table. No one else had sat there yet.

"So, they moved her?" Clarence asked as he started on his platter of macaroni and cheese, eating from the left side of the plate.

"This morning," I replied. "I'm going to visit her right after school."

"Your father, too?"

"No. He'll be there at night after his dinner meeting in the city, or so he says."

"Don't you believe him?" Clarence asked, surprised at my tone of voice.

I was silent, thinking about the last two days. Mommy's illness had rejuvenated Grandmother Beverly. She now had the strength and stamina of a forty-year-old. The morning following Mommy's being taken to the hospital, Grandmother Beverly was up ahead of Daddy. I heard her moving about the hallway and down the stairs.

Because Daddy was a broker on Wall Street, he had to be out of the house very early to make his commute and be ready for the opening bell at the stock market. I never saw him at breakfast during the week, but up until the last year or so, Mommy would get up to be with him. Grandmother Beverly sometimes didn't rise until I was about to leave for school, and she never rose early enough to say good-bye to Daddy in the morning.

Suddenly, she was doing it.

By the time I was dressed and down to breakfast, Daddy was already gone, of course; but Grandmother Beverly was still in the kitchen. I heard the dishes clanking as well as pots and pans. Curiosity quickened my footsteps. I stopped in the doorway and what I saw shocked and confused me.

"What are you doing?" I asked her.

She had taken all of the dishes out of the kitchen cabinets, and the pots and pans as well, and was reorganizing everything.

"This kitchen was never set up intelligently," she replied. "Cups and dishes and soup bowls all scattered about in different cabinets, and the pots and pans . . . why are they under the salad sink? They should be nearer the stove. You know how hard it was to find a can opener in this kitchen? Just ridiculous to have all this chaos."

"Mommy never has any trouble finding what she wants. She's going to be very upset when she gets home," I said.

"She'll get over it quickly, especially when she realizes how well organized it is now. If she gets home," she added in a mutter so low, I barely heard it.

"You can't do this," I insisted. "Put it all back where it was."

"Don't be silly, Cinnamon. Now get some decent breakfast in you and go to school," she ordered. "What do you have, eggs, cold cereal?"

"Does Daddy know you've done this?"

She turned and raised her eyebrows.

"You think I need my son to tell me what's right and what isn't? But to answer you, yes, he does," she continued and turned back to the cabinets. "Not only are things in the wrong places, but these cabinets need to be relined with cabinet paper. What good is it to wash your dishes and then put them on a dirty shelf?"

"They aren't dirty."

"Oh, you know? When was the last time you did any real housework here? When I was your age, I had to make all the beds and dust the furniture in the living room before I could go to school, even if it meant I'd be late."

"Brilliant," I said.

I turned and marched out of the house.

"Cinnamon!" she called after me. "Where are you going without your breakfast?"

I didn't answer. What she heard instead was the door slamming behind me.

Now, two days later, she had completed her revamping of the kitchen and was working on the living room and preparing our dinners. However, up until now, she had been left to eat them by herself. Daddy was working late and I didn't come home for dinner either night, going directly to the hospital to sit with Mommy. She slept most of the time I was there, and when she awoke, she was full of questions about Sacha and plans for what she would be doing when Sacha was released from the prenatal intensive care unit.

"I just know we'll both be better about the same time," she told me.

I wondered what she thought was supposedly wrong with her, but I was afraid to ask. I was actually afraid to ask her any questions. She would cry often and then say, "It's all right. I'll be fine."

I tried talking about the house, tried to get her interested in coming home quickly.

"Grandmother Beverly is changing things," I said. "You need to get better and come home quickly."

"Is she? That's all right. We'll just change it all back," she told me. For a moment I thought she was returning to her old self, but then she added, "I just can't wait to show her Sacha, to show her what a beautiful new granddaughter she has, a granddaughter she never wanted. How sorry she will be for the things she's said. Won't she be, Cinnamon?"

"Yes," I said weakly.

As long as Mommy was like this, Grandmother Beverly felt the power that comes with being right, predicting accurately and then never letting us forget it. She was practically beating Daddy over the head with this tragedy daily, shoving his face in the reality, washing out his mouth with her soap of truth.

The first two nights, he came to the hospital directly from work, looking fatigued, defeated. The market happened to be down, too, and that was depressing him. Some of his best clients were blaming him for his recommendations, he said.

"When they make money, I'm a hero. When they lose, I'm an idiot."

"Why did you ever want to be a broker, Daddy?" I asked while he and I sat at Mommy's bedside watching her drift in and out of sleep.

He shrugged.

"Money always excited me. There's nothing more beautiful than watching a small investment become bigger and bigger and then knowing when to sell. There's all that suspense. Right there in front of me events are transpiring that will affect people's lives, lose or make their jobs, destroy their retirement pensions or turn them into wealthy people. I like being part of that. I feel . . . plugged into the current that runs the country. Does that make sense?" he asked almost wistfully.

"I guess so," I said.

Actually, I had never heard him speak so passionately about his work before and for a few moments, I was actually mesmerized. Most of the time, he moved about so methodically, thinking and acting with a surgeon's care—analyzing, scrutinizing every little thing, right down to the portion of soap powder it took to wash floors. I was beginning to wonder if he was emotionally dead, if he cried or laughed or cared warmly about anything, especially Mommy and me.

"Are you upset about losing the baby?" I asked.

"Sure," he said. "But . . ."

"But what, Daddy? Don't say Grandmother Beverly might have been right. Don't dare say that," I warned him.

"No. Not exactly. I just wonder if Amber would have been strong enough for it, for raising a child from infancy again. She seemed so fragile, I began to wonder if we had done the right thing. Not because of her age," he quickly added. "I just wonder if she had the temperament for it."

"She had it. She would have been a wonderful mother to a new baby," I insisted.

He nodded, but not with any confidence. He simply nodded to shut me up.

We were both quiet then, both lost in our own thoughts, almost strangers on a train who just happened to be seated side by side. I had no idea where this train was heading.

All these events and discussions passed through my mind when Clarence asked me if I believed my father when he told me he would visit Mommy at the mental hospital after his dinner meeting.

"No," I finally replied. "I don't believe things he tells me these days. Lately, I keep finding his lies scattered all around the house."

"Huh?"

"Never mind," I said. "I have other things on my mind at the moment."

After school I got into my car and headed for the Chester Alton Psychiatric Hospital, a privately run institution outside of Yonkers where Mommy had been placed that morning. It was just far enough to be a good long ride. The car was really Mommy's car, but even before she had become pregnant and had her aches and pains, she had hardly used it. I already had logged twice as many miles on it than she had.

It wasn't just hard to believe I was on my way to visit my mother in a mental clinic; it was painful and actually very frightening. I could feel the trembling start in my legs and slowly vibrate up into my spine as I drew closer and closer to the clinic.

When I parked and got out, the building looked intimidating. It was so white that with the afternoon sun slipping out from under clouds, the reflection made me reach for my sunglasses. The moment I saw my image in the car window, a whole new persona came over me and helped me face what I had to do: visit my mother in a mental hospital. It was just too difficult to do it as her daughter.

I brushed back my hair, took a deep breath and moved forward like an actress about to step on a stage. It felt good, liberating. I walked differently, held my head differently and stepped up to the front entrance. Pretending was like wearing a mask and when I wore a mask, no one could see how terrible and how frightened I felt inside.

The lobby was deceiving. It wasn't that it was too immaculate—the tile floor gleaming, the furniture looking brand new. It was too cozy, too warm. I was expecting almost as much security as a prison with bars on all the windows and patients wandering about in house gowns, babbling or just staring vacantly at their own empty minds and sterile walls.

However, these walls had many pretty pictures, oils of pleasant country scenes, people with happy faces, bright flowers. There were fresh flowers in vases on tables and magazines neatly organized in a rack on the right wall. On the left was a small area with a television set. Three people sat on a sofa, all nicely dressed. I had the sense that one of them might be a patient, but there was no way to tell who were the visitors and who was the patient. Maybe they were all patients.

I thought the place resembled an upscale hotel lobby more than it did a psychiatric clinic.

A pretty young nurse sat behind a reception counter. She looked up and smiled at me as I approached.

"May I help you?" she asked. For some reason she reminded me of my dentist's assistant, her teeth glittering through that Colgate smile. I was almost expecting her to follow with, "Do you floss?"

"Yes," I said. "I'm here to see Amber Carlson."

"Amber Carlson?" She looked down at a large book and turned the page, reading. "Immediate family only," she muttered.

"I'm her younger sister," I said. "I've just flown in from Los Angeles and driven here directly from the airport."

"Oh."

"How is she?"

"Well, I don't have updates as to patients' conditions, but let me call the nurse's station and advise them of your arrival."

"Thank you." I gazed around as she dialed and informed the head nurse. She listened a moment and then thanked her and hung up.

"Mrs. Mendelson asked if you could please give them a few minutes. Your sister has just had a therapeutic bath and they're getting her back to bed," she said.

"Oh, fine."

"Los Angeles. How was your trip?"

"Smooth," I said. "I had forgotten how beautiful the foliage is here in the fall. Living in southern California," I said "you just forget the dramatic changes of season."

"Oh. What do you do in Los Angeles?"

"I work for a television production company. I'm a P.A."

"P.A.?"

"Production assistant. It's a way to get yourself into the business."

"What do you want to be?"

"An actress," I said as if it was the dumbest question she could ask.

"Oh, of course. You're pretty enough to be an actress. I bet you're good."

"I hope I am," I said. "My grandmother has such faith in me. She's the one who sends me enough money to keep trying. You don't make all that much money as a P.A., and it's so expensive to live out there. You need someone to be your patron, to support and believe in you."

"I bet."

"I auditioned for the part of a nurse recently," I said. "For a soap opera."

"Really? Which one?" she asked excitedly. "I follow one religiously."

"It's a new one, just starting. It's called *Transfusions*."

"*Transfusions?*"

"It's set in a hospital."

"Oh, right."

"I don't know if it will get on the air, but I tried out anyway. I'll hear next week. It's very nerve-racking."

"I bet," she said nodding.

"I was very upset when I heard about my sister. I know she wanted that baby very much. It doesn't surprise me that she's had this reaction to the disaster."

I held my breath, waiting for her to tell me that what happened to my mother was not all that unusual.

"I'm sure she'll get well soon," she said with little emotion. She obviously didn't know my mother's condition. The phone rang. She said hello and then nodded at me. "Take the elevator to the fifth floor and turn left. She's in the first room on your left," she instructed.

"Thank you."

I took out my compact mirror and glanced at myself. It seemed to me that would be a thing my mother's actress sister would do. When I looked at the receptionist, she smiled and nodded. I smiled back and sauntered over to the elevator.

When I stepped out of it on the fifth floor and turned left, I saw a nurse come around the desk and approach me quickly.

"I'm Mrs. Mendelson," she said. "She's still somewhat medicated, but I'm sure she'll be happy to see a familiar face."

"Thank you," I said. "I won't stay too long this first visit. Jet lag," I added.

She smiled.

"I understand."

She escorted me down to the room and paused at the door.

"She's still confused, suffering from traumatic amnesia. It's best you don't directly confront anything she says for the moment. She's like a patient with an open wound, but don't worry, she'll soon emerge from this and be fine."

"Thank you," I said and I entered.

Mommy was lying with her eyes open, her head supported by a large white pillow. She seemed smaller, paler to me. It brought tears to my eyes.

There were flowers in a vase on the stand beside her bed. I thought Daddy had sent them, but I looked and saw there was no card. It was probably just something the hospital did.

Mommy looked at me as if she didn't recognize me for a moment and I wondered if I had done such a good job of changing my personality that even my mother was confused. Then she smiled.

"Cinnamon," she said reaching up for me.

"Hi, Mommy," I said. I quickly kissed her and pulled the chair closer to the bed. "How are you feeling now?"

"Very tired," she said. "Have you seen Sacha today?" she asked without taking a breath.

"No. I just came from school, Mommy."

"Oh, right. I've lost track of time." She smiled. "I don't even know what day it is. What day is it?"

"It's Thursday, Mommy."

"Good, good. That's how many days now?" Her eyes blinked rapidly. "How many since her birth, Cinnamon? Three, four?"

"Three," I said.

"Three. Good. Every new day brings more hope. We've got to worry for a while, but she'll be fine, won't she?"

"Yes, Mommy, she'll be fine."

"Good." She closed her eyes. And then she opened them abruptly. "I want your father to get one of those baby monitors . . . you know, where you can hear if the baby cries? Of course, I'll have her sleep right beside us when we take her home, but even after she's out of danger, older, I want to have that. Too many babies die of crib death or choke on something. When you're that small and fragile . . . it's just a good idea, isn't it?"

"Yes," I said.

"Remind him, remind your father. He's so forgetful these days."

As if talking about him brought him to life, he called. I picked up the phone.

"Cinnamon. I'm glad you're there already. How's she doing?" he asked.

"The same," I said.

"Right. Don't worry though. The doctor assures me she's going to make a full recovery."

"What time are you arriving, Daddy?"

"I'm not sure at the moment. I just found out I've got to go to Brooklyn for this meeting. I was under the impression it was here in Manhattan. That's going to add at least an hour to my travel time."

"Can't you get out of it?"

"It's pretty important. Heavy hitters," he added.

"Mommy's been hit pretty heavy," I responded. He was silent a moment.

"She doesn't even remember if I'm there or not at the moment, Cinnamon."

"That doesn't matter. You'll remember you were here," I said sharply.

"Okay. Let me speak to her. Let's see what she says to me," he said and I handed Mommy the phone.

"It's Daddy," I said.

"Hello, Taylor?"

She listened.

"I need you to get something," she said and then she put the phone aside and looked at me. "What do I need? I forget."

"I'll tell him later, Mommy. Don't worry."

"Oh. Good. It's all right, Taylor. Cinnamon knows and will tell you. Is everything all right?"

She listened and nodded as if she thought he could see her through the wire, and then she handed me the phone.

"Hello?"

"I'll try to get there," he promised me.

"Whatever," I said.

"How are you doing?"

"I'm terrific. Matter of fact, Daddy, I think I'm going to win the Academy Award this year for the best all-around performance as a loving granddaughter. She was rearranging the living room when I left this morning. The bathrooms might be next, if she can pull up the toilets and tubs."

"All right, all right," he said in a tired voice. "I'll have a talk with her this week. I promise."

"You know what promises are, Daddy? Lies with pretty ribbons tied on them. I'll see you later," I added quickly and hung up.

Mommy stared at me and for a long moment, I thought she realized what was really happening and was coming out of it, crawling up from the dark pit of her temporary madness into the light of day like a restored heroine about to do battle with all the forces of evil. We'd be a team again.

Then she smiled that strange, distant smile.

"You know what I want you to do?" she asked. I shook my head. "I want you to sneak a camera into the prenatal intensive care unit and take Sacha's picture for me. Bring it here next time, okay. Will you?"

I took a deep breath to keep my throat from completely closing and nodded.

"Good," she said. "Good." She closed her eyes again. I reached for her hand and held it and sat there for nearly half an hour, waiting for her to open her eyes again.

She didn't and when the nurse looked in, I rose and

smiling at her told her I was tired, too. I'd be back tomorrow.

"She'll get better in a matter of days," she promised.

Another lie wrapped in a pretty ribbon, I thought and went to the elevator.

There was a different receptionist behind the desk in the lobby when I stepped out. She looked up at me, but I didn't feel like performing anymore.

I hurried out and to the car where I sat for a while, catching my breath. I dreaded going home, not only because of what else I might find my grandmother had changed but because Mommy's absence, the heavy silence in light of where she now was, would be hard to face. Instead, on the way, I stopped at a pizza place and bought myself a couple of slices. I sat in a quiet corner and ate them watching some younger kids talk animatedly, a pretty girl of about fourteen at the center, wearing headphones and listening to a portable CD player while the boys vied for her attention.

I envied their innocence, their wide-eyed fascination with everything they saw, touched and did. How had I grown so old so fast? I wondered.

After I ate, I decided to call Clarence. I needed to talk to someone.

He came out of his house to meet me in my car when I drove up. I told him what I had done when I arrived at the psychiatric hospital.

"And she believed you? You're so much younger than your mother," he remarked.

"She never doubted it."

He laughed.

"I guess you are good."

"It helped me go in and up to my mother's room, but

it didn't do me any good when I was with her. There are some things you can't pretend away," I told him.

He nodded.

"What about your father?"

I described the conversation.

"Maybe he just had to go to the meeting," he said.

"Maybe. Would you?" I quickly asked.

"I don't know. I guess I would try to get out of it. People should understand why and excuse him."

"Exactly," I said.

"Well, what are you going to do?"

"I don't know," I said.

"Miss Hamilton pulled me aside at the end of the day today. I was on my way out of the building. She wanted to talk about you. She said, 'I know you and Cinnamon are close friends.' "

He looked at me.

"I guess we are," he said.

"Of course we are—so? What did she want? To tell you how she'll be there for me or something?"

"No, she wanted me to try to talk you into going out for the play. She said you'd need something like being in a play more now."

"I'm already in a play," I said.

"What? Where?"

"At home. It's called, *A Happy Family*," I said.

Clarence laughed.

I started the engine.

"I'd better get home," I said. "I haven't even begun any homework yet and who knows? Grandmother Beverly might have moved my room into the pantry or something by now."

He shook his head and opened the door. For a moment

he just looked at me as if he were making a big decision. Then he leaned over and kissed me on the left cheek.

"Good night," he said quickly.

I touched my cheek.

Even that, I thought, even a kiss was a ritual for him and had to be done from left to right.

I laughed.

It was the only laugh I had had all day.

4

A Father's Lies

Grandmother had concentrated her efforts on Daddy's office this day. I didn't know how she had done it, but all by herself she had moved his heavy dark oak desk across the room so it faced the window on the east side, and once she had done that, she had to change everything: lamps, chairs, the small sofa, tables and even rearrange books.

"Why didn't you come home for dinner?" she demanded as soon as I entered the house. She had been watching one of her movies and keeping one ear turned to hear me or Daddy come home. The second I closed the door, she was in the hallway.

"I went directly to the hospital and visited with Mommy," I told her.

"You were there all this time?"

"It's not down the street," I replied without much emotion. "Don't you want to know how she is?"

"I've already spoken to your father about her," she told me.

"Really? Well considering he wasn't there, I'm sure he was very informative."

"He's been in contact with her doctor, which is more important," she insisted.

"Is it? You think that's more important than having your husband come see you, be with you, comfort you?"

"Don't start with your dramatics," she warned. "All of you children are so theatrical these days. It comes from spending so much time in front of the television set," she analyzed. "It's either that or staring into a mirror all day."

"I don't do either, Grandmother, and you know that. Matter of fact, you watch more television than I do, and you wear more makeup," I added.

"Don't be insolent."

"I'm not being insolent. I'm just stating facts."

"Never mind, never mind," she insisted. "There are far more important things to talk about and do. I'm getting this house intelligently organized. Come see your father's study," she told me.

It was really more of a command, but I was too curious not to follow her, and when I saw it, I smiled to myself.

If he doesn't like it, too bad, I thought.

"He works mainly in the afternoon when he works here on the weekends. He shouldn't be facing the sunlight. Don't you agree?"

"Fine with me," I said. Then I looked at her, my eyes small, determined. "Don't come into my room, Grandmother. If you move so much as a picture frame on the dresser . . ."

"I have no intention of entering your cave," she said. "You'll have to repair your room yourself."

"It doesn't need repairing. It needs to be left alone," I told her.

"Have you done your homework?" she cried after me when I turned away and started for the stairs.

I paused and looked at her, a half-smile on my face.

"Have I done my homework? Since when have you ever asked about that?"

"Well, with your mother gone, I thought I had better—"

"My mother isn't gone!" I screamed at her. "She's just recuperating. At least she's able to recuperate from her madness, which is more than some people can do."

I charged up the stairs, anxious to get away from her. She simply returned to her old movie, wallowing in it like she would soak in a warm bath.

It took me hours to calm myself down and do my homework. It was nearly midnight when I went to bed and still, Daddy had not come home. I fell asleep, but I woke to the sound of his footsteps on the stairs. Those stairs always creaked loudly, which was part of the charm of the house for me and for Mommy. Daddy didn't like it and Grandmother Beverly thought they should be ripped out and redone. She said the house was too old to be inhabited and complained vehemently about the creaks in the walls, the moans in the pipes, and the leaks in the roof. I would smile to myself, imagining her awake at night listening to the sounds, terrified that the house itself was coming alive and closing in on her. Footsteps on the stairway echoed with electric speed over the hallway floor and into her room as well as my own, but she didn't get up to greet Daddy.

I rose quickly and went to my door just as Daddy was passing my room.

"Daddy," I called in a loud whisper. He had his shoulders slumped like someone trying to tiptoe guiltily away.

"What are you doing awake?" he asked.

"I heard you coming up. Did you get to see Mommy?"

He shook his head.

"It was a horrendous trip. There were accidents and delays and I just managed to get home now. I'll get there tomorrow," he said, "but I did call and the nurse told me she was resting comfortably."

"She's drugged. How would they know if she was comfortable, Daddy?"

"All right," he said. "It's late, Cinnamon. Let's talk about it all tomorrow."

"When?"

"When I see you," he said. "Go to sleep. You're just going to make things more difficult for everyone by being contentious," he added and walked on to his bedroom.

I stood there and watched him go in, closing the door softly behind him.

He's not the same, I thought. He's just not the same. There's something more than Mommy's condition affecting him. I knew he would never tell me what it was. Could it be he was in trouble financially? Were we on the brink of economic disaster? Did he depend on Grandmother's money these days? Was that why he wouldn't contest anything she did?

Falling asleep with these questions in the air was like trying to walk over an icy road. Every time I drew close to drifting off, another troubling thought jerked me back awake, keeping me slipping and sliding until I finally passed out just before dawn. I hadn't set the alarm and my grandmother actually had to come pounding on my door.

"Are you getting up or not?" she cried from the hallway. I heard her try the knob, but I had locked it. "Who locks their bedroom?" she muttered. She knocked again. "Cinnamon, are you getting up?"

I groaned and looked at the clock, astounded at the time myself. For a moment I considered not going to school at all, and then, all my questions from the night before began to flood over me again and I made a quick decision. I was up and dressed in minutes.

"Why do you lock your bedroom door?" Grandmother Beverly asked as soon as I stepped into the kitchen. I went right to the coffee without responding. She made it too weak for my taste and even for Daddy's, but he didn't complain. I deliberately poured a cup and then poured it back through the coffee maker.

"What are you doing?"

"Trying to turn this tea into coffee," I muttered.

"A girl your age shouldn't be drinking so much coffee. It's not good for you," she insisted.

I started to look for one of my breakfast bars. She had moved everything around in the cabinets and literally nothing, not even a salt shaker, was where it had been. I started to shove things to the side more frantically.

"You're messing it all up. What are you looking for? Just ask," she said.

I turned.

"My breakfast bars! Where are they?"

"Oh, that garbage. It's candy. How can that be breakfast? I threw it all out," she admitted, proudly.

"Threw it all out? I had just bought them. They were mine. You had no right to do that, Grandmother, and for your information, they have a great deal more nutritional value than what you and Daddy eat for breakfast."

"Nonsense. Don't believe what they write on those wrappers," she said. "Now I'll make you some hard-boiled eggs." She put the pot under the faucet.

I gulped some coffee and marched past her.

"Cinnamon," she called after me. "Where are you going?"

"I'm too late to eat breakfast," I shouted back. "You eat it for me."

I rushed out of the house and to my car. My wheels screamed and stained the driveway with rubber as I accelerated. I was sure she had heard it. When I got to the road, I didn't head directly for school. Instead, I swung around toward Clarence's house and sure enough, I caught him sauntering along. He lived only about a half-mile from the school in the most elegant and expensive area. His house was actually as big as mine. He was surprised when I pulled up and honked the horn.

"What's up?" he asked after he opened the passenger door.

"I'm not going to school today," I said.

"Oh?"

"I have something else to do. Want to come along?"

"Where?"

"Into the city," I said. "Manhattan."

He thought a moment and then looked back as if someone was watching us. He shrugged and got into the car.

"I guess," he said.

I shot away from the curb and headed for the thruway.

"So what do you have to do?" he asked. "And don't say shopping. I hate shopping. If it's shopping, let me out. My mother used to drag me like a sled through the department stores."

"Hardly shopping. I'm going into the city to spy on my father," I replied.

"What? Why?"

"I have a feeling he might be losing his job or something," I said. "He might even have lost it by now. He's been acting strange and it's not because of what's happened to my mother. He's a bundle of secrets, wound up tight, and he won't let me inside. Sometimes, I feel like I don't care anymore, but then I think I should."

"Of course, you should," Clarence agreed. "Who else is going to care if you don't?"

From what he had told me about his own family life, he didn't have a much better relationship with his father who was a very busy attorney specializing in estate planning. His mother managed the new mall north of Yonkers and, according to Clarence, was busier than his father. He had a younger sister Lindsey in ninth grade, but they weren't close. Most of the time, they walked right by each other in school, barely exchanging a glance. He said she was very spoiled.

Funny, I thought, how you could be so alone in your own home, in your own family. Just because you had parents, it didn't guarantee you wouldn't be an orphan or a stranger if your parents were so wrapped up in themselves. Sometimes, I thought Clarence hung around with me and listened to my moans and groans just so he could feel like he was in a real family, even though it was mine and not his own.

"How are you going to spy on him?"

"I know where he works. We'll hang out there," I explained.

"Doesn't sound like you have much of a plan."

"I've got to do it. If you don't want to come . . ."

"No, it's all right. I'm fine."

It wasn't until we reached the Wall Street area that I felt I might have made a very silly decision. The traffic, the crowds and just the size of the buildings made what I had planned to do look as foolish as Clarence had made it sound.

"What do we do first?" Clarence asked, even more impressed with the task himself now.

"Find a parking garage as close to Daddy's building as possible," I said. I tried to look and sound like I knew what I was doing, like I was in the city often, but of course I wasn't. Mommy didn't like going to the city, except to shows. I saw my first Broadway show with her and Daddy when I was only seven. It was a musical, *The Phantom of the Opera*, and I remember being so mesmerized and excited, I could hardly speak.

"That's where you'll belong someday, Cinnamon," Mommy whispered in my ear and nodded at the stage.

I wondered. Did I? Could I?

I saw a few shows a year after that, but most of the time recently, it was just Mommy and me. Daddy was either working or meeting clients.

Parking was the easiest part of my skimpy plan today. It just meant spending money, which we did, and then we walked to Daddy's building.

"Have you ever been here before?" Clarence asked.

"Once, a long time ago. We had a day off but the market was open and Daddy decided to take me to see his offices and all the activity. I was in the fifth grade. Mommy came along and afterward, she and I went to a show off-Broadway, *The Fantasticks*. It was a very exciting day.

"I thought Daddy had a mad, crazy job. All that shouting and excitement. I couldn't understand how anyone kept track of anything or knew what he or she was doing. Daddy looked like the calmest person there."

Clarence listened, intrigued. He wasn't in the city that often, so his eyes were wandering everywhere, drinking in the activity, the endless flow of people, cars, the billboards and the variety of stores and restaurants. I wondered if your brain could shut down like some overloaded computer, all these sights and sounds coming at you at once.

"Now what?" he asked.

"There's a coffee shop in his building, in the lobby. Let's go there."

We went in and were able to get a table close to the window that looked out at the lobby. Having had nothing for breakfast, I was hungry and ordered scrambled eggs and a bagel. Clarence just had some coffee and watched me eat. I watched the elevators. There were four, with a constant stream of traffic, but soon it started to taper off. Most people had already arrived for work.

"What exactly do you think your father's doing?" Clarence asked as I ate.

"I think he's looking for a new job. That's why he doesn't tell his secretary exactly where he's going or where he can be reached or why he didn't answer a page the other day."

Clarence nodded.

"Yeah, that makes sense," he said. "He's probably got a lot of pride and doesn't want to feel like some kind of failure. My father has never made a mistake in twenty years of practicing law."

"Really?"

"That's what he makes it sound like, and everyone who works for my mother is a half-wit." He smiled. "I come from a pair of regular geniuses."

He made me laugh. Clarence is handsome, I thought. He has a twinkle in his eye that gets pretty sexy sometimes, whether he knows it or not. He acts like he doesn't, but I was always suspicious of people, especially boys. Their smiles and words were like little balls in the hands of a magician: now you see them, now you don't.

When I finished eating, I paid the check and lingered for a few moments.

"Now what do we do?" he asked.

"I want to be sure he's upstairs at his desk. I'll call and pretend I'm a client and ask for him," I said. "Afterward, we can go to the magazine and newspaper shop and then we'll hang out and wait until the market closes to see what he does. We've just got to keep inconspicuous."

We went to the bank of pay phones in the lobby and I dialed Daddy's number. His secretary answered and I asked for him.

"Oh," she said, "he's just this moment left. Can I switch you to Mr. Posner who's handling his accounts in the interim?"

"No," I said and hung up quickly.

"He left," I told Clarence excitedly. "Just now!"

We hurried back to the lobby and went into the newspaper and magazine store, pretending to be looking for something while I kept my eyes on the elevators. Moments later, Daddy emerged. He walked quickly toward the entrance and we shot out after him.

"We've got to be careful. I don't want him to spot us," I said as we stepped out.

Daddy was walking briskly down the sidewalk, his black wool scarf flung over his shoulders. He looked dapper, as dapper and handsome as Cary Grant in one of Grandmother Beverly's favorite old movies.

"I've seen this done enough on television," Clarence said confidently. "Just keep a good distance between us and him and try to stay behind someone."

Daddy never looked back, so it didn't matter. He crossed the street and continued down another busier street. Minutes later, he entered a coffee shop. It wasn't a very large one, but it had two big front windows. We could see everyone in it.

"He's just taking a coffee break," Clarence muttered. "He's not visiting any new firm."

I nodded, but Daddy strolled past the counter and paused at a booth. For a moment, because of the angle we were at, it looked like an empty one, but when he leaned over, we moved to our right and we caught sight of him greeting a woman, a very elegant looking blond-haired woman in a business suit. She seized his hand and held it as he slid into the seat across from her and for a long moment, they just looked at each other. Then Daddy smiled and sat back. She didn't let go of his hand.

I felt as if the air had just leaked completely out of my lungs and was quickly replaced with some steaming hot liquid burning in my chest and up into my mouth. It seemed like minutes flew by and still, they were holding hands.

"Maybe it's just a client," Clarence offered charitably.

My eyes clashed with his hopeful look.

"You don't hold hands with your clients," I managed to reply.

We both stood there, gazing through the window.

Whatever they were saying to each other pleased Daddy. His smile widened and then he leaned over the table to meet her halfway so they could kiss on the lips.

I looked at Clarence.

"Still think that's a business meeting?"

He let his eyes drift down and shook his head.

"Sorry," he said.

"Me too," I replied and turned abruptly.

I walked as quickly as I could. Clarence had to jog to catch up.

"It might still be something innocent," he offered.

"As innocent as Cain's murder of Abel," I replied. The tears in my eyes felt like they were frozen, stuck against my pupils, making the world appear foggy around me.

Mommy's lying sick and broken in a hospital room, was all I could think. It made my throat close.

I crossed the street quickly, nearly running toward the parking lot now.

"It's amazing that you decided to come into the city and be down here just at the right time," Clarence said trying to slow me down.

I stopped abruptly, so abruptly he almost stepped into another pedestrian.

"No, it's not really."

"What do you mean? You knew about this?"

"No. The spirits in the house made me go. The moment I woke up this morning, it was as if someone had whispered in my ear during the night or just before I woke up telling me to go. I felt pushed along."

"You're kidding. Aren't you?"

"No, I'm not. They look after me," I said. I walked on, Clarence hurrying to catch up again.

"You really believe there are spirits in your house? I

thought that was just something you wanted people to believe, something we had fun spreading around."

"It is fun, but I do believe it now. Yes," I said. I paused at the entrance to the parking lot. "You'll come over one night this week and go up to the attic with me and decide for yourself."

"Really?"

"Unless you're afraid," I said.

"No," he said shaking his head. He looked back in the direction of the coffee shop and then looked at me again. "No," he repeated, but this time, he didn't sound as confident.

"I've got to stop by the clinic to see my mother," I said. "Will you be all right waiting in the car?"

"Sure."

"Thanks," I said.

One of my frozen tears broke free and trickled icily down my cheek, but I had turned away in time to hide it from Clarence.

I didn't want anyone to see me crying over what Daddy was doing.

Sometimes sadness had to be kept as secret as love.

Sometimes, they were one and the same.

"Don't worry about me," Clarence said after I parked the car at the clinic. "I'll read what I was supposed to read for today's social studies class."

He smiled to give me some warm encouragement. All the way back from the city, I was quiet and didn't respond to any of his attempts to make conversation. I kept seeing Daddy kissing that woman in broad daylight, in a public place, unafraid or unconcerned. Maybe he thought no one knew him there anyway, or maybe he thought what if

someone did? What was he or she going to do, call
Mommy in the mental clinic to report it?

I nodded at Clarence and stepped out of the car. The
partly cloudy day had turned into a nearly overcast sky
with a much colder wind blowing into my face. I could
feel winter crawling up my spine, its icy fingers sliding
over my neck and shoulders. Zipping up my jacket, I
started toward the building, not knowing north from
south, east from west. I moved like someone in a trance
as though the upper part of me was being carried forward
against its wishes. Glimpsing myself in the window of
another car I passed in the parking lot, I saw how I was
holding my shoulders and my head back.

Now, I was sorry I had eaten so much for breakfast. I
ate more out of nervousness than hunger, and after seeing
Daddy with that woman, all the food in my stomach had
turned into balls of lead. It wanted to roll back up my
throat and out of my mouth. My legs were so heavy I
could barely lift my feet to go up the short stairway to the
front doors. I hesitated, took a deep breath, and then
entered.

An elderly woman was being escorted through the
lobby toward the hallway that led to the elevator. The
nurse with her gazed at me and smiled. When the elderly
woman saw me, she seized the nurse's hand and stopped
walking.

"It's Ida," she cried. She looked like she was an
instant away from bursting into happy tears.

"No, no, Rachael. That's not Ida."

"Sure it is. Ida, where have you been? I've been worried sick over you, dear," she told me.

The nurse smiled at me and shook her head.

It was as if there was a button in my head that when

pushed would open up the world of pretend. Maybe that was what all actors had in their heads.

"I was away," I said. "I came as soon as I could."

"Oh, dear, dear. I was worried about you, a young woman, all alone in Europe. Did my sister take good care of you?"

"Yes," I said. "And all she did was talk about you."

"Did she? That's nice. You have to tell me all about it," she said.

"She will," the nurse said, "after your nap."

"I will," I promised. "After you rest."

"Good. Don't forget now." She reached for me and I took her withered hand. The fingers were so slim, her paper thin skin seemed to have nothing between it and the bones. Her happiness gave her the strength to squeeze tightly. "I'm so glad you came home, dear. It's just the two of us now, just the two of us."

I smiled at her.

"We'll be fine," I said.

"Yes. We'll be fine." She nodded and then she continued along.

The nurse looked back at me with a smile of gratitude and then led her on toward the elevator.

I had a chill, a shudder running through me for a moment, when I envisioned that old, confused lady could be my mother years from now.

There was a new girl at the reception desk. I didn't pretend to be my mother's sister this time. I told the truth and she called up and then told me to wait because the head nurse was coming down. It put a panic in my chest and for a moment, I couldn't breathe.

"Why? What's wrong?" I demanded.

"Mrs. Fogelman will be here momentarily," the receptionist said. She nodded toward the pair of settees behind me. "Why don't you make yourself comfortable?"

I didn't want to sit, but my legs felt like they might simply melt beneath me, so I moved to the small imitation leather sofa and sat, staring at the elevators. Finally, one opened and a short, stocky woman with dark brown hair looking like it had been trimmed around a bowl, came out and hurriedly walked toward me. I rose.

"You're Mrs. Carlson's daughter?"

"Yes," I said. "What's wrong? Isn't she getting well?"

"I'm Mrs. Fogelman. The doctor was here earlier today and left instructions that I should personally greet any immediate family. There's been a little setback," she said.

"Setback? What does that mean?"

"Isn't your father with you?" she asked instead of answering.

I felt myself tighten like a wire being stretched to its limit. She actually looked past me toward the door.

"Unless he's invisible, I'd have to say no," I told her sharply. "What's wrong with my mother?"

"She's drifted into a comatose state," Mrs. Fogelman revealed after a moment of indecision. "However, the doctor feels it is only a temporary condition. We've moved her to our intensive care area and we're monitoring her carefully. I thought the doctor had reached your father and that's why you were here," she added.

"No, I think my father is unreachable at the moment," I muttered. "Can I see her, please?"

She nodded.

"Yes, that might be very good. She should hear your voice," Mrs. Fogelman decided. She smiled and we walked to the elevator.

"Are you in high school or college?" she asked me when the doors closed.

I hadn't been in many elevators in my life, but I always hated the deep silence, the way everyone avoided looking directly at anyone else, and waited uncomfortably for the doors to open again. The quiet moments seemed to put everyone on edge as if being closed in a small area with other human beings was alien to our species.

I barely heard Mrs. Fogelman talking.

"High school," I muttered. Who cares? I thought. What difference did that make now? What difference did anything make now?

She smiled at me and the doors opened mercifully one floor up. She led me down the corridor to the ICU ward and then to my mother's bedside. Her eyes were shut tight, the corners wrinkled.

"She looks like she's in great pain," I moaned.

Mrs. Fogelman didn't deny it.

"Mental pain," she said, trying to make it sound like it wasn't as bad as physical pain, but there was no hiding the truth. Mommy was in agony.

I reached for her hand and held it tightly in mine. Then I leaned over the bed railing and wiped some strands of hair from her forehead.

"Mommy, it's me, Cinnamon. Please, wake up, Mommy. Please."

Her face seemed frozen in that grimace of anguish. Her lips were stretched and white.

"What are you doing for her?" I demanded.

"We've got to be patient," Mrs. Fogelman said. "She'll snap out of it soon."

"What if she doesn't?"

"She will," she insisted, but my urgency and concern made her sound less confident.

"Do they always snap out of it?" When she didn't respond, I said, "Well?"

"Let's not think the worst, dear. The doctor is watching her closely. Keep talking to her," she advised and walked away quickly to get herself behind the sanctity of the central desk where she busied herself with other things and glanced my way only occasionally.

"Mommy," I pleaded, "please get better. You've got to get better and come home. I need you. We've got to be together again.

"Grandmother is taking over the house, just as you always feared. I want you to come home and make her put everything back the way it was. Please, Mommy. Please get better."

I sat there pleading with her until I felt my throat dry up and close. Then I kissed her on the cheek and looked at her face. Her eyelids fluttered and stopped.

"How are you doing, dear?" Mrs. Fogelman asked, coming up behind me.

I shook my head.

"Is your father on his way?" she asked.

I stared at her, bit down on my lip, and then smiled.

"The moment he gets an opportunity," I told her. "He'll rush right over."

She stared at me. Hadn't I said it right?

Or was it the rapid and constant flow of tears over my cheeks and chin that confused her?

I flicked them off, smiled at her again, looked back at Mommy and fled.

Clarence was so involved in his reading he didn't hear or see me until I opened the car door. By then, I had stopped crying, but he couldn't miss my red eyes.

"What's wrong?" he asked.

"She's worse. She's in a coma."

"Oh no. What do they say?"

I looked at him.

"They say what they're supposed to say. They say, 'Don't worry.' They say pretend this isn't happening. They say go on with your life and ignore it, ignore all of it, put on a good act, recite your lines, stay in the spotlights so you can't see the audience."

I started the car.

I saw rather than heard him mouth a curse.

I drove him home. He kept asking me what I was going to do now and I kept saying, "I don't know." He especially wanted to know if I was going to confront my father with what we had seen today.

"Would you?" I asked him.

He thought a moment and shrugged.

"I probably wouldn't be as surprised by it as you are," he finally replied. "But I'd like to help you," he said when I pulled up to his house. "Just don't be afraid to ask me for anything."

"Thanks, Clarence."

"Am I still coming over tomorrow night to meet your spirits?"

I smiled at him.

"Sure," I said. "We'll talk about it in school."

"I'll call you later," he promised. He leaned over to kiss my left cheek and then got out. I watched him walk away. He paused at his front door to wave goodbye and then I drove home. I don't know how I managed it. The car must have known the way by itself. One moment I blinked and the next I was pulling up the driveway.

The house never looked as lonely and dark to me as it did now. I didn't go inside. Instead, I walked around to the rear and then up to the knoll where the Demerests were buried. I stood before the old tombstones remembering the times Mommy and I were here.

The wind was blowing harder, the sky looking more bruised and angry, reflecting my mood. I could feel the cold rain threatening. We might even have flurries tonight, I thought, but I ignored the frigid air. Anger made my blood hot anyway. I could never understand the rage Medea felt toward her husband, Jason, when he betrayed her in the Greek tragedy. Now, I thought I could.

I charged toward a broken tree branch, scooped it up and dug into the ground, scratching away the earth like some madwoman searching for buried treasure. Finally, exhausted, I stopped. The hole was big enough for what I wanted anyway.

I reached around my neck and undid the charm necklace Daddy had bought me on my sixteenth birthday. I dropped it into the hole and covered it up.

It was as if I was burying him.

I jammed the stick into the ground like a grave marker and then I walked away without a backward glance.

5

Surprised by Love

The stillness in the house greeted me like a slap in the face. Grandmother Beverly's car was here, which meant she was home, but I didn't hear the television droning or any sounds coming from the kitchen. Was she already asleep? Good, I thought. I didn't want to face her at the moment. I started up the stairs, my head down, and lifted it only when I turned the knob on my bedroom door and was shocked to discover it wouldn't open.

It wouldn't open because a lock and a hasp had been installed and the lock was closed.

Both amazed and confused, I stepped back and cried, "What?" I had to touch it to believe it was really there. A lock on my own door?

"Grandmother!" I screamed. I spun around, but she didn't appear. I marched to her bedroom door and threw it open. She wasn't in her room, so I charged back to the stairway and pounded my way down, spinning at the bottom and rushing to the living room door.

There she was, seated comfortably like some queen mother, waiting for me.

"Why is there a lock on my door?"

She glared at me, her eyes small but so full of anger they looked capable of shooting out small flames in my direction.

"Where have you been today—and don't make up any ridiculous story about going to the hospital to be with your mother," she quickly warned. "I'm talking about the whole day from the moment you rushed out of this house without breakfast until now. Well?" she demanded, holding her body stiffly forward.

"Why are you asking me that and how dare you put a lock on my bedroom door?" I flared back at her, flashing my eyes with temper as hot and red as hers.

She sat back, a cold twisted smirk on her face.

"First, I'm asking because the school called here looking for you. Apparently, someone there was concerned about you and wanted to know how you were and why you weren't at school," she revealed.

Miss Hamilton, I thought to myself.

"Can you even begin to imagine how embarrassed I was when I had to reveal you weren't home and I didn't have any idea where you were?

"I called your father," she added, nodding. "I had to, of course."

"Really?" I replied, folding my arms under my breasts and placing my weight on my right foot, "and what did he have to say?"

"Fortunately for you, I was unable to reach him at the time."

"Is that so? Why? What did they tell you? Was he with a client, at a meeting, what?"

"That has nothing to do with our situation," she said. "Where were you?"

"Why is there a lock on my door?" I asked instead of answering.

"I put that lock on your door so you couldn't do what you always do when I question you or try to guide you . . . run off to your room and lock yourself inside. I'll unlock it when you tell me the truth. Now, where were you?"

"How dare you do this, Grandmother? That's my room!" I shouted at her, tears burning my eyelids.

"Until your mother returns, I have to be the one in charge of you, responsible for you. You are still a minor and your father is a very busy man with a great deal on his mind these days."

"Oh, yes," I said shaking my head, "my father is a very, very busy man. He's too busy to visit my mother. He's too busy to know she's fallen into a coma. That's a very busy man," I said.

"Mothers and daughters have to realize that their husbands and fathers can't be at their beck and call every minute. They're out there in the hard, cold world trying to make a living, trying to earn enough to provide and keep you comfortable. Who do you think pays the mortgage on this ridiculous relic of a house, and who pays for the food you eat and the gas you waste driving around in that car of yours, and who gave you that car and who—"

"And who cares?" I shouted, covering my ears with my hands. "Take it all back, everything!"

I turned and fled from her. When I reached my bedroom door again, I tried to pull the lock off, but I couldn't do it. Who could have ever imagined her doing something like this? Did meanness make people more inventive?

Instead of continuing my confrontation with her, I went up to the attic and threw myself on the small settee where I curled up in a fetal position and closed my eyes. My pounding heart calmed. The emotional tension had drained my body of all of its energy. I pulled the old afghan over myself, closed my eyes and almost immediately fell asleep.

The sound of my name hours and hours later woke me, but not abruptly. For a few moments it was as if the sound was inside me, in some dream, echoing. I groaned, my eyelids fluttered and then I felt someone touch my shoulder and I opened my eyes to see Daddy.

"Cinnamon. What are you doing?" he asked. "What in the world is going on here?"

I stared at him. Was this a dream? He had been in this attic so rarely that the sight of him here was more like a phantom of my imagination.

When I was a little girl, I could look at him and think my daddy was the perfect daddy, so handsome and warm, so loving and full of magic. There was magic in those hazel eyes. They could twinkle and make sickness go away, aches and pains flee, colds disappear and most of all, sad moments pop like bubbles. I remember his laughter. It was more like a song and whenever he said my name, it sounded like poetry. But that all seemed so long ago, truly like a dream, a fantasy. The memories were challenged now, cross-examined and scrutinized through my older, far more critical and discerning eyes.

His smiles were not as warm and held as long as I had thought. His words were not as soft and as comforting as I had wished. His promises were often forgotten, words written in the snow, melted and erased by the first touch of probing sunlight. He was merely a man.

I sat up, grinding my eyes to pull back the veil of sleepiness.

"Grandmother put a lock on my bedroom door," I said.

He stood up.

"I know. She told me about your not attending school today. Where were you? What did you do?"

"She put a lock on my bedroom door," I repeated, annoyed by the quivering in my voice.

"It's off," he said. "I unlocked it and took it off. Now, tell me where you were. What's going on with you?"

I looked up at him. The words were there, waiting to be born, launched at him like tiny knives. But I couldn't do it. I couldn't do it because saying them, sending them at him would cut me to pieces as well. I could only tremble at the thought of what it would all be like afterward with all of the ugly truth spilled before us.

"Don't you feel well?" he asked.

"No," I said.

"Well, why didn't you just tell Grandmother that?"

"She put a lock on my door," I muttered.

"I told you. I took it off," he said. "Where did you go?"

"Mommy's in a coma. Do you know that?" I snapped back at him.

He closed his eyes and nodded.

"I know. That's where I've been since I left work. The doctor assures me she will recuperate. He thinks it's just a temporary thing. She could be very much better tomorrow."

"Could she?"

"Yes. Now what did you do today, Cinnamon?"

"I had to be by myself today," I lied.

"We're all going through a very difficult time, Cinnamon. We've got to be strong, strong for Mommy," he said.

I couldn't look at him. I kept my eyes fixed on the floor. I thought I could hear my spirits, the Demerest women, all laughing at him. I guess it made me smile.

"Why are you laughing at what I'm saying?" he demanded. "Cinnamon, if you persist in this behavior, I'll have to have you examined by a doctor, too," he threatened.

That really made me laugh and made him furious.

"Go to your room," he ordered, "and you had better be in school tomorrow and behave or I'll take the car away from you. I mean it."

"Who pays for the mortgage and for the food and for the gas I waste . . ."

"What? You're not making any sense, Cinnamon. Go to bed," he ordered and turned away quickly.

I think he was actually afraid of me.

I sat there for a while, listening to the soft murmuring of the voices in the walls, the comforting rhythm of their words. A hundred years ago they came up here to escape from sadness too, I thought.

How little really has changed.

Daddy did take the lock off, but the hasp remained as a reminder of my grandmother's fury and power. She muttered around me all throughout breakfast the next day and followed me out of the house with a trail of warnings and threats, trying to make me feel guilty for putting more pressure and turmoil on our family at a difficult time.

"You're not the only one who's suffering here,

Cinnamon. Think of your father having all this on his head and having to have to do a good job at work at the same time. I know it's difficult for young people to be considerate of others these days. They've been spoiled and turned into self-centered little creatures, but I expect more from you."

Before I left, I couldn't resist turning on her and saying, "I'm not the self-centered one here, Grandmother. You should direct yourself more at Daddy," I fired. She raised her eyebrows and chased after me, out of the house and to the car.

"And what is that supposed to mean, young lady? What are you saying now? How can you say such a thing? Well?"

"Ask him," I said and got into my car.

I left her standing there, fuming.

Clarence was waiting for me at the lockers in the hallway when I arrived at school. One glance at his face told me something was very wrong.

"What?" I asked instead of saying hello or good morning.

"They called my mother at work," he said. "Told her I wasn't at school. She called my father and I'm grounded for a month. I can't go anywhere on the weekends."

"Oh. Sorry," I said. "They called my house too. Who knew they cared?" I added and pulled what I needed from my locker.

Clarence smiled.

"Get ready for the wisecracks," he said. "My sister already warned me they're talking about us."

"Good." I put my arm through his. "Let's give them something to really talk about then."

He looked surprised, but happy.

There wasn't an eye not directed at us as we made our way to homeroom. And that was the way it remained most of the day. We could see them all whispering, giggling, rotating their eyes with their fantasies and stories about us. I could tell Clarence was becoming more embarrassed by it than I was, but whenever he was embarrassed, his earlobes would turn red. The rest of him would grow pale and he would keep his eyes down, his lower lip under his upper.

None of the girls in my classes had the nerve to confront me directly. Even the girls who were so much bigger physically shied away from any face-to-face confrontation. Everyone was afraid of the evil eye, as my penetrating dark glare was called. The boys, however, were different. Eddie Morris, who liked to tease Clarence anyway, was full of witty remarks like, "Viagra Boy, can you keep up with her?"

Before lunch, Eddie and his buddies surrounded Clarence and tormented him with questions about our relationship. I was a little late because Miss Hamilton approached me in the hallway and practically shoved the script of her new school play into my hands.

"I want you to try out for the lead," she insisted. "Don't say no or anything until you read the play and see the part, Cinnamon. Please," she cajoled and I nodded and took it.

When I reached the cafeteria, Clarence was trying to get by four boys led by Eddie. Eddie kept poking him in the shoulder, baiting him with questions like, "Does she paint her nipples black too?"

Clarence lifted his eyes to see me coming and then, without any warning, swung his closed fist around and caught Eddie Morris on the side of his head. It took him by such surprise, he lost his balance and fell, spilling his books and notebooks over the floor. His friends, shocked, stepped back and Mr. Jacobs, the teacher on lunch duty, came charging forward, inserting himself quickly between Clarence and Eddie who was rising in a fury to retaliate.

He marched them both past me toward the principal's office. When Clarence went by, I caught a gleeful smile in his eyes.

"The spirits made me do it," he muttered and I laughed.

The other boys took one look at me and cleared away quickly. When Clarence returned, he came directly to my table and told me he had gotten a severe warning and two days detention.

"They're sending a letter home to good old Mom and Dad," he added, "but they don't have to. My sister will be blabbing about it at the dinner table tonight. Maybe my father will be at one of his famous dinner meetings. Maybe they both will be."

As it turned out, that was exactly what happened. Clarence called me to tell me so. Then he surprised me by asking when he should come over.

"I thought you were grounded," I said.

"I'll tell them I had to study with you for a math test or something. That usually works. Any excuse usually works," he added. "Ours is a house built on a foundation of lies everyone accepts."

"Come any time," I said and went to join my grandmother for dinner. It was the first time since Mommy had been taken away by ambulance.

But I was feeling better about Mommy because when I called the hospital, the nurse in ICU told me she had snapped out of the coma and was being moved back to a regular room. She said the doctor wanted to hold off visitors until the next day so she could get a full night's rest, but he was speaking with much more positive notes. It filled my heart with enough hope and warmth to even face my grandmother and be civil. The end, after all, was in sight. The madness in the house would stop.

What happened with Daddy was something else, something to postpone, but in my secret heart of hearts, I prayed there was some explanation and some end to that betrayal as well. Funny, I thought, how good news could turn you into a child again, permitting you to believe in happy endings.

At eight o'clock, the doorbell rang and I hurried down the stairs to get there before Grandmother Beverly. Daddy, who had called earlier to tell her he was attending an important business meeting, was not home for dinner and wouldn't be until quite late.

"Hi," I said after I opened the door and found Clarence standing there, looking shy and afraid. Was I the first girl he had ever visited?

He turned to gaze down the driveway as if he thought he might have been followed and then nodded, smiled and stepped into the house. His eyes were like hungry little creatures gobbling up everything in sight.

"Those two bare areas were where my mother had her favorite paintings," I said nodding toward the wall where Mommy's New Orleans paintings once hung. "Grandmother Beverly is in the process of replacing them with something more cheerful," I said under my breath. "When Mommy comes home, we'll put her pictures back."

He nodded and then stiffened and froze as Grandmother Beverly came out of the kitchen to see who had come to the door. The instant her gaze fell on him, her face expressed her disapproval: her lips stretching and flowing into the corners, her eyes flashing disgust. Clarence was wearing a ragged looking old bomber jacket and a tee-shirt with a picture of Bach and the words *Fugue Me* written beneath it.

"And who is this?"

"This is Clarence Baron, Grandmother. He and I are studying for a social studies test we're taking tomorrow. Is that all right with you?"

"Why didn't you ask before he arrived?" she countered.

"I couldn't imagine any reason why you wouldn't approve," I replied as sweetly as I could manage. "Maybe you've heard of Clarence's father, Michael Baron, one of the most prominent attorneys in the area."

She drew her head back as if she had flies in her nose and scrutinized Clarence as if she were considering him for a part in her play.

"Don't stay too late," she commanded, gave Clarence a threatening look of warning, and then returned to the kitchen.

I smiled at him.

"Now you see why she was the inspiration for the character of Freddy in *A Nightmare on Elm Street*," I said.

Clarence laughed and I hooked my arm into his and steered him toward the staircase.

"Quick, before she decides to take a sample of your blood," I said and hurriedly moved us up. I was embarrassed about the hasp on my bedroom door so I rushed him by and took him directly to the attic. I lit a stick of incense while he waited in the doorway, gazing in nervously.

"Don't worry. There's nothing here that will hurt you," I promised.

"I know that," he said, but not with great confidence, and entered.

"This was a favorite place for my mother and me," I began and then showed him the old pictures my mother had found, rattling off the names we knew and the names we had created, as well as a line or two about them, which was also mostly imagined.

"She is my favorite," I said showing him the picture of Jonathan Demerest's youngest daughter Belva. Clarence held it and studied her faint visage. Even awash in the sepia tint, her big eyes stood out.

"She looks so sad for a young girl," he said.

"Well, she fell in love with a young officer in her father's regiment, Captain Lance Arnold, and he fell in love with her even though she was only thirteen at the time."

"Thirteen? Really?"

"Yes. In those days women were engaged or married before they were twenty, you know."

"How old was he?"

"Twenty-three. Captain Arnold courted her and finally won her father's blessing. They were married when she was only fifteen and less than a year later, she was pregnant, but she and her baby died in a horrible birthing. Captain Arnold killed himself in grief."

"You're kidding?" Clarence said.

I wiped a tear from my cheek and shook my head. Then I took the picture from him and stared at it.

"She wrote exquisite but sad poems mourning the short life of beautiful things. She was a very sensitive person who liked to wander through the fields and forest and talk to the animals."

I closed my eyes and recited, "The color of roses lives in my eyes long after they have faded and gone. I lock the scent within my heart and when I sleep, they bloom once more."

I sighed and then looked at Clarence. He seemed about to cry himself. His eyes shone brilliantly with unused tears.

"Wow," he said.

"Sometimes, I really feel her beside me," I whispered. "When I'm very sad and alone, I close my eyes and I sense her fingers moving against mine."

I put my hand on Clarence's and he jerked back.

"You're kidding?"

"No," I said. "It's true. You can feel the love and the energy they left here. Close your eyes," I told him. "Relax and put everything out of your mind. Just conjure up her face. Go on," I urged and took his hand again. He let me hold his fingers and draw him closer to me.

We sat together, our eyes closed, holding hands, listening to our own hearts beat.

"Belva," I whispered. Then I leaned over and kissed him on the cheek.

He acted as if he had been stung.

"Why did you do that?"

"I couldn't help it. Belva made me do it," I said. "She takes me over sometimes. I think she sees you as her young captain when he was first courting her. She gets excited again and full of joy. Do you feel anything inside you?"

He cocked his head, considering.

"What should I feel?" he asked.

"A strange warmth, but a pleasant warmth. When you look at me, what do you see?" I asked bringing my face closer. "Look into my eyes, deeply."

He nodded.

"Yeah, I see what you mean, I think."

"Yes, you do," I told him. "I feel it, too. They're in us, taking us over."

I kissed him on the lips and then I did it again and he moved closer and put his arm around me, drawing me into him. I started to lie back, unbuttoning my blouse as I did so. He hovered over me, his eyes full of excitement, amazed. I reached up for him, drawing his face toward me, his lips to my breasts. He kissed me and for a moment I held onto him as if I were drowning. He moved completely over me and we kissed again and again.

"Wait," I said and sat up to strip off my blouse. I wasn't wearing a bra.

"God, you're beautiful, Cinnamon. I've been afraid to say it, but I always thought so. Right from the first time I set eyes on you."

"Yes. Captain Arnold said something just like that to Belva," I told him. "Don't you see? It's happening just the way it happened to them. We must make love," I decided. "We must make this night the most special night of our lives and then hold it in our hearts forever and ever."

He nodded and started to undress. I slipped my jeans down and moments later, both of us naked, we embraced. We kissed until we were breathless and then, as if coming to his senses, Clarence pulled away abruptly.

"I could get you in trouble," he said. He shook his head. "I feel like Mrs. Miller is standing next to us, warning us about safe sex like she does in health education. I'm not exactly prepared for this."

I smiled at him.

"You're always the gentleman, sir, considerate as well as loving. That's what Belva said to her captain."

"I want to make love to you, Cinnamon, more than anything," he said mournfully.

"Me too, but you're right, Captain."

He laughed.

"Wait," I said. "I have an idea."

I rose, wrapped the afghan around me and told him I'd be right back. He covered himself with his jacket. I tiptoed out of the attic, down the short stairway to Mommy and Daddy's room. Long ago, I had gone in there curious and explored. I discovered where Daddy kept his contraceptives. They were still where I had first found them. As soon as I had one, I rushed back to the attic.

Clarence was exactly where and how I had left him as if he feared a movement no matter how slight in either direction would shatter the magic. I stepped before him and opened my hand. His eyes widened. He reached for the contraceptive and turned to put it on while I slipped back beside him on the settee. Then he moved over me, lingering for a moment.

"I've fantasized about this so much, it feels unreal."

"It's real," I whispered. I put my hands around the back of his neck and drew his lips down to mine. It was a long, passionate, wonderful kiss.

"Oh Captain, my special, private, wonderful Captain," I whispered. "Take me to paradise."

There were moments when I thought maybe Clarence was right: I was making love in a dream. It did seem unreal, ethereal, but my blood was stirred by my pounding, hungry heart, a heart starving for love, for real affection, for warmth. My head echoed with our moans of pleasure, our reaching out for each other, into each other. I was afraid it would stop and when it did, I came down from my ecstasy reluctantly.

He softened and relaxed over me, his breath slowing until he was able to raise himself away and look into my face.

"Cinnamon," he said.

"No," I said putting my finger on his lips. "Call me Belva. I am Belva."

He smiled.

"Belva. I—I really love you."

"I'm glad, Captain. Now take me away from here," I said. "Take me someplace wonderful where we will always be happy."

"Okay," he said smiling.

I moved over a little and he scrunched down beside me. I pulled the afghan over us and told him to rest and be still and enjoy our wonderful, blissful aftermath. He closed his eyes. We held each other and soon, we fell asleep.

Grandmother Beverly's screams shattered our dreams. She was in the attic doorway, grimacing with revulsion, her eyes big, her mouth twisted.

"What depraved and despicable thing are you doing?" she cried.

Clarence trembled as if the house itself was shaking.

"Get out!" I screamed back at her. "This is my private place. Get out!"

"I knew it! I knew when I didn't hear a sound that you were wallowing in sin. Disgusting—and in your own home, right above my head."

I leaped up from the settee, forgetting my nudity, and closed the attic door in her face.

Clarence was rushing to get dressed.

"Oh wow, sorry," he said. "I'd better go. I fell asleep. I'm sorry."

"There's nothing to be sorry about. She had no right to spy on us."

I started to dress.

"You going to be all right?" he asked when he got his shoes on and reached for his jacket.

"I'll be peachy keen as always. Don't worry about it, Clarence. This is a glass house. The people in it can't throw stones."

He nodded and reached for the doorknob. I guess I couldn't blame him for being terrified. I hurriedly completed my own dressing and walked him down to the front entrance. Then I stepped outside. It had started to rain so we remained under the portico.

"I'll meet you at the lockers in the morning."

"Yes."

He kissed me quickly.

"Night," he said.

"Good night, Clarence. Clarence," I called when he stepped down. He turned.

"Yes?"

"You made a wonderful Captain Arnold."

He smiled and shrugged.

"Maybe I should go out for the play, too."

"Maybe," I said and watched him get into his car and drive away.

Then I turned and reentered the house. Grandmother Beverly was standing in the shadows. She stepped into the light so that the glow of the chandelier washed the darkness off her face. It glowed like ivory, her eyes twirling with anger.

"Your father will hear of this," she promised.

"Yes," I said, "and when you tell him, ask him what's worse, what I did or what he did? Ask him if adultery is worse," I threw back at her.

She raised her hands to the base of her throat.

"That's . . . a lie, but even so," she added quickly, "you're still a minor and . . ."

"I'm not a child, Grandmother. A hundred years ago, women were married and had children by my age. I'm a woman and what makes me age is not time. What makes me age is what the so-called adults around me do, to me, in spite of me. They won't let us be children. They kill the child in us quickly and then they ask us to be grown-ups like they are.

"I'd rather live in my attic," I spat and left her still mostly in the shadows, glaring out at me like some owl in the darkness waiting for easier prey.

I sprawled on my bed and gazed up at the ceiling until I felt my heart slow and my body calm down. Then I reached for the script Miss Hamilton had given me. It was a play entitled *Death Takes a Holiday.* I was familiar with the story. It was one of Mommy's favorites, actually.

A young woman is courted by a handsome man who turns out to be Death on holiday and when it's time for him to leave, he tells her who he is and she reveals she always knew and she's still willing to go with him.

Romantic slop?

Maybe.

But at the moment, I would gladly put my hand into his and run off.

I could do this part well, I thought.

I could do it so well, I'd frighten myself.

6

—⚜—

Seizing the Stage

Grandmother Beverly didn't tell Daddy about Clarence and me. She had a better way and a far more effective place to snap her punitive whip. Now it was Clarence's turn to be called out of class, only for him it was to meet with his father. Because Clarence didn't return for his afternoon classes, I didn't find out about it until I returned from visiting with Mommy. Instinctively, I knew something terrible was going on. Every time I thought about him, about our teacher calling out his name and telling him to report to the office, I felt my heart thump along like a flat tire.

When I drove into the clinic parking lot and entered the building, I tried to push my anxieties under a blanket of smiles. The last thing I wanted to do was lay my problems at Mommy's hospital bed. For her sake, everything had to look pleasant. She was a weakened vessel sailing in a tumultuous sea. Adding the weight of my problems to her own might sink her for good.

She had just finished having a cup of tea and was still sitting up in her bed. I could see from the brightness in her eyes that she had crossed through the darkness between her heart-breaking memories and the present. She still looked quite fragile, her lips trembling slightly, like the lips of someone on the verge of opening a dam of tears, but there was a significant change in her demeanor. It brightened my own spirits and I rushed to her side.

"Mommy, you're better," I cried and threw my arms around her. I kissed her and she did start to shed some tears.

"I was asking for you, Cinnamon," she said. "They told me some silly story about my younger sister coming here."

I laughed, and held her hand.

"That was me, Mommy. I pretended to be your sister the first time I visited."

She shook her head.

"Why?"

"I don't know," I said shifting my eyes guiltily.

She stared at me, her own eyes filling with understanding.

"Who wants to have a mother in here?" she asked gazing around. "I know how you feel." She sighed, closed her eyes and lowered herself to her pillow. "I lost the baby, Cinnamon. I lost her."

"It wasn't your fault, Mommy. You did everything the doctor told you to do."

She nodded.

"It wasn't meant to be," she said in a whisper. "Grandmother Beverly was right."

"No, she wasn't right. She's never right."

Mommy shook her head.

"This time, I'm afraid she was. Maybe I was too old. I had this hope that having a baby would make us a better family, improve my relationship with your father. Sometimes, you just can't force fate. It's almost a sin to try."

"Stop it, Mommy. Don't do this to yourself. That's why you were . . . sick before."

"Sick?" She nodded. "Yes, I suppose you could call it that. I don't remember very much. I found myself here and all they tell me is I suffered a slight nervous breakdown, but that I'm on the way to a full recovery. What happened, Cinnamon? What did I do that they would put me in here?"

I shook my head. Was I supposed to tell her?

"Please, honey. We don't keep things from each other," she reminded me.

"You thought you hadn't had the baby. You thought you were having labor pains."

I decided to leave out the bizarre drawing she had made on her body.

"Oh."

"Then you thought you gave birth prematurely and the baby was in intensive care. You kept asking me how she was."

She nodded, took a deep breath to keep her tears back, and shook her head.

"Is your father terribly upset?" she asked.

If I have any acting skills, I thought, now we'll see. My slight hesitation already had triggered some concern in her and her eyes snapped open and turned to peruse my face.

"He's been working harder to keep himself from thinking about it all," I said. "I haven't seen much of him."

She nodded.

"I don't blame him for working harder and not wanting to think about it. He wanted the baby very much."

I nodded, smiled and took her hand again.

"You must get stronger and come home as quickly as you can, Mommy. I need you."

Her eyebrows rose at the urgency in my voice.

"Grandmother Beverly making things hard for you?"

"Let's just say you've got a lot to do at home, Mommy," I replied and she laughed.

"Let her have her moment in the sun, gloat about what happened and how right she was. That's all she has, all she's ever had: her own self-righteousness," Mommy added. I felt my heart fill with joy. We were conspirators again, a team, turning the world into our stage, putting the lights where we wanted them, designing the set, filling it with our own props, writing the script as we went along.

"You mean you won't ignore her as much?"

"Exactly. I'll do exactly the opposite: pay too much attention to her. We'll agree with her, but of course, we won't."

"We'll haunt her. We'll even ask her opinions," I suggested.

She smiled gleefully.

"About every little thing, anything."

"Weigh her down with more responsibilities, more decisions."

"We'll yes her to death," Mommy said. "We'll overwhelm her with respect and cooperation until she runs off exhausted into the wings."

I laughed.

"Oh Mommy, I can't wait for you to come home."

She asked me about school and I told her about the play and Miss Hamilton's giving me a script.

"It's a wonderful play. Do go out for it, honey. I'd love to see you on the stage, a real stage with a real audience and not just our little attic room of make-believe, okay?"

"I'll think about it," I said.

"Good." She closed her eyes. "Good."

Her condition made it possible for her to turn on sleep in an instant. I saw her breathing become regular, slow, and felt her grip on my hand soften. Gently, I pulled away and sat back, watching her for a while.

She's coming home, I thought. Mommy's coming home.

I left the hospital with bounce in my steps. I felt I could do battle with anyone or anything again. I would go out for the play. I wouldn't be afraid of competing. I could even handle Grandmother Beverly until Mommy came home, and as for Daddy . . . I would pretend I knew nothing and let his own conscience boil in his heart.

Grandmother Beverly was in the kitchen, preparing dinner. I hated to admit it, but the aroma of the roast chicken and baked potatoes made me hungry. It all smelled so good. She greeted me and told me Daddy was coming home and would visit Mommy after dinner.

"So we're eating as soon as he arrives," she informed me. "Put your things away and come down to set the table."

"Mommy's better," I told her. "She's a lot better."
She nodded.

"I know all about it," she said as if that was the least important thing and went back to preparing dinner.

I hurried upstairs. I wouldn't return to the hospital with Daddy later, I thought. I didn't want to ride with him. I was afraid I wouldn't be able to keep what I knew to myself. Anyway, tomorrow were the auditions for the play and I did want to study the part, even memorize some of it to impress everyone.

Just as I put my books down and started to change my clothes, the phone rang. It was Clarence.

"I'm sorry I didn't call you sooner," I told him as soon as I heard his voice. "I went right to the hospital. My mother is better. She'll be coming home soon. She's better, Clarence."

"I'm glad," he said, but the heavy tone in his voice told me something was very, very wrong.

"What happened? Why did your father come to school for you?"

"Your grandmother called him this morning at the office," he said.

My heart stopped and started.

"What?"

"She told him everything she saw. She threatened all sorts of things, including a lawsuit. All this after I cut school and he had grounded me, too," he added. "Then he saw the letter about my fighting and it was like lighting a wick on a stick of dynamite. I never saw him this angry. My mother's just as angry. They had a meeting about me and they've decided to send me to the Brooks Academy. My father's always threatened to do that."

"Boarding school? When?"

"Immediately," he said.

"How can they do that?"

"You don't know my father. When he makes up his mind, he goes to work and moves mountains out of his way." Clarence took a breath. "I'm leaving tomorrow."

"Tomorrow! You're kidding?"

"I wish I was," he said.

"Well, why are you going? Don't go, Clarence."

"I've got to go. They've already removed me from school here."

"But—"

"He even suggested he might send me to a military school if I don't cooperate."

"Oh, Clarence."

"Maybe you can come up to Brooks once in a while. It's only about two and a half-hours' drive. I'll call you whenever I can, too. I can take my computer. Maybe we can e-mail each other every day."

"My grandmother did this," I groaned.

"I never saw my father as angry or afraid of anything or anyone."

I was quiet. I didn't know what to say. Who could I turn to for help and sympathy? My father? Hardly. I couldn't tell Mommy about this yet. I had to give her a chance to fully recover. Never did I feel as trapped and alone. I held the receiver to my ear, but Clarence was becoming fainter and fainter, a voice drifting away, a face diminishing, a memory thinning until it was nearly impossible to revive. He was on a boat floating into the darkness.

"I'm sorry," was all I could offer.

"I'll call as soon as I can," was his weak and despondent reply.

When I hung up, I felt as if I had closed my last window and was shut up in a room with no door.

"Cinnamon!" I heard Grandmother shout up the stairs. "Set the table. It's getting late."

You have no idea how late it is, Grandmother, I thought. No idea.

I decided to say nothing about Clarence at dinner. I wouldn't give her the satisfaction of knowing she had succeeded in getting exactly what she intended. Daddy was buoyant when he returned. He knew about Mommy's recovery, of course, and talked about how we were going to make things pleasant for her when she came home.

"When she's stronger, we can think about a nice little holiday, perhaps. In the spring. She's always wanted to go to Disney World. What do you think?"

"Ridiculous," Grandmother Beverly said. "Adults wanting to go to a children's playland."

"It's not only for children. Besides, the child in you never should die," Daddy countered.

I raised my eyebrows. It was rare to see or hear him disagree with her.

"You'll like it too, Mom," he said.

"Me? You want me to go to Disney World?"

"Why not? You'd be surprised at how you would enjoy it."

"Surprised for sure," she said.

He turned to me, smiling. "I spoke with Mommy late today and she told me you said you were going out for the school play."

"Maybe," I said.

"It would make her happy," he told me.

I glared at him.

"I know what makes her happy and what doesn't, Daddy. I know better than anyone."

His smile held, but lost its glow.

"Sure you do, Cinnamon. I know that." He glanced at Grandmother Beverly.

"What do you think, Mom?"

"She dresses like she's on some stage anyway," she said. "And she certainly needs more to do. Idle time leads to trouble," she added turning to me, her eyes small and hot with accusation.

I looked away, my lips struggling to open, my tongue thrashing about, anxious to fire off the furious words.

Don't give her the satisfaction, I told myself. Pretend nothing she does or says can have an effect on you. Defeat her with indifference.

That took all the control I could muster. Perhaps it was my greatest performance.

I smiled at both of them.

"Yes, I have decided," I said. "I'm going to win that part and be in the play."

"Good," Daddy said clapping his hands. "I have something wonderful to tell your mother tonight."

Of course, it was easier for me to say it, but even with Miss Hamilton's encouragement, winning the part was going to be a formidable task. The two other girls who I knew were going out for it were both veterans of the school's stage. One of them was Iris Ainsley, the prettiest girl in the senior class by far. I had to admit to myself that she looked the part more than I did. She had soft hair the color of fresh corn and eyes that looked as though God had taken them from the purest sapphire. She was an inch or so shorter than I was, but she had a dream figure, lithe with soft turns from her neck to her shoulders. When she walked through the school, she seemed to float. It was easy to see the looks of appreciation and longing in the eyes of some of the male teachers as well as the boys in school. She had a very pleasant speaking voice and she was an honor student.

If I had anything over her, it was my stronger desire to win the part, to win it for Mommy. Iris didn't have the same hunger, the same need and determination. She couldn't raise herself to the level of intensity. She was too comfortable being Iris Ainsley to really step out of herself and be the woman in the play. I only hoped others saw it as I did.

Auditions were held after school in the auditorium. I had been having a horrendous day. Rumors encircled me like a ring of fire now that everyone knew Clarence had been taken out of school. A little truth was mixed with a lot of exaggeration to create a recipe for disgrace. My role attracted the most exaggeration, especially from the lips of the boys. According to what some of the kids were saying, I had either raped poor innocent Clarence or taught him some nasty satanic rituals. Dirty remarks were cast my way in the halls and in the cafeteria. I found disgusting notes on my desk and shoved into my locker. I ignored it all and kept my focus on what I had to do: remain within that spotlight so that I couldn't see the world around me.

Most of the students who were going out for the play looked genuinely surprised I was there. Miss Hamilton handed out scenes from the play. She began by explaining the story and setting up the characters.

"Don't think about one character or another. Just read what I give you to read and leave it up to me to decide who fits each character the best. I appreciate you all coming out; it takes courage. And I would like to state right now that if you don't find yourself with a part, please consider being a member of our set crew, prop crew, lighting crew or publicity committee. My advice to all of you is to get involved any way you can," she added looking directly at me.

It filled me with dread. Was it a foregone conclusion that Iris would get the part I longed to have?

The readings began. Iris had done what I had done: she had memorized the lead's lines. I could see from their faces that everyone assumed she was going to get the role. I felt it was almost futile when I was called. The others didn't smile with disdain as much as they stared with curiosity. None of them had ever seen me do anything in front of an audience. I read in class, of course, and I made reports when I had to, just like they did, but this was different. This was truly being under the spotlight.

I stepped up on the stage. Dell Johnson was reading the role of Death. He had a very mature look and a deep, resonant voice. He sang lead in the chorus and had been in three major musical productions at the school. None of the boys trying out deluded themselves. They were here to get some other role. Dell owned this one by his mere existence.

He looked at me and smiled as if my daring to challenge Iris was a childish act of bravado. It stirred heat under my breasts. I straightened my shoulders and closed my eyes for a moment, conjuring up the very scene Miss Hamilton had chosen to be read.

And then I began, reciting, illustrating I had memorized the lines as well. I could hear a very audible gasp of surprise and a stirring in the group. Dell, who I knew had intended just to read his lines without much feeling, suddenly found himself actually acting. Later, Miss

Hamilton would tell me when someone is good, very good, it makes everyone else reach for his highest capability.

I looked at Dell. I moved toward him instinctively when the lines called for me to do so. I raised and lowered my voice, gazed into his eyes, drew him into the scene. We did so well together, we went beyond the pages we were given, and for a few seconds, no one, not even Miss Hamilton, realized it. Then she clapped her hands and we stopped.

"Well, thank you, Cinnamon. Thank you," she added with audible appreciation.

I glanced at Iris. She looked shocked, surprised, and angry at the same time, but that quickly turned to panic when she looked at Miss Hamilton and saw the depth of pleasure on her face. Then Iris turned back to me, long, glaring looks of envy delivered and redelivered as a series of visual slaps on my face. I walked off, feeling her eyes like two laser beams burning the back of my head. I ignored her and sat down to listen to the others, choosing whom I would select to play the various roles just to see how close I could come to what Miss Hamilton would do.

Surprisingly, I was nearly right about every one of them when I looked at the cast list posted the following morning. My name was prominent. I had won the part and that took over as the main topic of conversation in school. Most of my teachers congratulated me. Some looked genuinely surprised and impressed. Even Mr. Kaplan, the principal, stopped to wish me luck and encouragement. I was on pins and needles, anxious to rush out to the clinic to give Mommy the good news. Our first rehearsal was on Monday. Miss Hamilton assigned the pages to be memorized.

"I'm glad she chose you," Dell Johnson told me just before school ended. "I was afraid she wouldn't give you the chance."

"Thank you. Actually, she asked me to try out," I told him. That raised his eyebrows.

"Really?" He paused and looked around us to be sure what we said wouldn't be overheard. "You know, you'd better be careful about her," he advised.

"Why?"

"I've heard things, and I've got to warn you . . . Iris is pretty upset. She's already suggesting . . ." He rolled his eyes.

"Suggesting what?"

"Dirty stuff," he said. "Between you and Miss Hamilton," he added.

"She better not do it in front of me," I said.

"Don't worry, she won't. She doesn't work that way." He leaned toward me to add, "Just ignore them all, Cinnamon. Concentrate on the play. You'll be great," he said.

He sounded sincere, but I wondered if I could trust him. It was the beginning, I thought, the beginning of all the little intrigues that would surround and invade every dramatic project with which I would become involved. As always, the hardest part was acting in real life and the easiest thing was doing the actual performance. The line between the real and the imagined was blurred. Once again, I understood that life itself was an ongoing play. Shakespeare was right: the world was a stage and all of us merely players.

Well, it was my time to play and, I was now determined, I would.

*   *   *

Mommy was so ecstatic over the news, I thought she might get up, ask for her clothes and walk out of the clinic with me right then and there.

"I knew you would be chosen, Cinnamon. She would have had to be a dullard not to see your talents," Mommy told me.

"Sometimes, talent isn't what determines who does and does not get the good roles, Mommy," I said. "You taught me that."

She stared at me a moment, her eyes darkening.

"Of course you're right, honey," she said. "But I never meant to cause you to be cynical at so young an age. We need our childhood faiths sometimes. We need to believe in magic and wonder and have pure, innocent hope. Otherwise, the world out there is a very dark, disappointing place and frankly, it's the only world we have."

"I believe in the magic, Mommy, but it's magic we make for ourselves. Those who trust and have too much faith suffer the most," I said.

What she didn't know was that I was talking about Daddy and how much faith and trust she had in him. How would she react when she found out about him? Would she crumble and end up back in here? I would hate him forever, I thought.

"You're right, Cinnamon. I just want you to find a good balance."

"I will," I promised.

She wanted me to read from the play script and talk about the part. She was determined to get better quickly now and be there to help me give the best possible performance.

"When are you coming home, Mommy? Has the doctor told you?"

"He wants me to stay a few more days, to grow stronger and to be sure I am all right," she said. "Daddy thinks that's best, too."

"Really?"

"Yes. He seems so troubled these days, so distant. I feel sorry for him, sorry for what all this has done to him," she said.

"Don't you feel that way, Mommy," I charged. I was a bit too adamant.

"Why not?"

"You're the one who's suffered! You had all the pain and all the disappointment, Mommy."

"Okay, honey. Let's try not to talk about me anymore. Let's concentrate on you for a while. I can't wait to see you on that stage. Read some more," she urged.

I softened my hard heart and did what she asked. In fact, the play soon became my whole life. I rushed through my homework at night and then went upstairs to the magic attic room to read and recite aloud. It just felt better to do it in that room, our room for stories and dreams. I soon memorized the whole play, everyone's part as well as my own. I could deliver my lines and then Dell's, actually assuming his position and lowering my voice to sound like him.

It felt so good. I was safe, wrapped in the cocoon of the imaginary world, the characters, the time and the place. I was no longer here in a house where sad tears streaked the walls, where dark shadows brushed away our smiles, where old voices full of disappointments and trouble echoed in the silences that hung in every corner during the hours when darkness draped over us and the moon fell victim to night's long thick clouds.

The play was the thing, my everything, my new world. It filled the void that had been dug and created the day I spied on Daddy and saw him kiss that strange woman on the lips. I had someplace to go to avoid him, something else to think about and fill my head, shoving out the anger and the disappointment that followed the memory of that dreadful moment. It helped me tolerate Grandmother Beverly, to flick off her nasty comments and criticism or let it float on by, unheard, unrecognized. When she began one of her lectures, I stared at her and in my mind, I rolled off lines from the play, listening to the voices in my head instead of her. In a way I had become just like Mommy, able to ignore her.

Perhaps most of all, the play loomed as the one big thing that would restore Mommy, bring her happiness and pleasure, help her to forget her tragedy and depression and bring us together in our special way once more.

And then, as if Grandmother Beverly understood all this, she homed in on her opportunity to ruin it, to shut another door and maybe drive Mommy back into despair. This opportunity came from the ugliest and nastiest of the rumors that girls like Iris Ainsley kept swarming like angry bees around me. She was so beautiful and intelligent. She had more than most girls dreamed of having, but her jealousy was too strong. It replaced the soft blue in her eyes with a putrid green and turned those perfect lips into writhing corkscrews, turning and twisting words and thoughts until they spilled out around me in the form of accusations about Miss Hamilton and myself.

The clouds steamed in from the north, cold and dark, eager to close off my sunshine.

I couldn't let it happen.

I wouldn't let it happen.

I drew strength from my spirits, my old pictures in the attic and the voices in the walls.

And I went forth to do battle with all the demons inside my home and out.

7

—⚍—

Bright Lights Can Burn

It really began when Miss Hamilton decided to hold small rehearsals at her house on weekends. Mommy had returned home from the clinic by then. The doctor had given her some medication to keep her calm. She was still weak, fragile, tired by early evening. When she came home and saw the changes Grandmother Beverly had made, she was very upset, but Daddy quickly reminded her that she had to remain tranquil and not get herself so worked up that she suffered a relapse. He promised to restore whatever she wished restored, but he took his time doing it, so I found her pictures in the basement myself and took down the ones Grandmother Beverly had put in their place. Mommy supervised the restoration while Grandmother Beverly fumed in the living room, staring at her television programs.

It was more difficult to restore the furniture in the living room and to reconstruct the kitchen. Mommy wasn't up to working yet, which meant Grandmother Beverly still prepared the meals. As long as she was doing that, she wanted the kitchen to be "sensible and organized." Mommy and I removed as many of the changes in her and Daddy's bedroom that we could. I found their previous window curtains and we rehung them. I had to go to the department store to buy bedding similar to what they had before Grandmother Beverly had replaced it. She had thrown Mommy's choices away.

Everything we did, Grandmother Beverly challenged and argued over, but we didn't pay any attention. As Mommy had decided, we nodded, said yes and then did what we wanted. It was beginning to be fun again.

I took Mommy for walks. Color returned to her cheeks. Her appetite grew better and I was more hopeful and happier than I had been in weeks. I waited to tell her about Clarence and what Grandmother Beverly had done. He phoned a few times, but each time, he sounded terrified of talking too long. We made vague promises to see each other as soon as possible, but I sensed that we each knew our plans were fantasies. I could feel him letting go of my hand.

I felt heartsick, but helpless. My first disappointment in love, I thought, would certainly not be my last. By the time I decided Mommy was strong enough to hear about the whole incident, I decided there wasn't any point in upsetting her over something that no longer mattered. We were too involved in my play by now anyway. That absorbed most of our time together. Mommy enjoyed playing different roles and rehearsing with me. We would do it in the living room sometimes, which drove Grandmother Beverly away. Often, we would stop and throw lines back and forth, even at dinner. It was truly as if we had set up that *fourth wall:* impenetrable and protective. Grandmother Beverly couldn't do anything but look in at us.

My first weekend rehearsal at Miss Hamilton's seemed innocent enough because Dell and two other members of the cast were there as well. We came in the morning and then she sent out for pizza and we had lunch before putting in another hour.

The weekend rehearsals were important and better because we were all fresh for them, not coming to a rehearsal after a full day of school. We had more time to analyze the lines, talk about our characters and think about our reactions.

Miss Hamilton had a small house. The living room wasn't much bigger than my parents' bedroom, but it was a comfortable two-story Queen Anne with a patch of lawn in front and a little backyard. The house itself was done in a Wedgwood blue cladding with black shutters. She had a patio at the rear of the house and a sunroom off the kitchen. We rehearsed in the living room, pushing aside some furniture to get a wide enough space for stage movements. I learned about blocking, moving upstage and downstage, projecting to the audience and reacting to characters. She at least knew all the basic things about theater, and she appreciated my interpretations and insights into my character. Most of that came from the sessions Mommy and I had spent together.

The third weekend Dell was unable to attend rehearsal because he was going on a trip with his family. I thought Miss Hamilton would just skip it, but she suggested I come over anyway. She said she would play his part and we would refine my performance. The play itself had been criticized as too adult, not something the student body would appreciate and support, but she stuck to her choice, defending it as a significant dramatic work.

"Besides," she reasoned, "our students get enough fluff on television and at the movies. They deserve something different for a change."

There was already some resentment toward her because of that. However, she saw it all as a greater challenge, "We have to win their respect, leave them in awe, show them what real talent can do," she told me. "You'll never forget this, Cinnamon. Everyone starts somewhere."

It both amused and intrigued me that she believed I could be a real actress and make a living at it, perhaps even become famous. Was I permitting her own frustrated dreams to move over into mine? I supposed there was only one way to find out for sure and that was to be on the stage when the curtain opened and when it finally closed.

The applause will tell, I told myself, as well as the afterward. Would people really remember my performance? Would they talk about it a day later? It was truly exciting. I couldn't help but do everything possible to make it work.

That third weekend, I was surprised when I arrived at Miss Hamilton's and discovered none of the other members of the cast would be there.

"We're just doing your big scenes," she explained. "I didn't see the point in bringing them all here this time."

I suppose I was aiding and abetting the gossipmongers and hatemongers in my school, but I couldn't help being nervous alone in Miss Hamilton's house. Dell had successfully planted the seeds of suspicion in the darkest, deepest places of my imagination.

"She's nearly thirty," he told me, "and no one has ever seen her with a man. Why doesn't she have a boyfriend at least? She's not that bad looking, is she?"

"I don't care," I told him. "Her personal life is her own, and besides, you and everyone else can't know what she does or who she sees out of school."

He shrugged.

"I'm just telling you what people say," he replied.

I hated that, the pretended indifference and innocence people put on when underneath they are enjoying the spreading of rumors. When I mentioned it to Mommy, she nodded and said, "Life for most people is so boring, they have to find ways to make it interesting, even if it means hurting someone. Watch out for that," she warned. "It's not only the jealous who do such things, Cinnamon. It's sometimes just people who literally have nothing better to do. Sometimes, I think they're the worst."

Miss Hamilton began our rehearsal the same way as before: reviewing where we were in the script and then starting a discussion of what we were about to rehearse.

"When you are alone with Death, you've got to keep the audience thinking you don't know who he really is. Think of him only as a charming, handsome man, so when you reveal the truth, that you've known all along, it will both shock and amaze the audience," she said.

I knew this, but I listened as if I didn't. Then we began our rehearsal with her reading Dell's lines.

"I know it's hard for you to look at me and think of me as a handsome young man," she said after a few minutes, "but that's what you have to do."

She paused when I looked skeptical. She thought a moment and said, "A friend of mine who is an actress told me she had to do a love scene with a man she not only didn't like, but whom she said had bad breath, even body odor. She said just the thought of doing it turned her stomach. She was in tears about it. She thought she would do so badly she would hurt her career forever."

"What happened?" I asked.

"An older actor gave her some good advice. He told her to imagine the man was someone she liked, someone she actually loved, if possible, and see only that person. If she concentrated hard enough, he told her, she wouldn't smell a thing. She said it worked and she got through the performance."

"Why didn't she just tell the man he stunk?" I asked.

Miss Hamilton smiled and tilted her head, the small dimple in her left cheek flashing in and out.

"Now, Cinnamon, how do you think that would have gone over? What sort of relationship would they have on the stage? He might pretend to appreciate her honesty, but don't you think his ego would have been bruised badly? Remember that essay we read about the messenger? He was despised more than the message."

"I guess when the truth is painful, it's better to turn to illusion," I said.

"Yes." She smiled. "But don't go telling people I advised you to tell lies," she warned and we both laughed.

We started rehearsing again. She wanted me to keep eye contact, to look mesmerized by Death. She brought herself so close to me, to my lips, I felt my heart flutter in a panic. I think she saw it in my eyes finally and stopped.

She looked embarrassed for both of us.

"Well, let's take a short break. Would you like something to drink . . . tea, perhaps? It's always a good idea to have some tea and honey when you're on the stage."

"Fine," I said.

While I waited I looked about her living room. She had some pretty vases, some crystals on a shelf, inexpensive paintings of Paris, French villages, a seacoast scene that was somewhere in Italy. Were these places she had been or places she dreamed of visiting? What I realized was there were no pictures of family.

"Have you been to any of these places?" I asked nodding at the pictures when she returned with our cups of tea and some biscuits.

"Oh. No, but I will get there someday," she said. "Maybe even this summer. I've been saving."

"Where are you from, Miss Hamilton?"

"Well," she began setting the tray down and offering me my cup, "I'm from lots of places unfortunately."

"Why unfortunately? Was your father in the army or something?"

"No." She sipped her tea, looking at me over the cup for a moment as if she were deciding whether she should fall back on illusion or deal with the truth. She chose the truth. "I never knew my father, nor my mother."

"I don't understand," I said.

"I was an orphan, Cinnamon, then a foster child."

"Oh." I felt terrible asking personal questions now. "I'm sorry. I didn't mean to pry."

"It's all right. I think my being an orphan had a great deal to do with why I wanted to get into the theater first and then into teaching. When you're in a play, the whole cast becomes an extended family, especially if it has a long run. You're sometimes closer to your fellow actors than you are with your real family. At least, that's what they all used to tell me. Now I enjoy teaching, being close to my students, being a real part of their lives. Sometimes, I think I'm more involved, more concerned because I don't have a real family."

"Were you ever married?" I asked, nearly biting my own lower lip after asking.

She smiled again, sipped some tea, put her cup down and looked at me.

"You would think that nowadays people would be a lot more tolerant of women who weren't married or in a relationship by my age, but some ideas are branded in our social consciousness so deeply, we can't help being suspicious or critical of others who don't fit neatly in little boxes. Don't think I haven't been urged by older teachers and by administrators to settle down. As if it's my fault that Mr. Right hasn't come along," she added.

"I was almost married once, but in the end, we both decided it wouldn't have worked," she continued. "We were sensible and mature and lucky. Most people get involved too quickly these days and their relationships don't have the timber to last. Then, there's all that unfortunate business afterward . . . one or the other drifts away or things get unpleasant.

"You've got to really believe this is it for you. Maybe I'm more careful than most people because I never had a real parent-child relationship."

She paused and laughed.

"It's fun to be your own psychotherapist sometimes, but most of the time, I'd rather just let destiny unravel the spool called Ella Hamilton."

"Ella?"

"Yes," she said sipping her tea.

"Well if you had no mother or father, who named you?"

"Someone at the orphanage, I suppose. I never

minded my name. It means a female possessing super-natural loveliness. How's that?"

"That's very nice."

"Actually, it's a name that fits you better than it does me, Cinnamon."

I didn't blush as much as feel a warmth travel up my neck, a warmth that made me shift my eyes from her.

"You've got to get used to people complimenting you, complimenting your unique look and your talents," she said seeing my discomfort. "I'm glad you're not like so many of your classmates. You're far more mature. You don't giggle after everything you say and you have self-confidence.

"I know you're frightened inside. Everyone is, but you cloak it well and you've already developed the ability to keep it under control. That's why I'm so convinced you're going to succeed on the stage," she continued.

I lifted my eyes and looked at her. Now that we had gotten to know each other better, I wanted to like her. I wanted to lower that wall between us. I wanted to trust her. Why couldn't we be friends, honest friends, innocent friends? Damn the rumors. If I wanted to give her a friendly hug, I would.

"Should we get back to work?" she asked.

"Yes," I said.

We began the scene again and I did what she advised. I didn't see her. I saw Dell's handsome face, heard his vibrant voice. We were inches apart and I was really getting into the role when suddenly, we were both surprised by a flash of light that bounced off the mirror above the mantel. We both turned toward the window facing the street.

"What was that?" I asked.

She shook her head.

"I don't know." She went to the window and gazed out. "No one's there."

She shrugged.

"Maybe a passing vehicle reflected sunlight."

"It's cloudy, Miss Hamilton." I went to the window and looked out, too. The street just seemed too quiet to me. "It was someone," I muttered.

"Well, whoever it was is gone. It doesn't really matter now," she said.

Little did she know.

She had more innocence and trust in her than I would have expected for someone with her background.

I came from a family. I had parents.

And yet I knew in my heart something terrible loomed just on the other side of that *fourth wall* we so lovingly cherished. Hard lessons would teach me that it was far from enough protection.

Like a second shoe, it dropped two days later at school. I had just arrived and was walking toward homeroom when I noticed a crowd around the general bulletin board placed at the center of the main corridor. Most of the students were laughing. The crowd began to grow larger. I approached slowly with a thudding heart, and when those on the perimeter of the clump saw me, they stepped aside, clearing an aisle for me to walk down as I approached the bulletin board.

There, too high up to reach without a stepladder, was a picture of Miss Hamilton and me at her home, in the rehearsal, just at the point where we were standing inches from each other, our lips so close it did look like we were about to kiss. The caption under the picture was in big block letters and read: TEACHER'S PET OR SOMETHING MORE?

"Who did that?" I screamed.

"We thought you did," Iris Ainsley quipped from the outside of the continually gathering group. Everyone laughed.

I turned on her. I was so crazed with hate, my whole body shook. Those between us saw it and stepped back.

"You disgusting, jealous little girl. You were spying on our rehearsal this Saturday. You were the one who took this picture and you know we were just rehearsing."

"Do you have to rehearse to do that?" someone else cracked. The group laughed again.

"Do what?" I cried, twisting a sarcastic smile and glaring back at Iris. "Try to ruin someone's reputation? No, she doesn't have to rehearse for that. She's spoiled rotten and vicious enough without any training. Go on and laugh, but if any one of you take something from the princess here, she'll do something just as cruel to you."

Some smiles wilted as they considered what I was suggesting.

"What's going on here?" we all heard Mr. Kaplan demand. He came toward us and the students split up quickly, heading toward their various homerooms. Iris hesitated a moment, smirked at me and left. I stood waiting for him.

"What's going on, Cinnamon?"

By now I was sure the color had left my cheeks. I know I felt sick and wanted to flee the place.

"Iris Ainsley or one of her friends took that picture of my rehearsal with Miss Hamilton and put it up there with that stupid caption," I said nodding at the board.

He looked up at it, widened his eyes and glanced at me.

"Go to your homeroom before you're late," he ordered. Then he went off to get the custodian to bring a ladder and take the picture and the caption down.

Damage, however, was done. Mr. Kaplan called Miss Hamilton to the office and showed the picture to her. The blood that I was sure had drained from her face at the sight of the photo and its caption remained absent from her complexion most of the day. She looked pale and weak and in great anguish. I felt so sorry for her, but I was afraid to show too much affection and concern. Everyone's eyes were on us, just waiting for us to comfort each other. But she didn't speak to me or to anyone else until rehearsal began after school.

"Most of you are quite aware of what went on this morning. Some disgusting-minded person did a very nasty thing. Because of it, I've been asked not to hold any more weekend rehearsals at my home. I don't think it's going to hurt us. You're all too dedicated to this play to be set back, and I want you all to know how proud I am of the efforts you've made. We're going to show them," she declared.

Then she looked directly at me.

"If I've brought any of you any pain and trouble by not anticipating some of the disgusting things people can do, I apologize. I'll be a great deal more aware of the possibilities from now on, believe me.

"But I don't want this to color your enthusiasm with any gray. Let's work harder. Let's make this a success. Okay?"

"Absolutely," Dell cried. The rest of us applauded and the rehearsal began. Every time Miss Hamilton approached me or touched my arm, I could feel the self-consciousness seeping in. How I hated Iris Ainsley and her buffoons for doing this to us, but I couldn't let her win. I couldn't fall apart now.

It was more difficult than I anticipated because the picture was just a start. When I arrived home that day, I found that someone had called the house and given Grandmother Beverly an anonymous nasty message, which she quickly passed on to Mommy. She used the opportunity to tell her about the scene between Clarence and me in the attic and what she had done about it, warning Mommy that I was degenerating quickly and blaming it on Mommy's permissive attitude when it came to supervising me. Mommy looked devastated, weakened and pale by the time I arrived.

She was in her bedroom sitting in her soft chair, just waiting for me. The moment I saw her face, I knew what had happened.

"Did the principal call here?" I immediately asked.

"No, why would he call, honey?"

I told her about the picture, how it had happened and what some nasty, jealous students had done. She nodded as she listened and then began to tell me about her conversation with Grandmother Beverly.

"Why didn't you tell me anything about Clarence Baron, Cinnamon?"

"It was over and I didn't see why I should trouble you, especially since you had just come home from the clinic," I explained.

She nodded.

"But you should have told me by now, don't you think?"

"Maybe. I'm sorry."

"Your father hasn't mentioned it either. I'm sure he knows too, right?"

I looked up at her.

"No, I'm not so sure," I said. "Grandmother Beverly doesn't need reinforcements when she goes into battle."

"He's never spoken to you about it?" she asked.

I shook my head.

"How odd," she muttered and looked thoughtful. "Well, maybe you're right. She's such an overbearing woman. She thinks she's been ordained to run all our lives or something. But, I am troubled by all that's happened, honey. What did Miss Hamilton do today?"

"She ended our weekend rehearsals. I think the principal forced her to do that. She's really hurt. I felt worse for her than I did for myself."

"Yes. Sometimes, innuendo is enough, too much." Mommy looked at me. "There's not a shred of truth to the ugly stories, is there?"

I shook my head slowly, the tears coming hot and heavy into my eyes.

"How could you even ask?" I said.

"You're right," she replied quickly, "but you see what the power of suggestion can be? Even I was worried for a moment, Cinnamon. I shouldn't have been, but it's only natural, I suppose. I'm your mother. I have to worry."

"I hate them. I hate them so much," I said. "I wish I did have spiritual powers and could put a curse on all of them."

She smiled.

"They'll put a curse on themselves with their own actions. It might take a while, but those kind always end up eating out their own hearts, honey. Come here," she said and held out her arms.

I stepped forward and she hugged me tightly.

"I love you, Cinnamon. I trust you and I believe you."

"Thank you, Mommy," I said.

"What happened to Clarence?" she asked and I told her.

"You don't want to see him anymore?"

"I think he's moved on, Mommy. We were good friends and maybe we should have left it that way."

She nodded.

"I understand. More than you know," she added with a cryptic look in her eyes.

Either nothing was mentioned to Daddy, or if it was, he chose to ignore it. Grandmother Beverly made some veiled remarks at dinner, but Daddy seemed very distracted, lost in his own thoughts. Mommy noticed, too.

"Is something troubling you, Taylor?" She asked.

"What? No," he said quickly, far too quickly.

"You can't treat me like a thin-shelled egg forever," Mommy told him. "It will make me feel worse."

He gazed at Grandmother Beverly and then smiled at Mommy.

"It's just this market, with the Feds making everyone nervous threatening to raise rates, not to raise rates," he explained. "Some of my clients are driving me bonkers."

"I wish you thought about getting yourself into something else, Taylor. You used to talk about establishing your own financial group for estate investments instead of doing battle daily in that madhouse called the stock market."

He nodded.

"Maybe soon," he said.

Grandmother Beverly made a small, throaty sound of

skepticism and then nodded to me to start clearing away the dishes.

Mommy glanced at me and I at her. We were spiritual sisters. We shared a sensitivity that told us something wasn't quite right. I had my own ideas about it, of course, and I made the mistake of looking away too quickly. Later that evening, Mommy called me into her bedroom.

"Is there something you know, you all know, that Daddy doesn't want to tell me, Cinnamon?"

I shook my head. How could I ever tell her what I had seen?

"You know, worrying about something terrible happening can make you almost as sick as the terrible thing itself," she said.

I nodded, but kept my eyes down. I felt so trapped.

"All right, honey. I don't want you to worry either. You have too much on your mind these days with your schoolwork, your tests and the play coming up. Let's just think about the good things," she suggested.

I smiled and nodded.

"Okay, Mommy."

The week before the play was so intense. We had three evening dress rehearsals in a row so the lighting, the sets, the props and, of course, our performances could be sharpened and coordinated. We made so many mistakes, I was convinced it would be a total disaster. People like Iris Ainsley would get what they wanted, their sweet, vicious revenge. It might very well destroy Miss Hamilton's career as well, I thought. What terrible thing had I done when I took this role and assumed this awesome responsibility?

Miss Hamilton tried to assure us that blunders during dress rehearsals were a good thing.

"Let's make all our mistakes these nights and be perfect in front of the audience," she said.

The evening before the play opened, I had a nightmare that I had lost my voice. When I stepped onto the stage, I couldn't make a sound and the whole audience broke into a fit of hysterical laughter. I saw Iris's face burst into a fat, happy smile and Mommy's face streaked with tears. I woke and found my heart was pounding. It seemed impossible to fall back to sleep and that made me even more nervous. If I'm not rested and I'm exhausted, I'll forget lines, moves, everything. When the alarm sounded in the morning, I woke in a panic. My eyes looked bloodshot. I wanted to stay home, but I knew if I didn't attend school, the principal could keep me from performing.

Mommy rose to have breakfast with me and encourage me.

"I know this is a big day for you. You'll be floating, hardly hearing or seeing anything, Cinnamon, but you've just got to stay firm, stay confident. You'll be wonderful," she assured me.

Here she was recently recovered from a terrible emotional crisis in her life giving me comfort and boosting my morale. How I loved her, I thought, and hugged her tightly before I left for school. She was right about the day. It seemed to take forever. I spent most of my class time glancing at the clock, longing for the sound of the bell, hardly hearing the teachers. Thankfully, none had scheduled an exam. In the cafeteria I sat with members of the cast. We had gravitated to each other out of a mutual sense of anxiety, drawing comfort from each of us freely admitting he or she had trouble sleeping the night before, and everyone confessing fear of forgetting lines.

"Don't worry about it," Dell assured us. "When you step onto that stage tonight, you won't remember being afraid and you won't be tired. You'll be so juiced."

I didn't see how that was possible. When school finally ended, Miss Hamilton stopped me in the hallway and told me to just go home and rest. We had an early call for makeup and then it would begin.

Or end.

At home Mommy had gotten herself back into the flow of activity. She took over preparing our dinner because she wanted to be sure I ate something light. Daddy had promised to get home early. Grandmother Beverly was coming to the play, too, "to see if all this time had been wasted."

Mommy looked so much her old self, hovering around me as I prepared to leave for the school theater. All I could think was if I failed, she might regress. It added to the pressure.

"You'll do fine, honey," she told me as I started down the stairs. "Just being part of something like this is wonderful. You'll see."

We hugged. Daddy was still not home, but he had called to say he was on his way. Miriam Levy, the head of our student makeup crew, was coming by to pick me up. I headed out, looking back once to wave to Mommy in the doorway, and then I released a hot, anxious breath and got into Miriam's car.

There was so much commotion in the makeup room, it was hard to worry. Miss Hamilton was busy with details, putting out small fires. We had no time to talk. Finally, twenty minutes before the opening curtain, she gathered the cast together and gave us her pep talk.

"I want you all to know that I'm proud of you already.

In my short life in the theater, I learned that what makes the difference is not perfection, but the ability to deal with imperfection. Mistakes will happen. Expect them, but stay on your feet and react to them so that the audience never knows. Good luck, gang. Thanks for giving me so much of yourselves," she concluded, her eyes fixed solely on me.

We took our positions. Someone cried, "The place is full!"

My heart dipped like a yo-yo in my chest and touched the bottom of my stomach. I thought I would vomit and was happy Mommy had made sure I had a very light dinner. When the curtain opened, there was applause for the set and it began.

Like a baby duckling just realizing it can swim, I glided through the lights. I could feel myself growing stronger, more confident with every successful line delivered. Dell was as strong as ever—even stronger— and our performances enhanced each other's. I felt as if I had been on the stage all my life. Maybe it was remembering Mommy and myself in the attic, all those stories we acted, those people I portrayed. Whatever, I didn't miss a word or fail to hit my marks.

When it came time for Dell's and my most dramatic scene, I could sense that the audience was rapt, but I didn't think of them. I thought of who I was in the play and what I was saying and what was happening. How much I wanted the sense of calm and completion my character had at this moment. How brave her love had made her. The sweet tragedy brought tears and when the final curtain closed, the applause was thunderous.

I had avoided looking directly at the audience all evening. The lights had helped block them out, but when we took our curtain calls, and I came out on the stage, I was overwhelmed by the sight of all those people rising to their feet. I glanced at Miss Hamilton. She was glowing so brightly, she looked like a little girl again.

The moment I stepped off the stage, we hugged.

"Thank you," I told her.

"No, Cinnamon, thank you. Thank you for being who I thought you were. This is just the beginning for you," she promised.

Afterward, friends and family came backstage. Mommy looked so beautiful and so healthy, my heart burst for joy. Daddy couldn't stop complimenting me and I saw how much he enjoyed the accolades other people were lavishing on him.

"She's a natural."

"What a talented young lady."

"You must be so proud."

In the background, looking overwhelmed herself, stood Grandmother Beverly. She, too, welcomed the praise and was glad to take credit for being a member of my family.

"I knew you would do well, honey," Mommy whispered. "Our spirits assured me.

"And you know what?" she added.

"What?"

"They were here, too. I could hear them clapping for you."

We laughed.

Was the world really this wonderful after all?

8

My Turn to Shine

"There's someone I'd like you to meet," Miss Hamilton told me when the crowd began to thin out.

Mommy, Daddy and Grandmother Beverly had left while I cleaned off my makeup and changed. They were waiting in the lobby. I turned from the makeup mirror and looked up at a tall, thin man with small dark eyes, a sharp straight nose and a square-boned, cleft chin. He had thin, arrogant lips and styled dark brown hair. He looked impeccably dressed in a gray, pin-striped suit and tie. There was a small twist in the right corner of his mouth that made him look lofty, condescending.

"Cinnamon, I'd like you to meet a good friend of mine, Edmond Senetsky."

"Hello," I said, gazing quizzically at Miss Hamilton. It was obvious to me from the way she was gloating that this man was important to her.

He extended his right hand, a slim hand with long fingers, one of which was dressed in a gold and diamond

band. It wasn't a wedding ring, just a very expensive
piece of jewelry.

I stood up quickly and shook his hand. He had a soft,
unremarkable grip, more like the grip of someone just
letting go.

"Edmond is a theatrical agent, Cinnamon. I once had
illusions of him representing me," Miss Hamilton said.
She laughed, but he didn't.

"I think the worst thing you can do to someone is give
them false hope," he declared firmly. He looked at Miss
Hamilton and added, "Those who can, do; and those who
can't, teach."

She didn't stop smiling, but I thought that was a mean
thing to say and stopped smiling at him.

"He's right, Cinnamon," Miss Hamilton said quickly.
"There's no disgrace in being the teacher either. You get
to live on through your students."

"Precisely," Edmond said. He wasn't English, but he
tried to speak so perfectly, he sounded like someone imitating a distinguished Englishman.

"Anyway, honey, you might have heard me mention
Edmond's mother, Madame Senetsky who was once a
very famous Russian stage actress and who now operates
one of the most prestigious dramatic arts schools on the
East coast. Actually, she takes on only a handful of new
students every year. Edmond thinks you could be one of
them."

"I didn't say that exactly," he corrected quickly, showing some annoyance. "You've given a passable performance tonight for a high-school girl."

"Passable, Edmond?" Miss Hamilton pushed.

"Well, perhaps somewhat more remarkable than that,
but I must warn you, the *crème de la crème* auditions for

my mother every year. It's one thing to compete with your classmates in a school this size, but quite another to go head to head against the best in the country."

"You're going to frighten her away, Edmond," Miss Hamilton told him.

"If I do, she's meant to be away," he said. He drew a step closer to me. His eyes were beady, his lashes long enough to make any girl green with envy. "Let me tell you this one truth about the theater, the movies, television, modeling, anything that has to do with performance, Miss . . ."

"Cinnamon," Miss Hamilton said. "Cinnamon Carlson."

"Yes, Cinnamon. All of it is at least thirty percent perseverance. Then there is about thirty percent luck, being in the right place at the right time. The rest has to do with talent. If it's in you to do it, you'll do it, if not . . ."

"I'll teach?" I countered.

Miss Hamilton laughed.

"Or take tickets at the entrance," he shot back. He turned to Miss Hamilton. "You will have the information you need." He looked at me. "Good luck."

"That's thirty percent," I said.

He almost smiled. His eyes brightened with some appreciation. Then he nodded, thanked Miss Hamilton for inviting him and left.

"Who *was* that?" I grimaced.

"He really is a very powerful agent, Cinnamon, and his mother's school is really the most sought after in the country. All her graduates go on to find success in a most competitive world. I want you to think about auditioning. Two weeks from now, in New York. I'll go with you, if you like. I'll get all the information to you and your parents."

"I don't know, Miss Hamilton."

"Talk it over with your family. I'll mention it to your mother and father when I see them out in the lobby now. You were wonderful, Cinnamon. Really wonderful."

She left me wondering what all this meant. Most of my fellow students were already planning their futures and applying to colleges. Daddy wanted me to go to his alma mater, NYU, but I had yet to submit the application. I was anxious to see how Mommy reacted to Miss Hamilton's suggestion.

By the time I arrived in the lobby, there were only a few stragglers left. Mommy and Daddy and Grandmother Beverly, who looked impatient, were still talking with Miss Hamilton.

"Here's our little star," Daddy said and gave me a kiss on the cheek. "We're all very proud of you, Cinnamon, very proud."

Miss Hamilton stood there, beaming. However, I saw how Grandmother Beverly was looking at her, her eyes fixed with accusations.

"I'm tired," I declared.

"Of course, you are, sweetheart," Mommy said. She put her arm around my shoulders. I said good night to Miss Hamilton and we left, my triumph hovering around me like an angelic light. Anyone left in the lobby and in the parking lot shouted their congratulations. I couldn't help but wonder where Iris Ainsely and her friends had gone to pout.

"Miss Hamilton told me about Edmond Senetsky," Mommy said after we started away. She and I sat in the rear and Grandmother Beverly sat up front because she hated sitting in the back. She said it made her feel like she was in a taxicab. I wondered why it didn't make her feel like she was in a limousine, but her answer was she hated that feeling, too.

"We'll have to learn more about this school," Daddy admonished.

"Ridiculous," Grandmother Beverly said. "What kind of an education will she get in a school run by an old woman?"

"She's not just an old woman. She's a famous international actress," I said.

"It sounds very exciting," Mommy declared.

"It's very competitive, Mommy. I don't see how I can get chosen."

"Of course you will," Mommy decided. "Look what you did tonight."

"We'll see. It does sound very, very competitive," Daddy said, punctuating the air with a heavy note of caution. He glanced at Grandmother Beverly who simply shook her head and stared at the road.

I suddenly felt like the two of them were coconspirators, conspiring against Mommy's dreams and mine. My pride rose quickly up my spine like some flag of defiance.

"I'd like to try nevertheless," I announced, almost more out of spite than desire.

"Good," Mommy squealed and hugged me. "I'm so terribly proud of you, sweetheart, so very, very proud."

Dare I say I was proud of myself, too? Or was that being arrogant?

I didn't have to say it. Mommy could see it in my face. She was the only one who could, but that was enough, I thought. That was enough.

The next evening our second performance went as

well as the first. During the curtain call, the president of
the student government came up to present me with a
bouquet of red and white roses. The audience was on its
feet applauding. Mommy and Daddy had come again,
but Grandmother Beverly had remained at home to
watch one of her old movies.

When I arrived at school on Monday, the accolades
continued. All of my teachers lavished so much praise on
me, I felt myself in a constant blush. Iris Ainsley was
never so quiet and in the background. She and her friends
were chased off like mice into the corner of the cafeteria,
whispering among themselves. They looked small and so
insignificant, I chastised myself for ever taking them
seriously enough to feel bad after anything they had said
or done.

The cast remained close. We ate lunch together and
all of us basked in the continuing adulation. Then, on
Wednesday, Miss Hamilton gave me the information
about the audition. It was being held in a week at a small
off-Broadway theater Madame Senetsky used every year
for this purpose. I clutched the paper containing the
details in my hand. My parents had to call to make the
appointment.

"If you want me to go with you, I will," Miss
Hamilton offered again. "But it might be something you
and your parents should do together, a family thing," she
added. "I don't mean to interfere."

"I'm sure my mother would want you to go if I go," I
said.

"Give it a try, Cinnamon. If you don't, you'll always
wonder. Believe me. Those kinds of questions haunt you
for your whole life."

I nodded, but I was so nervous about it that I almost

decided not to tell Mommy when I arrived home that afternoon. She was reading and listening to music in her room, but I could tell from the way she sat and from the tightness of the lines in her face that she was upset about something. Was it something Grandmother Beverly had done or said? I wondered.

"Hi, honey," she said lowering her book.

"What's wrong, Mommy?" I asked immediately. Her face was a book I could easily read.

She smiled at me.

"We're too alike, you and I. How can I ever hide anything? Your father was supposed to take us out to dinner, to celebrate your success, but he called just a half hour ago to tell me he was called to a very important meeting and wouldn't be home until ten tonight. Grandmother Beverly made one of her famous bland meat loafs."

My heart raced, chased my own rage.

"Let's go out for pizza," I suggested.

"Really?"

"Yes, Mommy. I'll change into something more pizza-ish and we'll just go ourselves," I said, my voice laced with defiance. She laughed.

"Yes, why not? Grandmother Beverly doesn't mind eating alone. She's alone when she's eating with us anyway," Mommy said.

We laughed and I went to change. Mommy informed Grandmother Beverly of our intentions.

"She didn't say a word," Mommy told me when we got into my car and I started for my favorite pizza hangout. "She barely nodded."

"She uses silence like a sword," I said.

"I can't help feeling sorry for her sometimes, Cinnamon. She has no real friends, no one from her past life with Grandpa Carlson who cares to stay in touch with her, just a bunch of busy-bodies looking for juicy gossip. She puts so much emphasis on taking care of Daddy and competing with me that she doesn't have time to nurture relationships. But the truth is your father seems oblivious to the both of us these days," she added sadly.

Should I tell her what I knew, what I had seen? Was she ready, strong enough? What if it set her back, wounded her so deeply she had to return to the clinic? How could I live with myself? How could I ever look at Daddy, much less live with him afterward? It was hard enough doing it now.

I swallowed the story back and stuffed it tightly in the dark drawer under my heart.

Mommy loved the pizza place. She said it reminded her so much of her own childhood and teenage years. She talked incessantly, almost with a nervous energy that made me suspicious, but she did tell me stories about her youth that I had never heard, stories about boyfriends and girlfriends and her own fantasies.

"I didn't want to be an actress. I wanted to be a singer. I had an old aunt, Grandma Gussie's sister Ethel who told me that you could train your voice or turn it into a good singing voice if you found a place where you could get a good echo. I found one about a half-mile from our house, a little canyon, and I used to go there and practice the scales. I think I frightened off not only the birds and squirrels, but the insects. I did go out for chorus, but I was never chosen to do anything more than sing along.

"Fantasies die slow, quiet deaths. They're like cherry blossoms breaking away and sailing down slowly, still holding onto their color and their softness and beauty, but ending up on the ground to be blown about by cold winds.

"Don't let that happen to your dream, Cinnamon," she warned. "This is more than a fantasy. You've got something, a gift; and don't let anyone or anything stop you. Promise me. Promise me you won't let anyone discourage you," she begged.

I promised and then I showed her the paper Miss Hamilton had given me.

"Then this is real, an opportunity!" she cried. She was happier for me than I was for myself, I think. I hated myself for even harboring a hesitation. "I'll take care of this in the morning."

"Miss Hamilton offered to go with us if we'd like her to," I said.

Mommy seemed to lose some of her excitement and glow. I shouldn't have told her, I thought.

"Of course, if you'd like her to go with us, she can."

"It's not that important, Mommy. I think she's just so excited for me. She's an orphan, you know."

"Oh?"

We both ate some pizza and I told her as much as I knew about Miss Hamilton.

"No," Mommy decided after she heard the details, "she should go with us. She is the one really responsible for all this. Why shouldn't we make her part of it? Besides, if I treat her like I believed those nasty rumors, I would be as guilty as someone spreading them."

I nodded.

Then we went back to giggling, eating our pizza, listening to the music and acting like a couple of teenage sisters. It turned out to be the best time we had together since she had come back from the clinic.

When we got back to the house, I went to do my homework and study for a math test. Mommy returned to her reading. Daddy didn't come home at ten. It was nearly eleven-thirty when I heard his footsteps on the stairway. He went by my room quickly and quietly. I heard their bedroom door close and then the silence of sadness closed in around me, driving me to the sanctity of sleep.

The next day Mommy had all sorts of information for me when I returned from school. Madame Senetsky's administrative assistant told Mommy to have me prepare a speech from *The Taming of the Shrew*. We had a collection of Shakespearean plays and Mommy had already found the pages.

"We're going Saturday," she told me. "Ten A.M."

"Saturday! That's only two days away!"

"Don't worry. We'll practice plenty," she declared. Then she added, "Tell Miss Hamilton and ask her for any suggestions, too."

Meanwhile, Mommy and I began that evening. She thought it would be so right for me to practice in our attic room where my dramatic life had really had its beginning.

"Besides," she said almost in a whisper, "the spirits will be with us as they were with you on that stage."

Who was I to doubt it? I thought.

We went up right after dinner. Daddy came to see what we were doing because we were there so long. He listened a little and then he left, shaking his head and smiling. At dinner Friday night, Grandmother Beverly gave voice to her disapproval.

"Why shouldn't she be chosen?" she asked. "Don't believe all that business about it being very competitive.

I saw that paper. I saw how expensive it is to attend that so-called school of dramatics. It's a waste of good money—and while she should be at a proper school learning something useful."

"It is expensive," Mommy agreed. I looked up quickly. Daddy stopped eating, too. "I was going to ask you to release some of the trust fund that Grandfather Carlson and you established for her."

"She's not to touch that until she's twenty-one," Grandmother Beverly declared.

"I know, but that wasn't well thought out. Young people need college money and they need that before they're twenty-one."

"But this isn't a college. It's . . . it's . . . a foolish indulgence. I won't agree to waste a cent on such nonsense."

"It is a hefty tuition," Daddy said softly.

"Yes, but it includes everything. She lives at the school, is taken under wing by Madame Senetsky."

"Lives at the school," Grandmother Beverly practically spit. "It's just some old New York house. She's running this scam to meet her expenses because she was probably a great failure."

"That's a lie," I cried. "I read all about her. She was a very famous actress and people from everywhere try to get into her school. I probably won't even have a chance."

"Lucky for you," Grandmother Beverly said.

Mommy looked like she was going to burst a blood vessel.

"Yes," I said calmly, softly, almost sweetly, "if I don't make it, it's probably lucky because I won't chase a foolish dream. You're so right, Grandmother Beverly."

Mommy's eyebrows went up and then she looked at

me and I at her and we both burst into a fit of laughter that surprised Daddy and drove Grandmother Beverly from the table mumbling to herself.

Daddy woke up with a terrible sinus headache on Saturday morning. He had said he was going with us and would take us all to a nice lunch in Greenwich Village, but Mommy told him to stay home and nurse his head cold instead.

"You'll only be uncomfortable and take Cinnamon's attention from her work," Mommy added.

He didn't put up a great deal of resistance and, of course, Grandmother Beverly agreed.

"You should all stay home," she said.

"You don't want to come then?" Mommy asked her. "We could have a nice day in the city."

"Me? I hate the city," she replied, but she looked unsure of Mommy's motives, almost as if she wanted to believe we really hoped she would come. For the first time I wondered if Mommy was right about her: she was just a very lonely old woman we should pity.

We left and picked up Miss Hamilton. On the way in she talked about the auditions she had undergone during her acting days.

"Everyone is nervous. If you're not, you just don't care enough," she said.

"That's very true," Mommy agreed. "I imagine if you're too nonchalant, you give off an air of indifference and turn off the director."

"The trick, if there is a trick, is to not think of yourself in that theater on that small stage, Cinnamon. Get into the play. You know it so well. We read it in class earlier this year," she told Mommy.

"Yes, Cinnamon loved it, and actually went around reciting some of Kate's lines long before this."

"That's wonderful," Miss Hamilton said. "Then this is meant to be."

They got into a discussion about plays they had seen and by the time we arrived at the little theater, they were laughing and joking together like old friends. It made me happy and took away some of my nervousness, but I was still so terrified, I thought my legs would surely fold up beneath me the moment I stepped onto that stage.

When we entered the theater, we were surprised to see no other candidates. The room itself was dark and there was just a small spotlight turned on, dropping a circle of light upstage.

"Edmond told me this might be the case," Miss Hamilton whispered. "She doesn't like other candidates sitting around, watching someone else audition."

"Someone else?" Mommy said. "There's no one here at all!"

"Not true," we heard a strong, deep female voice state.

At the rear of the auditorium, seated in the shadows so that we could barely make her out was who we imagined to be Madame Senetsky herself. Her pewter gray hair was pulled tightly up into a coiled chignon at the top of her head and clipped with a large, black comb.

"Madame Senetsky?" Miss Hamilton asked.

"Of course. Please have your candidate take the stage immediately. Promptness is essential in the theater, as it should be in life itself," she added.

"Why is she sitting in the dark?" Mommy wondered in a whisper.

"Go on, Cinnamon," Miss Hamilton said. She moved

into an aisle, taking the second seat and leaving the aisle seat for Mommy.

"She could greet us at least," Mommy muttered but sat.

I started for the stage, my heart not pounding or thumping so much as it was tightening in my chest. It felt difficult to breathe. Why should I be so nervous? I wondered. There's only one person in this audience, I told myself. It's not like it was at the school play with nearly a thousand in attendance. One pair of eyes and one pair of ears are out there.

Mommy was right. Why didn't she have the decency to greet us and at least make me feel comfortable? What arrogance, I thought. I grew angrier with every step toward the stage.

Who does she think she is? She didn't win an Academy Award, did she? Most people won't remember who she is. It's impolite not to have greeted Mommy and Miss Hamilton. I felt like turning around and unleashing a tirade that would shake that chignon loose.

Instead, I stepped onto the stage, took a deep breath, closed my eyes and told myself to be Kate, to move forward into the play, to do such a good job, I would make that pompous woman feel terrible about her treatment of us.

"Well?" she cried.

If that was intended to throw me off, to unnerve me and see whether I would crack and run off the stage, it didn't work.

"Well, indeed," I whispered.

I stepped forward and began . . .

"Fie, fie . . ."

I loved Kate, loved her fury and her defiance, but I also loved the way she was conquered, convinced and

ultimately wooed to love Petruchio. In the end they were
the most romantic, loving and considerate couple on
earth. I dreamed I would have such a romance someday
and such a marriage.

Miss Hamilton and Mommy clapped at the end of my
speech. I stood there waiting to hear something, but there
was just silence after that.

Then the spotlight went out.

"What the . . ."

There was just enough light from the aisle lamps for
me to make my way back to them and for us to find our
way to the exit doors. When we looked for Madame
Senetsky, we saw no one.

"I don't understand," Mommy said. "Where is she?
What are we supposed to do now?"

Miss Hamilton shook her head.

"I don't know any more than you do. I'm sorry."

"This is a ridiculous way to treat people. Who does she
think she is?" Mommy cried. "Hello! Anyone here?"

We waited a moment and then Mommy said, "Let's
get out of here."

We stepped out in the bright sunlight, all of us squint-
ing.

"You were wonderful, Cinnamon," Mommy said. "If
that woman had any insight, she would see it."

"Yes, you did great," Miss Hamilton said. "I'll call
Edmond."

"Don't bother to waste your time and money," Mommy
said. "She must be some kind of a nut or sadist. Let's have
some lunch," she added, "and enjoy the rest of the day."

We did enjoy it. In the restaurant Mommy did an imitation of Madame Senetsky sitting in the rear of the theater. She seized her hair and pulled it up so tightly, her

eyelids stretched. Miss Hamilton and I laughed. I knew the both of them were trying to make me feel better and I appreciated their efforts and pretended not to be bothered.

But I had left that theater feeling so exposed, so embarrassed. It was as if a doctor had asked me to undress and then left me naked in the examination room.

On the way home, Mommy and I decided we wouldn't tell Grandmother Beverly anything. If we did, she would just gloat and chant how right she was about such schools and why it was a great waste of time and money. We told Daddy I performed well and we'd see, but I had no hope. He wasn't feeling much better and went to sleep early that evening.

The next day Miss Hamilton called to tell me she had phoned Edmond Senetsky and he had told her that was the way his mother conducted her auditions. She didn't have the patience for small talk and she didn't see the point of conversation before or after the audition. The audition was all that mattered to her. As to my chances, he repeated his admonition that there were dozens of candidates parading past her this week. She had seen six the day I was there, in fact.

Early the following week, I completed my application to NYU and to some state schools the guidance counselor had recommended for me. I was busy studying for tests. Acting began to drift back toward that place reserved for fantasies and dreams in my mind. Every day I entered her class, Miss Hamilton's eyes widened a bit in anticipation, but one look at my face told her I had no news, and soon she stopped anticipating any.

In the end Grandmother Beverly was probably right, I told myself. Just because she said everything in a hard, cold manner didn't mean it wasn't couched in truth. The thing is it was harder to accept reality when someone like Grandmother Beverly, unhappy with reality herself, presented it to you or forced it on you. What did she dream about now? I wondered. When she laid her head upon her pillow and closed her eyes, what helped her sleep? What were her secret wishes and hopes? Or was her head always full of warnings and skepticism, turmoil spiraling forever behind her closed eyelids?

"Pity her," Mommy kept telling me now. It was as though her bout with her own demon and trouble had made her a far more compassionate person, full of little mercies instead of little terrors. In my heart of hearts, I thought she might even pity Daddy if she knew what I knew.

She still suspected something. He was more distant with every passing day. I feared the coming of his confessions and what it would bring down on this fragile house and family.

And then the letter came, the letter that would force so much truth upon us we would nearly drown. Mommy was waiting for me in the living room with it when I came home from school. She called to me and she held it out, unopened.

"It's come," she said.

"Why didn't you open it?" I asked taking it from her.

"It's yours, honey, yours to open."

I tore the envelope and pulled out the papers.

The letter was so dripping with presumption and arrogance that I was sure it had either been written or directly dictated by Madame Senetsky herself.

Dear Ms Carlson:

You are to report to the Senetsky School of Performing Arts on July 7 at 10 A.M.

All tuition costs must be paid at that time.

Below is a list of required clothing and attached is a list of rules to follow while you are residing at the school. Any violation of any rule, no matter how small or insignificant it might appear, will result in expulsion and the forfeiture of tuition paid.

The contract is included and must be signed and returned by a parent or legal guardian within two working days of receipt of this letter.

Yours truly,
Madame Senetsky

I handed it to Mommy and she read it quickly, burst into laughter and then stopped abruptly and considered.

"I don't know if she's a madwoman or what. She treats us like nothing and then accepts you."

"What should I do?"

"Well, you'll go, of course. It's what you wanted, isn't it?"

I shook my head.

"I don't know. I'm so confused."

"Of course you'll go, honey. This is a great opportunity."

I went right to the phone and called Miss Hamilton. She was so happy, she started to cry. I told Mommy and she cried, too. All of us were crying and it was supposed to be a happy, wonderful moment.

A few minutes later, we heard the front door open and stepped out to greet Daddy.

"What's up?" he asked.

Mommy handed him the letter.

Daddy's expression as he read the letter and immediately afterward told me he was not only not expecting it, he was hoping it would never come. His low-keyed, "This is nice," took Mommy by surprise, too.

"Nice?" she countered. "Nice is all you can say?"

He glanced at me and then forced a smile.

"Well, I mean it's nice to have options, to be wanted in many places."

"Options? This isn't the stock market, Taylor. It's your daughter's future," Mommy snapped.

He nodded. I never saw him look this uncomfortable, not even in the mental clinic.

"I know that. I'm referring to all the choices she can have. It takes some thinking. You want to be sure you make the right decisions for yourself, Cinnamon," he told me. "Let's review it all, consider everything. That's all I'm saying," he told Mommy.

She smirked and stepped back.

"You've been listening to your mother too much, Taylor."

"Well, she's not all wrong. I bet if you looked into it, Cinnamon, you'd discover that most successful actors nowadays started at something else first. It's a very difficult, challenging thing and you might be better off attending a regular state university or something and getting a well-rounded education. While you did that, there would be nothing to stop you from going out for the plays and building experiences, right? Then, if you were still inclined to pursue it, you could audition again," he said as if it was as simple as fastening a seat belt.

Mommy shook her head.

"Why are you saying these things now, Taylor? Why didn't you say them when Miss Hamilton told us about the performing arts school? Why didn't you say them before we took her to the audition? Why didn't you say them all these days that have gone by since?"

Daddy looked pained.

"From what you told me about it, I have to admit, I never expected this," he said holding up the letter.

Mommy plucked it from his fingers.

"You should have had more faith," she said and turned away from him. "I'm getting dinner together. Your mother hasn't come back from the dentist yet."

"Oh? I thought she had a four o'clock appointment. She should have been back by now."

"Maybe she's shopping for a new bedroom set for us," Mommy muttered and walked off.

I stared at Daddy. His shoulders sagged, there were heavier bags under his eyes and he looked tired and pale. I didn't want to feel sorry for him, but I couldn't help it. He glanced at me and saw something different in my eyes. It made him look twice.

"I'm sorry if I upset you with my suggestions, Cinnamon. And it's not something Grandmother put into my head. It's only meant to be sensible."

He started up the stairs, lifting his legs as if each weighed as much as his whole body. I saw him take a deep breath at the top and then continue toward his bedroom. I turned to go to the kitchen to help Mommy with dinner, but just as I did, I heard a loud thump from above. For a moment, I just stood there, listening. Then Mommy came back into the hallway.

"What was that?" she asked.

I shook my head and lunged for the stairway. When I reached the top, I saw my father on the floor, lying on his side. His right leg twitched as he struggled to get up.

"Daddy!" I screamed and ran to him. Seconds later, Mommy was at my side.

His eyelids fluttered.

"What is it, Taylor? What happened?" Mommy asked him.

"Got dizzy," he said. He tried to rise again and grimaced. "Pain," he said touching his chest.

"Don't move, Taylor. Don't try to get up. I'm calling for help. Stay with him, Cinnamon," Mommy told me and hurried to the phone in their bedroom.

I lowered Daddy's head gently to my lap. His lips looked blue, but he kept his eyes on me and forced a smile.

"It's all right," he said so low I could barely hear him. "I'll be all right."

I could barely see him through the glaze of tears on my eyes.

"Listen," he said. He beckoned me closer.

I leaned as far as I could.

"I'm sorry about all I said. I'm proud of you, proud they want you. It was the cost, but we'll find a way," he promised. He closed his eyes.

"The paramedics are on their way," Mommy cried coming from the bedroom. "How is he?"

"I don't know," I said.

She knelt beside him.

"Taylor, I'm here. I'm with you," she said grabbing his hand and holding it with both of hers. She wiped strands of hair from his forehead. His eyelids fluttered and then opened.

"Sorry," he said.

I couldn't help but wonder what his apology included.

Epilogue

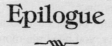

Daddy didn't die, but he was diagnosed with a heart problem serious enough to require a pacemaker. Grandmother Beverly blamed his condition on Mommy, of course. She didn't come right out and say it, but she dropped her hints around the house like rat poison.

"It's no surprise," she remarked when the diagnosis was made. "Not with all he's had on his mind these days."

"Any man who carried his burdens would have dropped dead long ago."

"He was always a healthy man, but ever since I moved in here, I've seen him dwindling, eaten away."

Finally, one night before Daddy came home, Mommy was the one who dropped her fork on the plate and turned to Grandmother Beverly with critical eyes after she made another one of these remarks.

"Beverly," she said. I knew something hard was going to follow because she rarely called her Beverly. "I think you should seriously consider moving out of here, finding your own little place."

"What? You can't be serious," Grandmother Beverly said smiling. "Why, you need me more than ever around here now."

"I need you less than ever," Mommy retorted. "We need our own lives, without any interference and certainly without any static. You don't like this house and you are not happy living here. Because you're not happy, you do everything to make everyone else miserable.

"Maybe if you're living somewhere more to your liking, you'll be more satisfied. We'll have you for dinner often, of course, and you can visit whenever you like."

Grandmother Beverly nodded.

"I *should* go. I really should teach you a lesson and leave."

"Please, teach me," Mommy replied softly.

Grandmother Beverly looked at me and I looked down.

"Very well, I'll take one of those garden apartments where Mrs. Saks lives."

"Good choice," Mommy said and picked up her fork without skipping a beat.

"Taylor will be upset," Grandmother warned.

"Well, we'll tell him it's what you wanted, won't we?" Mommy asked her with a smile. "That way, we won't risk his being too upset, okay, Beverly? I know that's what you want too."

Grandmother Beverly pressed her lips together and nodded slowly.

"He married you against my wishes; he should suffer the consequences of his actions."

"We all do, Beverly," Mommy said. "We all suffer the consequences of our actions in the end."

I held my breath.

Grandmother Beverly rose, looked at us, and went to her room.

Two days later, she was moved out of the house, and a day after that, Daddy came home.

Despite all that had happened and all the commotion and tension, Mommy had remembered to sign and send in the letter of acceptance to Madame Senetsky. I was surprised when she told me.

I was worried, too, because Daddy had revealed the financial burden was his main concern. Madame Senetsky's school was twice as expensive as a private college and there would be other associated expenses as well.

One afternoon, almost a week after Daddy was home, I came home from school and saw he was sitting on a chaise longue out back, getting some sun. Mommy was still at the supermarket. I wandered out and sat across from him. He looked like he was sleeping, but he opened his eyes immediately.

"Hey," he said.

"Hey."

"How's it going? School's coming to an end."

"Uh-huh."

"Graduation is always an exciting time," he said. He stared ahead for a moment and then he looked at me. "I've got to tell you something, Cinnamon. When I was being taken into the operating room for the pacemaker, I had one great fear."

"What, Daddy?"

"That I would die without telling you something,

something I had to tell and something I couldn't tell your mother. I was afraid of what it might do to her. I'm still afraid."

I held my breath.

"I did something wrong a while back and I had to work my way out of it. I'm ashamed of it, but I realize you're old enough to know that your father's not perfect. No one's perfect. When you're young, you can believe the people you love are perfect and that's fine. It makes the world seem safer, but you're about to go out into the real world, the competitive cold world and you'd better know it's not a walk in the sun."

"I know it isn't, Daddy."

"Yes, I think you're a much smarter, more mature young lady than most your age, and I've got to credit your mother for that. She's done a great job with you while I had my face buried in stocks and bonds."

He paused, looked away and then spoke softly.

"Some time ago, I used a client's investment money to speculate on a stock I was sure would have a very big return. It would have, if something hadn't come up that caused the Food and Drug Administration to call back the company's product. I lost most of the money and I had to confront the client and tell her."

"Her?"

"Yes. She's a wealthy woman, a widow. The reaction she had and what she wanted was quite unexpected. I was prepared to borrow on life insurance policies, the house, everything and anything, but she knew she had me in a box. What I did would cause me to lose my license and be thrown out on the street."

"What did she want, Daddy?"

"She wanted me to pretend . . . to pretend she was

someone I admired . . . loved," he said. "She had a fantasy and I had to be part of it for a while. Finally, I was able to restore her funds and break loose of her hold on me." He shook his head. "Crazy thing is, she wasn't upset. She was satisfied and has gone on to another fantasy. She even still invests with my firm."

"Why did you tell me this, Daddy?"

"When I was faced with the possible end of my life, I felt I had to get it off my conscience. The other day when Grandmother Beverly visited me, she told me about an accusation you had made and that got me thinking. Why did you tell her that, Cinnamon?"

Now it was my turn to look away. He waited. Tears were building under my lids.

"One day I cut school . . ."

"Yes, I remember that."

"And Clarence Baron and I went to the city to spy on you. I thought you were trying to get another job or that you were in some financial trouble."

"I was."

"But that's not what I thought it was," I said. "I followed you to a coffee shop and saw you kiss a woman on the lips."

"Ah," he said. "You're not going to believe it, but I had the feeling I was being watched. Your mother's and your spirits," he muttered. "This house . . ." he said looking up. "So that was it."

"Yes, Daddy."

"Well, I'm glad we had this talk," he said. "I hate secrets between me and the people I love. I can only imagine how terrible you must have felt and how angry, but you couldn't have hated me more than I hated myself."

"I never hated you, Daddy," I said. "But I was angry."

"Sure. You should have been. I would have been, too. I say I hate secrets, but I don't see any good in telling your mother about this."

"That's up to you, Daddy, you and Mommy."

He nodded and smiled.

"You are very mature and very perceptive. I'm glad you're going to that school, Cinnamon."

"What about the cost?"

"Well," he said. "I had a good talk with your Grandmother Beverly and she agreed to free up your trust."

"She did?"

"Yes," he said laughing. "Your mother was right about her. She's happier living somewhere else, anywhere else but in this house," he said.

"Do you hate our house?"

"Hate it?" He thought a moment. "No. I used to be afraid of it, afraid those spirits of yours would get me. Maybe they did. I deserved it if they did. But, the place kind of grows on you," he said.

He rose.

"I'd better go in. Your mother will be home any moment and I want to help her."

"I'll be there, too."

"Naw, don't worry. We can handle it," he said. He stood there looking at me.

And I ran into his arms and we held each other for a long, precious moment.

"I love you, baby," he said. "And you make me proud, very, very proud."

He kissed my forehead and walked into the house.

I sucked in my breath and started for the hill. When I got there, I looked at the tombstones and then I rushed forward and pulled the stick out of the ground. I dug like a mad dog until I found my charm necklace, the one Daddy had given me. I brushed it off and put it back on quickly.

Then I looked at the stones once more, turned and walked back toward the house.

Toward the future.

Toward tomorrow when I would be on another stage in front of another audience.

Under the spotlight.

Ice

Prologue

———m———

When I was a little more than six years old, my first-grade teacher, Mrs. Waite, pulled me aside after school to tell me that if I didn't talk, if I didn't answer questions in class, and if I continued to behave like a mute, all the thoughts in my head that should have been spoken would eventually expand, explode and split my head apart.

"Just like an egg!

"There's a warehouse in your brain for storing thoughts, but there's just so much room in there," she explained. "You've got to let more thoughts out and the only way to do that is to speak. Do you understand me, Ice?" she asked.

Mrs. Waite always grimaced when she pronounced my name and spoke through clenched teeth as if she hated it and as if simply pronouncing it made her teeth chatter with the chill.

During the one and only parent-teacher conference

Mama attended when I was in grade school, Mrs. Waite questioned the wisdom of naming me Ice. I was sitting there in my little desk and chair with my hands clasped (as they were supposed to be every morning when our day began) listening to her talk about me as if I was listening to her talk about someone else. It embarrassed me, so I turned my attention to a sparrow pacing impatiently back and forth on the window ledge.

I really was more interested in the sparrow. I imagined it being bothered by our presence and wondering why human beings were here making human noises, interrupting her private singing rehearsal.

"It's more of a nickname than a name," Mrs. Waite said aggressively. "Doesn't she have another name, a real name?"

"That is her real name." Mama turned her lips in when she spoke. She did that whenever she was very angry. Her ebony eyes practically glowed with rage.

It was enough to intimidate my petite teacher who wasn't much bigger than some of her students. She was barely five feet tall with childlike features and very slim. She cowered back in her chair and glanced at me and then at Mama who kept her eyes fixed on her as if deciding whether or not she would lean forward and slap her on the side of the head.

"What do you mean by asking me if my daughter has a real name?"

"Well, I . . . just . . . wondered," she stuttered, instantly backpedaling, "I mean, she gets teased a great deal by the other students. I thought if we could do something about it now, she would avoid any of that as she grows up. You know how cruel other children can be, Mrs. Goodman."

"She'll take care of herself just fine," Mama replied, twisted her lips, nodded at me and then stood up. "Is that it?"

"Oh no," Mrs. Waite cried, "no. Please don't leave just yet," she pleaded.

Mama took a deep breath, lifting her very feminine shoulders and firm breasts. She was proud of her beautiful figure and wouldn't wear a bra even to a school conference. Mama had me when she was only eighteen, and despite her smoking and drinking, she could still pass for a high-school senior. Her complexion was as smooth as the color of a fresh coffee bean. Daddy, who was a big, burly man with a stark black mustache that began to show some gray hairs before he was even thirty, was often teased about having a child bride or bringing his daughter around. Mama loved that. In fact, Daddy would occasionally accuse her of deliberately dressing and acting like a teenager just so it would happen. Mama would spin around on him and vent her outrage; the words flung at him so fast and sharply, they were like a handful of rocks.

"What are you accusing me of, Cameron Goodman? Huh? What are you saying about me? You saying I'm some sort of street girl? Huh? Well? What?"

Daddy would throw up his hands, shake his head and step back.

"You do what you want," he'd say.

"And what are you looking at me like that for?" she would ask me while I stood in the corner watching them argue. I didn't say anything. I stared at her and then went back to whatever I was doing.

Their arguments weren't pleasant to hear or to watch, but they weren't yet having the all-out, slam-bang quarrels they would have when I was older. That was to come. It loomed in the shadows and corners of our Philadelphia apartment like bats sleeping, waiting to be nudged, disturbed. Eventually, they circled us on an almost daily basis, eager to swoop in at the slightest sign of dissension.

"What else do you want me to know about my daughter? She sass you?" Mama asked Mrs. Waite.

"Oh no, Mrs. Goodman. I couldn't ask for a more polite child."

"So then?"

Mrs. Waite looked at me and leaned toward my mother as if she was going to whisper, only she didn't. She wanted me to hear it all.

"It's nice to have a shy girl these days. So many of the youngsters lack decorum."

"What's that?" Mama asked with narrow eyes of suspicion.

"Good behavior, respect for their elders. Too many of them are loud and undisciplined."

"Don't I know," Mama said bobbing her head. "Especially that Edith Merton. I tell Ice to keep away from her. She can only learn bad habits from a girl like that. I know she smokes. Right, Ice?"

I nodded.

"And she's only what? Nine? Huh?"

I gazed at the two of them. Mama knew how old Edith Merton was.

"What I was starting to say, Mrs. Goodman, is it's nice that Ice is a well-behaved girl, but she's too introverted."

"Intro- what?"

"She's reluctant to communicate, to express herself. It

worries me and I've told her so many times, so this isn't a tale told out of school," Mrs. Waite said looking at me.

"Tale told out of school? We're in school," Mama pointed out and laughed. "Ain't that right, Ice?" She winked at me. "So what is it you want me to do, Mrs. Waite? I'm not following you here."

"If she continues to be so reluctant to talk, to express herself, we'll have to have her tested by the school psychologist," Mrs. Waite warned. "Not that it's a bad thing to have that done," she quickly added. "Because we've got to be concerned."

"Psychologist?" Mama pulled the corner of her lips in, puffing out her cheeks. "You saying something's wrong with her mind?"

"Something is keeping her all locked up inside," Mrs. Waite insisted. "The technical term for her problem is elective mutism."

"Elective?" She grimaced with confusion. "You mean like voting?"

"Precisely. She's choosing to be this way."

Mama raised her eyebrows. She kept them trimmed pencil thin, tweezing them almost daily because she believed the eyebrows were the most important facial feature. It was practically a religious ritual for her. She'd light incense on her vanity table and begin, humming or listening to her New Age music because the girl down at the beauty shop told her it took stress lines out of your face. Mama stared at her image in the glass and checked every inch of herself. Her gilded-framed oval mirror was her altar.

"She's choosing to be a mute? How do you know that?"

"Because she has no physical disability or language

problems. In other words, no clear reason for being like she is."

"So why do you want her to see that psycho- something?"

"To evaluate her more and see if we can help her overcome whatever it is that keeps her so closed up." Carefully, now close to a real whisper, Mrs. Waite asked, "How is she at home?"

"She's a good girl there, too," Mama said, looking at me. "She knows she better be," she added filling her voice with threat. It was like blowing air into a balloon and then letting it out. She shook her head. "Election mute. That girl talks when she wants and she certainly doesn't keep her mouth shut when it's time to sing. She's the best singer in the children's church choir, you know? The minister told me so himself about a thousand times."

"No," Mrs. Waite said, her eyes wide with surprise. "Really?" She looked at me as if she had just realized I was there. "She sings?"

"The minister calls her Angel Voice. She takes after my side," Mama said proudly. "My mama was a church singer, too. Okay," she said standing again, only this time with more determination. Her quick movement sent the sparrow flying from the window ledge.

"Ice," Mama snapped.

I looked up at her.

"You talk more in school. You hear me? Don't make me mad now."

I continued to stare up at her.

"Look at the girl. She look afraid? No. She look upset? No. Don't you see, Mrs. Waite? She got ice in her veins. She's as cool as can be. She never cries even when she gets slapped. She didn't cry much when she was a baby either. That's why her name fits her, no matter what you say about it. I gotta go," she added after looking at her watch. "C'mon," she told me and I rose to follow her, looking back at Mrs. Waite who shook her head and bit down on her lower lip, frustrated. Mine was probably her worst parent-teacher conference.

My reluctance to talk didn't affect my schoolwork. I wasn't a bad student. I did well on all the written work assigned and on all our tests. When I had to recite something, I did it reluctantly, but at least I did it, even though I did only what was required and spoke so softly it was nearly impossible to hear me. Mrs. Waite often complained that I never raised my hand to ask a question. If I had to go to the bathroom, I just got up and went for the bathroom pass.

"You should ask first," Mrs. Waite said. She wanted to hear me speak so much, she tried forbidding me to take the pass without asking and she soon saw that I would endure the pain of holding it in more than the pain of speaking. When she saw the agony in my eyes and saw how I squirmed in my chair, she finally offered the pass and I hurried out to do my thing.

Mrs. Waite was clairvoyant when it came to her predictions about my future in school, however. It never took my classmates long to begin teasing me after the start of a new school year. My reluctance to speak, to read aloud, to recite anything drew quick, curious and critical eyes. My behavior, along with my name, gave my tormentors a warehouse full of tortures to inflict.

I don't know how many times I heard someone in one of my classes say, "Her name's Ice because all the words are frozen in her mouth."

Once, when I was in the seventh grade, a group of

girls decided they would make me talk for as long as a
minute. They ganged up on me in the girls' locker room
after our teacher went to see about a sick student. They
stripped off my gym uniform and held me down dangling
my clothes around me and threatening to keep me naked
until I spoke for the full minute. Thelma Williams held
up her wrist and called off the numbers on her watch.

"Talk," they chanted, "talk."

"Or we'll throw all your clothes and your uniform out
the window and push you into the hallway."

"Talk!"

I cried and struggled, but they were relentless. Finally,
I closed my eyes and began to sing an old Negro spiritual:

> "I'm gonna sing when the spirit says, 'Sing!'
> I'm gonna sing when the spirit says, 'Sing!'
> I'm gonna sing when the spirit says, 'Sing,'
> And obey the spirit of the Lord!
> I'm gonna pray, I'm gonna pray all night,
> All day, angels watching me, my Lord.
> All night, all day, and obey the spirit of the
>   Lord!
> I'm gonna shout, shout, shout
> When the spirit says, 'shout, shout, shout.' "

"Shut her up!" Thelma Williams cried. She was in the
church choir, too, and couldn't stand that I was singing
one of our hymns. It actually frightened her and some of
the others, who quickly released my arms and legs and
dropped my things at my feet.

"She's nuts. Leave her be," Carla Thompson declared.
It satisfied most of them and they left me alone for a while.

As I grew older, I became a little less introverted, but I was never as talkative as the other girls in my classes. Once, when another one of my teachers remarked about my quiet way, a boy named Balwin Noble—who played piano so well he was the pianist for our school chorus— said, "She's just saving her vocal cords for when it counts the most."

I looked at him and thought, maybe I was.

Maybe that was something I did naturally.

It just seemed to me that words flew all around me as undistinguished as flies with just a few as graceful and important as birds. I didn't talk just to hear the sound of my own voice or need to talk in order to make myself seem important. Silence was often a two-edged sword. It worked well by keeping me invisible, almost forgotten when and where I wanted to be forgotten. Sometimes merely waiting to speak, holding back, made every word I said seem like a gem. People listened to me more because I spoke less, whether they were my teachers or my friends.

Finally, the second of Mrs. Waite's predictions came true. I was ordered to see the school psychologist when I was in the ninth grade. Mama and Daddy had to come too, and Mama was asked to come back. She didn't want to, but the principal made her do it. I met with the psychologist a half dozen times afterward. Mostly he asked questions and I either ignored him or gave him as simple an answer as I could.

I was smart enough to realize that the psychologist, Doctor Lisa, had a theory that I was trying hard to remain invisible because my mother didn't want to be a mother and my existence reminded her she was. I had to admit to myself I had stood by quietly many times when I was much younger and wished I was invisible, especially when Mama told new friends I wasn't really her child. She'd lie and say I was her younger sister's child, a sister who was promiscuous, and she was just keeping me for a few years. She hated taking me places with her, and Daddy was often left home watching me while Mama went shopping or out to the movies with some girlfriends.

I could count on my fingers how many times we did anything as a family, especially when I was very little. Whenever Daddy offered to take us out to eat, Mama would complain, "What kind of night out is it with a child, sitting at a table with a high chair in a restaurant and either you or me having to feed her? We'll get a baby-sitter."

Mama was never terribly particular about the baby-sitter either. Any warm body old enough to carry me out in case of fire or use a telephone was considered good enough. I was often left shut up in my room, ignored or put to bed hours before I was supposed to be asleep. Many of the baby-sitters had girlfriends or boyfriends over. When I was only seven, I saw Nona Lester letting her boyfriend fondle her breasts and put his hand up her skirt. They seemed to think it was funny to have me as an audience.

Did all this cause me to be an elective mute?

I never talked about any of it. I kept it to myself, swallowed it down like some bad-tasting medicine and tried to keep it from ever coming back up. Some of it did, of course. Some of it rode in the nightmare train that rattled and rushed through my dreams making me toss and turn and wake in a sweat with a small cry.

Sometimes the cry brought Daddy, if he wasn't working at night. It never brought Mama.

No wonder I thought I hadn't even uttered a sound.

What difference did any sound make?

Silence greeted me; I greeted it back with silence.

It was like staring someone down.

The darkness backed off. The train of nightmares came to a halt. I lowered my head to the pillow, took a deep breath and closed my eyes again.

Music entered, seeped into my mind from every available opening until my head was an auditorium in which a full orchestra played and I began to sing.

My voice transcended every ugly sound. I couldn't hear car horns, people screaming at each other or screaming in fear. I was traveling high above it all, floating on the notes.

Music gave words their souls.

What was the point in using them without it?

I used to wish real life was an opera or a musical like *The Phantom of the Opera* in which everyone sang when he or she spoke.

Mama would be the elective mute then.

Most unhappy and mean people would. They actually hated the sound of their own voices.

Not me.

I just kept it special, kept it waiting in the wings, waiting for the music.

—⁓—

Mama's Plan

Whenever I was alone in our apartment, which was quite often, and if I was very quiet, I could hear the sounds of other families below and around us. They traveled through the thin walls and in or over the pipes. I could move my ear from the wall on one side of the room to the other or take myself to another room, preferably the bathroom or kitchen, and press my ear to the walls there and hear different noises—what I thought of as the symphony of the Garden Apartments. It was almost like changing stations on a radio.

There were families who always seemed to be at war with each other, complaining, screaming, threatening in growls and shouts. There were those who spoke softly, enjoyed some laughter and even some singing. And there were often the sounds of someone crying, even sobbing, as if someone was walled in forever like in the short story by Edgar Allan Poe. Of course, I could hear television sets and hip-hop music. There were at least a half-dozen white families in our project, but their music wasn't very different, and I often heard as much shouting and crying from them as well.

I didn't know any other person who paid as much attention to the symphony of the Garden Apartments as I did. They were too busy making their own noises to listen to anyone else's and rarely did an hour pass in their homes when silence wasn't broken. Silence, I learned early on, frightens people, or at least makes them feel very uncomfortable. The worst punishment imposed on my school friends seemed to be keeping them in detention, forcing them to be still and shutting them off from any communication. They squirmed, grimaced, put their heads down and waited as if spiders had been released inside them and were crawling up and down their stomachs and under their chests. When the bell that dismissed them finally rang, they would burst out like an explosion of confetti in every direction, each talking louder than the other, some even screaming so hard that veins strained and popped against the skin in their temples.

Mama wasn't any different. The moment she entered the apartment, she turned on the radio or clicked on the television set, crying, "Why is this place like a morgue?"

If she had done some drinking with a girlfriend, she would dance and laugh, calling to me to join her while she fixed dinner; if I didn't come or if I made a reluctant face, she would pounce on me and accuse me of being strange, which she blamed on my daddy and his side of the family.

"Never seen a name fit better than the name I gave you, girl," she would declare. "The only time I ever see a smile on your face is when you're singing in that church. You going to be a nun or something? Wake up. Shake your booty. You got a nice figure, honey. You're lucky you don't take after your daddy in looks and be big boned like that Tania Gotchuck or somebody similar.

"You got my nose and mouth and you're getting my figure," she said with her hands on her hips, turning as if she were surrounded by mirrors.

Mama didn't need mirrors to look at herself though. She could spot her reflection in a glass on the table or a piece of silverware and suddenly fix her hair or touch her face and complain about aging too quickly. She wasn't. She was just anticipating it with such dread that the illusion of some tiny wrinkle forming or a single gray hair put hysteria into her eyes and panic in her voice.

"You wouldn't be so crazy nervous about yourself if we had another child," Daddy told her. "It would give you something more important to worry about."

He might as well have lit a firecracker in the middle of our living room, but for as long as I could remember, Daddy wanted to have more children. I know he wanted a son badly. However, Mama grumbled that giving birth to me had added a half-inch or so to her hips and another child would surely turn her into another one of those "walruses waddling around here with a trail of drippy-nosed brats they couldn't afford to have. Not me. I'm still young enough to turn a head or two."

"That's all that makes you happy, Lena," Daddy retorted. "Being the center of attention."

He didn't make it sound like any sort of accusation or even a criticism. It was just a matter-of-fact statement. Even so, Mama would go off on one of her tirades about how he wanted her to be fat and ugly so other men wouldn't look longingly at her anymore.

"You used to be proud to have me hanging on your

arm, Cameron Goodman. I could see how you would strut like a rooster, parading me in front of your friends, bragging with your eyes. I let you wear me like some piece of jewelry and I didn't bitch about it, did I? So why are you complaining now?"

"I'm not complaining, Lena, but there's more to life now. We're settled down. We have a home, a child. We should be building on this family, too," Daddy pleaded, his big hands out, palms up like someone begging for a handout of affection and love.

"I told you a hundred times if I told you once, Cameron. We can't have any more children on your salary," she replied and turned away quickly to end the argument or to run from it.

That wasn't fair or even a good excuse. Daddy made a decent salary. He had always done well. Now he was the head of security for Cobbler's Market, a big department store on Ninth Street. He had been a military policeman in the army; after he came out, he started working different security positions until he was chosen to head up one and then another.

It wasn't just his size that recommended him for the job, even though he stood six feet four and weighed two hundred and twenty-five pounds. He was considered a clear-thinking, sensible man who could manage other men. I know for sure that his calm, patient demeanor helped him get along with Mama. It took a great deal more than it took most men to get him to lose his temper. He seemed to know that when he did, he would unleash so much fury and rage, he couldn't depend on his power to rein it in. He was truly someone who was afraid of himself, of what he could or would do.

Amazingly, Mama never seemed afraid of him, never

hesitated or stepped back even when it looked like she was treading on thin ice. I have seen her throw things at him, push him, even kick him. He was like a tree trunk, unmovable, untouched, steady and firm, which only seemed to get Mama angrier. Finally, frustrated with her inability to get the sort of reaction from him she wanted, she would retreat out of exhaustion.

"You're just like your father when it comes to your cold personality," she accused, pointing her long, right forefinger at me like some prosecutor—because to her way of thinking not to be outgoing and emotional was truly a crime. "There's where the ice comes into your veins. Certainly not from me, child. I'm full of heat," she bragged. "A man looks into these eyes and he melts."

She would wait for me to agree or smile or look like I was envious, but I didn't do any of that and that brought a sneer to her lips.

"What is with you, girl? You think you're better than everyone around here or something?"

I shook my head vigorously.

"Because I never did anything to make you believe that. I never pumped you up with compliments and such until you walked around with your head back, looking like you got flies in your nose or something, did I? Well, did I?"

I knew she would keep at me until I spoke.

"No, Mama."

"No, Mama," she mimicked. "So?" she said, her hands still on her hips, "why are you home all the time, huh? Why don't you have girlfriends and boyfriends? When I was your age, my daddy put a double lock on the door to keep the boys out. Here you are seventeen," she said, "and you ain't been out on a real date yet. I don't hear the phone ringing either," she complained.

It nearly made me smile to hear her grievances. All the other girls my age were constantly moaning and groaning about how their parents came down on them for being on the phone too much or being out too late and hanging around with bad kids.

"Are you ashamed of this place, ashamed of us? Is that why you hardly ever utter a word? Your family embarrass you? Huh?"

I shook my head again.

"Because the worst kind of girl is a snob girl," Mama declared. "She's worse than the other kind who teases and such. Are you a snob? Is that what your friends think, too? You think because you have a nice singing voice, you can't waste it on us ordinary folks? Is that it? Because if it is, that's a snob. Well? Answer me, damn it."

"I'm not a snob, Mama," I insisted. "I'm not ashamed of you or Daddy either."

Tears tried to come into my eyes, but I slammed the door shut on them.

She raised her eyebrows, surprised she had gotten so strong a verbal reaction from me.

"No? Well, what are you then? What's your problem, girl? Why do people talk about you being strange and mute? People here say good morning and you just nod or they ask you how you are and how your family is and you smile instead of talk. I hear about it. Some of them like rubbing it into me like oil or something. Is that why you don't have a close girlfriend and no boyfriends? I bet it is," she said nodding. "I know boys don't want to waste their time on someone who acts deaf and dumb.

"You ain't ugly, far from that, child. You look too

much like me. What is it then? You just shy? Is that it? Was that grade-school teacher right about you years ago? You're Miss Bashful?" She drew close enough to me that I could smell the whiskey on her breath. "Huh? You got no self-confidence?" She poked me in the shoulder. "You afraid they going to laugh at you?" She poked me again. "Well?"

I put my hand over my shoulder where it was getting sore, but I didn't cry or even grimace.

"What?" she screamed at me.

"No one interests me yet," I said calmly.

That stopped her. She thought about it a moment and then shook her head.

"Well, you don't have to think of every boy as your future husband, Ice. Don't you just want to go out and have a good time once in a while?"

I didn't answer.

"You're shy," she decided, nodding firmly. "You're just too much like your daddy. He was so shy, I had to kiss him that first time. How's that? It surprise you to know that big, strong, bull of a man was afraid to kiss a girl? That's right. He was shaking in his shoes so bad, I could have pushed him over with one finger," she said, smiling. "I have that effect on most men. And you could, too, if you'd just listen to me. You don't even put on lipstick unless I hound you, and you still ain't trimmed those eyebrows the way I taught you."

Mama had spent six months in a beauty school when she was seventeen. It was her one real attempt at any sort of career for herself, but she lacked the sense of responsibility and the discipline to follow through. If she woke up tired, she just didn't go in, and soon they asked her to leave. However, she had learned a great deal.

"You need the arch," she pursued, running her forefinger over my left brow. "You put the high point directly above the middle of your iris. Brows are the frames of your eyes, Ice. Don't be afraid to tweeze them! Why should you be afraid of something like that anyway?"

"I'm not afraid, Mama," I said stepping back.

"Well then, why don't you do it? You can make your eyes look bigger. Remember what I told you: tweeze the hairs from underneath, not from above. Best time is after a shower. It's less painful, but a little pain can go a big way."

I looked down, hoping she would get bored as usual and start on some other pet peeve of hers, like how small our apartment was or how she couldn't buy the new dress she wanted because it was too expensive. Usually, she ended up threatening to go get a job, but she had yet to apply for work anywhere. Most of her day was spent looking after her hair and her skin, doing her beauty exercises or meeting her friends for lunch, which usually ran most of the afternoon. She always had too much to drink at those lunches and always reeked of smoke.

I once asked her why she smoked and drank if she cared so much about her looks and she responded by throwing a water glass across the room and accusing me of being too religious. She threatened to keep me from attending the church choir or make me quit the school chorus.

"It's the only time I ever see you show any interest in anything. What kind of a young life is that? Even birds do more than just sing."

Actually, both our school chorus and the church choir were award winning and were often asked to sing at government and charity events, but what did Mama know about that? She rarely came to hear me sing.

"You'll end up mealymouthed and fat, worrying about your everlasting soul day in and day out instead of having any fun," she rattled on. Now that she was on a roll, she seemed driven by her own momentum like some car that had lost its brakes going downhill.

"My mama was like that and that's why I was glad to get out of that house when your daddy came along and made me pregnant," she said without the slightest shame.

Other mothers would hide the fact that you were an accident, but not mine. Depending on her mood when she talked about it, she was either seduced by Daddy or clever enough to get herself pregnant and married as a means of escaping imprisonment at home. Whatever the reasons, however, my birth had been a blow to her youth and beauty. She never stopped reminding me about that added inch on her hips besides the strain it was on her to care for a baby.

"If you looked after yourself more, you'd have boys asking you out, Ice. As it is, they won't give you a second look unless you become one of them easy conquests."

Her eyes widened with her own imaginings: me on a street corner or in the back of some parked car.

"You do that and I'll throw you out on the street," she threatened. "I'm not having people talk dirt about a daughter of mine."

I stared at her as if she was really talking nonsense now.

"Don't look at me like that, girl. It doesn't take much to turn a nice girl into a street tramp these days. I see it going on all around us. That Edith Merton might as well put a sign on her door out there," she declared, pumping her finger at our front door. "That whole family oughta be evicted."

The Mertons lived at the end of the hall. Edith's father was a city bus driver. She had a ten-year-old brother and her mother worked in a dry-cleaning and laundry shop. Edith's double trouble was to have developed a heavy bosom at age thirteen and to have parents who were so busy working to keep a roof over their heads and food in their mouths that she was left on her own too much.

Mama's obsession with herself and her youthful looks had one good result, I suppose. She was terrified of disease, especially anything that affected her complexion. I was prohibited from ever going into Edith's apartment, and I was never to invite her into ours. Mama saw her as walking contamination and pointed to every blotch on her face as evidence of some sexually transmitted disease.

As a result of what I learned people would call a bad neurosis, Mama wanted our home to be immaculate. If she did any real work, it was to keep our house and our clothing clean. Of course, I was the one who did a major part of all that, but I didn't complain. Except for my singing in the church choir and the school chorus and doing homework, I had little to compete for my time.

However, shortly after Mama and I had our most recent one-sided conversation about my anemic social life, Mama came to the conclusion that it was finally beginning to reflect poorly on her.

"I go out with my girlfriends," she complained, "and before long they're all talking about their kids in some new romance, bragging about the way they get all spruced up or how pretty they are and I got to sit there with my mouth as sewn tight as yours usually is, just listening and hoping no one's going to ask me about you. But I know what they're thinking when they look at me: 'poor Lena. She got that great burden to bear at home.' How do you think that makes me feel, huh?" she whined.

"I'll tell you," she said knowing I wasn't going to offer any answer. "It makes me feel like I got some kind of a retard at home, a girl who never gets her hair fixed in a beauty shop, never listens to me about her makeup, never asks for a new dress, never does nothing but read or listen to her music and go singing with some travel agents to heaven. You're an embarrassment!" she declared finally. "And I mean to do something about it once and for all."

I had no idea what she meant, but I did look at her with curiosity, which made her smile.

"You need a push, girl. That's all. Just a little head start. Even your daddy says so," she told me.

I doubted that. More than likely, she went into one of her tirades when he had just come home from work late and was tired and he couldn't offer much resistence. To shut her up, he probably nodded a lot, grunted and looked like he agreed, but my guess was he wouldn't even remember the topic of conversation the next day if he was asked about it.

At least, I hoped that was true. Daddy never lied to me or ever criticized me for being too quiet or too withdrawn. He liked the tranquility he and I enjoyed when Mama wasn't around to lecture us on one failing or another. More often than not, he and I would sit quietly, both of us reading or listening to his jazz records. We said more to each other in those silences than most people did talking for hours and hours.

"Listen to that trumpet," he would say and I would; he

would nod and look at me and see that I understood why he loved jazz so much.

He had a valuable collection of old jazz albums that included Louis Armstrong, Lionel Hampton, Art Blakey on drums, and female vocalists like Carmen McRae, Ella Fitzgerald and Billie Holiday. He loved how I could listen to Carmen McRae singing "Bye Bye Blackbird" and then imitate her. He said I did a wonderful job imitating Ella Fitzgerald's "Lullaby of Birdland." He would play it and I would sing along. I could see the deep pleasure in his face whenever I performed for him. If Mama was there, she would thumb through one of her beauty magazines and look up at me occasionally, torn between giving me a compliment and complaining about me being content at home with them or my disinterest in the music girls my age loved.

"You're turning her into some weird kid. She doesn't listen to hip-hop or any of the music kids her age listen to and it's because of you, Cameron," she would grumble.

"I'm just listening to real music," Daddy would reply. "And she enjoys it. What's wrong with that?"

"*Real* music," Mama muttered. "My idea of real music is going somewhere to hear it and dance and have a good time, not sitting in your living room tapping your fingers on the side of an armchair."

They did go out on weekends occasionally, but Mama was never happy about the places Daddy took her. The people there were either too old or too calm or out of touch with what was really happening.

"You're not out in the world like I am," she would tell him. "You just don't know."

Daddy didn't argue. He drew his music around him

like a curtain of steel and sat contented, as contented as someone soaking in a warm bath. I listened, sang, learned about tempo and beat, phrasing and rhythm while Mama pouted or went into her bedroom to turn on the television set very loud. Those nights, we drove silence out the window.

Finally, Mama really decided to do something about me, to take control of my destiny, just as she had threatened. She was back to that idea that some girls just needed a little push. Well, she was going to give me more than a little push. She was going to give a firm shove.

She returned one afternoon, stepped into my bedroom while I was sprawled on my bed doing my math homework, and made an astonishing announcement.

"Thank your lucky stars, girl. I got you a date with a handsome young man."

"What?" I asked, turning.

"I got you a date for Saturday night. We got to go out and buy you something decent to wear and then I have to help you get yourself togther, fix your hair, do your makeup. When you go out with someone, you represent me, too," she declared. "People gonna say that's Lena Goodman's daughter and by the time I'm finished fixing you up, people gonna say, 'I would have known anywhere that was Lena's girl, a girl that pretty has to be her daughter.' "

"What do you mean, a date?" I asked, my heart thudding like a fist on stone.

"I know you kids don't like to think of it as a date. Somehow the word became old-fashioned. You just what—'hang out with someone' nowadays?" She smirked and shook her head. "Well, to me a date's a date.

The man picks you up, takes you somewhere nice, and pays for everything. That's still a date in my book."

"What man?" I asked, sitting up.

"Louella Carter's younger brother Shawn. He's gonna be home from boot camp on leave this weekend, and we arranged for you two to be together Saturday night. He's a very good-looking boy and a boy in the army is gonna be well mannered, too. I spoke with him on the phone myself and he was all, 'Yes ma'am' and 'No ma'am' and 'Thank you, ma'am.'"

"I'm not going out with someone I never met, Mama," I protested.

"Of course you are. Didn't you ever hear of something called blind dates? You either got your nose in your schoolbooks or your father's old record albums, but you must've heard of that."

"I don't like blind dates," I said.

"You've never been on one! You've never been on any date, blind or otherwise, so how can you say you don't like it, Ice?"

"I just know I don't," I said.

"Well, this time you're gonna make an effort to like something I do for you. I didn't just go looking for a date for you, you know. I screened a lot of young men first. Louella's a girlfriend of mine and her brother's got to be a good boy who won't take advantage of an innocent girl such as yourself. I'm not saying he won't want to kiss you and such, but you know when to stop."

She thought a moment.

"Don't you?" she asked. "I mean, you learned all about that stuff in school, right?"

I nodded.

"Good. Then it's all set."

"Nothing's set," I said.

She glared at me a moment and then she stepped farther into my room, her eyes heating over, her jaw tightening, her hands folding into small fists pressed firmly into her thighs as she hovered over me.

"I said it's set. You're going to get all dressed up and have a good time whether you like it or not, and you're going to make me proud and give me something to brag about when I'm with my girlfriends, hear? This is one Saturday night you're not going to be shut up in your room singing to yourself or out there with your father and me listening to his antique records."

"But—"

"No buts, Ice. I want you to make a good effort toward having a good time. Do it for me if not for yourself," she added in a softer tone, practically begging. Her face looked pained with the effort.

I stared at her a moment and then looked down.

"Well?"

"Okay, Mama," I said.

"Good. Good. You're going to be thanking me afterward," she predicted. "You should be grateful that you have a mother who knows how to dress up and look good, too. Other girls depend on their friends or something they see in a magazine and usually look pretty stupid. I'm right here, at your side, giving you the knowledge I have from real experience.

"First thing we got to do is get your hair cut right."

"What? No, Mama. I don't want to cut my hair," I moaned.

"Of course you do. You don't know it right now, maybe, but once you're in the shop and my personal beautician Dawn starts working on your mop, you'll be very happy about it," she practically ordered. "You can't just keep your hair brushed down all the time. It looks drab."

She reached out and touched my hair

"And it doesn't have the body and silky satin feel it should. Men like to touch nice hair and see a woman whose face is framed right. You're not taking advantage of your good qualities, Ice. I've been after you for months to do something about this . . . this mess, well now we have a reason to do it and we will.

"After that, we'll go look for a dress. Maybe we'll take advantage of some of those discounts your father gets, discounts we don't use enough. You'll need some new shoes, too."

"I don't want to cut my hair, Mama."

"I already made your beauty parlor appointment. It's tomorrow at nine."

"Tomorrow at nine? But I'll be in school, Mama."

"Not tomorrow, you won't."

"But—"

"You don't ever miss a day, Ice. You can miss one and don't tell me you can't. I see some of the girls in your class hanging around here during the school day, pretending to be sick or something and having a good old time of it. No one comes around to check on them either. At least you have a good reason not to go."

"Getting your hair done is not a good reason to cut school, Mama."

"It is to me, especially when you don't ever go and get it done, and especially when you have an important occasion coming up," she insisted.

"Important occasion," I mumbled under my breath.

"Yes," she said wagging her head, "it is an important

occasion. It's like what they call those debutante balls or something, a coming-out."

I started to smile and her face turned hard and cold.

"Are you laughing at me, Ice?"

"No, Mama."

"Don't you go showing your stuck-up face to me."

"I'm not being stuck-up. But Mama, this is not anything like a debutante ball."

"It is to me and it should and will be to you. Now that's it. You can thank me later," she added and left me stunned and anxious about what she had done.

It was almost like the old days when parents arranged the marriages their children would have. If any of my classmates found out what she had done, I would really be the object of ridicule, I thought. Knowing Mama's girlfriends, it wasn't hard to believe the gossip would fly.

"Ice's mother has to find her a date. She can't get one on her own," they would say. They'd tease me and ask if my mother could find them a date, too.

I've got to find a way to get myself out of this, I thought. I could go to Daddy, but if I went to him, it could become a big blowup between them and they had been having quite of few of those lately. The last thing I wanted to do was be the cause of another.

Maybe I could pretend to be sick, I thought.

No, she wouldn't go for that. She's so excited about this, she'd send me out with a temperature of a hundred and five and a face covered in measles.

Maybe Louella's brother wouldn't show up. Maybe he would change his mind. Maybe he wouldn't like being made to go out with a high-school girl on a blind date. Maybe . . .

Maybe you might just have a good time, another voice inside me said. Maybe you'll like him.

Just maybe, your mother might be right. Don't try to tell yourself you never dreamt of having a nice time with a really nice young man.

Yes, your mother might be right.

I'd soon know, I thought and settled back into the inevitability of what was to come like someone floating on a raft toward Niagara Falls.

2

—❧—

The Makeover

From the way Mama talked and behaved, anyone would
have thought I really was being prepared for a debutante
ball. She couldn't wait to tell my daddy when he came
home from work that evening, a little after ten. When he
worked the later shift, he would have a sandwich for dinner, but that was never enough for a man his size, so
Mama would prepare leftovers for him if she was home
when he returned. If she wasn't, I would come out of my
room as soon as he was home and warm up his dinner.

"Ice has a date Saturday night," I heard her tell him at
the table.

We had a small, separate dining room and a four-chair
yellow Formica breakfast table in the kitchen. She served
the late dinner in the kitchen, ostensibly because she
didn't want to mess up a clean dining room just for a left-
over dinner. It made no sense to me because she would
have to clean up the kitchen again anyway.

Despite her complaints, our apartment was a good size

for the rent we paid and Daddy was always pointing out that the building was rent-controlled and we wouldn't get as much for our money if we did what Mama wanted and looked for another place to live. He tried to make it nicer to please her. He had friends who laid carpet and put up wallpaper and got some very good deals at the mall. No matter what he did though, the place was still "a dump" to Mama.

"Date? What kind of date?" Daddy asked. I could hear the concern in his voice, which took me by surprise. He rarely asked me anything about my friends or any boys at school. He never pushed me to go to dances or asked me why I wasn't going out on weekends.

"A nice date," Mama said. "I arranged it myself," she boasted.

"You arranged it? What do you mean? How?"

"I arranged for Louella Carter's brother Shawn to take her out. He's an army boy on leave from boot camp."

"Army boy? What kind of an arrangement is that? What are you saying, she never met him?"

"Now you tell me, Cameron Goodman, how is she going to meet anyone shut up in this place listening to music with you on weekends and such, huh? You think there's some sort of billboard out there with her face on it, announcing Ice Goodman's here, come and ask her out?"

"This doesn't sound good to me," Daddy said, his voice ringing with alarm.

"Oh no? And why is that, Cameron? Huh? Why? Because I made it all happen?"

"It just doesn't sound like it will be good. Army boys are a different breed," he warned. "Don't forget I was an MP. I know what being shut up with other men does to them, especially a boy just released from boot camp."

"Well, this time it will be good," she insisted. "Louella's a very nice girlfriend and I'm sure her brother's a nice young man. Besides, what have you been doing to help that child be a normal girl, huh? Nothing. You're content just keeping her home listening to music. How she ever going to meet anyone and get married that way?"

"She's only seventeen and still in high school, Lena. It's not exactly a crisis."

"How old was I when you married me? Huh? Well?"

"It was different," Daddy said almost under his breath. "You were different."

"What's that supposed to mean? You think she's better than us?"

"No. That's not what I'm saying," he said, but he didn't say it firmly enough for her.

"Blowing that child's ego up to make her think she's the Virgin Mary or something, raving about her singing all the time. No one's ever going to be good enough for her. Maybe that's what you want, Cameron Goodman. Maybe you want to keep her at your side all your days. Her hair will grow gray alongside yours listening to music. It's unnatural, that's what it is."

"Stop it, Lena."

"She's going on a date. She's going to be a normal girl who talks. And she's going to make me proud. Come aboard or swim to shore, Cameron, but don't you dare say one word against it, hear? I'm warning you."

Daddy was quiet. He wasn't happy, but he retreated as he usually did. His lack of enthusiasm and his warnings, however, put even more steam into Mama. Now she had to prove she was right. She couldn't wait to get me up and out to the beauty parlor the next morning. She made such a production out of it, I was truly embarrassed when we arrived.

"Here she is!" she cried as soon as we stepped through the doorway.

All the women in chairs turned to look and every one of the beauticians stopped work. Dawn, a dirty blond no taller than my old grade-school teacher, Mrs. Waite, emerged from the rear of the shop and looked me over as if I was someone just brought to civilization.

"She's got potential," she declared. "I see what you were saying, Lena."

Mama swelled with pride.

"But we've got some work here," Dawn added cautiously as she circled me. Everyone else was still looking at me.

"Pretty girl," the woman in the first chair said.

"Tall, like a model," the man working on her commented.

Dawn fingered my hair. "You're really dry, girl," she said. "And doing a lot of shedding."

"I knew it," Mama said. "She just hasn't looked after herself right. I've been hounding her, but you know young people today. You can't tell them anything."

Dawn didn't respond. She kept circling me, which made me even more nervous.

"We have to shampoo and condition plenty," she said. "Add moisture."

"Exactly," Mama said nodding.

"What have you been using on your hair, hand soap?" Dawn asked me. Everyone laughed, even Mama.

I looked down, debating whether I would just turn and run out or stay.

"Well, let's get you in the chair and get started," Dawn said. "We'll make it right."

"Go on, Ice," Mama coached.

Reluctantly, I walked across the shop, past the other chairs and women and got into the chair reserved for me. Dawn came around and started to prepare the sink for my shampoo.

"You use a blow-dryer too much," she began, "especially with your dry hair. Why don't you give your hair a break and put it in cornrows?"

"No," I said sharply.

One of the women who was having it done turned to look my way.

"It's not for me," I added and gave Mama a look that told her I would get up and leave if they didn't listen.

"Just suggesting," Dawn said. "What do you say we do a press and cut, Lena? I'd bring it to here," she said pinching my hair at my chin. Mama nodded. Dawn looked at my face and smiled. "You've really never been to a beauty shop before, huh?"

"Not because of me," Mama said.

"This is going to look great," Dawn told me. "I'm going to insert a full head of weave, apply styling mousse and set your hair with a flat iron, curling the front down and the back up. You'll see. Great," she said.

Mama stepped back, nodded at Dawn and they began. I closed my eyes like someone about to go into an operating room and tried to shut out all the talk and laughter by listening to Daddy's music replay in my head.

When it was finally over, Dawn turned me around and stood behind me as proud as any artist. I gazed at myself in the mirror, amazed at the difference in my appearance. Not only did I appear older and more sophisticated, but

Mama was right: I did have most of her good facial features, maybe even better because of my stronger mouth and bigger eyes and more prominent cheekbones—features I had inherited from Daddy.

"Well?" Dawn said. "You haven't said a word all the time I've been working. What do you have to say now?"

"She loves it. Don't you, Ice?" Mama asked, her eyes pressuring me to respond positively.

I nodded.

"Yes, I think I do," I admitted.

Mama let out a trapped breath, and she and Dawn laughed. Mama really looked pleased and that made her face even softer and younger. Anger always aged her instantly, like a dark hand waved magically in front of her.

"Now we'll do her eyebrows and I'll get her straight on her makeup," she told Dawn. "We're off to get her a nice dress."

"Are you going to a prom or something?" Dawn asked me.

I looked at Mama.

"No, she's going on her first real date."

"First? You're kidding me, Lena Goodman."

"I wish I was," Mama said. "We've got a lot of time to make up."

Dawn raised her eyebrows, looked at me and nodded.

"I bet," she said. "And I bet she will," she added.

Everyone but me laughed.

"Okay," Dawn said, "I gave you the best cut I could. Remember, before you go to sleep every night, prepare your hair for its own beauty rest. Apply a small amount of the moisturizer your Mama just bought for you, and to stop hair breakage, don't wear no hair band. We have satin sleep caps, Lena. Maybe you oughta get one for her."

"Yes," Mama said. "Absolutely."

Mama was on a tear now, spirited by our success at the beauty parlor. We took a cab to the Gallery at Market East and to Drawbridge's Department Store where Daddy had a twenty-percent discount. When I saw the price of the clothes, I didn't think it mattered if he had a discount or not, but cost didn't matter to Mama. She wouldn't let a little thing like breaking our budget for a couple of months stand in her way.

"I don't want you wearing those granny clothes young girls parade around in these days. Most of them look like sacks from thrift shops. And those clodhoppers they wear . . . I swear it's like girls are ashamed to show what they got anymore, or else they don't have it and don't have anything to show."

I tried to explain styles and trends to Mama, but she wouldn't hear of it.

"What makes you look good is in style and what doesn't is out of style in my book," she said.

We wandered through the teen fashions unsuccessfully. Mama didn't like anything. I thought she would give up on Drawbridge's, but she decided to go into the adult section, and she stopped in front of a manikin wearing what was called a princess cut blouse and skirt. It was a black and silver polyester jacquard material with a floral pattern on the blouse and a modest leaf pattern on the skirt. Because of the curve-enhancing princess shape in front and back, Mama thought it was sexy and stylish.

When I stepped out of the fitting room, Mama and people around her looked impressed. Other customers paused to look at us, too. I was embarrassed by the attention.

"What a perfect fit and what a beautiful figure your daughter has, Mrs. Goodman. She could model for us," the saleswoman said. "She looks like she's in her early twenties."

"Her father will have to sit at the door with a shotgun, you buy her that dress," a woman just passing said to Mama.

Mama was bursting with pride, her eyes electric, her shoulders hoisted.

"That's the latest fashion, you say?" she asked the saleswoman.

"Yes ma'am. It just came in yesterday, matter of fact."

"We'll take it," Mama decided.

It was an expensive outfit because of its designer, but Mama was determined.

"Your father can pick up some overtime," she told me when I showed her the tag.

"I don't need anything this expensive, Mama."

"Of course you do," she said. "The better you look Saturday night, the nicer you'll be treated. He's not going to take you to any Denny's in this," she said laughing. "That's for sure."

"Maybe he can't afford to do anything else, Mama," I said. After all, I didn't know anything about him and Mama really didn't know much either.

"That doesn't matter," Mama said. "When a woman impresses a man, he doesn't think of budgets and bank accounts and what he can and can't afford. He just thinks about one thing: impressing her. I know men, honey. And before long now, you're going to know them too, know just what to expect.

"Your education is starting a little later than mine did, but you have the benefit of me," she decided, nodding. "Truth is, I wish I had me when I was younger. I didn't have an easy time of it. My mother thought sex was such a dirty word, she had me and my sister and brother thinking we had been born through some sort of pollination, you know, like flowers? It got sprinkled on her stomach and we got created."

I smirked at her attempt at a joke, but she laughed.

"I'm not being funny. All she knew was the birds and the bees and that's what bees do; don't they spread the pollen? Bet you didn't think I knew so much about science, huh?

"I got a lot of surprises up my sleeve, Ice."

Suddenly, I was afraid she was telling the truth.

My heart ticked like a time bomb as Saturday night drew closer. That night after we had done all our shopping, Mama made me put on the outfit we had bought so I could model for Daddy. First, she worked on my makeup. She sat me in front of her vanity table and stood behind me gazing at my face in the mirror, scrutinizing. She decided I needed a little eye shadow. I thought it was too much, but she claimed my eyes were my strongest feature and I should do all I could to make them stand out.

"You have a natural pout," she told me, and decided to enhance it by dabbing a sliver of lip gloss onto the center of my lower lip. She showed me a trick to prevent lipstick from getting on my teeth. I was to put my finger in my mouth and close my lips. When I withdrew my finger, it removed any excess color.

"Someone once told me a beautiful woman's face was

like an artist's palette. The artist sees the picture there and brings it out. You got to do the same with your face, Ice. Make it a work of art. That's what I do," she said softly, but with deep feeling.

I remember looking up at her and thinking with surprise that she had more depth to her than I had ever imagined. Looking at myself in the mirror and at her behind me, standing there so proudly, I realized my mama had nothing but her good looks to rely on to give her meaning and purpose in life. Most of her girlfriends did look at her enviously and wanted to be in her company because her beauty had a way of spreading to them, embracing them, keeping them under wing. People, especially men, looked their way because Mama strolled along in the center. Maybe with the right management and some lucky breaks Mama could have been a model. As she sat there night after night, thumbing through those beauty magazines and gazing at the women who advertised beauty products or fashions, she had to be tantalized, taunted and frustrated knowing how much more beautiful and special she was.

It was funny how all this came to me in those moments before her vanity mirror. We had never had a real mother-daughter conversation about such things. Through the endless flow of complaints and moans she voiced in our small world, I was burdened with the task of understanding what she really meant and really felt. I had to read between all those crooked lines until I suddenly realized who she was.

Mama was a beautiful flower that had been plucked too early and placed in the confines of some vase where it finished blossoming and then battled time and age to keep from losing its special blush. Now she was looking at me and thinking I would complete her, I would do all that she had been unable to do and be all that she had dreamed she would be.

"Children are our true redemption," the minister told us all one Sunday. "We believe they will redeem us for failing to be all that we had hoped to be, that they will do what we dreamed we should do and be whom we thought we should be. That's a healthy thing. 'Go forth and multiply,' " he recited.

The burden of such responsibility was heavy and something I didn't want, but I didn't have the hardness in me to turn around and say, "All this is your world, Mama, not mine. I don't need to be in the spotlight. I don't mind being in the chorus. It's the music that matters most."

Of course, I kept my famously shut-tight mouth zipped.

"All right," she declared when we were finished. "Put on your dress. Let's show your father how blind he's been by treating you like a little girl."

I was almost as nervous dressing for Daddy as I was to be dressing for Shawn on Saturday. Mama came into my room to make sure I had everything right. She had bought me a pair of shoes to complete the outfit and had given me her precious pieces of jewelry to wear: her pearl necklace on a gold chain with the matching pearl earrings.

"Turn down that music, Cameron Goodman," she cried from my doorway, "and get yourself ready for a real surprise."

I felt like I was a runway model when I crossed from my room to the living room. Daddy obeyed Mama's command, turning down his music, and then she brought me into the living room. When he looked up from his big cushioned chair, his eyes did a dance of their own, enlarging, brightening, blinking and then suddenly narrowing with a kind of dark veil of sadness. I could see it clearly in his face. It was as if his thoughts were being scrolled over his forehead in big white letters: *My little girl is gone and in her place is this beautiful young woman who is sure to be plucked like her mother and taken off to be planted in someone else's garden. All I will have are the memories.*

"Well?" Mama demanded. "Don't just sit there acting mute too, Cameron Goodman. Say something. I spent a lot of time and energy on all this."

"She's . . . absolutely beautiful, Lena."

"You like the outfit?"

"Yeah," he said nodding emphatically.

"Good. You're going to need to remember that when you see the bill."

His smile froze, but he didn't show any anger or displeasure.

"She reminds me a lot of you, Lena, when I first set eyes on you," Daddy said.

Mama absolutely glowed.

"Told you," she whispered and squeezed my hand. "She's prettier than I was, Cameron. I didn't know anything about hair and makeup then."

"You were a natural."

"There's no such thing. Every woman needs to have her good qualities highlighted," Mama insisted.

Daddy sat back, his smile warming again. Then he drew a serious expression from his thoughts.

"Where's this Shawn taking her?" he asked.

"How am I supposed to know? The man isn't here, is he? And when he comes, I don't want you treating him like one of your suspects or something."

"I don't have suspects," Daddy said. "Besides, there's nothing wrong in knowing your daughter's whereabouts when she goes out."

"I'm warning you," Mama replied. "I went through a lot of trouble to make this night special for her. Don't do anything to mess that up or I'll heave your precious old records out the window."

Daddy's face turned ashen for a moment and then he forced a laugh, shook his head and put up his hands.

"Yes, boss," he said and gazed at me. "I want you to have a good time, honey. I do."

I didn't say anything. My heart was doing too many flip-flops and there was a lump in my throat big enough to choke a horse.

Mama returned to my room with me to watch me put my new things away. She mumbled about Daddy not appreciating her efforts enough but blamed it on his being a man.

"Men expect too much and appreciate too little," she lectured. "They think you go into your room, fiddle about for a while and then come out looking like a million dollars. If you're taking too long, they moan and groan, but if you didn't look your best, they'd be unhappy because they wouldn't get all the congratulatory slaps on the back from their jealous friends.

"Men tell you they don't want other men gawking at you, but believe me, Ice, that's exactly what they want. It's like everything else they own. They want to drive a fancy car so everyone will look at them and be jealous. They want expensive watches and rings to draw green eyes. It's the same with their women."

I guess my eyebrows were scrunched. She stopped talking and smirked.

"You don't believe me, do you? What? You don't think men think of women as another possession? You still living in your books, girl. Forget all that romantic slop. What I'm telling you is the truth, is reality. You're going to start learning about the real world now and you'll come back to me and say, 'Mama, you were right. Tell me more so I know how to deal with it all out there.'

"That's what you'll be doing," she said nodding to herself and hanging up my skirt and blouse. "And I'll have lots more to tell you, too, more than you could ever learn from books and music."

She turned to me and looked thoughtful, looked on the verge of a decision. She made it quickly.

"Your daddy isn't the only man I've been with, Ice. I can see in your face that the news surprises, even hurts you, but a daughter becomes a woman when she can sit with her mama and hear about her mama's love life without squirming and hating her for it."

She was quiet. Maybe she was waiting for me to say I was ready, but I wasn't and maybe never would be.

"Don't worry," she concluded. "I'll know when it's the right time to tell you more about the real world."

She started out and stopped in the doorway, smiling.

"I wish I could be invisible, like one of them tiny angels, and ride on your shoulder tomorrow night and whisper advice in your ear when you need it.

"But you'll be fine," she decided. "You're my daughter. You got to have inherited something more than my good looks. Just don't be afraid to have some fun," she advised. She looked angry. "Don't be listening to those church choir songs in your head either. Last thing any man wants is to be holding hands with a saint or someone who's there to remind him he's headed for everlasting

Hell just because he thinks you're pretty and wants to kiss you.

"If you got to sing anything, sing something lively," she said and left.

Poor Mama, I thought. She thinks this is all one big movie or musical.

And the irony was she thought she was getting me prepared for the real world.

Maybe there was no real world. Maybe it was all makeup and lights and curtains opening and closing.

And when you fell off the stage, that was when you were really dead or forgotten. No applause, no music, nothing but the silences so many people seemed to fear.

3

---⟊---

The Kit-Kat Club

In my mind, Saturday morning began with a drumroll. The moment the light slipped in around my window curtains to caress my face and nudge my eyelids open, it started. I had dreamt I was in the circus and Mama was the ringmaster, snapping her whip at the lions and tigers and drawing the audience's attention to the small circle in the center where I stood spotlighted in my new outfit, all dressed up and ready for "The Greatest Date on Earth."

As if she had been aware of my dreams, Mama swept into my room almost immediately after I had woken and had started to rise.

"I don't want you doing all that much today, Ice. You need to rest and do a beauty treatment."

"What's that?"

"You'll see," she promised.

After breakfast, Mama set out her creams and lotions. I never realized all that she had and did to herself before

she ventured out in public. She had products to reduce
tension, soften the skin, relax the eyes. She had creams
for her hands, her feet. Later in the day she had me lie on
the bed with slices of cucumber over my eyes.

Daddy was annoyed and disappointed because he
received a phone call early in the day from his boss asking
him to come in to work. He was supposed to be off, but his
replacement had called in sick. Now he was worried
because he wouldn't be home to greet Shawn when he
arrived to pick me up. He wondered aloud if he shouldn't
call to get someone to substitute for him so he could be
here. Mama insisted it was unnecessary.

"I think I know the right things to say, Cameron, and
besides, what's your being here going to do, huh?"

"I have enough experience to know what to look for
in a soldier, Lena."

"Oh stop. You'll frighten the girl with that kind of talk
and that's no way for her to be on a first date with someone. You need a can opener to get words out of her mouth
as it is. If you keep up this talk, you'll put stress in her
face," she added, "and ruin all my work."

"She didn't need all that work to start with," Daddy
muttered.

Mama glared at him for a long moment. I thought it
was going to turn into one of their bad fights, her eyes
heating and brightening with her riled temper. She
looked ready to heave something at him. Daddy glanced
at me and quickly walked away.

"See what I mean about men?" Mama said nodding in
his direction.

Actually, I was hoping Daddy would meet Shawn
and I was more disappointed than he was, but I was
concerned about making any sort of comment about it

because Mama would feel I didn't trust her enough to do and say all the right things. She was so excited all day and hovered over me with reports from her girl-friend Louella telling her when Shawn would arrive, what he looked like when he did, and how much he was looking forward to this date, too.

"He's very excited about meeting you," Mama came by to tell me late in the afternoon. I was lying on my bed with those cucumber slices over my eyes, feeling very silly. "Louella said he's more excited about you than he is about seeing his family."

I took off the slices and sat up.

"How can that be, Mama?" I asked. "He doesn't know anything about me, not even what I look like."

She shifted her eyes guiltily away.

"Mama?"

"Well, I told Louella stuff about you and I gave her a picture to send him."

"What picture?" I asked.

"That one we took a month or so ago when we cele-brated my birthday. I just cut me and your father out of the picture and sent you."

"I guess this is only a blind date for me then," I said.

"It doesn't matter, Ice. Any date with any new man is a blind date, no matter what people tell you about him. Believe me about that. If you hear about a man from another woman, it's half lies or exaggerations, and if another man tells you about him, you got to color in green for jealousy. There's only one person who can tell you what you got to know about a man and that's you."

She smiled.

"Maybe I oughta be writing a newspaper column of advice for lovers, huh?"

I widened my eyes and she laughed.

Nothing I could recall in our recent history made Mama so young, bright and happy as my impending date. I was afraid to utter one negative comment or iota of hesitation.

Before Daddy left for work, he stopped by and just stood in my doorway.

"I hope you have a good time," he said, "but if for any reason you're not happy out there, you don't hesitate to demand to be taken home, Ice. You make it clear and sharp, just like the orders he's growing used to in the army. Men need to be made straight right off. That's all I'll say," he added, "and that you're looking mighty pretty."

"Thank you, Daddy."

He nodded, kissed me quickly on the cheek and left.

Mama came rushing in immediately afterward.

"What that man say to you, Ice? He say anything to make you afraid?"

"No Mama. He just wished me a good time."

"Umm," she said still full of suspicion.

I looked at the clock.

"Getting about that time," she said. I really did feel like someone preparing for an opening, a big performance. "You dress in my room, use my table and stuff," she told me.

She hovered over me, making sure I put on the makeup she wanted as she wanted it, fixing every strand of my hair and then fussing over my new outfit. When I was completely dressed and ready, she surprised me by bringing out her camera and taking a picture.

"I want one of you and Shawn, too," she said.

"Oh Mama, it's going to embarrass him."

"Nonsense. Any man would want his picture taken with you, Ice," she said.

I wondered if she was right. Was I really as pretty as she was, and was it only because of my reputation of not talking very much that boys avoided pursuing me?

Exactly at seven, the door buzzer rang. I thought it stopped my heart. Then I heard the pounding in my ears. I tried to swallow, but couldn't.

Mama had gotten herself pretty dolled up, too, putting on her V-necked red dress and her pumps. She strutted from her room, glanced at me waiting in the living room, smiled and went to the door.

"Evening, ma'am," I heard a deep, strong voice say. "I'm Shawn Carter, Louella's brother."

"Aren't you though?" Mama said. "And look how handsome in your uniform."

"Thank you, ma'am."

"Come right in. Ice is waiting for you in the living room, Shawn."

I felt my whole body tighten, my ribs feeling as if they were closing like claws around my insides. Mama came in first and then stepped aside to let Shawn enter. He stood there with his hat in his hand, gaping at me. For a moment neither of us spoke. I gulped a view of him and digested it.

He was about my height with broad shoulders, almost as broad as Daddy's, but he was nowhere nearly as handsome. He looked almost bald because of how closely his hair had been cropped and how far up his forehead his hairline sat. The close haircut emphasized his large ears. All of his features were big except for his eyes, which were small, beady ebony marbles. His lower lip was a little thicker than his upper and his jawbone was emphatic.

His smile softened his initial appearance, however. It made him look younger.

"Hi," he said.

I was far from stuck-up, but a little voice inside me whispered: "No wonder he was so excited about taking you out, girl. You're probably the prettiest girl he's ever been able to date. Without the army uniform, he would be so ordinary you wouldn't give him a second look and maybe not even a first." Mama didn't really think he was so handsome, I concluded, unless she was bedazzled by a uniform. However, I was the first to agree that a book shouldn't be judged on its cover. It took time to learn if someone was truly handsome or beautiful inside.

Mama looked at me, her head bobbing, urging me to speak.

"Hi," I said.

"You look very, very pretty," he said. "Much prettier than you are in that picture my sister sent me."

"Bad camera lighting," Mama said. "Ice is very photogenic most of the time."

"Oh, she don't look bad in the picture," he quickly corrected. "She just looks a helluva lot better in person."

His smile widened and Mama laughed.

"Of course she does. Well, have a seat, Shawn and tell us a little about yourself before you two head on out. Unless you have a deadline to meet for dinner."

He nodded.

"Well, I was hoping we'd meet up with some of my buddies and all go to the Kit-Kat," he said.

"Oh. I don't believe I heard of that place," Mama said.

"It's a restaurant that has a jazz band," he told her.

"Jazz? Well now, Ice will appreciate that, I'm sure.

Her father and her are jazz-a-holics," Mama offered and laughed.

"Jazz-a- what?"

"Never mind, never mind. Well, I won't keep you then," she said. "Ice, you'll need my light coat," she told me. We had already decided I would, but Mama pretended it was a last-minute decision. "I'll just get it for you. Pardon me," she told Shawn.

"Yes, ma'am."

"Oh, I just love that polite talk, don't you, Ice?"

Shawn smiled and looked at me. Mama waited for me to say something and then sucked in her breath with disappointment and went for the coat.

"Your mother's real nice," Shawn said.

I stood up.

"You know my sister?" he asked.

I shook my head and muttered, "Not really."

He nodded. His struggle to find the right words, or any words, was clearly visible on his face, especially in his eyes. He didn't want to look at me unless he had something to say. He kept his gaze low, nodding slightly as if his head was on a spring.

"You're in the twelfth grade, a high-school senior?" he asked.

I nodded.

"You look older," he said and then quickly added, "not old, just older."

I stared at him, wondering how he could have ever thought I'd think he meant old.

"Here we are," Mama cried bringing me her coat. She held it out and Shawn practically lunged to take it from her and help me on with it. Mama stood by beaming her approval.

"Oh wait," she cried. "Before you put that on her, I want a picture of you two."

I raised my eyes toward the ceiling.

"Fine with me," Shawn said. "Put me down for two copies. One goes right on my locker at the barracks."

Mama laughed and picked up her camera that she had placed on a table in the living room in anticipation.

"Just stand over there," she nodded a bit to our right. "Go on and put your arm around her, Shawn. She won't break," Mama advised.

I closed my eyes and bit down on my lower lip. His arm went over my shoulder and his big hand closed on my upper arm, pulling me closer to him.

"You can smile better than that, honey," Mama said. "Shawn here has a nice smile."

I forced my lips to turn and curl and she snapped the photo.

"One more," she said. "Just in case."

When that was over, I stepped forward out of Shawn's embrace and reached again for Mama's coat. He hurried to help me on with it.

"Well, thank you, Mrs. Goodman," Shawn said. "I'll show her a good time."

"I'm sure you will, Shawn. Don't be too late now," Mama called as we headed for the door.

"No ma'am," Shawn replied, but what did that mean? What was too late? Daddy would have been more definite, I thought.

"Have a really good time, Ice, honey," Mama called before the door closed behind us.

"We will," Shawn promised. He looked at me. "Okay, let's go burn up the town, huh?"

I started for the elevator and he took my hand. He

grabbed it so quickly and firmly, he startled me for a moment. Then he pushed the button for the elevator.

"You grow up here?" he asked as the door opened.

I nodded.

"Me too. I didn't finish high school, though. I decided to take that program the army has where you finish your diploma while you're in the service. I got started late in school," he explained. "My mother traveled around a lot with us before she settled in Philly. When I was fourteen, she took off with some computer salesman and left Louella and me. Louella had already gotten a good job so we were able to take care of ourselves," he continued.

As the elevator descended, he seemed determined not to let a moment of silence occur.

"I asked my sister how come your mother named you Ice and she said it was because you're a cool cat. Is that true?" he asked.

"No," I said and stepped into the lobby.

"Well, why'd she call you that then?"

I shrugged and he opened the front door. It was colder than I had expected. I closed the coat and held the collar tightly shut, waiting for him to direct me to his car. All I saw at the curb was a pickup truck with a cab over the back. I turned to him.

"I borrowed my friend Chipper's truck. My sister doesn't have a car and I haven't gotten around to getting one of my own yet."

We walked to the truck and he opened the door for me. When I got in, I smelled what I was sure was whiskey. The seat was torn in the middle and looked very ratty. I hoped there was nothing on it that would stain my new outfit. I saw a wrench on the floor and had to push it out of my way with my feet. He got in and started the engine.

"Here we go," he said. When he pulled from the curb, an empty beer can came rolling out from under the seat.

"Chipper ain't much of a housekeeper," he told me. "So, you ever hear of the Kit-Kat?"

I shook my head.

"They'll be checking IDs at the door," he said.

"I'm only seventeen."

"That's all right. Don't worry. We know the guy doing it. He's a friend of mine's brother. Besides, you look at least twenty. There's cigarettes in the glove compartment if you want one," he added nodding at it.

I shook my head.

"You don't smoke? That's good. I only smoke once in a while. Cigarettes, that is," he added laughing. "So, I bet you go out a lot, huh?"

I didn't know whether to tell him the truth or not. If I did, he would probably assume he was important and I knew instinctively that I didn't want him thinking that.

"A girl like you has to be popular. Not only are you good-looking but, from what Louella tells me, you're a singer, too. Where did you do your singing so far?"

"Chorus," I said.

"Chorus? That's it?" He laughed. "Hell, I was in chorus, too, but I'd never call me a singer."

He kept talking, describing his experiences at boot camp, the new friends he had made, the drill instructor he hated, and where he hoped he would be stationed someday.

Finally, he turned to me and smiled.

"My sister warned me you don't talk much. Why is that, if you have such a nice voice?"

"I talk when I have something to say," I told him.

He laughed.

"You'd fit right in at boot camp. My instructor is always shouting, 'Keep your hole closed unless I tell you to open it.' He gave Dickie Stieglitz KP for a week because he was mumbling complaints under his breath when we were in formation. The guy has radar for ears or something. He don't even have to be nearby to hear you.

"Hey, I'm going to get hoarse in the throat doing all the talking. Can't you tell me anything about yourself?"

"I like jazz," I offered.

"Great. Great. We're going to have a good old time of it. What's your drink?" he asked when we parked in a lot across from the nightclub. "Vodka? Gin? Beer?"

I shook my head.

"Bourbon, rye, what?"

"I don't drink," I said.

"Sure you don't," he replied with a laugh. "Hey, don't worry. I don't tell my sister about my dates, if that's what's troubling you. Your mother's not going to know anything from these lips," he promised.

I didn't say anything, so he opened his door and got out. Now that we were away from Mama's eyes, he didn't come around to open my door for me. Gone were the "Yes, ma'ams" and "No, ma'ams," too, I noticed.

When we stepped into the club, his friend checking IDs looked me over from head to toe, nodding with a smile so sly and licentious he made me feel naked.

"Nice," he told Shawn. "You're late," he continued. "Everyone got here already in your party."

"We'll make up for it," Shawn told me and ushered me into the club.

Right off the entrance to the right was a long bar

with tinsel over the mirrors that made it look like Christmas. The stools were all occupied and the bartender was so busy, he could barely raise his head. I noticed that the men were dressed well, jackets and ties, and most of the women were wearing expensive-looking clothes, too.

On a small stage, a five-piece jazz combo played a Duke Ellington number I recognized. Shawn led me down the aisle to a table in the front at which three other young men in army uniforms sat with three girls—all looked years older than I was. The moment the men saw us, they started shouting and laughing, which I thought was impolite, considering people around them were enjoying the music. Of course, that drew a great deal of attention to us, especially to me.

"Where the hell you been? We thought you went AWOL on us," the tall, red-headed young man on the right cried. The girl with him looked unhappy, almost in pain. She had very short, dark hair and a mouth so soft, the lower lip looked like it was unhinged in the corners.

"Had to do the please-the-parent-thing first," Shawn explained. "This here's Ice. Ice meet Michael," he said nodding at the tall, red-headed man, "Buzzy," he added pointing to a stocky African-American man who looked older than everyone else, "and Sonny," he continued. Sonny looked the youngest. He had a caramel complexion with dark freckles peppered on his cheeks and forehead.

They all said, "Hi," and then Michael introduced the other girls. The one with him was Jeanie and the one with Buzzy was Bernice. She was stout and big busted with light brown hair that not only was the color of straw, but looked like it had the texture of it as well.

He paused before introducing the girl with Sonny and said, "What was your name again, honey?"

"I'm Dolores," she said, very annoyed that he didn't remember. She looked Latin, maybe Mexican. I thought she was the prettiest of the three because of the dazzling color of her dark eyes that flashed when she showed her temper. She got over it quickly, however, and continued moving in her chair, enjoying the music. "When are we going to stop all this talking and dance?" she cried.

"Sonny, get up and dance with the girl, will you?" Michael said. "Her engine's been running at high speed all this time and you're in park."

They all laughed.

Shawn took my coat off and put it over my chair. All of his friends stared at me as hard as the one at the club's entrance. It made me wonder if I had done something wrong. Mama had insisted on my wearing one of those wonder bras. I know I was showing a lot more cleavage than I would have liked.

I sat and Shawn quickly ordered a gin and tonic for himself and then looked at me and said, "Give her the same."

I didn't say no, but I thought I wouldn't drink it if I didn't like it.

"Why are you called Ice?" Buzzy asked leaning over the table. "You don't look cold to me."

They all laughed again, even Jeanie who seemed incapable of smiling.

"She's not cold," Shawn said. "She's cool."

"Ice, you can dip your finger in my drink anytime," Sonny quipped. They all laughed again.

"How long you know this work of art?" Michael asked me indicating Shawn.

I thought a moment.

"Twenty minutes," I replied and he roared and told everyone else what I had said. That seemed to be the funniest thing they had heard their whole lives. I thought the laughter wouldn't end.

The music stopped and the audience applauded. Our drinks came and Shawn nearly finished his in a single gulp.

"I needed that," he said. "Meeting a mother always makes me thirsty."

"I bet you've met a few," Buzzy said. "Are you from Philly?" he asked me.

I nodded. There was so much noise in the club, you had to shout to be heard and I knew what that would do to my throat in short order.

"You know how dangerous this guy is that you're with?" Michael kidded.

I shrugged.

"His life story is X-rated."

"You're right," Buzzy said after more laughter. "She's cool. She doesn't look a bit worried, Shawn. In fact, I think you'd better start worrying."

The music began again.

"You like this music, Ice?" Sonny asked, grimacing.

"She loves it," Shawn said. "She's a jazz-a-holic."

"Sure," Michael said. "You know this one?" he asked nodding at the band.

I smiled.

"It's a Benny Goodman tune," I said. They all turned to me. "Called 'After Awhile.' It's about 1929," I told them. Their mouths opened, jaws dropped.

"She's kidding, right?" Buzzy asked Shawn.

He shook his head.

"Her mother said she's into it and guess what," he added, "she sings, too."

"No. All this and talented too?" Michael cried. The other girls looked annoyed at the attention I was getting. Dolores finally got Sonny to get up and dance and then Shawn asked me if I would like to dance. I smiled to myself, remembering some of the steps Daddy had taught me.

I nodded and we got up. Shawn had no rhythm and couldn't do much more than pretend, but I ignored him, closed my eyes and let the music into me. I didn't realize how I was stealing the attention of the entire audience until the music ended and people applauded, looking more at me than they did the band. The leader, a tall black man with gray temples and friendly eyes, smiled.

When we returned to our table, the boys were all raving about me and the girls were looking much more annoyed. Shawn ordered another drink for himself. I had just taken a sip of mine.

"C'mon, drink up," he urged. "We've got a lot of night ahead of us."

More reason to drink slowly, I thought, but everyone was ordering another drink by now.

We danced some more. Dolores tried to capture more attention with some very sexy moves. When Sonny asked me to dance, she looked like she would leap over the table to scratch out my eyes.

"Go on, give him a thrill," Shawn told me.

"I'd rather not," I said as gently as I could.

It seemed to take the laughter from all their eyes. When everyone was drinking and being silly, there was no room for any serious thoughts, I realized. It put a damper on things.

"That's being cold," Michael told Sonny. "Now I see the ice."

"Hey, give her a rest," Buzzy said. "Besides, it's time she sang."

I shook my head.

"No," I said.

He didn't listen. He jumped up and went to the bandleader, who looked my way and nodded. Buzzy beckoned to me.

"Go on," Shawn urged. "Show them a thing or two."

"No," I said shaking my head. People in the audience were all looking at me.

"What's the matter, this crowd's not good enough for you?" Jeanie asked me.

I looked at her.

"I never sang a solo," I said, hoping that would be enough.

"Tonight's the night you do," Michael declared.

Shawn started to help me up.

I shook my head again.

People were clapping on the right, urging me to get up. I continued to shake my head, but by now they were all cheering at our table, the girls the loudest, hoping I would make a total fool of myself.

For once, I thought Mama had named me correctly. My blood seemed to freeze in my body. I was numb with fear. And then, suddenly, I heard a familiar voice behind me.

"Go on, Ice."

I turned to see Balwin Noble, the senior at school who played piano accompaniments for our chorus.

"Balwin! What are you doing here?" I cried.

"I thought you said she doesn't talk," Sonny shouted at Shawn.

"I come here often and play with Barry Jones. Do 'Lullaby of Birdland,' " he urged. Occasionally, when no one else was at the rehearsal yet, he and I would fool around and I'd sing. Like Daddy, he loved my rendition of Ella Fitzgerald's hit song. "I'll get on piano."

"Really?"

"Who the hell is this?" Shawn demanded.

"I play piano for the school chorus," he told him.

"Well, this ain't school, stupid."

"I won't go up unless Balwin can," I declared.

The audience was getting impatient. People were clanking silverware against their glasses. Shawn looked around.

"Let him go," Michael said. "What do you care?"

Shawn stepped aside and Balwin and I walked to the small stage. They all did know him. The piano player got up to let Balwin take his place.

"Hey, Balwin," the bandleader said, "you sure about her? This isn't an easy crowd tonight."

"She's in the chorus. She makes it," he bragged. Then he leaned over and said, "C'mon, let's show them." He turned to the bandleader. "Do 'Lullaby,' " he told him.

"You've got it."

My heart wasn't pounding. It was clamoring, raging like a caged beast in my chest. The only thing that gave me some comfort was seeing Balwin at the piano. His familiar face and smile gave me encouragement.

"Wipe the doubt off their smug faces," he said.

I was given the microphone. Buzzy took his seat. My table all gaped at me, the girls looking furious. Then the music started, I thought about Daddy and me in the living room and his happy smile and I began;

soon, I wasn't in the Kit-Kat, I was back home. I was safe, and the song kept me safe.

When I finished, the audience was on its feet; even the girls at my table reluctantly stood to clap.

"Come around any time you want," the bandleader told me.

Balwin looked so proud.

"I knew you could do it," he said.

"I wouldn't have if you weren't here, Balwin."

"I'm glad I was," he said.

Shawn stepped up between us quickly.

"Nice," he said. "Really nice. C'mon. We're all going to Michael's house to party and celebrate."

"What? Why? What's wrong with staying here?"

"We're finished here," Shawn said.

I looked at the group getting up from the table and I thought about my father's advice.

"I don't want to go to anyone's house, Shawn," I said firmly.

"Why not?"

"We were supposed to go out to dinner. We haven't even eaten yet."

"We'll get something to eat there," he said.

"Maybe you should just take me home," I told him.

"Are you kidding?"

I shook my head and the smile of incredulity turned to a look of annoyance.

"Why?"

"I don't want to go to anyone's house," I said.

"I thought we were going to have a good time. Don't you want to have a good time?"

"Yes, but I don't want to go to anyone's house for it," I said.

"Aw, c'mon."

"No," I said as firmly as I could.

He glared angrily at me for a moment. Then he went to his friends to tell them, and they all started on me.

"We were just going to listen to music, have something to eat, enjoy the night."

"We can really party."

"What's the problem?"

I didn't reply to any of them. I sat at the table, my arms crossed under my breasts, fixing my attention on the stage and ignoring their comments and pleas.

"You got yourself a chunk of ice all right," Sonny told Shawn.

He stared down at me furiously.

"I'm leaving and going to Michael's," he finally said. "You coming or not?"

I looked up at him.

"No means no," I said as hotly and as firmly as I could. He snapped his head back as if I had slapped him across the face.

"Fine. Then let the fat boy take you home," he cried and turned away from me. "Next time my sister wants to fix me up with someone, I'll tell her to think twice. Go call *your* sister, Delores," he told her. "I should have listened to you and taken her out. This one's jailbait anyway."

All the girls laughed. I glared back at them and then turned away.

"Hey," Buzzy said leaning over to whisper in my ear. "You ever want to go out with a real man, call me. I'm in the yellow pages under Real Man."

He laughed and they all walked up the aisle, leaving me sitting by myself at the table. I was sure everyone around us was staring at me. Whenever I lifted my eyes from the table and turned, I met someone else's. I felt so stupid and frightened, very much an adolescent drowning in the world of adult quicksand. But I didn't move.

"What happened?" Balwin rushed over to ask me as soon as they all had left the club.

I told him quickly.

"How could he just leave you like this?"

I didn't reply. I stared at the table, my whole body still trembling. I felt his hand touch my shoulder gently.

"Hey, don't worry, Ice. I got my mother to give me the car tonight. I'll take you home," he said. "Do you want to go home?"

I nodded.

"I heard you say you haven't eaten. How about we stop for some pizza on the way? I'm hungry too. I'm always hungry," he confessed.

"Okay," I said. I would have agreed to anything to get out of here.

But as I rose to walk out the door with Balwin, I thought about Mama.

She was surely going to hate me.

4

—···—

Allies

I decided not to tell Mama. Both she and Daddy were watching television when I arrived. I tried to be very quiet about it, but the moment I opened the door, Mama was up and in the living room doorway.

"Where's Shawn?" she asked looking past me. "Didn't he escort you to the door?"

I shook my head.

"Doesn't surprise me," Daddy called from the living room.

"And that doesn't surprise me," Mama shot back. She threw a suspicious glance at me and said, "Well, come in and tell us how it was."

"Fine," I said.

"Fine? That's it? Fine?"

Daddy looked up at me.

"I heard he took you to the Kit-Kat. They got Barry Jones playing there, right?"

I nodded.

"See, Lena, you didn't want to go there when I asked you to go last month, and here Ice goes and has a good time. Talented combo. What did they do?"

"Ellington, some Benny Goodman, a good Miles Davis," I recited. Daddy's eyes lit up.

"Oh, that you can talk about in detail, but when I ask you a question, I get 'fine.' What's all this talk about the music? What about Shawn Carter?"

"What do you expect her to tell you about him after only one time?" Daddy asked.

Mama shook her head at him and turned to me.

"Did you have a good time with him?"

I shrugged. "It was all right."

"Doesn't sound anything like a nice time to me," she muttered. "Ellington, Goodman, Miles Davis, they had a better time. Did you meet his friends? How were they? Did you make any new friends? Are you going out with him again?"

"Why don't you give her a chance to answer one question before you ask her another?" Daddy said.

"I'm waiting for her to say something that tells me something, anything, Cameron, thank you. I put in a lot of work for this and we spent a lot of money to get her out of this cocoon she's wrapped herself in, no thanks to you."

"They were all older girls, Mama. I don't think they want to be friends with me. I'm still in high school."

"You don't look like a high-school girl, Ice. They should want to be friends with you. I bet you were the prettiest one there, right? Huh?"

"You're embarrassing her, Lena."

"She oughta be proud of herself and of me and what we did together. You can brag a little, Ice. Well?"

"I suppose I was, Mama." I looked at Daddy. "I sang 'Lullaby.' "

"You did what?" Daddy was almost up and out of his chair. "No kidding? With Barry Jones?"

I nodded.

"How did it go?"

"They all stood up and clapped," I said.

"You hear that, Lena? They all stood up and clapped."

"And what was Shawn Carter doing when this was going on?" Mama asked.

"Listening and clapping, too, I suppose," Daddy replied for me.

I nodded.

Mama narrowed her eyes.

"What kind of a date was this? You sang with the band?" she wondered aloud.

"She had a good time, Lena. Leave it at that."

"I'm tired," I said. "Good night."

"All she talked about was the music," Mama moaned behind me. "When I went out with a man, I had a lot more than that to say."

"I bet," Daddy quipped and she turned on him.

I shut my door on the bickering and let out a hotly held breath.

I was hoping it was over. Mama would stop asking questions and eventually the whole thing would fade away, but almost as soon as I entered the kitchen the next morning for breakfast, she was on me again. Daddy was still in bed.

"What kind of a dinner did you have? Was it expensive? I bet you had something to drink, huh? I bet they didn't even ask you for identification. Well?"

"Shawn ordered me a gin and tonic, and no one asked me to show them any identification, but I didn't drink any of it," I told her. I was still traveling on the truth.

"Men like to ply you with liquor, so they can soften you up a bit. It's no harm done as long as you play your cards right. I always pretended to be tipsy, but I always knew what was going on around me. The rest of them drank plenty, huh?"

I nodded.

"You and Shawn just stayed at the Kit-Kat all evening?"

"Yes," I said, but I looked away too soon.

"He wanted to take you somewhere else?"

I nodded.

"Where? Damn, girl, why do I have to pull every word out of you? Why don't you just tell me the whole story at once? You ever say two sentences together?"

"He wanted me to go to one of their houses for a party, but I said no."

"That so? Well, that's all right. He should respect you more for that. It was only your first date, after all. You did right. I'm sure he understands. He did, didn't he?" she asked.

Just as I was about to burst and tell her all of it, the phone rang. We both looked at it. Mama smiled and I picked up the receiver.

"Hi," I said with enthusiasm after I heard who it was.

"That Shawn?" Mama whispered, hovering over me.

I turned my back without answering. It wasn't Shawn; it was Balwin.

"No, it's all right. We're up," I told him.

"I got a phone call just five minutes ago," he said, his voice rife with excitement, "from Barry Jones. They just got in from the evening. After the Kit-Kat Club, they go to another hip jazz joint and play until morning. Then they go for breakfast and after that, go home and sleep all day."

"What a life," I said.

"Musical vampires. Anyway, he wanted to call me before he forgot. He was impressed with you."

"Really?"

"Yeah, but someone else was, too, someone named Edmond Senetsky, an entertainment agent from New York who was there with a client, sitting in the back of the club. He heard you sing and asked Barry about you and Barry told him he didn't know you, but he knew someone who did. That was me, of course."

"Well . . . what does he want?"

"Barry said he told him that you should audition for his mother's performing arts school in New York."

"New York?"

"What about New York?" Mama asked from behind me. "He wants to take you to New York?"

I shook my head.

"Yes," Balwin said. "He said you should prepare a couple of numbers for the audition and he gave Barry his card for you to call to get the details. Barry read the telephone numbers to me. You want me to give them to you now?"

"No," I said emphatically.

"Why are you saying no? You can go," Mama coached from the sidelines. Again, I shook my head.

"Well, should I come over later with it? This is a big opportunity for you, Ice. At least, Barry thought so and he knows. I heard of this school too. If I wasn't already going to Juilliard, I might be considering it."

"Let me think about it."

"Sure. I'm home all day today. I don't know if I ever told you, but I've been composing songs. My parents got me a piano and put it in the basement. It's nothing like a studio, but I can record quietly and no one bothers me down there. Boy, I'd love to have you try one of my songs," he said.

"Okay, thanks."

"I'm going to call Mr. Glenn to see what he knows about this school in New York," Balwin said, referring to our vocal instructor. "We'll get his opinion about it all."

"Right," I said. "Bye."

"Call me as soon as you can," he said quickly and I hung up.

"What was that all about?" Mama pounced.

I stood there, staring at the phone for a moment and then I turned to face her.

"It wasn't Shawn Carter, Mama. It was Balwin Noble."

"Who's Balwin Noble?"

"He's a boy at school, the one who plays piano accompaniments for our chorus. He's that good," I emphasized, but she didn't look impressed.

"So? What's he want? What was that about New York?"

"He was at the Kit-Kat Club last night when I was there with Shawn," I began.

"Who was?" I heard Daddy say as he came through the kitchen doorway. He scrubbed his hair with his dry hands, yawned and stretched and looked at us. "What's up, you two? You make so much noise, a dead man couldn't sleep."

"If we lived somewhere where the walls weren't made out of cellophane, we could have a conversation without waking each other up in here," Mama retorted.

"Well, what's all the talk?"

"I was just asking about her date, that's all," Mama said.

"Oh, that again," he said. He went for a cup of coffee.

"Yes, that again. Then there was this phone call for Ice and I'm asking about that now. Is all this okay with you or do I need special permission to talk to my own daughter?"

Daddy didn't respond. He drank some coffee and began to prepare himself some eggs. He made omelets better than Mama, but I was afraid ever to say so.

"You eat yet?" he asked me. I shook my head. "Lena, you want an omelet, too?"

"No, I don't want any omelet. Damn," Mama said frustrated. She sat looking stunned for a moment. I went to put up some toast. "What was I saying?" she muttered, squeezing her temples between her thumb and fingers. "Oh yeah, New York . . . what about this boy, Balwin? What's he want?"

I took a breath, turned to her and began.

"When I was singing last night, Balwin was playing the piano. He's a very talented musician and he goes to the Kit-Kat occasionally to sit in with Barry Jones."

"Wow," Daddy said. "He must be very talented to have them let him do that."

"He is, Daddy."

"Well, that's just wonderful for him," Mama said, "but what's it got to do with you?"

"Barry Jones called him this morning to tell him a New York entertainment agent was there and heard me sing and wanted me to audition for a school for the performing arts."

"No kidding?" Daddy said. "That's terrific."

"What's terrific about it? How she going to go to a school in New York? You know what kind of money that means," Mama practically shouted at him.

"Well, let's see about it first," Daddy said.

Mama stared at him. Her frustration had made her eyes bulge and whitened her lips. She looked at me with growing suspicion now.

"Who brought you home last night?" she asked. "Well?" she demanded when I hesitated.

"Balwin," I confessed.

"Thought so."

"What's this?" Daddy asked, turning from the stove. "What happened, Ice?"

"I told Mama they all wanted to go to someone's house for a private party and I refused to go. Shawn didn't understand, Mama, and he didn't respect me for saying no. He got belligerent and he left me there."

"He did what? I told you . . ." Daddy stammered.

"Oh, shut up, will you, and let the girl talk, finally," Mama said.

"They were drinking a lot and Shawn was too. We never even had any dinner."

"That's what I expected," Daddy said nodding.

"Oh, you *expected*. What are you, a fortune-teller now?"

Mama sat there fuming.

"You didn't act mute or nothing all night, did you?" she asked with accusation written all over her face. "You didn't make them all think you were stuck-up?"

"No, Mama. I talked when I had something to say and

when they asked me questions, but the other girls didn't want to hear me talk."

"I bet," Daddy said. "What a mess you put her into!"

"Me? I did no such thing. I tried to get her out with people, to become someone. Don't you go making statements like that, Cameron Goodman."

"It wasn't Mama's fault, Daddy. There was no way for her to know what it would be like."

"A woman with all her worldly experience ought to have known better," Daddy muttered and returned to his eggs.

Mama took the plate on her table, lifted it above her head and smashed it at his feet. He jumped back instinctively, accidentally hitting the handle of the pan, which sent it sliding over the range and onto the floor, spilling our omelets. It was all over in a split second, but it was as if the roof had caved in on our apartment.

"Look what you've gone and made me do!" Daddy cried.

"I'm tired of you making remarks about my past as if I was some kind of street girl, Cameron. I've told you that a hundred times, and I especially don't appreciate it in front of our daughter.

"Now, you've gone and filled her head with so much nonsense about this music thing, she thinks she can run off to New York and be a show star or something. She goes out on a date and gets up on a stage. I bet Shawn felt stupid."

"Why? He should have been proud she was with him. He should have appreciated her more."

"A man likes his woman to give him all her attention, not flirt with some piano player."

"I didn't flirt with him, Mama. He's just a friend. He plays for us at school. He—"

"Oh, I heard all that. You went and showed them you were nothing but a high-school girl. All my work and all that expense down the drain," she moaned, rose, glared at Daddy once and then marched out of the kitchen.

I started to clean up.

"Don't worry about her," Daddy said. "She'll get over it. You did the right thing not going to that house party. You'd a been trapped with a bunch of drunks," he said. "She knows that, too. She's just . . . frustrated," he added and helped pick up the pieces of Mama's broken dish.

This was my fault, I thought.

I should have just insisted on not going out.

I should have stayed home and not tried to be Mama.

Balwin called again in the early afternoon to tell me he had spoken with Mr. Glenn and Mr. Glenn had told him the Senetsky School was so special only a half-dozen new students get in it a year.

"It's not just a school. You live there and she teaches you how to handle the entertainment world, how to behave, dress, act—everything. Her graduates are all in Broadway shows or in television and film. As soon as you graduate, her son becomes your agent, and he's a very successful agent. It's the closest thing to a guaranteed successful ride into show business, whether you act, sing, dance, play instruments, anything she thinks shows real talent. You've got to do this, Ice. You've just got to give it a shot. I'll help you," Balwin added.

"I don't know," I said still trembling from the battle Daddy and Mama had in the morning because of me. The house had become a tomb—no one speaking, no music, barely any movement. Daddy sat in the living room rereading the same newspaper and Mama was lying down, a wet cloth over her forehead, fuming. I was afraid to make a sound. I was practically whispering on the phone.

"Something wrong?" Balwin asked.

"No," I said quickly.

"Well, I know this sounds like short notice, but why don't you come on over and we'll tinker around with some possible pieces you could use."

I didn't respond.

"You know where I live, right?"

"No," I said.

He rattled off the address and then added directions.

"It's only about a ten-minute walk from where you are," he concluded.

Balwin lived in a nice neighborhood. I had been down that street before, but I didn't know anyone who lived there, until now.

The night before he had told me a lot about himself. His parents were both professionals. His father was an accountant and his mother was a dental hygienist. Like me, he was an only child. He was about twenty pounds or so overweight for his five foot ten inch frame, but he had a nice face with kind, intelligent black eyes and firm, straight lips. He was definitely the best-dressed boy in school and was often kidded about his wearing dress slacks and a nice shirt. They called him Mr. Noble, making "Mister" sound like a dirty word. Some of our teachers called him Mr. Noble, too, but they weren't teasing him. They were showing him respect because he was a good student, polite and very ambitious.

"Okay," I decided quickly. "I'll be there."

"Great. This is going to be fun," he said and hung up before I could even think of changing my mind. It

brought a smile to my face, which had become like a
desert when it came to smiles these days.

I put on my jacket and called to Mama and Daddy
from the doorway.

"I'm going out for a while," I shouted.

"Bring back a carton of milk," Mama screamed back
at me.

"Okay," I said.

I knew they both assumed I was just going for my
usual walk around the block or maybe past some of the
stores to look in the windows.

It was a cool, gray day with some wind. Spring was
having a hard time getting itself a foothold this year.
Winter just seemed to be stubborn, refusing to be driven
off. We had had flurries in early April and only one day
more than seventy degrees. Today it was in the low
fifties. People walked quickly, some regretted not wearing their heavier coats and hats. The weather made them
angry, as angry as people who had been cheated and
scammed by some con man or woman. In this case, the
villain was Mother Nature who had offered a contract
with the calendar and then broken it with northerly winds
and heavy clouds.

I wore a light-blue sweater and skirt along with a pair
of black buzzin' boots with three-and-a-half-inch heels. I
liked feeling tall. I heard some catcalls and whistles from
men in passing cars, but I kept my eyes forward. Once
you look their way, they think you're showing some
interest.

A gust of wind brought tears to my eyes as I quickly
whipped around a corner and headed down Balwin's
street. I was practically running now. When I got to his
door and pressed the buzzer, he opened it so quickly, I

had to wonder if he hadn't been waiting right in the entryway the whole time.

"Looks nasty," he said glancing at the way the wind had picked up some discarded paper and chased it up the gutter.

I took a deep breath and nodded.

He looked nervous and started to talk so quickly, I thought he would run out of breath.

"I should have taken my father up on the car offer. He put a dollar value on my weight, offering to deposit so much for every pound I lost. I was to be weighed every morning before he went to work and he was going to keep this big chart up in his home office, but I never cared if I had my own car or not and he withdrew the offer."

He smiled.

"Maybe eating was just more important. Sorry. I could have picked you up tonight if I had my own car. My father won't let me use his car, and they took my mother's car tonight, which was the car I used to take you home from the Kit-Kat. They went to New York to see a show and have dinner," he said finally pausing for a breath. "Let me take your coat and hang it up for you."

I was shivering, but I gave it to him and he put it in the hallway closet. Whenever I visited anyone who had his or her own house, I understood Mama's constant longing to get us into something better. Odors from whatever other people on your floor were cooking didn't permeate your home. Noise and clatter were practically nonexistent. You had a true sense of privacy.

Balwin's house was a little more than modest. His parents had decorated it well. The furniture looked new and expensive. It was all early American. There were thick area rugs, elegant coffee and side tables, interesting pole and table lamps and real oil paintings on the walls, not prints. A large, teardrop chandelier hung over the rich, cherrywood dining room table.

"You want anything warm to drink? I'll make you some coffee or tea, if you like."

"Tea," I said nodding.

"Milk or sugar or honey?"

"Honey."

"That's good. That's what singers should drink," he said smiling.

I followed him into the kitchen and gazed at the modern appliances and the rich cabinets. When he ran water into a cup and immediately dipped in a tea bag, I gasped.

"You forgot to heat the water," I said.

He laughed.

"No, this faucet gives boiling water immediately."

"Really?" I took the mug and felt the heat around it.

"C'mon, I'll show you my studio," he said proudly and led me back through the hall to a door. We went down a short flight of stairs to a large room with light oak panelling and wall-to-wall coffee-colored Berber carpet. The piano was off to the left. On the right was a bar and a pool table, a built-in television set to the left of the bar, and a small sitting area consisting of a settee and two oversized chairs, one a full recliner.

Against the wall on shelves were neatly stacked tapes, records and CDs, below them was Balwin's sound system.

"These amplifiers are four hundred watts," he began, beaming with pride. "I've got multitrack recording capability with nonlinear track mixing and editing as well as digital mixing on this sixteen-track, twenty-four bit studio recording workstation."

One look at my face brought a laugh to his.

"Sorry," he said. "I get carried away sometimes and talk the talk."

"I don't know much about these things."

"It's all right. The main thing I'm trying to say is we can produce a CD of your singing if we have to, but whatever we record, it will be very high quality. Just in case they ask for something like that."

"I don't have money for this, Balwin."

He laughed again.

"You don't need any money, Ice. I'm taking care of all that."

"Why?"

"Why?"

He looked flustered for a moment, glanced at his piano, and then smiled and said, "Because I love music and I love to hear it done well and you do it better than anyone at our school," he explained.

Embarrassed by his explanation, he moved quickly to the piano and scooped up some sheet music.

"Look these over. I sifted through my collection to pick out what I thought you might like to do and what you could do well," he said.

I put the mug of tea down on a small table and went through his suggestions. One brought a quick smile to my face. It was Daddy's favorite, "The Birth of the Blues." He loved Frank Sinatra's rendition. I pulled it out of the stack.

"What about this?" I asked.

He nodded.

"That's the one I would have chosen for you, too," Balwin said. "Let's tinker with it."

He went to the piano and began to play. I didn't need

the sheet for it. I had sung it enough times, singing along with Daddy's Sinatra recording.

"Jump in any time you want," Balwin said.

I did. He played to the end and then nodded.

"Good," he said, "but you're going to do a lot better before we're done."

I laughed at his tone.

"You sound like Mr. Glenn talking to our chorus."

"I'll try to be for you," he replied. "Ready? We'll do it a few times, record it, listen to it and correct whatever we want to correct."

I smiled at him. The night before he had tried so hard to cheer me up after what had happened to me at the Kit-Kat Club. His first thought was that I was unhappy about not being able to please Shawn Carter. He wanted to know how long we had been going together; when I told him it had been my first and only time with Shawn, he looked relieved and surprised.

"I don't hang around with anyone in particular at school," he told me as he turned from the piano, "so I don't know about everyone's social life, but that was the first time I've seen you at the Kit-Kat. Where do you usually go on dates?"

"I don't," I told him.

"I don't understand," he said.

"I haven't gone on many dates."

The more he learned about me, the happier he became.

"Why are you smiling?" I finally asked him.

"You're a lot like me," he said. "All this time, I thought you were so quiet and reserved because you were so far ahead of everyone else at the school socially. That's why I wasn't surprised to see you with the army guys."

I looked at him quizzically. Was it just him or did others at my school think that of me?

"I mean," he quickly added, thinking he had somehow put me down, "you definitely could be in an instant, if that's what you wanted."

I laughed to myself. Why did everyone, including and especially Mama, think I was so special?

"I'm not trying to be above or ahead of anyone, Balwin," I told him.

He smiled and after a moment softly said, "You don't have to try, Ice."

Was he just trying to make me feel good again? Or was he saying these things because he was as much a loner as I was and I had come to his house? My guess was I was the first, the first girl at least.

Did he ask me because he really, truly believed in my talent or because I was a girl?

Questions, doubts, suspicions.

Why can't you just accept a compliment and leave it at that? I asked myself. What are you afraid of, Ice Goodman?

Being too much like your mother?

She would certainly ask the question.

Maybe, deep down inside, you're really afraid of not being enough like her?

Shut up and sing, I told myself. Just sing.

5

A Song of My Own

I thought our first rehearsal went just all right, but Balwin was more enthusiastic. When he referred to me, he used words and expressions like "terrific," "amazing talent," "a prime candidate for any school." Of course, I assumed he was just being nice. I knew what it meant to compete in the world of entertainment. Daddy had told me lots of stories about singers and musicians he had known in his life, people who were talented and yet failed to get anywhere because they didn't have the breaks they needed or the grit to keep trying.

"It's much easier to accept failure and become comfortable with it than it is to keep coming at them, Ice," he said. "You blame it on destiny or fate or luck and just settle into mediocrity. Lots of good people I know lost the fire in their spirits and now smoulder in some dark, small place, drowning their ambitions and dreams in alcohol or drugs."

The way Daddy spoke about it made me wonder what

had been his private dream. When he finally revealed that he had once hoped to play the trumpet because his teacher had encouraged him, I was surprised. He had never even hinted at it before. Then he dug down in a dresser drawer to show me his trumpet mouthpiece. His maternal grandmother had bought him the instrument.

"It's all I have of the trumpet I once had," he said. "I blow on it from time to time when I get nostalgic."

"What happened to your trumpet, Daddy?" I asked.

His eyes darkened and he shook his head.

"My father made me pawn it, only I pretended to have lost the mouthpiece. He beat me for that," he said.

"Why didn't you go back to playing, Daddy?" I asked him.

"I guess I was afraid," he said. "I was afraid I would get so I couldn't live without it and that would make it terrible, Ice."

I had never known my grandfather. He had died when I was only two, but if he was alive now, I wouldn't be able to look at him without hating him. Amazingly, Daddy didn't sound hateful or angry.

"Didn't you hate him?"

"No." He smiled. "He couldn't see how it mattered in my life then and the money was sure handy that month," Daddy said.

Hearing him speak about it made me wonder about all the secrets people buried in their hearts, all the dreams that had been crushed and interred. Those were the real silences, the ones they were afraid to disturb. It frightened me and did the most to make me hesitant when it came to my own singing and dreams of success. Dare I dream?

It was probably why I just shook my head at Balwin

and thanked him for his compliments as if I knew he was doing it just to be nice. I could see the confusion and even the anger in his eyes.

"I mean it," he insisted. "You're going to make it, Ice. I love music too much to lie about something like that," he added.

"Okay," I said. "I'm sorry. Thank you."

We scheduled another rehearsal. As if he was afraid talking about it or even referring to it during the school day might put a hex on it or something, he actually avoided me. I quickly realized he was the shy one when it came to being with someone from the opposite sex. Like me, he used his music as both a shield and a way to communicate with others. Without it, he was almost as much a mute as I.

Even at chorus rehearsal, he didn't say anything special to me. When I said I would see him later, he nodded quickly and turned away, afraid someone nearby would notice.

Mama wasn't home for dinner. She had gone to a movie with two of her girlfriends. Daddy had another one of his late nights. I expected to be home before either of them, so I didn't leave a note telling them where I was.

Just as the first time, practically the instant I rang the doorbell, Balwin was there.

"Hi," he said and I stepped in. He looked nervous, jittery. Without another word he started for the doorway to the basement studio.

Just before we reached it, however, a tall, lean man with a patch of gray hair encircling his shiny bald head stepped into the living room doorway. He was holding a neatly folded copy of the *New York Times* and was dressed in a three-piece pin-striped gray suit and tie.

His lean, long face was as shiny as the top of his head. His skin was so smooth in the reflected hallway light, he looked like he shaved with one of Mama's tweezers. I saw a resemblance in his and Balwin's mouth and eyes and the shape of their ears.

"Who's this?" he asked sternly.

Balwin glanced at me as if he had smuggled me into his home and been caught in the act. I saw a look of abject terror take over his face, his eyes shifted guiltily away and down as his shoulders slumped and his head bowed slightly to make him look like a beaten puppy.

"Her name is Ice Goodman," he said almost too softly for even me to hear.

"Ice!"

Balwin raised his head and nodded.

"If you have a friend coming over, why don't you tell your mother or me and why don't you make a proper introduction instead of stealing away to your bunker?"

"I wasn't stealing away. We were . . ."

"Well?" his father demanded.

Balwin stepped forward, glanced at me and then said, "This is my father, Mr. Noble. Dad, this is Ice Goodman, a girl from school who is in the chorus."

"I see. And you are here to do what?" he asked me.

"She's here for a rehearsal," Balwin said before I could reply.

His father glared at him and then turned back to me, his eyes narrowing.

"Rehearsal? Why would you rehearse with only one member of the chorus and why can't you do this sort of thing at your school?"

Although he was asking Balwin these questions, he continued to stare at me.

"It's not a chorus rehearsal," Balwin said.

"Oh?"

He turned to him.

"And what exactly is it then?"

"She's going to audition for a special school and needs to prepare some music. I'm helping her," Balwin explained.

"Is that so?" He looked at me again and then turned to Balwin. "Am I correct in assuming you've completed all your homework?"

"Yes sir," Balwin said.

"What school is holding this audition?" he asked me.

"She's auditioning for the Senetsky School in New York," Balwin replied quickly.

"I was asking her," his father said. "She's a singer, you say, but I have yet to hear her utter a sound."

"I was just—"

His father's glare was enough to snap Balwin's mouth shut. I had never seen such obedience coming from such terror.

"It's the Senetsky School," I repeated.

His father barely looked at me before turning back to Balwin.

"I see. Well, your mother has a bad headache this evening, so don't make your music loud," he ordered.

"Yes sir," Balwin said.

His father snapped the paper in his hands like a whip, turned and disappeared into the living room. I could see Balwin visibly release a trapped breath.

"C'mon," he said and continued to the stairway.

"I don't want to cause any trouble," I said before starting down.

"It's all right," Balwin said looking up at me. "My

father doesn't think much of my music, my composing. He likes to recite statistics about how difficult it is to succeed in the creative arts. Everything I have here, I've bought with my own money, and money my mother gave me. Please close the door behind you," he added and continued down the stairs and to the piano.

I looked at the living room doorway and then stepped down and closed the basement door.

"When I sell something for a lot of money, my father will change his tune," Balwin muttered.

It was hard getting myself back into the spirit of singing. Every time I raised my voice, I thought about his father hearing me and becoming enraged. He wasn't half as wide or as powerful looking as my father, but there was something more terrifying about Balwin's father. His name should be Ice, I thought. Those eyes looked like they could stab someone with a sharp, hard glare.

"Don't be afraid to get into it," Balwin said after we had run through it twice. "My mother won't be able to hear you and even if she did, she wouldn't complain like he says."

"I don't want to get you into trouble."

"You won't," he insisted. "C'mon. I want to make a CD soon. You'll be able to play it for people."

We started again and I gave it more energy, which brought a smile back to his face.

"That's more like it," he said after we finished. He played the recording he had made and we listened and followed the music. "Right there you should give it more authority," he said, using one of Mr. Glenn's instructions for the chorus.

I smiled.

"Don't you agree?"

I nodded and he looked embarrassed. When the recording was finished, he asked if I would like something to drink.

"I can make tea down here. I've got a microwave behind the bar."

"Okay," I said and watched him do it. As he prepared a cup for himself and me, I walked around the basement, looking at the posters on the wall and some of the photographs in frames.

"Your mother's pretty," I said.

"She's gained a lot of weight since that picture," he told me. "I guess I take after her in that respect. Maybe in most respects," he added.

He put my cup of tea on the bar and I sat on a stool. He remained behind it, sipping from his mug and watching me mix in some honey.

"My father is so precise about everything he does, including eating. He's proud of the fact that he hasn't gained or lost a pound in twenty years. He once tried to starve me to make me lose some weight," Balwin revealed, shame in his face.

"Not really?" I said.

He nodded.

"I could only have a glass of apple juice for breakfast and then he had everything I ate for dinner weighed on a small scale. Of course I snuck candy bars and ate what I wanted at school. He actually searched my room the way someone might search it for drugs and found two Snickers bars and a box of malt balls. I love malt balls. He went into a rage and put a lock on my piano and threatened to sell every piece of equipment if I didn't lose five pounds that month.

"My mother was so upset and cried so much, I had to

do it. Finally, he relented and took the lock off the piano. But I regained the weight the following month and he threw his hands up one night and told me he was giving up on me."

He looked away to hide the tears that had come into his eyes. When he turned back, he put on a smile quickly.

"It's all right. We've got a sort of fragile truce in the house now. At least he's happy about my grades. I guess he loves me. He's just one of those people who have a hard time revealing it. He thinks it's weak to show too much emotion. He came from a very poor family background and made a success of himself. He says no mature adult can blame failure on anyone but himself. There's always a way to get around an obstacle or solve a problem if you really, truly want to do it.

"I guess he's right."

He sipped some more tea and then shook his head.

"I'm sorry. I didn't mean to blab like that."

"It's okay," I said and smiled.

"You're cool, Ice. Sounds funny to say that, I know, but I can't imagine you blabbing. I bet you would have been great in silent movies."

I laughed.

"No, really. You say more with your face, with your eyes, than most of the girls do talking all day. I like that. The fact is," he said looking down, "I've written a song about you. I hope you don't mind."

"Me?"

He nodded.

"It's not that great."

"Where is it?"

"In here," he said pointing to his temple. "I haven't written it down yet. I'm still playing around with it."

"I want to hear it," I said.

He took a deep breath and looked almost as terrified as he had upstairs in front of his father.

"Please," I begged.

"If it sounds terrible, promise you'll tell me the truth, okay?"

I nodded.

He walked around the bar and went to his piano. I followed and stood by it, waiting. He glanced at me, looked up and then began his introduction. He sang:

> *There is music in the silence of her smile.*
> *There's a melody in her eyes.*
> *She glides unheard through the clamor that's*
> *   around her,*
> *but it's in the harmony of her that beauty lies.*
> *Listen to the patter in my heart; listen to the*
> *   drums within my soul,*
> *see how she can make the chorus sing and see*
> *   how she can make the symphony start.*
> *Play, play this song of you.*
> *Play for the old and play it for the new.*
> *Play at the break of day and play in the*
> *   twilight hour.*
> *Play away the sadness and the sorrow.*
> *Walk before the saddest eyes you see.*
> *Walk and bring the music back to me.*

He stopped and stared down at the piano keys.

"That's all I have so far."

He looked up.

It had been a long time, a very long time since anyone or anything had brought tears to my eyes, tears I couldn't hold back, tears with a mind of their own that surged forward and out, streaking down my cheeks; glorious tears, unashamed, proud to reveal that my heart was bursting and I had been moved.

"Well?" he asked.

I walked around the piano and answered him by kissing his cheek. He was so surprised, his eyes nearly popped. I had to laugh and flick away the tears from my cheeks.

"Thank you. It was beautiful," I said.

He beamed.

"It's not finished, like I said. I'll work on it every day. I'll have it perfect. I'll—"

"How long is this rehearsal, as you call it, to go on?" we heard and looked at the stairway where his father stood midway down.

How long had he been there? Had he seen and heard Balwin singing the song to me? Did he see me kiss him?

"We're just finishing up, sir," Balwin said.

"Good."

He turned and stomped back up and out, closing the door.

"Sorry," Balwin said. "He gets that way sometimes."

What's he afraid of? I wondered, looking after him.

"I've got to get home anyway. My father is coming home late and I have to get his supper. My mother's out with friends," I said.

"Okay. We'll meet again tomorrow night, if you want."

Balwin saw my eyes go to the upstairs doorway.

"It'll be okay," he added.

I nodded and started up the stairs. I was so quiet. Balwin's father didn't seem to mind silence. There was no sound of television, no music, just the heavy ticking of the grandfather clock in the hallway.

"Good night," I told him at the door. "Thanks."

I stepped out quickly. The wind greeted me with a slap in the face and cold fingers in and under my unzipped jacket. I quickly did it up and hoisted my shoulders for the walk home. Just before I reached the corner, I heard a car slow down and turned to see two young men looking out at me, one with a ski cap and the driver with a cowboy hat. The one with the ski cap wore sunglasses even though it was night. I recognized them as former students at my school. I was surprised they knew me.

"How about a ride, Ice baby?" he asked. "It's warm enough in here to melt you."

"Real warm," the driver shouted.

I kept walking, but they continued to follow.

"What's a pretty girl like you doing out here alone anyway?" the one with the sunglasses continued. "You and your boyfriend have a fight?"

I walked a little faster, my heart thumping and echoing in my ears like a pipe being tapped with a wrench in my building. Suddenly, just as I was about to turn the corner, they pulled ahead of me and the door swung open. The one with the sunglasses stepped out and made a sweeping bow and gesture toward the car.

"Your chariot awaits, m'lady."

I stopped, terrified.

"Ice!" I heard and turned to see Balwin running to catch up with me. He stopped, gasping for breath. "Sorry. I had to do something first," he said looking toward the car and the man with the sunglasses.

"Who's this? Balwin Noble? Can't be your boy-

friend. He'd crush you," the man with the sunglasses said
and laughed. His friend laughed, too.

"Forget it," the driver called to him.

"You missed out, honey," he told me and got into the
car. We watched them drive off.

"I was watching out the front window and saw them
slow down," Balwin said. "I'll walk you home."

I started to shake my head.

"I should have offered to anyway. My father gets me
all wound up in knots sometimes. Sorry," he said and
started. "C'mon," he urged.

We walked on together, Balwin with his hands deep in
his pockets.

"I'm going to go on a diet tomorrow," he said.
"Really."

I smiled to myself and we walked on, Balwin doing
all the talking, me doing all the listening, but feeling
good, feeling warm and protected.

We said good night in front of the apartment building
and I thanked him.

"I'll ask my father for the car tomorrow. When he
hears I'm going on a diet, he'll be nicer to me."

"Okay," I said. "But don't make any trouble on my
account."

Balwin smiled.

"Can't think of a better reason for it," he said, leaned
forward to give me a quick peck on the cheek and then
turned and hurried away as if he had truly stolen a kiss.

Daddy got home earlier than I had expected. He was
already in the kitchen, sitting at the table, eating what he
had warmed for himself. My look of surprise appeared to
him to be a look of guilt and worry, I guess.

His eyebrows lifted and he peered suspiciously at me. "Where were you, Ice? You didn't go and meet that Shawn again, did you? Your Mama didn't go and make another one of her special arrangements, I hope."

I shook my head.

"So, where were you?"

"Rehearsing," I said and entered the kitchen. "Sorry I wasn't home to fix your dinner, Daddy."

"That's no bother. What do you mean, rehearsing? Rehearsing for what?"

I shrugged.

"C'mon, out with it," he said.

"I know I'm just wasting my time," I said.

"Ice, what is this? What are you talking about?" he asked slowly.

I lifted my gaze from the floor and looked at him.

"My audition piece for the New York school," I said quickly.

"Really?" He sat back nodding. "That's good, Ice. That's good. Where were you rehearsing?"

I told him about Balwin and how he was helping me.

"Very nice of him. I'm glad about this." He turned to me quickly. "And don't go saying you're wasting your time. I don't want to hear that defeatist stuff from you, hear?"

"But it will be too much money, won't it, Daddy?"

"You just let me worry about that when the time comes to worry about it, honey." He nodded. "We'll manage it somehow. I'm not going to let you miss such an opportunity, no sir, no ma'am."

I smiled to myself and started to clean the pot and the stove while he finished eating.

"Your mother say where she was going tonight?"

"Movies."

"Movies, huh? If she went to all the movies she says she went to, she'd be seeing stars and I don't mean the movie stars," he quipped.

He was trying to be funny, but I could see the concern in his face. It put a cold shiver in me.

"Can't make that woman happy anymore," he muttered, mostly to himself.

I saw how quickly his elated mood turned sour and dark. He stopped eating, stared blankly ahead for a moment and then rose and went into the living room to play one of his Billie Holiday albums while he waited for Mama to come home. After I finished in the kitchen, I went in to sit with him.

"You look tired, honey," he told me nearly an hour later. "Go on to bed. I'm all right by myself. Go on. Get some rest," he ordered. "You got school tomorrow."

I rose, kissed him on the cheek and went to bed. I couldn't fall asleep. I kept hoping I'd hear Mama's footsteps in the corridor and then the front door opening, but an hour passed and then another and, still, she wasn't home. This was going to be a very bad night, I told myself. My stomach churned like a car without fuel, grinding and dying repeatedly. I tossed and turned and tried desperately to think of something else, to sing myself to sleep, anything. Nothing worked.

When the front door finally opened, it was close to three in the morning. Mama didn't just come in, either. It sounded like she fell in.

I sat up to listen and heard her muffled laugh. She was very drunk.

"What are you doing on the floor, Lena?" I heard Daddy ask her.

She laughed and then she told him the heel broke on her shoe. I could hear her struggle to her feet, still giggling to herself.

"Where were you all this time, Lena?"

"Out," she said. "Having a good time. Ever hear of such a thing? Know what that is anymore? I doubt it," she told him.

"Where were you?" he repeated.

"I said out," she snapped back at him.

I heard him step forward and then I heard her short scream.

I rose from bed and opened my door just enough to see the two of them.

Daddy had his hands on her upper arms and he was holding her up like a rag doll, her feet a good foot off the ground. He shook her once.

"Where were you, Lena?" he demanded.

"Put me down, damn you! Put me down."

"Where were you?"

"I'm not one of your suspects, Cameron. Put me down."

"I'll put you down," he threatened, "like they put down dogs if you don't tell me where you were."

"I was with Louella and Dedra. We went to eat and then we went to a movie and then we went to Frank and Bob's just like we always do."

Daddy lowered her slowly.

"I'm tired of you coming home drunk," he said.

"People drink because they're unhappy," she spit back at him.

"Why are you so unhappy? If you got yourself a job, maybe or . . ."

"Oh, a job. What kind of a job could I get, huh? You

want me working in some department store or at a fast-food place?"

Her face crumpled as she started to sob.

"I wasted myself. I should be on a magazine cover or doing advertisements. I should be somebody instead of . . . of what I am," she moaned. "But do you care?" she asked, pulling herself up and tightening her lips. "No. You and your music and your stupid work hours."

"I'm doing my best for us and . . ."

"Best," she muttered. "You don't care about what's happening here. We got a daughter who's like some deaf-and-dumb person, who should be making me proud, and I blame that all on you, you!"

"She's a beautiful girl, a talented girl. She's going to make us proud, Lena."

"Right. I go and work on her and get her a date and it all falls apart."

"You know that wasn't her fault."

"I know. It was mine," she screamed at him. "Who else would you blame?"

"Nobody's blaming anybody, Lena."

"Leave me alone," she said. "I'm sick. I'm not feeling good."

"Why should you after what you did to yourself?"

"You did it to me," she accused.

"Me?"

"You made me pregnant when I was young and beautiful and had a chance, Cameron. And then you promised to do things for me, but look at what you've done . . . nothing. Nothing but tie a lead weight around my neck.

"I'm drowning!" she screamed at him. Then she seized her stomach, doubled over and hurried to the bathroom.

He stood there looking after her, his face as broken and sad as I had ever seen it. He felt my eyes and turned to my doorway.

We looked at each other.

Was I the weight Mama said was around her neck? Did he hate for me to have heard such a thing?

The pain in his eyes was too great for me to take.

I closed the door softly and returned to bed, to the darkness and to the pursuit of fugitive sleep.

6

---~m~---

Out of Tune

There were many times when the mood and atmosphere in our house resembled an undertaker's parlor. I call it *morgue silence* because to me everyone who is infected with it seems to be imitating the dead. I've been to funerals where people sit in the presence of the corpse and keep their eyes so still and empty, I imagined they have just deposited the shell of their bodies in the funeral hall for a while and then have gone off to kill some time at some livelier place.

However, when the singing started, it was always like everyone had turned into Lazarus and risen from the grave. As a little girl, I was so impressed with the energy and the emotion some people exhibited at these wakes that I often wondered if they wouldn't revive the dead man or woman whose eyes would suddenly snap open and then sit up in the coffin and begin to join in the singing. Once, I imagined it so vividly, I thought it actually had happened. Mama saw me sitting there with my eyes so wide and full of amazement, it made her nervous. She insisted on taking me home because she thought the funeral was making me crazy.

"And she's crazy enough with her elective mutism," she told Daddy. She loved using that term ever since she had first heard Mrs. Waite use it at the parent-teacher conference.

Everyone was an elective mute in my home the morning after Mama's late night out. We had *morgue silence*. Mama didn't rise from her bed, but she wasn't asleep. I looked in and saw her staring up at the ceiling, her lips tightly drawn like a slash across her face. Daddy sipped his coffee and stared at the wall. I felt as if I had to tiptoe about the apartment, getting ready for school. He didn't say anything until I was ready to leave.

"I've got a double shift today," he told me. "Training two new men. I won't be back until late, but don't fix me any dinner. I'll have enough to eat this time," he said, his voice trembling with anger and disgust. "She might put poison in my food anyway," he muttered glaring in Mama's direction. "Blaming everyone but herself for her unhappiness."

"I can make you something, Daddy."

"No, it's all right," he said. "I might be later than usual. Don't worry about me," he ordered. He was wound so tight this morning, I was already feeling sorry for anyone who crossed him at work.

I nodded and finished my breakfast without another word and left for school.

The moment I arrived, I sensed something different. I knew from the way other students (especially some of the girls in my class) looked at me; hid smiles behind their fingers, spread like Japanese geisha-girl fans; or

deposited whispers into each other's ears that I was once
again the object of some ugly joke. Usually, having a
thick skin came naturally to me. Whatever darts of
ridicule they shot from their condescending eyes or
spewed from their twisted, vicious lips bounced off the
back of my neck and fell at their own feet like broken
arrows. Most of the time, ignoring them as well as I did
brought an end to their little games. They grew bored trying to get any sort of reaction from me, and when I
looked at them with a blank stare, a face that could easily
be lifted and used as a mask of indifference at a Stoic's
convention, they retreated and searched for a more satis-
fying target.

Today was different because I could feel their determination and their satisfaction growing with every
passing minute—from homeroom to my first class of
the day—despite my apparent disinterest. I was confused by it and couldn't help being curious. Was it
something my mother had done? Or had said? Were
they all just learning about my blind date and laughing
at the results? What could possibly be the reason for all
this whispering and laughing behind my back? It followed me from room to room like a string of empty
cans tied to some poor dog's tail. The faster I walked,
the louder the whispering and laughter became. When I
sat in my classes, I merely had to turn slightly to the
right or the left to see all eyes were on me, girls and
boys mumbling over desks, making such a thick under-
lying flow of chatter that our teachers had to reprimand
them a number of times and threaten to keep the whole
class after school.

Their persistence began to make me nervous, but I
was able to keep the lid on my emotions, walk with my

eyes focused straight ahead, behaving as if there was no one else in the world. Finally, just before lunch, Thelma Williams and Carla Thompson stepped in front of me as I walked to the cafeteria. They wore identical wry smiles and with their books in their arms, their shoulders touching, presented themselves like a wall thrown up to block my way.

"What?" I demanded when they continued to just stand there, grinning.

"We were wondering if you and your boyfriend Balwin would like to come to a party at Carla's house this weekend?" Thelma asked in a phony sweet tone of voice.

"What?"

"We've never invited you to anything because you never showed any interest in boys before," Carla said.

"Some of the girls were worried you might be gay, you know. They don't like undressing in front of you in the locker room," Thelma emphasized.

I shook my head and started to go around them.

"How long have you been secretly seeing Balwin?" Carla asked as they stepped to the right to keep me blocked.

I stared at them. Balwin? Could Balwin have said something to someone about me? It seemed unlikely.

A small crowd began to gather behind them.

"What we were wondering is how does he make love with that big belly of his in the way," Thelma said. The others were starting to giggle. "I told Carla you would always have to be on top, right?"

"You're disgusting," I said.

"There's nothing wrong about being on top," Carla said. "As long as there's something to be on top of."

That brought a loud laugh. Some boys passing nearby stopped to listen.

"I've got to go to lunch," I muttered and stepped forward again, but they didn't part to make room for me.

"Well, are you coming to the party or not?" Thelma asked. "We'll have Carla's bed reinforced to handle the extra weight."

She turned to the appreciative crowd and smiled before turning back to me.

I fixed my glare on her.

"You must be very sexually frustrated," I said. That drew a loud howl from the boys on the rim of the circle.

"Not so frustrated that I'd be going to Balwin Noble's house. You've got to find his thing with a tweezer."

Laughter rolled like thunder down the hallway and over me. My heart pounded. Rage rose in my blood.

"You've got that wrong, Thelma," I said so calmly I could have been talking about a problem in biology. "It's your brain that has to be found with a tweezer."

I forced my way between her and Carla as the boys roared with laughter, most of them now turning to tease Thelma. She cursed them. Before I made it to the cafeteria doors, I felt her books slam against my back. She had heaved them after me. They fell to the floor. I paused, took a deep breath and then just walked on, passing Mr. Denning, the cafeteria's teacher monitor, who nodded and smiled at me. He heard the commotion continuing outside and turned his attention to it, ordering the crowd to disperse.

They did, but shortly afterward, there was a great deal more noise in the hallway and Mr. Denning had to rush out again. A group of students gathered at the doors to watch and then everyone scattered to his table when three other teachers appeared.

What was going on now?

I was shaking in the lunch line and still trembling when I finally sat down with my tray of food. Arlene Martin and Betty Lipkowski, two white girls who had always been pleasant and friendly, were already seated at the table. They were in the chorus, too.

"I guess Mr. Glenn's going to be accompanying us on the piano today," Betty said.

"Why?" I asked.

"Didn't you see what was going on out there just now?" Arlene asked me.

"I saw enough out there," I muttered.

"Balwin got into a bad fight."

"What?"

"He and Joey Adamson had to be pulled apart by Mr. Denning. He took them both to the principal and you know fighting is an automatic three-day suspension, no matter who's to blame," Betty said.

"How does it feel?" Arlene asked.

I stared at her.

"What?"

"You know, to have a boy get into a fight over you?"

I looked down at my food. I had to keep swallowing to stop what I had already eaten from coming back up.

"Sick," I finally said.

"What?" Betty asked.

"Sick. It makes me sick," I said, rose and walked out of the cafeteria.

The remainder of the day passed in a blur. My teachers' voices ran into each other in my mind. I moved like a robot, unaware of how I went from one room to another.

When Miss Huba called on me in my last class of the day, Business Math, I didn't even hear her. I guess I was staring so blankly and sitting so stiffly, I frightened her. She came to my desk and shook my shoulder.

"Ice? Are you all right?"

I gazed up at her, and then looked at the rest of the class. Everyone stared, all looking like they were holding their collective breath, waiting to see if I would scream or cry or laugh madly.

"Yes," I said softly. Her previous math question entered my brain as if it had been waiting at the door. I rattled off the answer. She smiled.

"That's correct. Okay, let's turn to the next chapter, class," she said.

When I looked at the others again, their expressions varied from amazement to disappointment. After Miss Huba made the assignment and gave the class the last ten minutes to begin, a silence thickened around me. Then, Thelma Williams, who sat in the last seat in the third row, loudly muttered, "Give her a tweezer." The whole class roared. Miss Huba looked up confused. And I . . . I felt as if each syllable of laughter was like a pebble thrown at my face.

Finally, I gave them what they wanted so desperately.

I covered my face with my hands, rose and ran from the classroom. Miss Huba's amazed voice was shut off by the door I slammed behind me.

I didn't go to chorus rehearsal. I went straight home. I was glad for once that Mama wasn't there to greet me. I dreaded her questions, her demands to know exactly why I had cut my chorus rehearsal, especially with the concert coming up in a little over a month. She would dig and scratch until she got all of it out of me.

Of course, I felt terrible. Balwin had only tried to do me a favor, had only tried to help me with my future and now found himself not only the target of ridicule, but in trouble at school, probably for the first time. I shivered thinking of what his father might do to him.

About an hour later, I heard Mama come home. She was mumbling to herself, not realizing I was already home. I let her go to her room and then I came out of mine, expecting to see her any moment and gearing myself up for her cross-examination. She didn't come out. I waited and waited and finally went to her door and peered in. She was in bed again and fast asleep with an opened bottle of aspirins on her night table. I decided it was best not to wake her.

When I started making some supper, I heard her call to me and I returned to her room. She had risen and gotten herself a cold washcloth, which she had over her forehead.

"This has been the worst hangover of my life," she moaned. "I'll never drink cheap gin again. Don't you ever do it, Ice. If you drink, insist your man buys you the best," she advised.

"I don't drink, Mama."

"Yeah, yeah, but you will someday," she insisted.

"Are you hungry?"

"Not with my stomach," she complained. "I tried to eat some lunch today and it nearly came up as soon as I swallowed. Just make me some coffee, will you, honey?" she asked.

I nodded and did so. I gave her a steaming mug of black coffee, which she sipped, closed her eyes, and sipped again. Then she looked up at me sharply.

"Where's your hardworking father?" she asked.

"He's doing a double shift today, Mama."

"Figures. The day I need him around here, he's baby-sitting some department store."

She dropped her head to the pillow as if her head was a solid chunk of granite and closed her eyes.

"Get me two more aspirins," she ordered.

After she swallowed them, she said she wanted to just sleep until next week.

I returned to the kitchen and continued making myself some supper. Before I sat down, however, there was a loud, strong knock on our front door. I listened and heard the knocking again.

"Yes?" I asked with the door closed.

"I'd like to speak to you, Miss Goodman," I heard. The voice was strangely familiar. I churned through my memory desperately, trying to recall where I had heard it before and then realized. It was Balwin's father!

I looked back toward Mama's room, waiting to hear her ask who it was, but she didn't call out to me.

"I'll just take up a few minutes of your time," I heard Balwin's father say.

With trembling fingers, I opened the door and stepped back to let him in.

He stood there gaping in at me. Dressed in his dark gray pin-striped three-piece suit and his tie with his gold cuff links visible, he looked almost as alien in this building as someone from outer space. His lips were pressed tightly shut, which drew the skin on his chin into a small fold.

"Thank you," he said stepping forward. He gazed around as he closed the door behind him, nodding softly as if what he saw confirmed what he believed and expected.

"What do you want, Mr. Noble?" I asked.

I had already made up my mind to stay away from Balwin and would agree to it immediately as soon as he demanded it. I expected to hear his complaint, how I had caused his perfect student son to misbehave seriously for the first time ever, proving I was a bad influence on him.

"I'm here to ask for a favor," he began, "but not a favor I expect to be gratis," he quickly added.

He gazed at the doorway to the living room.

"Are your parents at home?"

"My mother is, but she isn't feeling well and she is in bed," I said.

He nodded.

"Well, can we sit down for a moment?" he asked.

I led him into the living room. He looked over every possible seat as if he wanted to be sure to choose one that wouldn't leave a smudge on his immaculate suit. Our apartment was far from dirty. The furniture might look worn, but there wasn't any dust nor were there any stains. He chose to sit in Daddy's chair. I remained standing.

"Well, now," he began, his fingers touching at the tips, "I suppose you're aware of what went on today."

I nodded.

He tilted his head and almost smiled.

"I was obviously quite taken by surprise when I received the phone call from the principal. My Balwin? Fighting? I remember girls on the playground pushing and kicking him around and him not lifting a finger to defend himself—or even to voice a complaint, for that matter. I thought he was without any self-respect. Other children his age could wipe their shoes on him and he would stand there obediently as if he were a living rug. I can tell you how much that bothered me, and when he began to gain weight, I thought it was just a logical consequence of the softness in his spine. He has no pride."

"That's not true," I cried.

He snapped his hands apart as if I had driven mine through them.

"No," he said nodding, "I realize now that there are some things that will motivate him to stand up for himself, to care about his self-image and the image he presents to others. One thing at least, I should say," he concluded, gazing up at me and nodding.

I waited, my arms now wrapped around my body, under my breasts.

"You know I'm referring to you. This fight today was over you, as I understand it. He was defending your honor. Of course, he received three days' suspension at just the wrong time of his high-school life, when he's expected to do well on his exams and prepare to enter a prestigious institution. He's got his heart set on this Juilliard, but I have gotten him to at least apply to Yale and Harvard."

"Mr. Noble—" I began, but he put up his hand to stop the traffic of my words.

"How, I asked myself, how can I take advantage of this rather embarrassing situation so it won't be a complete loss? I make my living doing that for others in a sense, so I should be able to do it for myself, don't you think?

"For the longest time, I have tried without much success, to get Balwin to look at himself in the mirror and see what everyone else sees. I have tried to explain, to demonstrate, to emphasize just how important appearance is in this world. People, for better or for worse, most often judge others on the basis of their looks, the image they present. Clothes do make the man, Miss Goodman, and so does your personal hygiene and your physical self.

"In Balwin's case it's deplorable. He has nice clothes to wear and he takes good care of his wardrobe, but you can't turn a pig into a swan merely by dressing it in pretty feathers."

"Balwin is not a pig," I blurted.

He stared at me and then closed his eyes for a moment, as if he had to seize control of his raging emotions.

"No," he said opening his eyes again. "He's not a pig in spirit even though someone looking at him might think he overindulges, as do pigs."

"What do you want from me?" I demanded, growing tired of listening to Balwin's father tearing him down.

"I want you to get him to lose weight," he said.

"What?"

"You heard me. I want you to get him to shape up, to improve his self-image. I know you can motivate him now because of what's happened. That shows some commitment to something other than his music.

"Of course, I don't expect you to do this without receiving some compensation so I am prepared to make this offer . . . I'll give you ten dollars for every pound you get him to shed from now until the end of the school year," he stated.

I simply stared at him.

"Twenty pounds gets you a quick two hundred dollars. I'm sure you could use it," he said, glancing around the living room. "No," he said after another moment of my silence and my famous penetrating stare, "I should improve this offer. Tell you what. I'll increase the dollars per pound with every five pounds so that pounds one to five, you'll get fifty dollars, but pounds six to ten, you'll get double that, a hundred dollars, and then pounds ten to fifteen, we'll make triple and quadruple the amount for fifteen to twenty. Anything more than twenty, I'll give you fifty dollars a pound. How's that sound?"

"Stupid," I said. "Insulting. Depressing, disgusting and insensitive," I concluded. "Balwin will lose weight when he wants to lose it and not because I tell him to lose it."

Mr. Noble smiled.

"Please, Miss Goodman. We both know that a boy who has a crush on a girl, as Balwin has on you, will do almost anything the girl asks him to do. All I'm asking is you . . . lead him on a bit. I don't have to tell you how to get a boy to do your bidding, I'm sure. Only this time, you can earn some good money for it.

"I might even be inclined to throw in a bonus if you succeed in making a difference in a few months. It will be a nice graduation present and what harm will you have done? Nothing. But you will have helped Balwin immensely. Wouldn't you like to do something good for someone and make money doing that as well?"

"I don't need to be paid to do something good for someone," I said.

I heard Mama's distinct groan and looked toward her bedroom, expecting her to make an appearance and be shocked at the sight of Mr. Noble. It grew silent again, however, so I turned back to him.

"My mother's not well, Mr. Noble. I'm sorry, but you should leave."

"Fine," he said, standing. "Think over my offer and get back to me. You can continue to come to the house to practice your music, of course, and benefit that way, too."

He walked to the front door, opened it, and stood there a moment.

"Don't be so quick to condemn a father for trying to help his son," he added and then slipped out gracefully, closing the door softly behind him.

I stood there for a moment staring after him. Then I heard Mama behind me. I turned and saw her shaking her head.

"I raised a fool," she said. "I heard all that. You just went and threw out hundreds of easy dollars."

"I couldn't take money from Balwin's father for something like that, Mama. I'd feel like a traitor or something," I said and started for the kitchen.

"Why? Who you betraying? Some fat boy? Believe me, Ice, you don't get a chance to take advantage of men much in this world. It's usually the other way around. Think of that Shawn Carter. Didn't he try to take advantage of us? Of you? It just comes natural to men, so why shouldn't you benefit from an opportunity, huh?"

I started to shake my head.

"If you don't want the money, take it and give it to me, for godsakes."

"I can't, Mama," I said.

She smirked and nodded.

"Right, you can't. And what have you been doing over that boy's house anyway, huh? C'mon, tell me all of it."

"We've been practicing music for my audition," I revealed.

"Thought so. Your father know about this?"

"Yes," I admitted.

She pulled herself up.

"Well, that figures, too. Secrets. You and him keep secrets."

"No, Mama," I cried. "He didn't find out until last night when I came home. I would have told you, too, but you didn't come home until very late . . ."

"Sure, blame it on that. He blames everything on me, too," she said.

She took a deep breath, turned and went back to her bedroom. I wanted to follow her and explain more, but I thought she would only close her ears as tightly as she closed her eyes. Later, I tried to get her to eat something and she finally relented and had some toast and jam.

"You take that money," she told me when I brought it into her. "Don't be the fool I've been. Take whatever you can while you can. It doesn't last long. Before you know it, they're looking at younger women and you might as well be invisible," she complained.

I went to my room to finish my homework. Just before ten, Balwin called.

"I guess you heard what happened," he began.

"I'm sorry, Balwin. I never wanted to get you into any trouble," I told him.

"It's not your fault. Jeez, Ice, you can't blame yourself for what those idiots do. I shouldn't have let him get to me," he said, "but I wouldn't let him say those things about you."

"I know," I said. I wondered if he had any idea his

father had been to my house. "Was your father very angry?" I asked.

"Not as angry as I expected he would be. He didn't even ask about the cause of the fight and he hasn't said a bad word about you, Ice. I don't mind the days off. I'll work on my music. I'll finish your song, too," he vowed.

"Balwin . . ."

"You'll come over after dinner tomorrow night, won't you? Please? I'll feel like a total idiot if you don't," he explained. "Like it's all been for nothing, a waste."

I smiled to myself.

"Are you sure, Balwin? It won't stop at school, you know."

"I know. I don't care. Matter of fact," he said, his voice deepening, "I think I'm going to start to enjoy it. They're just jealous, that's all.

"Here, the prettiest girl in the school and the most talented, too, is friends with me, coming to my house," he bragged. "I guess they just don't understand the power of music as well as we do, right, Ice?"

He waited.

"Right?"

"Right, Balwin," I said.

"Okay. Same time, okay?"

"All right, Balwin," I said.

"I can't think of anyone I would rather get in trouble over than you, Ice," he said. Then he quickly said, "Good night," and hung up.

It was just like before when I felt he had stolen a kiss.

It brought a deeper smile to my face.

Music is powerful, I thought. It can make you feel so much better about yourself and your life, it can help you visualize your dreams, it can give you hope and strength.

Just like Daddy, Balwin and I would wrap our music about ourselves snugly and shut out the nasty world.

Let them curse and laugh, ridicule until they're blue in the face.

All we'll hear is the rhythm and the blues or the melody of Birdland.

I'll sing louder, better and longer.

And I'll drown them all out.

7

—~—

Sweet Harmony

I decided not to say anything to Balwin about his father visiting me. Of course, Balwin was confused as to why his father was so cooperative about my coming over to practice music, giving him the car to pick me up, never questioning what we were doing and never complaining about the noise. It filled him with suspicions, and he often wondered aloud about it when I was there. I thought it would just break his heart even to think that I might be seeing him only because his father was paying me.

"It's almost as if he's happy I got into a fight at school," Balwin said. "My mother was far more upset than he was about it. In fact, she was the one to suggest I should stop seeing you."

"Maybe you should," I quickly said.

"No, no, it's all become nothing," he promised.

He was back in school and back at the piano for our chorus rehearsals. An unexpected and happy result of the fight and of all the trouble we both had with other students was Balwin's loss of shyness. He was no longer reluctant about talking to me and sitting with me at lunch. It was as if the fight had been some sort of initiation he had to endure in order to be accepted. Almost immediately afterward, fewer and fewer boys teased him, and those who did, didn't do it with any enthusiasm.

"They're making things up about us behind our backs anyway," Balwin rationalized after I had made a remark about it. He gazed around the cafeteria, still searching for wry smiles and sly glances.

"We never needed their permission to talk to each other, Balwin," I told him.

"Right. Who even cares about them?" he asked with his new bravado.

Despite my fury toward his father and the insulting proposal he had made to me, I had to admit to myself that what he had predicted was coming true anyway. Balwin began to take better care of himself. He loosened up, wore less formal clothing, actually had his hair styled and began to do more vigorous exercise and lose weight. I started to wonder if Balwin didn't suspect something because he began to report his losses to me on a regular basis, almost as if he believed I had some sort of personal stake in his physical improvement. After two and a half weeks, he was down ten pounds and it became very apparent in his face. His cheeks lost their plumpness and I thought he looked a lot more handsome.

Exercise made him proud of his budding muscularity. One afternoon, he just had to roll up his sleeves to show me his emerging biceps.

"My father's happy because I'm finally making use of

the expensive weight lifting equipment he bought me three years ago."

I felt funny encouraging him. I couldn't help experiencing the guilt, even though I had specifically and vehemently turned down his father's offer. Nevertheless, Balwin was so excited and proud about his progress, I had to compliment him.

He no longer avoided physical education classes and he began to make friends with boys who previously had no use for him. Now they were inviting him to participate in their pickup basketball games and then, nearly a month after the fight he had had with Joey Adamson, I saw the two of them talking and joking with each other between classes as if they had been lifelong friends.

Even Thelma Williams began to eat her own words because some of her girlfriends were making positive remarks about Balwin's new look. Reluctantly, she approached me after our physical education class and said, "Looks like you're having a good influence on your man."

She spoke the words as though they each left the taste of rotten eggs in her mouth.

"Whatever he does, he does because he wants to do it. Not because of me," I said. "And he's not my man. He's his own man," I snapped.

Everyone's eyebrows went up. Even I was changing, talking more these days, and they all took note of it.

Thelma smirked, looked at the others and shook her head.

"Sure," she said. "Just shut him off and you'll see whose man he is and whose he isn't."

They all laughed and walked on, leaving me pondering what they all believed. Balwin and I had hardly exchanged a friendly kiss. What made them assume otherwise? Was it simply our spending so much time with each other?

"It's the music," I told Arlene Martin and Betty Lipkowski one afternoon when they asked me why I spent so much time with Balwin as compared to some of the better-looking, more outgoing boys who had shown interest in me.

"Music?" Arlene asked.

"Balwin feels it like I do. When we're doing a song together, we're connected. We touch each other more deeply. In here," I said with my hand over my breast, "and here," I added pointing to my temple.

They sat there staring at me for a moment. Then Betty shook her head and smiled.

"You make it sound like sex," she said with an air of jealousy.

"Maybe it's better than sex," I said.

The two looked at each other and then gazed at me as if I was truly insane. Soon, there was something else about me and Balwin, something else to fill the pot of gossip and to be stirred and spread. Betty and Arlene were telling people we were in some kind of weird, kinky relationship related to music. It kept us on the idle-chatter theater marquee, kept us moving through spotlights and made us aware of every word we said to each other, every touch or smile. It was as if we both felt we were under glass, in the camera's eye, being recorded. Ironically, it made Balwin even more self-conscious about his appearance and he looked more handsome.

When I sang in chorus now, I could feel everyone's eyes and ears on me, watching how I gazed at Balwin behind the piano, all of them looking for some special light, some special sign that would reveal the magic we shared. I suppose I sang even better. I know I sang louder, but Mr. Glenn was very pleased.

"This will be the best concert ever," he predicted.

Two nights before the concert, Balwin picked me up for another special rehearsal at his house. He had completed his song about me and wanted me to hear all of that as well as complete our preparations for my second audition number. His father, pleased with Balwin's physical changes, was talking about buying him his own car.

"He told me if I was going to have girlfriends and dates and such, there would be a greater need for my own transportation. I didn't even bring it up!" he cried, ecstatic over his father's new face.

Whenever his father greeted me now, he always wore a very pleased smile. Balwin said it was having an effect on their whole family. When his father was happy, his mother was happy.

"I can't believe the changes that have come over my home these past few weeks," he told me as we drove to his house. "My father and I actually talk to each other these days. I don't know how to explain it, but I'm sure it has a lot to do with you," he added.

"Me? Why?" I asked quickly.

He shrugged.

"I said I don't know how to explain it. All I know, Ice, is ever since you and I started working together, the world turned into rainbow colors from the gray and black it used to be. You're just going to have to accept the compliment," he insisted.

I turned from him, feeling my heart skip beats. These were nice things to hear said about me, but somehow they made me very anxious. It was as if my heart knew more than my brain and with every beat was warning me that rainbows don't come until after the storm.

We had yet to have the real storm.

Balwin's house was always very quiet, but this evening it seemed more so. His father didn't make his usual appearance in the living room doorway either.

"My parents are having dinner at the home of one of my father's clients," Balwin explained. "My mother wanted me to go, too, but I told her I had already made plans. My father said it was fine," Balwin quickly added before I could complain that he shouldn't have turned her down. He smiled at me and shook his head. "He is the one who always insists I go along to show my respect for his clients. I sure can't figure him out these days," he said and continued down the basement stairs.

A dark shadow moved over the hallway toward me, but it was only a cloud floating across the moon, shutting down the light that passed through the windows. I followed Balwin who was already at the piano.

"It's ready," he declared. "I've finally figured out the last verse."

I knew he was speaking about the song he had written for me.

I stood at the side of the piano and he began, singing through the part I had heard before and then looking at me during the finished final verse, he sang:

Yes, there is music in the silence of her smile.
There is a melody in her eyes.
When she looks at me,
I feel my heart begin to sing.
I feel the glory that her lips can bring.

I understand the true reason for the spring
The burst of blossoms, the song of birds
And I lift my own lips and eyes to be caressed
   by her bejeweled voice.
So play, play this song of you.
Play for the old and play it for the new.
Play at the break of day and play in the
   twilight hour.
Play away the sadness and the sorrow.
Walk before the saddest eyes you see.
Walk and bring the music back to me.

When he lifted his fingers from the keys and sat back, I just stared at him. The music was still ringing in my ears. He formed a tentative, insecure smile.

"Is it all right?" he finally asked.

I nodded and then he stood up quickly, his face twisted with confusion.

"Ice," he said, "Ice, there are tears streaking down your cheeks. What is it?" he asked stepping closer. He touched one of my tears as if he had to feel it to believe it. Then he brought his fingers to his lips.

"Beautiful," I whispered.

"Like you," he said.

His face moved toward mine in such small incremental movements, it was truly slow motion, but I didn't step back or turn away. We kissed, a soft, long kiss, neither of us lifting our hands from our sides. When he pulled away, his eyes were still closed as if he was trying to savor every lingering delicious moment.

"When I kiss you, it's like bringing the words to the music, making it complete," he said.

I smiled and he kissed me again. His left hand went to

my waist and his right to my shoulder. I put my arms around him and we held each other, our lips holding us as though all the magnetic magic was there at our mouths.

"The song was the only way I could tell you how I felt about you," he said softly. "I feel it all here," he added, placing his hand over his heart.

I nodded and he took me by the hand and walked me to the settee. We sat beside each other just looking at each other. When someone has so much creativity and talent inside him as Balwin has, I thought, it becomes a more solid identity, far deeper than any mask of male good looks. His feelings for me weren't only in his eyes and on his lips; they were in his very being. I was overwhelmed by his sincerity and his hunger for my approval and love.

Yet, I couldn't help feeling a little afraid as well, but not afraid for myself as much as I was afraid for him. Such total love as Balwin was expressing for me made someone, especially someone like him, as vulnerable as a turtle out of its shell. I did not know myself if I loved or cared for him half as much as he apparently cared for me. He longed to hear me say so. His eyes told me that.

But I did not know if what I felt for him at the moment was all or as much as any woman could feel for any man. Was this what love was? Instinctively, I felt that love meant caring for someone more than you cared for anyone else, even yourself, but I also understood that you needed him to feel the same way or you were incomplete, lost. Could I feel anywhere as intense about Balwin as he obviously could feel about me? Wouldn't he feel incomplete, lost, if I didn't? It took the greatest trust to utter the words, "I love you," to anyone because he might laugh or reject you and leave you as exposed as that turtle.

What would happen then?

Would you be afraid to ever utter those words again?

Silence, I realized, was so safe.

As if he could hear the debate in my mind, Balwin leaned forward to end it with a long and far more passionate kiss. He moved his lips over my cheek and up to my eyes. He kissed my forehead, my hair and then my lips again. I did not stop him or pull back and his excitement built faster and faster. I thought I could hear his heart beating against mine, or was that only my own, pounding?

"Ice," he whispered, his hands slipping under my blue cotton blouse and then up to my breasts. His fingers moved in quick side motions over my nipples, hardening them. My back softened and I lowered myself as he moved over me. I felt my bra clip snap and then his fingers on my skin, making every place he touched feel like a tiny firecracker had been lit over it, exploding, the heat building up and down my stomach and my chest, circling my ribs and making me soften and soften until I felt so helpless, so willing to be touched everywhere, kissed everywhere.

I closed my eyes and felt as if I was sinking into the settee.

"I love you, Ice. There, I said it without singing it," he bragged.

I opened my eyes and looked into his to see the great happiness. He kissed me again, his tongue slipping over mine and then he struggled with his own clothes until I felt his naked thighs and his hardened excitement emerging. It had the opposite effect from what I imagined it was supposed to have. It was more like a wake-up call, a quick splash of cold water or even an electric shock.

What was I doing?

Was this what I wanted to happen? And even so, was it what I wanted to happen now?

Had I already passed that moment when you could still think and decide, that moment before the heat in your blood took control and turned you into an obedient slave to your own passions?

"Wait, stop," I said. "Please, Balwin. Don't," I cried sharply.

He lifted himself from me and looked down, his eyes so hot, I could see the fire burning inside him. I shook my head.

"Oh," he moaned and then looked down at himself as if he just realized what he had been doing. "Oh. I'm sorry," he muttered and struggled to get himself dressed.

I sat up and fixed my bra. He rushed about, getting his clothes on, hurrying like someone who had to flee the scene of some crime. I reached out to touch his shoulder and he stopped and looked at me, his face full of desperation.

"I'm just not ready for that," I said.

He looked like he would burst into tears. He nodded quickly and completed dressing. Then he rose and for a moment looked in every direction.

"Well . . . we . . . well . . . let's get back to work," he said.

I watched him hurry back to the piano and sift through pages of music, keeping his eyes off me.

"I'm sorry. I know that wasn't fair of me," I said.

He looked up and started to shake his head.

"No, it wasn't fair of me. I wasn't sure myself," I

admitted. I thought about a spiritual I often sang. "You weren't the only one in muddy waters," I told him.

He smiled.

"You mean you never . . ."

I shook my head.

He looked relieved.

"I'm no expert," I said, "but it seems to me it's better if it takes its proper time. If it's meant to be, that is," I added.

"Like a baby being born?" he suggested. "You shouldn't rush it, huh?"

I laughed.

"Maybe. I'm no expert when it comes to that either," I said and he laughed too.

"Back to the music," he said and I rose to join him at the piano.

It was truly as if we had rid ourselves of some cobwebs, some of the darkness and the shadows that always hung between us like Spanish moss, draped over our every expression, our every word. We had to get past the feelings, the need to touch and know each other in more intimate ways before we could draw closer to each other than we already were. Once we had done that, the music followed, blossomed. His fingers were freed and so was my voice. We sounded so good together, we both cried out for joy, both knowing it was special.

"If you sing like that, you'll get in that school for sure," Balwin declared when we finished.

"I will if you come along to accompany me. Can you?"

"We've got to find out if they permit it first," he said. "If they do, sure I will."

"Thank you, Balwin. You've given me so much," I said.

I hugged him and he held on to me a moment longer, his head pressed to my bosom, his eyes closed.

"You've given me much more," he whispered, his voice cracking.

I lifted his head away, looked down at his loving face and lowered myself to kiss him. The music, his devotion, made him the most handsome man in the world to me at that moment. His hands reached around my waist and pressed my rear as he brought his lips to my lower stomach and then lower and lower until I felt a rush of excitement shoot with lightning speed through my blood to my heart. He looked up at me again, his eyes drawing me. Did I have the strength to say, "stop," again?

Moving together, touching each other, even through mere looks and words, was like trying to navigate a minefield in which passion could explode at any time if we accidentally triggered it through a deeper look or an innocent caress.

"Step back, Ice," I told myself. "Hurry before it's nearly too late again."

However, my own fingers, like little traitors, betrayed me. They came around to undo my pants. Balwin began to lower them over my hips. His lips moved over my naked stomach, pushing into the waistband of my panties. I moaned as his hands went under them to grip my buttocks and hold me.

He breathed deeply as if he wanted to commit every aspect of me to his memory. Then, he lowered his arms, surrounding my legs behind the knees, and stood, lifting me.

"See how strong I've become?" he asked, smiling. I kissed him again and we were back on the settee. This time, I lay there quietly as he carefully and patiently removed every piece of clothing from my body, including my socks. Then he knelt at the settee and put his forehead on my stomach. My blood felt like it was at a boil. When he lifted his head and perused my body, I looked at him and saw the pleasure and the utter amazement and joy building in his eyes. He hovered over me, taunting me with his lips and his fingers.

"Turn off the lights," I whispered.

He rose to do so.

"I understand," he said. "You're not ready to see me like this yet. Got a ways to go, huh?"

"That's not it at all, Balwin."

"Sure it is. That's fine," he said. "I'll be there soon," he vowed.

He slipped out of his clothing and then lay beside me. We kissed and held each other.

"Muddy waters clearing any?" he asked.

I was so deep down in the well of passion, his voice seemed to reverberate above me. I was losing the battle. In fact, it might be all over, I thought. My own curiosity and excitement were pushing caution away from the controls. Alarms were being drowned out by the drumroll in my heart, the parade of desire and lust marching up from my thighs to the back of my neck and around to my lips.

He moved closer, closer . . .

And then, we heard the upstairs door open and close and his parents' voices, his father's laugh and his mother's following.

Balwin practically flew away from me, scurrying like a rodent over the floor to gather his clothes. I rushed to get mine on as well.

"The lights!" I cried. "They'll wonder why we're down here in the dark."

He flicked on the lamp at the piano just as we heard the door to the basement being opened. I rushed around the corner to keep out of eyesight as I completed dressing. Balwin tapped out some notes, pretending to be working at the piano.

"Hey!" his father called down. "You still working with Ice down there?"

"Yes, Dad."

"Getting late, son," he said and closed the door.

I came around quickly and we looked at each other. Most of the lights had been off. Surely, it looked suspicious and strange.

"It's all right," Balwin said trying to reassure me. "Don't worry."

"I'd better get home," I said. He nodded and we started up the stairs.

When we stepped into the hallway, his father appeared in the living room doorway, gazing at us, a wry smile on his face.

"Making music down there?" he asked.

Balwin looked at me, his eye shifting every which way as he searched desperately for just the right answer.

"Yes," I said for him.

"Good," his father said. He smiled at me. "Good," he continued and turned away.

We hurried out and to the car.

"Sorry about all that," Balwin said as we drove off.

"Maybe we had better cool it for a while," I suggested.

"Just awhile," he said nodding. "We'll start again after the concert Saturday, okay?"

"We'll see," I said.

Little did I know what my hesitation would come to mean to him, but then, I had no idea myself.

*   *   *

Our annual spring concert was always a very well-attended affair. We had an excellent, award-winning orchestra as well as an award-winning chorus. Many people attended who didn't even have students participating. They just knew they would get their money's worth buying a ticket to one of our concerts.

Most of the proceeds went toward a scholarship for a worthy musical student. The winner or winners were announced just before the final choral number of the evening. Mr. Glenn called up the principal to make the presentation. Everyone was sure that Balwin would be this year's recipient. After all, he had volunteered his services for the chorus for more than two years now and had even performed solo at past concerts, always bringing the audience to its feet.

Despite his father's reluctance to praise Balwin for his musical abilities, the accolades and the congratulations he and Mrs. Noble received made it impossible for him not to at least appear proud. It wasn't hard to see, however, that he had hopes Balwin would eventually go on to pursue a career that held more financial promise. Balwin told me that if he hadn't been chosen in an early admissions program to attend Juilliard, his father would surely have pressured him to go to Harvard or Yale, both of which had accepted him, and then get an MBA.

"He's got to get it out of his system," was Mr. Noble's favorite expression whenever anyone talked to him about Balwin's pursuit of music. It was as if he believed music was like an infectious disease or something, a flu or virus he had to purge from his soul. Mr. Noble seemed to think that with time, Balwin would simply outgrow it.

All this applause was nice, he told friends, but when it

came right down to it, applause didn't put food on the table or pay for an elegant home or provide a good living. For that, Balwin would eventually have to turn his attention to more mundane things like following in his footsteps perhaps and becoming a financial advisor, manager or even a company chief financial officer. He could always buy a piano and play for people on holidays, couldn't he?

"After all, how many people do you know," his father would ask someone, "who make a very good living on entertainment?

"We all can't be Frank Sinatra," he pointed out with a laugh.

I heard him say these very things in the auditorium lobby during the concert's intermission. Balwin heard them, too, and was embarrassed enough to try to lose himself in the crowd.

"I've got to check on something," he told his mother and slipped away.

My mama and daddy had come to the concert. I was surprised Mama had actually shown up, even though she had gone into her room to prepare long before I left. She always thought the music was too stuffy and made her sleepy. I had to admit that she looked very nice, dressed in a dark blue dress with her pearls and her hair and makeup perfect. She was enjoying a lot of attention, and every once in a while, glanced at me with her eyes dancing, brightly filled with pride. Daddy looked somewhat uncomfortable beside her, his tie like a hangman's noose on his neck. He flashed me a smile and made his eyes roll toward Mama who had just let out one of her sweet sounding laughs while she absorbed a compliment from someone else's father.

We were called back in to finish the concert. The second half began with three orchestra numbers and then a chorus number, after which the auditorium grew very quiet. Mr. Glenn introduced the principal who stepped forward and announced that this year the school had extremely worthy recipients for its prestigious music scholarships. He then began with a very detailed rendition of all of Balwin's accomplishments. I had forgotten myself how he had often gone over to the elementary school to help that chorus rehearse and once had performed a small assembly program for the primary classes.

The audience rose to its feet when he was called forward to receive his scholarship. I clapped as hard as I could. He glanced my way and smiled and then stepped up and thanked the school and his parents. He promised to make good use of the scholarship.

Again, there was a hush in the crowd. The principal put on his reading glasses and began by describing someone who was truly a discovery, "a jewel so covered in modesty, someone could walk right by her. Until," he added lifting his head to look out at the audience, "you heard her sing. Then, there is no question. It is with great joy that we present a scholarship to someone who has the potential to make us very proud citizens of this school, Ice Goodman."

At first, I didn't realize he had uttered my name. I stood there, waiting for another name. Mr. Glenn turned to me, beaming, and the others looked at me, too. All their eyes brought the reality home. I thought I would be unable to take a single step, but Mr. Glenn came forward and reached for my hand to escort me to the podium. Balwin's face was so full of joy, his eyes glittered like tiny stars in the footlights. I thought I would surely faint. My heart was beating so fast, I couldn't find a breath.

The principal handed me the envelope and stepped back. I knew that meant I had to say something. Everyone in the auditorium was looking at me, waiting.

"Thank you," I said. Then I turned and hurried back to my place.

No one applauded.

The principal stepped forward, laughing.

"She makes up for all that when she opens her mouth to sing, folks. Just sit back and enjoy the final number."

The audience finally applauded.

I did sing hard and strong until the final note, after which Mr. Glenn congratulated me first and then most of the chorus. Balwin and I remained backstage waiting to greet our parents. Mama was in her glory. She feasted on the accolades and compliments as if she had expected them, and then Daddy revealed that they had been informed of my impending award so that they would be sure to attend the concert.

"We're very proud of you, honey, very proud," he said hugging me.

Some of the men he knew pulled him off to shake hands and receive their congratulations. Balwin and I stood close to each other, greeting people like the victors of some Olympic event. Finally, his father came up to me.

"I guess your working together helped you both in different ways," he began. Balwin was shaking hands, but listening with one ear turned our way.

I nodded, smiled and started to turn away from his father, when he reached out again and took my hand.

"You deserve this," he said. "And now that I know

you've got a promising future, it will be put to good use, I'm sure. Thanks for fulfilling the bargain," he said.

I opened my hand and looked down at five crisp hundred-dollar bills.

Balwin gazed at it as well and then he looked up at me, his face full of confusion and pain.

"No," I said shaking my head. "I don't want your money, Mr. Noble," I cried. "I told you . . ."

He turned his back on me and walked into the crowd. I looked at Balwin.

"I told him I didn't want . . ."

He didn't wait for me to finish. He moved away quickly, disappearing into the crowd. I started after him, but Mama seized me and started to praise me in front of her friends, claiming how much she encouraged me to sing in church. Half of me listened.

The other half was off, screaming into the night.

8

—∽—

Wounded

The silence I had once embraced as a friend soon turned into a despised enemy. It was the silence I heard growing between Balwin and me almost the instant the incident with the money occurred in front of him. The pain he felt was so deep, I thought I could never reach down far enough to wipe the salve of my explanations over it. He would always suspect, distrust, even detest me as long as he had any reason to believe I had been part of a conspiracy hatched by his father.

Full of a thousand anxieties, I tried calling him as soon as I was home from the concert, but he didn't answer his phone and when his father picked up their main phone, he told me Balwin was already asleep.

"You did a despicable thing handing me that money in front of him, Mr. Noble. He thinks everything between us was planned, contrived, done for the money," I said, tears burning under my eyelids.

"Wasn't it?" his father asked coldly.

A hot rush of blood heated my face.

"No!" I screamed, "and I want you to take your money back."

He laughed.

"Sure you do," he said. "Mail it to me," he challenged and hung up.

I found an envelope immediately and addressed it. Then I stuffed the money in it and set it out to mail it to him first thing in the morning. Balwin's mother answered his phone the next day and told me he had gone for a ride with some friends. I didn't know whether to believe her or not. I asked her to tell Balwin I had called and she said she would, but I didn't hear from him, and I decided not to keep calling.

Of course, we saw each other in school the following Monday, but as soon as he set eyes on me, he turned and headed in the opposite direction. His avoidance of me caused more of a stir than when we had begun to be together. Everyone wanted to know what was going on, but I ignored the questions and the comments, all except one: Thelma Williams's implication that Balwin was upset he had to share the award with me.

"The only reason why you don't know how stupid that is," I told her, "is because you're so stupid."

It nearly started a bad fight. If Balwin heard about it, he didn't say anything to me before the day ended. Chorus was over for the year so we didn't meet after school, but on my way home, I saw him driving his car in my direction. When I rounded the corner to my street, I found him parked alongside the curb. He was staring ahead, waiting.

I got in and closed the door.

"I heard about you and Thelma Williams," he began. "Thanks for defending me."

"It was a dumb thing for her to say."

He nodded and then he squinted at me.

"I just want to know if everything you did was paid for with that money my father gave you," he said.

"Nothing was paid for, Balwin. I've been trying to tell you that, but you won't listen."

He stared at me, the pain and hurt tearing at his eyes.

"Why didn't you tell me what my father had done? Why didn't you ever say anything about it?"

"I thought you would always be suspicious. I thought you would never believe it wasn't true," I replied. "I also thought your father would get so angry, he would forbid you from ever seeing me."

"You should have told me," he repeated, shaking his head. "If you like someone, really like him, you trust him. Trust is a very important thing, Ice, very important."

"I know. I'm sorry, Balwin. Really, I am. I sent the money back to him. When I called and told him, he said I wouldn't and he laughed at the idea."

"You called?"

"A few times. I called your phone and spoke to your mother, too. Didn't anyone give you the messages?"

He shook his head.

"I guess they thought my usefulness was ended," I said. I was feeling so sorry for myself, I wished someone would dig me a well to cry in. "Your father didn't have to pay me to like you and to help you feel better about yourself, Balwin."

I turned on him, my eyes burning with unrequited tears.

"I enjoyed every minute we were together and the song you wrote for me will always be something special to me."

Balwin glanced at me and I stared at the floor. I was afraid to look directly at him again, afraid I really might start to cry and never stop. I think he sensed it. His voice turned so much softer.

"I should have given you more of a chance to explain, Ice. I'm sorry about that, but I was so hurt, so angry. I felt betrayed."

"I know."

"Will you come back?"

"No," I said. "I don't think I'll feel comfortable there just now."

"Well, then let's keep practicing at school. Mr. Glenn will let us use the chorus room, okay?"

I was silent.

"Ice? Okay?"

"If that's what you really want," I said.

"I do."

"Then, okay," I said and got out of the car.

"Tomorrow, after school?" he called.

I nodded.

Then I turned and walked away. He watched me walk all the way to my apartment building before he started his car and left. I watched him drive off.

Music, I thought, music was still the tie that binds. The rhythm, the melody and the words flowed through my heart as well as my mind. I could face anything if that was always true, I thought.

I was soon to be put to the test.

It came in the form of a loud knock on our apartment door just a little after eleven that same evening. Mama was already asleep and when she fell asleep, she was pretty much dead to the world. Sometimes, she even put cotton in her ears to keep anything from disturbing her.

I thought the knocking was part of a dream I was having. I tossed and turned all night, fretted in and out of the nightmare trying to settle in my brain. I heard the knocking continue and finally opened my eyes. I listened, heard a voice and more knocking and then rose quickly, scooping up my robe and shoving my feet into my slippers.

"Who's there?" I called through the closed door. There were two robberies this month in the building, and both had happened because someone had opened her door too quickly.

"Mike Tooey, from the agency," I heard. I knew that was Daddy's security company and I knew Mike Tooey. I looked toward Mama's bedroom, but she hadn't yet woken.

"Just a minute," I said and undid the locks. I opened the door and faced him. He had his hat in his hands and he was in full uniform. "What is it?"

"Your dad," he said, "was shot about an hour ago. He was stopping a robbery."

I pressed my hand to my breast. My whole body felt as if I had fallen into a large pot of boiling water. I could barely move a muscle.

"How is he?" I finally managed to ask.

"He's in intensive care at the hospital. You and your mother should get over there," he said. "Sorry."

Sorry? It sounded so simple, so nonchalant, so nothing. Sorry to wake you. Sorry I stepped on your foot. Sorry I snapped at you. Sorry I bumped into you. Sorry your father was shot.

"I can take you two there," he offered. "I'll wait outside in the company car, okay?"

I nodded, closed the door, took a deep breath and started for Mama's bedroom.

There was no music in my mind, just the continuous, ominous roll of parade drums.

Almost as if she knew she would be facing unhappiness when she woke, Mama stubbornly clung to sleep as I shook her. I shook her again and called her and shook her until finally her eyelids fluttered, closed, and then snapped open.

"What?" she practically screamed at me.

"Daddy's been shot," I said.

She stared up at me a moment and then she sat up so quickly and firmly, I stepped back.

"What?"

"Mike Tooey is outside waiting to take us to the hospital in the company car," I said. "Daddy stopped a robbery."

"Oh Jesus," she muttered, "oh Jesus, Jesus."

She rose and began to get dressed. I hurried back to my room to do the same. Less than ten minutes later, I was ready, but Mama was still brushing her hair.

"I look a mess," she moaned at her own image in the mirror.

"I don't think that matters at the moment, Mama," I said dryly.

She paused and looked at me as if I had gone crazy.

"It always matters, child. You think I want your father looking at a hag when I get there. The better I look, the better he's going to feel," she predicted, finished her hair and then joined me at the door. "I shoulda bought that wig the other day," she muttered as we hurried out. "You got a wig, you just throw it on and don't worry. I should have bought it."

Mr. Tooey either really didn't know very much or was too frightened to give us the details. However, we were told everything almost as soon as we arrived at the ER. Daddy had taken two bullets; the first had lodged in his shoulder, but the second had hit him in the abdomen and nicked his spine as it passed through. He had lost a lot of blood and was in critical condition.

"Is he going to live?" Mama demanded from the doctor.

"We'll see," was the doctor's best reply no matter how much Mama pressured him.

Different places have different kinds of silences, I thought as we waited in the lounge anxiously. Hospitals weren't really quiet places. Staff workers, interns, nurses, all spoke rather loudly to each other. There was much activity going on, too: people being pushed along in wheelchairs or on stretchers, doctors talking to relatives or to the patients themselves, technicians rolling machines from one room to another, nurses and doctors shouting orders across hallways.

The silences I did see and hear were the silences in the eyes of the worried wives, mothers, husbands, brothers, sisters and friends who lingered in corridors, quietly comforting each other, holding each other, standing in the shadows and gazing absently at the floors or walls or looking out the windows at nothing, just waiting in a world where all time seemed to have stopped, where everything said or done seemed so far off reverberating into the darkness.

There were many elective mutes here, many people who didn't want to speak, to hear the sounds of their own voices for fear it would make them crumble or turn to tears and cries of pain.

"Will my daddy die?"

"Will Bobby get better?"

"When will the doctor tell us anything?"

"When will my mommy come home?"

It was so much better not to hear these and similar questions, not to have to answer, not to have to look into the face of reality and recognize what tomorrow could be like. It was better to wait quietly, to hold your breath and not think about anything, anything at all.

Mama couldn't do that. She talked incessantly, commenting to everyone who would listen, complaining about the waiting, the world today, the criminals out there, her poor husband's miserable fate, moaning and groaning, drawing all the sympathy she could to herself until finally, exhausted, she sputtered like some boat running out of fuel on some lake, her words growing farther and farther apart, half spoken, and soon altogether stopped.

She stared along with the others and waited and looked at me and took a deep breath and closed her eyes.

Time tormented us. Minutes took longer. Hours stretched. We were stuck in forever, until eventually, almost like an afterthought brought back from some dark corner of the hospital, the doctor made his way toward us, his face glum, a doctor's face full of ifs and maybes.

Daddy was still alive. The next twenty-four to forty-eight hours were critical. If he lived, it would be a long recuperation with a lot of therapy. He would most likely regain his ability to walk, too, but it was all somewhere way out there like a promise at the end of a rainbow.

It was best we went home and returned the next day. There wasn't much left to do, but wait.

"He's a strong man, Mrs. Goodman," the doctor told her. "A lesser man would be gone by now," he said. I could see he meant it sincerely.

Mama nodded. For once, she seemed speechless. She threaded her arm through mine and we left to get a cab to take us home. All the way she rested her head against my shoulder. As soon as we arrived, she went right to sleep.

I sat in the living room for a while, looking at Daddy's empty chair and humming some music to myself. Finally, I went to bed and fell asleep, too exhausted to entertain a single dream.

I was up and out of bed the moment my eyes snapped open in the morning. Mama was still asleep. I went right to the phone and called the hospital. When they heard I was immediate family, they forwarded my call to the nurse on duty who told me Daddy was stable, but there was nothing more to say until the doctor came to evaluate.

I rushed about the apartment, putting up some coffee first because I knew Mama wouldn't budge without some. Then I called to her and woke her. She mumbled and cursed and cried, but finally rose. I showered and dressed and had her coffee poured and waiting when she emerged from her room, practically sleepwalking to the table. I told her I had called the hospital and what the nurse had said.

"We've got to get there as quicky as we can, Mama. We've got to talk to the doctor."

"Why rush? All they do is make you wait and wait until they're good and ready," she said.

"We don't want to miss him," I insisted. "If you're not ready, I'll leave without you," I threatened.

She looked up at me with surprise and then shook her head and complained all the rest of the time and all the way to the hospital, moaned about how I had hurried her so much she couldn't fix herself properly to face the world. I was to be blamed for her mediocre appearance. I worked hard at closing her out of my mind and soon her words bounced off my ears like raindrops off the top of an umbrella.

I was right about being there as soon as we could. The doctor was on his way to another hospital after seeing Daddy and we wouldn't have gotten any direct information if we hadn't been there.

"He's improved far faster and better than I had anticipated," he told us. "I believe he's out of danger, but he's going to begin a long recuperation. Prepare yourselves for that," he warned, his eyes on Mama as if he could sense how difficult it was going to be for her, maybe even more difficult than it would be for Daddy.

He told us we could see Daddy later in the day when he was conscious. I had the hardest time keeping Mama at the hospital to wait for the opportunity. She wanted to go home and dress herself all over again. We ate some lunch in the hospital cafeteria and then went back to the ICU waiting room and waited for the nurse to come out to get us.

"You can stay ten minutes," she said. "He's conscious now."

"Well, Hallelujah!" Mama muttered.

We followed the nurse in to Daddy's bedside. Even on his back with all the tubes and monitoring devices attached to him, he still looked big and powerful to me.

He smiled when he saw us.

"Now look what you've gone and done," Mama told him immediately. "I bet you didn't have to stick your big neck out, Cameron Goodman. I bet you just couldn't wait to be a hero, huh?"

"Hi Daddy," I said. I kissed him.

Mama looked around, held her face of chastisement, but kissed him, too.

"Now, what are we supposed to do?" she asked him.

"Mama," I whispered. "Don't cause him any worry now."

"You'll be fine," Daddy said. "Money comes in anyway. Insurance. Don't worry," he said.

"Great," Mama said. "And you have a long recuperation. You'll be hanging around the house playing that music all day and night now. I'm telling you right now, Cameron, I'm no good as a nurse," she warned.

Daddy smiled at me.

"Well, I'm not. I won't be carrying bedpans and breaking my nails changing bandages and such."

"There's home nursing care when we need it," Daddy told her, his voice just above a whisper. "Stop your worrying, Lena. You'll be fine. We'll all be fine."

"Right. Getting in the way of a bullet. I do declare, Cameron, I never wanted you to do this job. You shoulda . . . shoulda drove a taxi or something."

Daddy widened his smile, but I could see he was fading again fast.

"Don't worry," he whispered and fell asleep.

"You'll have to leave," the nurse said quickly.

"Leave? We haven't been here five minutes!" Mama cried.

"Please," the nurse insisted.

I took Mama's arm and practically walked her out forcibly. She muttered to herself until we were in the hall.

"You see his face when he looked up at me? I knew I wasn't looking my best," she cried. "We rushed here for five minutes. I'm going home," she said. "I'll be back tomorrow or when I can see him for a sensible visit. I'm so tired from all this, Ice. It's as if the bullets hit me, too."

Mama was more comfortable feeling sorry for herself and getting me to sympathize. I took her home, checked on Daddy with a phone call later and then made dinner for Mama and myself. She wanted me to return to school the next day, but I wouldn't do it. I went to the hospital and saw Daddy without her in the morning. He had improved some more and was stronger and more alert.

"Don't let this stop you from following your plans, Ice. Please," he begged me. "I was so proud of you at the concert."

"I don't know, Daddy. We've got so much more to think about now."

"There's nothing more. I'll be fine and so will your mama," he insisted. "Promise me," he insisted. "Promise."

"Okay, Daddy," I said. "I promise."

"Good." He closed his eyes with some relief. "Good," he said and fell asleep.

The news about Daddy spread fast through the school. When I returned the next day, everyone, especially my teachers, asked about him. Balwin was very attentive, feeling even worse about the misunderstanding that had occurred between us.

"You're still going to work on the audition, aren't you?" he asked.

"I don't know," I said. "Our lives are changed now. Daddy's going to require a long period of recuperation and I'm not sure about costs and money. I don't know," I told him.

He looked sicker about it than I was.

"Well, you should practice and keep up anyway," he said. "Just in case it works out."

"I don't know where I'll find the time," I said.

Now, as soon as school ended every day, I rushed over to the hospital to be with Daddy. Mama didn't visit as much and hated being in a hospital. I started to complain about it, but Daddy stopped me and said he was better off being around her only when she was happy. I understood and ignored her selfishness as best I could.

When Daddy was moved to a room, I found I could be a real help, assisting the nurse's aides, getting him things he needed or wanted or just amusing him. Every once in a while, he would look at me and make me repeat my promise to go forward with my plans. Finally, one day it dawned on him that I was spending so much time in the hospital, I couldn't be practicing my music.

"You've got your homework and end of the year exams, I know," he said. "Why are you spending so much time here, Ice? That boy still wants to help you, right?"

"Daddy—"

"You promised me, child. You telling me you're not keeping up the promise? You're my hope, Ice. I don't want to get out of this bed if you don't try. Well?"

"All right, Daddy," I said. "All right. I'll go back to practicing."

That satisfied him. It was left as an understanding between us, however, that I wouldn't discuss it with Mama. We both knew it would just create more tension in an already tense household.

She made her appearances when she thought she looked pretty enough. She paraded in as if she had just come off a model's runway. We could smell her perfume ten minutes before she arrived. When Daddy told her so, she shook her head angrily and said, "Well, I've got to do something to keep these putrid hospital odors out of my nose, don't I? You walk out of here smelling like a nurse if you don't," she insisted.

Daddy and I looked at each other and laughed.

"Go on, make fun of me, if you like, but I know I'm right," she insisted.

When Daddy was well enough to begin some therapy, I decided to meet with Balwin and go over my music. I still had my audition date for the Senetsky school scheduled. He and I practiced after school. It was very difficult for me to start again. It was as if we had never worked on the songs before, but Balwin was patient and kept giving me encouragement.

"Sometimes I think this is more important to you than it is to me," I told him.

He laughed.

"You just don't know yet how important it is to you," he assured me. "But you will. Someday, you will and then you'll be happy you did this, Ice."

I smiled at him and then, almost as if it was a reflex action, I gave him a kiss. His eyes brightened like candles just lit.

"Tomorrow," he said, "I'd like to visit your father with you. I'll take you there after school," he said.

I thought that was very nice of him and when we arrived, Daddy was very happy to see him. They talked about music as if they had been old friends. Daddy was impressed with Balwin's knowledge of jazz. At the end, he thanked him for helping me.

"Your father's a great guy," Balwin told me. "I found it easier talking with him than I do with my own father," he added.

I felt sorry for him. At least I had someone who wanted the same things for me that I wanted for myself, someone encouraging me, standing beside me. Balwin was far lonelier than I had imagined, even lonelier than I was.

The next day Mama found out that Balwin had accompanied me to the hospital. She cross-examined Daddy about it and when I returned home, she started on me.

"What have you been doing with that fat boy?" she demanded.

"He's not a fat boy anymore, Mama. He's still trimming down nicely and—"

"Oh, I don't care about none of that. What's going on, Ice?"

Reluctantly, I revealed that our practicing for the audition had continued and she went off on me like she never had before, screaming at the top of her voice, tossing things around the kitchen, straining her neck and her eyes to the point of bursting blood vessels.

"First, where we ever going to find the money for such nonsense, and second, how am I supposed to handle your father with you gone, huh? You can forget all that talk about going to some fancy school and stop wasting everyone's time, Ice. I'm going to need you right here."

I didn't argue with her, but that didn't stop her. She threatened to complain to Daddy about it. She even promised to tell him to stay in the hospital if I was going to leave for some school. Terrified of what damage she would do, I finally promised her I would stop practicing and cancel the audition. She was satisfied and calmed down, but slowly, muttering to herself almost until she fell asleep.

I told Balwin the next day. He tried to argue with me, but I wouldn't listen.

"We've only got one more week, Ice. Don't give up now," he pleaded.

I shook my head.

"It was silly of me to do this, Balwin, and wrong of me to waste your time too. I'm sorry. It's all so impossible, don't you see?"

"No," he said.

"Well it is," I told him and left.

I went home and put my music sheets away, took care of the chores in the house and made dinner, but Mama didn't come home for dinner. I ate alone. I thought she might have gone to the hospital and went as soon as I had cleaned up, but she wasn't there. I tried not telling Daddy about her, but he could read my face as if my thoughts were behind a glass wall.

"The woman's just frustrated," he said. "Don't fret about her. She'll be all right once I'm out of here," he promised. "How's your work going with Balwin? It's getting close to that time, right?"

I called on all my powers to hide the truth, but there was something so strong between Daddy and myself that he could feel the vibrations in my body. His eyes grew small with suspicion.

"Ice?"

"It's foolish to waste time on something like this, Daddy. Where are we going to get the money and you'll need me for a while. Maybe—"

"Ice," he nearly shouted. He was in a wheelchair and we were in the corner of the recreation room in the therapy area. Some people looked our way for a moment. Daddy reached out and seized my hand.

"You don't know what this has come to mean to me," he began. "I put all my dreams in you. All my disappointments are piled up and waiting to be crushed. You're the hope, honey. I watched you grow into this, take on the music like some magnificent, beautiful gown and go strutting across the stage. You've brought me the only joy I've had these years. And you're just starting. I know it, Ice. I know it in here," he said holding his hand over his heart. "Don't give up on me now.

"Don't be me," he declared firmly. "You go right home from here and you go into my third dresser drawer. You lift the clothes in the right corner and you take out that trumpet mouthpiece, understand?

"You hold it tightly in your hand and you think of me selling my trumpet and spending my whole life wondering 'what if?' And you take that mouthpiece with you to the audition. Do it for me and forget all the rest.

"Will you? Will you?"

"Yes, Daddy," I promised.

He reached out and touched the tear zigzagging down my cheek.

And he smiled.

"You're melting, Ice," he said laughing, "and it's just fine.

"Just fine."

Epilogue

—⁓—

Balwin drove me. We had asked and been given permission for him to be my accompanist. Mama knew nothing about it. She thought I was going to school as usual and then going to visit Daddy.

I think my heart pounded all the way to New York City. When we arrived at the little theater, I was so terrified, I couldn't move my legs. I looked at Balwin and he laughed.

"I've seen stage fright and I've seen stage fright," he said, "but you've got stage terror."

"It's not funny, Balwin. I'm going to make a fool of myself," I cried.

"Then you'll make one of me, too," he declared firmly. He held out his hand and I got out of the car. "Take a deep breath," he said. "Close your eyes and take a deep breath. Go on. Relax yourself. This is nothing. If she doesn't like you, it's her loss, not yours."

"Right," I said. "Sure."

He laughed and we entered the theater. It was so quiet and empty, I thought we had come on the wrong day. Suddenly, a tall, thin dark-haired woman emerged from the shadows, her heels clicking on the tile floor of the small lobby.

"Are you this Ice Goodman?" she asked holding a paper in her right hand. She had large brown eyes and a sharp nose, so pointed at the tip, I thought she could cut steak with it.

"Yes," I said.

"You're ten minutes early, but that's fine. Madam Senetsky is in the theater. And this is your accompanist?" she asked nodding at Balwin.

"Balwin Noble," Balwin said extending his hand. She simply looked at it and nodded.

"Go right to the stage and begin," she ordered, turned and retreated into the theater.

"Ready?" Balwin asked.

"No," I said.

"Good," he said and led the way.

It was dark except for some small light on the stage. It took a moment for my eyes to get used to the auditorium. At first I thought there was no one there and then I saw someone sitting all the way in the rear.

Balwin continued down the aisle to the piano. He sat, set out the music and looked at me. Then he nodded at the stage.

"Just do it as we have been," he said.

I looked back toward the woman in the rear. She was like a manikin. I couldn't make out much detail, but I saw that her hair was pulled tightly up into a coiled chignon at the top of her head, a little toward the rear where it was clipped. Why weren't there more people here, I wondered, and where was that tall, sour-looking woman who had greeted us?

Shaking, I stepped up onto the stage. Balwin had me do a quick warm-up and then I looked at him and he nodded. I took a deep breath and he began.

I sang as best I could. As I went on, I felt myself relax and I thought only of the song itself and then, as if by magic, I thought I saw Daddy sitting in the first row, looking up and me and smiling.

And in his hand was his trumpet mouthpiece.

I did my second piece, too. No one spoke to us afterward. In fact, the elderly woman was gone when I stepped off the stage. We stood for a while and then realized no one was going to talk to us, so we started out, looked in the lobby and found no one.

"Why couldn't someone at least thank us for coming or say good-bye?" I muttered.

Balwin shook his head.

"I guess they don't thank you. You thank them," he said and we left.

He was very quiet most of the way home. I knew what he was thinking. It was a disaster. It was so bad we didn't even rate a good-bye and thanks for the effort. I felt sick to my stomach. The only thing that cheered me a bit was knowing Mama would be happy I failed. I wasn't going to tell her anything though. She would be so angry that I had gone to the audition in the first place.

I didn't forget about the audition, but all of the days right before graduation and the school year's end seemed full of small explosions and exhilaration. You could hear it in everyone's voices, how they burst with happiness and excitement. Lives were being planned. There was talk of colleges and jobs. It seemed as if a grand doorway was slowly opening for everyone to pass through into a new world, everyone but me.

Daddy made more progress with his therapy and there was talk now of his coming home. He and I didn't discuss the audition. It was left hanging in the air like some dream. I think he was afraid of my being disappointed and what that would do to him as well.

Mama carried on more about the new demands that would be made on her, but I could see she was happy about Daddy's impending return, too. With it was the promise of some sort of restoration. Daddy even added to her optimism by talking about their moving to a nicer place. He had compensation funds and he was promised a softer, easier job when he could return to work. He was, after all, something of a hero to the company.

When I had filled out my application, I had indicated I wanted Madam Senetsky to respond to Mr. Glenn at the school. I was afraid of anything arriving at the apartment and Mama finding it first. Finally, three days before the last day of school, the principal called me to his office. Mr. Glenn was there, too. The moment I walked in, I knew something astounding had occurred. Their faces radiated with congratulations.

I read the letter of acceptance signed by Madam Senetsky twice before really absorbing it. Once more in my life, I was muted, unable to speak. They laughed and congratulated me again. Mr. Glenn had Balwin called to the office. When he heard what had happened, he started to cry. It wasn't sobbing; it was just the emergence of some tears he quickly flicked away.

He and I left the building with the principal's permission and Balwin drove me to the hospital. Daddy was doing some upper body exercises in his wheelchair. The therapist turned when Daddy stopped and stared at us entering the therapy center.

I didn't speak.

I didn't have to speak.

What I did was hold up his trumpet mouthpiece.

He cried out and then, to the amazement of his therapist he stood up and took a few unassisted steps toward me. I ran into his arms.

"Mama will be furious," I said.

"So what's new about that?" he replied and we laughed.

"How can we do it, Daddy?"

"We can," he insisted, "and we will. I mean, you will."

Balwin nodded in agreement.

Outside the therapy room window, on the ledge, a sparrow paraded and flapped its wings.

And I remembered a little girl, afraid to speak, finding a voice in the music, the same music that helped the sparrow lift itself away to soar in the wind.

Rose

Prologue

When I was a little girl, I thought the bogeyman was hiding in shadows, watching for an opportunity to scare or hurt me. He lived in the darkness. I saw him in the quick movement of a silhouette, heard him tiptoeing over creaky floorboards or whispering through the walls. He entered my mind through nightmares and made me whimper and cry out for my mother or my father.

When I grew older and wiser, I realized the bogeyman is not in the shadows, not in the darkness outside. He is in the hearts of evil people, selfish and envious people, and they urge him to frighten or hurt us. They whisper our names into his ear and point him in our direction.

And the only weapon we have against him is the power of love. We can turn it on him like a great light and chase him back into the evil hearts that gave him life.

It was a lesson I learned painfully. It took away my innocence and my trusting heart. It made me cautious and skeptical. I questioned every smile, every laugh, every kind word, scrutinizing all to be sure the bogeyman wasn't somehow involved.

I had to become older, mature, and be strong.

But how I longed for my childhood faith and the simple wonder that came with the sun that woke me to every new day.

It was hard to leave all that behind.

It was the saddest good-bye of all.

1

Daddy

I always believed there was something different about my father. He was whimsical and airy, light of foot and so smooth and graceful, he could slip in and out of a room full of people without anyone realizing he was gone. I don't think I ever saw him depressed or even deeply concerned about anything, no matter how dark the possibilities were. He lost jobs, had cars repossessed, saw his homes go into foreclosure. Twice, that I knew of, he was forced to declare personal bankruptcy. There was even a time when we left one of our homes with little more than we carried on our very selves. Yet he never lost his spirit or betrayed his unhappiness in his voice.

I used to imagine him as a little boy stumbling and rolling over and over until he stopped and jumped right to his feet, smiling, with his arms out and singing a big "Ta-da!" as if his accident was an accomplishment. He was actually expecting applause, laughter, and encouragement after a fiasco. He once told me that when he received a failing grade on a test in school, he took joy in having a bright red mark on his paper while the other, less fortunate students who happened to have passed had only the common black. Defeat was never in his vocabulary. Every mistake, every failure was merely a minor setback, and what was a setback anyway? Just an opportunity to start anew. Pity the poor successful ones who spent their whole lives in one town, in one job, in one house.

Daddy, I would learn, carried that idea even into the concept of family.

He was a handsome man in a Harrison Ford sort of way, not perfect, but surprising because his pastel blue eyes could suddenly brighten with a burst of happy energy that made his smile magnetic, his laughter musical, and his every gesture as graceful as a bull fighter's. He stood six feet one, with an unruly shock of flaxen-blond hair that somehow never looked messy, but instead always looked interesting, making someone think that here was a man who had just run a mile or fought a great fight. He was athletic-looking, trim with firm shoulders. He never had the patience or the discipline to be a good school athlete when he was young, but he was not above stopping whatever he was doing, no matter how important, and joining some teenagers in the neighborhood to play a game of driveway basketball.

Daddy's impulsiveness and childlike joy in leaping out of one persona into another in an instant annoyed my mother to no end. She always seemed embarrassed by his antics and depressed by his failures, yet she held onto him like someone clinging to a wayward sailboat in a storm, hoping the wind would die down, the rain would stop, and soon, maybe just over the horizon, there would

be sunny skies. On what she built these sails full of optimism, I never knew. Maybe that was her fantasy: believing in Daddy, a fantasy I thought belonged only to a
young and innocent daughter, me.

Or maybe it was just impossible to be anything but
optimistic around Daddy. I truly never saw him sulk and
rarely saw him look disgusted. Of course, I never saw
him cry. He wasn't even angry at the people who fired
him from his jobs or the events that turned him out of one
opportunity after another. It was always a big "Oh, well,
let's just move on."

At least we remained in one state, Georgia, crisscross-
ing and vaulting towns, cities, villages; however, it soon
became obvious that Daddy anticipated his inevitable
defeats. After a while—our second mortgage failure, I
think—we stopped buying and started renting for as
short a period as the landlords tolerated. Daddy loved
six-month leases. He called every new rental a trial
period, a romance. Who knew if it was what we wanted
or if it would last, so why get too committed? Why get
committed to anything?

Of course, Mommy flung the usual arguments at him.

"Rose needs a substantial foundation. She can't do
well in school, moving like this from place to place. She
can't make friends, and neither can I, Charles.

"And neither can you!" she emphasized, her eyebrows
nearly leaping off her face. "You don't do anything with
other men like most men do. You don't watch ball games
or go out hunting and fishing with buddies and it's no
wonder. You don't give yourself a chance to build a
friendship, a relationship. Before you see someone for the
second time, you're packing suitcases."

My father would listen as if he was really giving

all that serious thought and then he would shake his head and say something like, "There's no such thing as friends anyway, just acquaintances, Monica."

"Good. Let me at least have a long enough life somewhere to have acquaintances," Mommy fired back at him.

He laughed and nodded.

"You will," he promised. "You will."

Daddy made promises like children blow bubbles. At the first suggestion of approaching storm clouds, he blew his promises at us, perfectly shaped, rainbow-colored hopes and dreams, and stood back watching them float and bob around us. When they popped, he just reached into his bag of tricks and started a new bubble. I felt like we were all swimming in a glass of champagne.

Bursting through the front door at the end of his workday, whatever it happened to be, he cried out his wonderful "I'm home!" He bellowed like someone who expected everything would be dropped. Mommy and I would come running out of rooms with music blaring behind us. She would put down her magazine or book, or stop working on dinner. I would leap from my desk where I was doing homework or spring from the sofa where I was sprawled watching television, and we would rush into the hallway to hug him and be hugged by him.

That stopped happening so long ago, I couldn't remember if we had ever done it. Now when he bellowed his "I'm home," his voice echoed and died. He still greeted us with his big, happy smile, looking like someone who had returned from the great wars when all he had done was finish one more day of new work successfully enough not to get laid off.

At present, he was a car salesman in Lewisville,

Georgia, a small community about forty-five miles
northwest of Atlanta famous for its duck ponds and its
one industry, Lewis Foundry, which manufactures auto-
motive cast-iron braking components and employs over
seven hundred people. Small housing developments
sprouted up around it and from that blossomed retail
shops, a mall, and four automobile distributorships, one
for which, Kruegar's, Daddy worked selling vans and
suburban vehicles and Jeeps.

How Daddy found these places was always a mystery
to us, but for the past two years, which was a record, we
had been living here in a small house we rented. It was
actually the most comfortable and largest home we had
ever owned or rented. It was a Queen Anne with a gabled
roof and a front porch. It had a small backyard, an
attached garage, a half-basement, and an attic. There
were three bedrooms, a nice size dining room, a kitchen
with appliances that still functioned, and a modest living
room. Since we didn't have all that much furniture anyway, it was quite adequate for our needs, and the street
was quiet, the neighbors pleasant and friendly.

Everyone liked Daddy pretty much instantly. He was
so outgoing and amiable, always greeting them with a
smile and a hello full of interest. Daddy was a glib man.
He could stop and talk politics, economics, books and
movies, and especially hunting and fishing with anyone.
He always knew just enough to sound educated on an
issue, but not really enough for any deep analysis. He
hadn't gone to college, but he knew how to agree with
people, to anticipate what they felt and thought, and find
ways to escort them down their paths of beliefs, making
them think he was a sympathetic voice, in sync with
whatever theory or analysis they had. Mommy always

said Daddy missed his calling. He should have been a politician. He even could talk his way out of a speeding ticket. By the time he was finished, the poor policeman almost felt guilty.

Daddy's verbal skills and friendly manner did make him a good salesman. When he failed at a sales job, it wasn't because he couldn't do it. I always thought it was either because he lost interest or saw something over the horizon that attracted him more. He would slack off and eventually cause his boss to decide it would be better if Daddy moved on, and move on he did. Daddy was so agreeable, I'm sure his bosses found firing him was almost a cheerful experience.

Now, we were here, still here, hoping to stay, hoping to build a life. Mommy was permitting herself to make close friends, to join organizations, to make commitments. I was doing well in school, and since I was at the beginning of my senior year, we were expecting I would graduate at this high school. I hadn't yet decided what I wanted to do with my life. I had been in school plays and I was told I had an impressive stage presence and carried myself like a seasoned fashion model, but I knew I didn't have a strong enough voice, and I was never very comfortable memorizing lines and pretending to be someone else.

Mommy didn't pressure me to be anything special. Her advice was more along the lines of what to do with myself socially. Lately, she was more strident-sounding than ever with her warnings.

"Don't give your heart to anyone until the last moment, and then think it over three times."

Her dark pronouncements came from her own regret in having married so young and ending what she called her chance for really living before she had even started. She and Daddy had been high school sweethearts and consequently married soon after graduation, despite the admonishments of her parents, who refused to pay for any wedding. Daddy and she eloped and set up house as soon as he acquired the first of what was to be a long string of jobs.

Because of our lifestyle, I knew that Mommy now considered herself well beyond her prime. I could see it in her eyes whenever she and I went anywhere. She would take furtive glances at men to see if they were looking her way, following her movements with their eyes, showing any interest. If a younger woman pulled their attention from her, the disappointment would settle in her face like a rock in mud, and she would want to get our shopping over quickly and go home to brood.

Over the years, she had taken odd jobs working in department stores, especially in the cosmetic departments, because she was a very attractive woman. When Daddy lost his positions, Mommy would have to give up hers, no matter how well she was doing or how pleased her bosses were with her work. After this happened a number of times, Mommy simply gave up trying to work.

"What is the point?" she asked Daddy. "I won't be able to hold down the job or get promoted."

"I'd rather have you at home anyway, my homemaker, Rose's full-time mother," Daddy declared, avoiding any argument. He acted as if the added income was superfluous, when it sometimes was all we had.

Now, because we had lived in Lewisville so long, Mommy was considering returning to work. I was old enough to take care of my own needs, to help out in the house, and she had lots of free time to fill. Daddy didn't oppose her when she brought all this up now. In fact, they rarely had marital spats. Daddy was too easy for that. He would never disagree vehemently. Nothing seemed to matter that much to him, nothing deserved his raising his voice, putting on an angry face, sulking or being in the slightest way unhappy. His reaction to it all was always a shrug and a simple, "Whatever."

It had become our family motto. Whatever I wanted; whatever Mommy wanted. Whatever the world wanted of us, it was fine with Daddy. He loved that old adage, "If a branch doesn't bend, it breaks."

"How about not breaking, Charles, but not having to bend either?" Mommy asked him.

He shook his head, smiling.

"Monica, there's no place in the world where there's never a wind."

Mommy showed her frustration and started to go into a depression and brood, but Daddy would come up with that rabbit in his hat almost all the time. He would have flowers sent to her, or he would secretly buy her some new perfume or some piece of jewelry. She would shake her head and call him an idiot, but she was always too pleased to keep up her growling. In the end, Daddy's charm overwhelmed everything. I started to believe he might be right about life. There was nothing worth stress. He lived the Edith Piaf song he played when he sat quietly with his martini in the living room. *Je Regret Rien:* I regret nothing.

Whatever happened, happened. It was over and done with, in the past. Forget it. Look to the future. It was a philosophy of life that turned every rainy day into a sunny one. You put your Band-Aids on your scrapes and bruises, choked back tears, and forgot about them.

"There should be only happy tears, anyway," Daddy told me once. "What does crying get you? If you're miserable, you're defeating yourself. Laugh at life and you'll always be on top of things, Rose."

I looked at him with wonder, my Daddy, the magician who seemed incapable of *not* finding rainbows. The ease with which he captured people impressed me, but what impressed me more was the ease with which he tossed it all away or gave it up once he had succeeded. Was that ability to let go with no regret a power or a madness? I wondered. Was nothing worth holding onto at any cost? Was nothing worth tears?

It wasn't long before I had an answer.

According to Mommy, it was Daddy who insisted on naming me Rose, quoting one of his favorite Shakespearean lines, "A rose by any other name would smell as sweet." It wasn't only because he insisted I had the sweetest face of any baby born that day. He argued that a rose always brought happiness, good times, bright and wonderful things.

"What happens whenever you place a rose next to something?" he asked her in the hospital. "Huh? I'll tell you, Monica. It makes it seem more wonderful, more delicious, more enticing, and more desirable. That's what will happen every time she comes into a room or into anyone's life. That's our Rose."

Mommy said she gave in because she had never seen him so excited and determined about anything as much as he was about my name. She said my grandparents thought it was just dreadful to have a name like that on a birth certificate.

"She's a little girl, not a flower," Grandfather Wallace,

Daddy's father, had declared. He favored old names, names garnered from ancestors, but Daddy had long since lost the ties with family that most people enjoy. His father never approved of the things he did with his life. Both of his parents closed all the blinds on every window that looked out on him. They shut down like a clam, but Daddy didn't mourn the loss.

"People who drag you down, who are negative people, are dangerous," Daddy told me when I asked him about my grandparents and why we had so little to do with them. "Who needs that? Before long, they make you sad sacks, too. No sad sacks for us!" he cried and swung me around.

When I was a little girl, he was always hugging me or twirling my strawberry blond hair in his fingers, telling me that I was a jewel.

"Your eyes are two diamonds. Your hair is spun gold. Your lips are rubies and your skin comes from pearls. My Rose petal," he cried and kissed the tip of my nose. Laughter swirled in his eyes and dazzled me. Everything my daddy did was fascinating to me in those early years. He even made every meal we had a special event, assigning names and stories to each and every thing we ate. Mommy told him I laughed too much at dinner and I would have stomachaches, but Daddy didn't believe that happy things could do any harm in any way.

"Glum people have stomachaches, Monica. We don't, right, Rose?" he would ask.

Of course, I always agreed with him then. To me it seemed the right thing to do, the right way to go, the right way to be: carefree, happy, unconcerned.

"Your father just never grew up," my mother told me. "He's a little boy in a man's body. Yes, he makes people feel good, but one of these days, he's going to have to become substantial. I just hope it's soon," she would tell me.

Worry darkened her eyes. She took her deep breaths and waited, worked when she could, and made the best of every home we had, but I couldn't help feeling this same anxiety as I grew older and wiser and saw the shine begin to dull on Daddy's face and ways. Despite his attitudes and behavior, he was growing older. Gray hairs sounded small warnings and began to sprout like weeds in that flaxen cornfield. Lines were deepening under his eyes. He was less and less apt to drop everything and rush onto a basketball court to match himself against young boys. The world he had kept at bay was seeping in and under every door. He was beginning to show wear and tear. He had to search harder and harder to find ways to deny it, or avoid it.

Daddy kept his little escapes private. He did a little more drinking than Mommy liked, but he didn't do it in salons and dingy bars with degenerate friends. He kept his whiskey in a paper bag and drank surreptitiously. Even his drinking was solitary. All of his means of relaxation were. He loved to go duck hunting, but he never went with a group. He was a true loner when it came to all this. It was as if he didn't want to share those moments of doubt or admit that he needed his retreats from reality.

One weekend morning, as usual, he rose early and left the house before Mommy and I rose. He didn't leave a note or any indication about where he had gone, but it was fall and duck season, so we knew he was off to some solitary place he had discovered, some little outlet from which he could launch his rowboat and sit waiting for the

ducks. He never shot more than we could eat, and
Mommy was very good at preparing duck. She said it
made him feel like some great hunter providing for his
family. He was always saying that if we had to return to
the days of the pioneers, he was equipped to do so.

The night before he went hunting, he had come into
my room while I was doing my homework. I had started
it on a Friday night because I had been given a lot to do
over the weekend, including beginng a social studies
term paper. He stood there a while, watching me quietly,
before I realized he had entered. He smiled at my surprise.

"Daddy? What?" I asked him.

He shook his head and sat beside me on the floor with
his legs curled up under him. It had been a while since he
had done this. Unlike the parents of most of my friends,
Daddy didn't hover over me daily or even on a weekly
basis checking on my schoolwork and questioning my
social activities. In some of the houses of my school
friends, their parents behaved like FBI agents. One girl
revealed that her parents had actually bugged her telephone because they suspected she was in with a bad
crowd, and another told me her parents had hired a private detective who followed her when she went out on
dates. She said it was by pure accident that she had discovered it. She inadvertently pressed the answering
machine playback in her father's office and heard the
detective's report about her most recent date.

These parents made me feel grateful I had a father
who was so casual and trusting. Nothing I did ever displeased him greatly. He didn't yell. He never even so
much as threatened to hit me, and if my mother imposed
a punishment like "Go to your room for the night," or

"Stay in all weekend," my father would intercede to say, "She knows she's made a mistake, Monica. What's the point?"

Frustrated, my mother would throw up her hands and tell him to take charge and be responsible. Daddy would turn his big, soft eyes on me and say, "Don't get me in trouble, Rose. Please, behave." I think that plea of his, more than anything, kept me from misbehaving. It was funny how I hated the idea of Daddy ever being sad. If he should be, it would seem as if the world had come crashing down on us. I was afraid that once my daddy lost his smile, the sunshine would be gone from our lives.

"There's nothing in particular," Daddy replied to my question when he sat on the floor beside me. "But it's Friday night. How come you're not going anywhere with your friends—a movie, a dance? You're probably the most beautiful girl in the school."

"I'm going out with Paula Conrad tomorrow night, Daddy, remember? I told you and Mommy at dinner."

"Oh. Right."

He smiled.

"Just you and Paula?"

"We'll probably go to a movie and meet some other kids."

He nodded.

"And I assume other kids includes boys."

"Yes, Daddy."

"So how are you really doing these days, Rose? Are you happy here?"

A small patter of alarm began in my heart. Daddy often began a conversation this way when he was going to explain why we were about to move.

"Everything is good, Daddy. I like my teachers and

I'm doing well in my classes. You saw my first report card this year, all A's. I've never gotten all A's before, Daddy," I pointed out.

He nodded, pressing his lips tightly.

"And I was in the school plays last year, so I was thinking of going out for the big musical in the spring. The drama teacher keeps reminding me. I don't know why. I can't sing that well."

"You're the jewel, Rose. He wants his show to sparkle," Daddy said, smiling. "Don't be too humble," he warned. "Act like sheep and they'll act like wolves," he warned.

I knew he was right, but I was afraid to wish anything big for myself. I guess I've always been modest and shy. Maybe that was because I was afraid of committing myself to anything that required a long-term effort. We had been so nomadic, moving like gypsies from town to town, city to city, so often I was terrified of becoming too close to anyone or too involved in any activity. Good-byes were like tiny pins jabbed into my heart. How many times had I sat in the rear of the car looking through the back window at the home I had just known as it disappeared around a bend and was gone forever?

However, Daddy wasn't the only one who used superlatives when remarking about my looks. I should have been building up my confidence. Wherever Mommy took me, even when I was only six or seven, people complimented me on my features, my complexion, my eyes. I was often told how photogenic I was, and how I should be on the covers of magazines.

When I was about eleven, I sensed that my male teachers looked at me and spoke to me differently from the way they did the other students and especially the

other girls. I could feel the pleasure I brought merely
being in front of them. In my early teen years, my male
teachers seemed to flirt with me. Other girls with green
eyes of envy muttered about my being Mr. Potter's pet
or Mr. Conklin's special girl. They complained that I
could do no wrong in the opinion of my male teachers.
They even assumed my grades were inflated because I
knew how to bat my long, perfect eyelashes or smile
softly so that my eyes were sexy, inviting.

I suppose it was inevitable that Mommy would want
to enter me in a beauty contest. Six months after we had
arrived in Lewisville, Mommy heard about the Miss
Lewisville Foundry beauty pageant and discovered that
through some oversight there was no minimum age
requirement. She decided I could compete with women
in their late teens and twenties and filled out the application. She made Daddy ask his boss to consider sponsoring me, and I was brought to the dealership to meet Mr.
Kruegar, a balding forty-year-old man who had inherited
the business from his father. It was the first time I was
paraded in front of someone who looked at me like some
commodity, a product—in his case, like a brand-new car.
He even referred to me as he would refer to one of his
new model vehicles.

"She has the chassis. That's for sure, Charles," he
said, drinking me in from head to foot, pausing over
my breasts and my waist as if he was measuring me for
a dress. "Nice bumpers and great chrome," he added
and quickly laughed. "You're a beautiful girl, Rose. No
wonder your father's proud of you. Sure we'll sponsor
her, Charles. She's a winner and I can't get hurt by the
publicity. Not if she's going to wear a Kruegar T-shirt
and a Kruegar pin. That's for sure."

Mr. Kruegar wiped the tip of his tongue over his thick, wet lips and nodded as he continued to scrutinize me with his beady eyes. I felt like a dinner for a cannibal and wanted nothing more to do with the contest or him, but Mommy assured me he would have little to do with what happened.

"You probably won't see him again until the actual event," she promised.

With a good budget now for my preparations, Mommy set out to buy me an attractive evening dress, a new bathing suit, and a pretty blouse and skirt outfit. The contest took only one day. Like the Miss America pageant, there was the question and answer period, which at least pretended an interest in our minds as well as our bodies. Then there was the swimsuit competition, and finally, the evening when we could sing, read poems, dance, whatever. I did a Hawaiian folk dance I learned off a videotape Mommy had bought. After we were all finished with our talent show, we paraded in front of the judges for the final evaluation, supposedly based upon poise and grace.

I knew the older women were infuriated that I had been entered. None of them were friendly. As it turned out, a woman named Sheila Stowe won the title. I was first runner-up. Everyone in the audience, except Sheila's family, thought I was cheated because Sheila, as it turned out, was a relative of the Lewis family.

After the contest, people insisted on calling me Ms. Lewisville Foundry or just Miss Foundry whenever they saw me. They sympathized with my mother, cajoling and insisting I was the true beauty of Lewisville. I can't say it didn't put daydreams in my head. I began to imagine myself on the covers of the biggest and most glamorous magazines, eventually developing products under my name. I started to think of elegance and style more seriously, and began to dare ambition.

"I'm expecting you to become someone very special, Rose," Daddy told me as he sat there in my room. "I have high hopes. I know that I haven't exactly made things easy for you and your mother, but," he said, smiling, "you're like some powerful, magnificent flower plowing itself up between the rocks, finding the sunshine and blooming with blossoms richer than those of flowers in perfectly prepared gardens. Just believe in yourself," he advised.

Daddy hardly ever spoke so seriously to me. It kept my heart thumping.

"I'll try, Daddy," I said.

"Sure you will. Sure," he said. He played with the loose ends of my bedroom floor rug for a moment, holding his soft, gentle smile. "I guess I never had much faith in myself. I guess I move on so much because I'm afraid of making too much of an investment in anything. It would make failure look like failure," he said, looking up, "instead of just a temporary setback I can ignore.

"Don't be like me, Rose. Dig your heels into something and stick with it, okay?"

"Okay, Daddy," I said.

He stood up, leaned over, and kissed me on the forehead, twirling my hair in his forefinger and reciting: "Your eyes are two diamonds. Your hair is spun gold. Your lips are rubies and your skin comes from pearls. My Rose petal."

He laughed, kissed me again, and walked out.

I never heard his voice again or his laugh or bathed in his happy smile.

2

Gone

Mommy was up almost as early as Daddy Saturday morning. When I came down to breakfast, she told me she must have just missed him. She was sitting at the table, flipping the pages of her cookbook, searching for a new and interesting recipe for duck.

"I'm tired of having duck, but if we don't eat what he brings home, he'll make me feel like I've committed a sin, having him kill a duck for nothing."

"You always make it delicious, Mommy," I said.

"Um," she replied, her eyes on the recipe she had found. "I've got to go to the supermarket to get some of these ingredients."

"I'm going to the movies tonight with Paula Conrad," I reminded her.

She nodded, half-listening.

"Mommy. Daddy didn't say anything about us having to move soon, did he?" I asked, and she brought her head up so fast, I thought she would snap her neck.

"No, why?"

"I don't know. He was talking so . . ."

"What?"

"Seriously. I just got that feeling," I said.

"I won't go. I won't," she insisted. "This time, I'm going to plant my feet in cement. I've got an interview with Mr. Weinberg who owns that insurance agency on Grant Street. He's looking for a receptionist and book-keeper and I can make a good salary. I won't go.

"Besides," she continued, "you've got to finish your senior year here. Did he actually suggest moving?"

I shook my head.

"It was just a feeling I got, Mommy."

"Um," she said, her eyes narrowing with suspicion. "I should be wary. Whenever he starts going off by himself regularly on weekends and increases his drinking, it usually means something. No one can blame me for being paranoid," she added.

She sat there, pensive for a long quiet moment, and then she slammed her palm down on the table so hard, she made the dishes jump and clang.

"I'm not going and that's final."

She rose and marched out of the kitchen before I could even try to calm her down. I felt guilty for putting her ill at ease and probably clawing and barking at Daddy the moment he returned from hunting. All day long she built up her fury. I could see it in the brightening fire in her eyes and could hear it in the way she pounded through the house, slammed doors, and ran the vacuum cleaner. She was pressing down so hard on the handle, I was sure she was sucking up the very foundation of the house.

Early in the afternoon, she set out for the supermarket. She asked me to go along. I was afraid even to hesitate. It was an unusually warm day for late October, with just a few puffs of cotton white clouds barely moving across the turquoise sky. The world looked so vibrant, all the colors sharp and rich in the grass, the flowers, the picket fences. Days like this encouraged people to wash their cars, cut their lawns, paint and spruce up their homes. The freshness and the sharpness around us underscored how good we both felt about our present home and how much we wanted to hold on to it.

"How could he even dare to contemplate a move now?" Mommy muttered.

Once again, I emphasized that I didn't know he was for sure. It was just a feeling.

She looked at me and nodded, convinced of the worst possible scenario.

"He is," she said. "You're right on it. I live in denial most of the time and ignore all the signals until they're plopped right in my face.

"I'll make him a duck dinner," she fumed, making it sound more like a threat. "I'll make him a duck dinner he'll never forget."

She carried her fury into the supermarket and stomped around the aisles, pushing the cart like a lawn mower, plowing anyone in her way to the right or to the left before they had to meet her head-on. When anyone said hello, she fired her hello back as if they had cursed her. Her reply of "I'm fine, thank you very much," was almost a challenge to declare otherwise. I saw some people shake their heads as we continued by.

At the checkout counter, Jimmy Slater gave me his usual big grin as he packed my mother's groceries.

"How's Miss Lewisville Foundry today?" he asked me.

"I'm not Miss Lewisville Foundry," I said for the hundredth time.

"You are to me," Jimmy insisted.

My mother glanced at him with her eyes askance and almost smiled at me as we headed out to the car. At home I helped her unpack and put away our groceries, and then I went up to my room to continue my homework. Around five o'clock, I expected to hear Daddy's Jeep pulling into the driveway with its usual squeal of tires. I leaned toward my window, which faced the front of our house, and looked down, anticipating his arrival any moment. At five-fifteen, I heard Mommy pacing in the downstairs hallway.

"If that man expects a duck dinner tonight, he'd better be here in five minutes," she declared. "I don't serve greasy duck. It takes a few hours to make it right."

She pounded back to the kitchen and then, twenty minutes later, she returned to the living room to look out the front windows. I came down the stairway and stood in the living room doorway. She was standing there, her arms folded, glaring at the street. For a long moment, neither of us moved or spoke. Then she turned and looked at me, her face twisted with anxiety and anger.

"I don't know why I'm surprised. Why should time matter to a man like that now? It never has before," she said.

I glanced at the miniature grandfather clock on the mantel above our small fireplace. It was now five-forty-five. Twilight deepened. Shadows were spreading like broken egg yolks over the street.

"You go make yourself something to eat. I know you're going to the movies," Mommy told me.

I nodded and went to the kitchen, but I had very little appetite. My anxiety over what would go on when Daddy returned had turned my stomach into a ball of knotted string. Every once in a while my heart would pitter-patter like a downpour of rain against a window.

Six o'clock came and went and still we were waiting for Daddy's Jeep to pull in. Mommy came into the kitchen and banged some pots and pans and then started to put things away.

"If he thinks I'm going to make a duck dinner now, he's got another think coming," she muttered.

At six-thirty, Mommy's lines of anger began to slip and slide off her face to be replaced by folds of anxiety and concern in her forehead. Small flashes of panic lit her eyes as she walked back to the front windows.

"Where is he?" she cried.

When the phone rang, we both looked at it for a moment. Then I lifted the receiver. It was Paula, telling me she would be by to pick me up at ten after seven. I looked at Mommy. I couldn't leave her until Daddy had arrived, I thought.

"I can't go, Paula."

"What? Why not? We're supposed to be meeting Ed Wiley and Barry Burton. We practically promised, Rose."

"I can't go. My father hasn't gotten home yet from hunting ducks and we're worried about him," I said.

She was silent.

"Oh, go to the movies," Mommy said. "You're not going to do me any good sitting here and clutching your hands. I'll eat something and watch television. I'm sure he's just gone a little farther this time."

"Why wouldn't he call us, Mommy?"

"Why? Why? Don't start asking me why your father does this or that. We'll be here forever thinking of answers. Go on. Be with your friends."

"Are you sure?"

"Yes," she insisted.

"Okay, Paula," I said. "Come on over to get me."

"Good," Paula said and hung up before I could change my mind.

I didn't see how I was going to have a good time, but I went up to fix my hair and put on some makeup. At seven o'clock, Mommy hovered over a plate of cold salmon and some salad, but she had eaten very little.

"Two hours late, Mommy."

"I can read a clock, Rose. When he comes through that door, I'm going to hit him over the head with it, in fact," she threatened. I knew it was a very empty threat. When he came through that door, all the air she was holding in her lungs would be released and all the tension in her body would fly out. We both spun as if we were on springs when we heard a car pull into the driveway.

"See if that's him," she ordered, and I went out to look. It was only Paula arriving a little early.

Paula was tall and slim with long dark brown hair and round hazel eyes. She was the captain of the girls' basketball team and very popular in school. The real reason we were going out together was that the boy she was after, Ed Wiley, was best friends with Barry Burton, who I heard was interested in me, but was very shy. Paula had practically begged me to go out with her.

"Hi," she cried enthusiastically as soon as I opened the door.

My mother stood in the hallway, her arms folded, gazing at us and forcing a smile onto her face. Paula looked from her to me and raised her eyebrows.

"Your father still not back?"

I shook my head.

"He'll be fine. Don't worry about it," Mommy assured me. "Go on. Have a good time, girls."

"Thank you, Mrs. Wallace," Paula replied instantly.

Was her budding romance so important to her that she could ignore our worries? I wondered. One look at her told me most definitely.

"Let's go," she urged, practically pulling me out the door.

I glanced back at Mommy and felt so terrible leaving her.

"Go on," she ordered in a loud whisper.

"I'll call after the movies, Mommy," I promised. She nodded and we left.

Paula babbled about the boys all the way to the theater complex. I was only half-listening. Daddy's behavior the night before had made me nervous, and his considerable lateness on top of that had practically turned me inside out.

"Stop worrying," Paula finally cried as we drew closer to the movies. "He's probably with some of his buddies in some bar. My father's done that dozens of times."

"My father hasn't," I said dryly.

She shook her head and looked at me as if I lived in a bubble.

When we arrived at the theater, the boys were waiting in the lobby. Paula went right after Ed, swooping in on him as if she was afraid to let him have a moment without her voice in his ear and her face in his eyes. He looked overwhelmed, and glanced back at Barry, who

just smiled and escorted me quietly to our seats. I liked
Barry well enough. He was a good-looking boy and
seemed very nice. His shyness was actually calming
and refreshing. Most of the boys I knew thought they
were God's gift to women and spent more time on their
coiffure, complexion, and clothes than most of the
girls.

But I was a poor date this night. Even the movie, an
exciting thriller about a woman and her seven-year-old
daughter imprisoned by a mad family after her car broke
down on an old country road, didn't keep my attention.
My mind continually drifted back to Mommy standing in
that hallway, looking so small and fragile under the cloak
of fear and anxiety. I couldn't wait for the show to end so
I could get to the pay phone to call her.

She answered on the first ring, which told me she was
hovering over the phone in anticipation.

"Mommy, isn't he back?"

"No," she said, her voice cracking. "I don't know
what to do. Should I call the police? I just know what
they'll do about it . . . nothing, I bet. A man doesn't come
home to his wife for hours. That's probably not so
uncommon, but your father hasn't done something like
this before. He's done lots of things I could wring his
neck over, but this isn't something he's done. Of course,
there's no telling if he's starting some new outrage for
me to tolerate."

I realized she was babbling to me.

"Call the police anyway, Mommy," I said. "Let them
be the ones to tell you not to worry, but at least let them
be aware of your concern."

"I don't know. It's embarrassing," she said. "But
maybe you're right. Maybe . . ."

"Do it, Mommy," I insisted.

Finally, she agreed and hung up.

I turned to the others.

"I've got to go home," I said.

"What?" Paula cried, her face practically sliding off her skull. "We're going to get some pizza and then we're going to Ed's house and . . ."

"I've got to go home," I repeated. "I'm sorry. My father hasn't come home from hunting and it's almost ten o'clock. My mother's calling the police."

"Wow!" Ed said.

"Oh pooh," Paula groaned.

"I'll take her home. You two go for pizza," Barry said.

"Really? Okay," Paula said quickly. She scooped her arm into Ed's. "We'll just go ahead in my car." She practically tugged him out of the movie lobby.

"Thanks," I told Barry.

We left the theater quickly.

"I'm sorry to spoil everyone's good time," I said after we got into his car.

"No problem. There'll be other good times," he replied and I understood why I liked him. He wasn't really shy. He had a more mature way about him, a quieter, far more self-assured manner than most of the boys in my class. He was a contender for valedictorian, only half a percentage point separating him from Judy McCarthy, a girl the other students called "Dot Com" because of her computer-like brain and zero personality.

Barry tried his best to reassure me as we drove to my house. He talked about duck hunters who lost track of time, uncles of his who went to such out-of-the-way places for their secret spots it took half a day to get back.

"Maybe your dad just met up with one of the old-

timers here who took him to his special pond or whatever. Some of these guys travel hundreds of miles to
shoot a duck."

"You don't go hunting?" I asked him.

He shook his head.

"I fish a little, but I've never been into guns. My father
wishes I was. He'd like me to go with him, but I never
took to it. Bugs, mud, ugh," he said, and I had my first
smile since Daddy hadn't arrived at five.

I thanked Barry and got out of his car quickly when
we pulled into my driveway. I could see that Daddy's
Jeep was still not there.

"I'll call you," Barry shouted as I hurried to the door.

I waved back at him and practically lunged into the
house.

Mommy was in the living room staring at the wall. I
caught my breath and waited.

"I phoned the police and it was just as I expected.
They told me he'd have to be gone longer for them to
consider it any sort of police matter. I asked how long
and the dispatcher said longer. He wouldn't give me a
specific time."

She lifted her hands, palms up.

"What do we do?"

"What can we do, Mommy? We wait," I said and sat
beside her.

She took my hand and rocked a bit and then she
leaned against me and we both sat there, our hearts
pounding as one, waiting in silence.

"Put on the television set," Mommy said after a while.
"I need something to distract me."

I did. We gazed at the picture, heard the voices of
the actors, but it all ran together. Near midnight,

Mommy fell asleep beside me. I rose to turn off the television set when I saw the car headlights pulling into our driveway. My heart did flip-flops. *Daddy,* I thought. *Finally.*

But when I stepped up to the window, I saw it wasn't Daddy. It was a police car, with the emblem on the side identifying it as a Georgia State Police vehicle. Two officers stepped out, put on their hats, and walked toward our front door. For a moment, I couldn't move; I couldn't breathe. I just watched them approaching. Then I turned to Mommy. I thought I said, "Mommy," but she didn't stir and I wasn't sure if I had spoken or shouted in my own mind.

The sound of the door buzzer made her eyelids flutter. The policemen pressed the buzzer again and Mommy opened her eyes, looked at me, and sat up.

"Was that our front door?"

"Yes, Mommy," I said. I couldn't swallow.

"Well, who would be here at this hour?"

I glanced out the window and then back at her.

"It's the police, Mommy."

"The police?"

She smothered a cry. She seemed frozen. Her hand hovered near her throat. Something horrible exploded in my heart just watching her reactions.

"Go," she finally managed to utter.

I went quickly to the door and opened it. They had their hats off again. Both looked so tall and impressive, larger than life, beyond reality, like two characters who had emerged from the televison program we were barely watching.

"Is this the home of Charles Wallace?" the slightly taller one on the right asked me.

"Yes."

"Is Mrs. Wallace here?"

"Yes." I'm glad they didn't ask another question. I didn't think I could say more.

They stepped in and I backed up. The second patrolman closed the door behind him.

"May we speak with her?" the first patrolman asked me.

I nodded and went to the living room doorway. They followed.

"Mrs. Charles Wallace?" he asked.

Mommy nodded—slightly, stiffly. Quickly, I went to her side and she reached up for my hand.

The patrolman approached us. In the light his face looked pale, his eyes two ebony marbles.

"I'm sorry, ma'am, but your husband appears to have been in a serious hunting accident. A few hours ago, a farmer out in Granville Lake called the local police to report a row boat with a man slumped in it."

A long sighed escaped from Mommy's choked throat. She swayed and would have fallen forward, if I hadn't held tightly to her hand.

"The patrolman on the scene reported what looked like a gun accident, ma'am. Searching for identification, he came up with your husband's license and other items. He had a fatal wound in his chest area. I'm sorry," the patrolman said.

"My husband . . . is . . . dead?" Mommy asked. She had to hear the definite words.

"I'm very sorry," he replied, nodding. "It's too early to tell, but preliminary examination suggests he was killed instantly and some time before he was discovered."

"I called the police to report him being very late,"

Mommy said, as if that should have prevented it. "They told me I would have to wait longer."

The patrolman nodded.

"Yes, ma'am. What we have here is an unattended death, ma'am, so there is a mandatory autopsy."

My legs finally gave out on me and I crumpled to the sofa and sat beside her. Mommy just stared at the two patrolmen.

"Maybe there's someone you should call," the second patrolman directed to me.

I shook my head.

"Someone will be here in the morning to tell you more," the first patrolman continued. "Is there anything we can do for you at the moment?"

Mommy shook her head.

I didn't feel myself. I thought I had turned into pure air and a breeze would come along and simply scatter me everywhere. My daddy was dead? He wasn't coming home for his duck dinner. He was never coming home again. Mommy and I were alone forever.

The second patrolman stepped forward and held out a plastic bag with Daddy's personal things in it. I saw his wallet, his watch, and his wedding ring. Mommy just looked up at it. I reached out and took it.

"We located his vehicle about a mile upstream," the patrolman said after I took the bag. "After we examine it, we'll have it brought back."

"This is very unfortunate, ma'am. Did your husband go out by himself, do you know, or did he go with some-one else?" the first patrolman asked softly.

Suddenly, I felt we really were in a television movie. The police were trying to determine if Daddy's death was truly accidental.

"Himself," Mommy managed to utter.

"You're positive, ma'am?"

"He didn't go out with anyone," I said sharply.

The patrolman nodded.

"Was he upset when he left today?" he continued.

"Upset?" My mother smiled. "No, not Charles. Not Charles, never upset."

They stood there silently. What were they after? What were they trying to say?

"What could have happened?" I asked.

The second patrolman shook his head.

"He could have tripped and accidentally discharged the gun," he suggested. "It's not the most uncommon thing to happen."

"It's never wise to go out alone," the first patrolman said, as if we could learn an important lesson from this.

"Tripped?" my mother muttered.

"Well, we did find he was drinking some, ma'am. There was a bottle of bourbon in the boat. Guns and whiskey just don't mix," he added. Another valuable lesson.

Mommy just stared up at him. I looked at the floor. The words were all jumbling in my mind, stacking up and sprawling out like some product on an assembly line in the Lewis Foundry going awry.

"You're sure there's nothing we can do for you?" the second patrolman asked.

Mommy shook her head, her eyes so glassy they looked fake.

"Please accept our condolences, ma'am."

They stood there a moment and then both turned and walked out the door. We heard them open the front door and close it behind them. I looked down at the plastic bag containing Daddy's things in my hand. Mommy followed my eyes and stared at it, too.

She reached out and took the bag, plucking the ring gently from the bag and turning it in her fingers.

"Charles," she said and she started to sob, deep rasping sobs emerging from her throat, but no tears yet from her eyes. It was all taking hold slowly, but firmly, the realization, the reality that this was not some nightmare. This had just happened.

I saw the words and the thoughts forming in her eyes.

Her husband was gone.

I took a deep breath. I had to let reality in, too. I had to let the thought take shape.

My daddy was gone.

3

—∾—

Secrets

After my daddy's death, the nightmares and bleak thoughts that had shadowed our lives for so long finally took more solid shapes and crossed over the line between the darkness and the light. One discovery after another descended on our small, fragile world with the force of a sledgehammer. Mommy made the shocking discovery that Daddy had neglected to pay his life insurance premiums. Somewhere along the rough and uneven line of our lives, he had simply overlooked it, or in his inimitable fashion had decided, why worry about dying?

Thinking back now, I realized we never spoke much about death in our house. My father had become so estranged from his parents that he didn't attend his own father's funeral. He did go to his mother's, but he didn't take me or my mother along. It was almost just another business trip because he attached an interview with a prospective new employer to his itinerary and when he returned had nothing to say about his relatives.

My mother's parents had long since disowned her and put all their attention and love into her younger brother and sister. She tried to restore a relationship, but my grandfather was a stubborn, unforgiving man whose reply and philosophy was "You made your bed. Now lie in it."

I had only vague memories of both of them, and the one picture Mommy had of her father was of him staring at the camera, almost daring it to capture his image. Mommy told me he didn't believe in smiling for pictures because it made him look insubstantial and foolish, and he hated being thought anything but important. Looking at him in the picture frightened me so much, I had nightmares.

Neither he nor my grandmother responded to the announcement of my father's death and more importantly didn't offer any assistance. It compounded my mother's sorrow and laid another heavy rock on her chest.

The only time I could actually recall my father talking about death was when he said, why talk about it?

"As I see it, there are things over which you have some control and things over which you don't, Rose. Just forget about the ones you don't. Pretend they don't exist and it won't bother you," he told me.

However, for us, that translated into all sorts of big problems—beginning with no money for a real funeral, a grave site, or a tombstone. When Mommy lamented about these things, I wondered why she had permitted it to happen, too. Why hadn't she insisted on facing realities? Why hadn't she seen to it that these things were addressed? Why did she bury her head in the sand Daddy poured around us? I wanted to scream at her, demanding to know why she had put up with all of this irresponsibility.

But how do you ask such questions and say such hard things to a woman who looked like she was being dragged over hot coals by a cruel and indifferent Fate? Was there any way to have such a sensible conversation with someone who looked stunned, who barely could eat or talk or dress herself in the morning? She was always a woman who paid attention to her appearance, and now, she didn't care how washed-out and haggard she looked.

Fortunately for us, Mr. Kruegar decided he would pay Daddy's salary for two more months and help with the funeral costs. Apparently, he really did like Daddy and enjoyed his company at the dealership. As soon as the news of Daddy's death was out, Mr. Kruegar was the first one to come calling, and that was when he made all these offers.

"We got a lot of new business out of sponsoring you in the beauty contest," he told me as we all sat in our living room. It was so still and quiet, it did seem as if the world had been put on pause. "I'm glad your father asked me to do it."

I simply stared at him. *How could he talk about something like that at this horrible time?* I wondered.

He smiled at Mommy. She nodded, but she looked like she would nod at anything, even if he merely cleared his throat.

"You know, next month is Kruegar's twenty-fifth anniversary. I'm thinking of having a big celebration. Refreshments, balloons, little mementos to give out, special discounts on the new cars and used cars, stuff like that. I'm going to have the local television network there and a radio station broadcasting from my site. I'd like you to come down and be one of my hostesses," he told me. "Maybe you could wear that beauty contest swimsuit and do that hula-hula dance you did. You'll be on television.

"I'll pay you a hundred dollars a day that weekend," he added.

Mommy raised her eyebrows and looked at me.

"I don't feel much like parading around in a bathing suit and dancing, Mr. Kruegar."

"Oh, I know that. Not now, but next month. Give it some thought, okay? I'd like to do what I can to help you people. I'll miss him. Great guy, great salesman. Broke a record in March, you know. I gave him that thousand dollar bonus for it."

He turned to Mommy, but she shook her head and I realized Daddy had never told her. I wondered why. I think Mr. Kruegar realized it, too, because he suddenly looked embarrassed and made his excuses to leave.

Some of my school friends came to visit and a few of the women Mommy had gotten to know and be friendly with brought baskets of fruit and flowers, some coming with their husbands, but most coming alone. Everyone wanted to know what we were going to do now, but few came right out and actually asked. I think they were afraid she might ask them for help.

Mommy was still considering going to work at the insurance company. We were in very bad financial condition, even with the two months' salary from Mr. Kruegar, because Daddy's income really came from commissions. We had little in a savings account and all our regular expenses loomed above and around us like big old trees threatening to crush us. In the evenings Mommy would sift through her possessions, considering what she could sell to raise some money. I felt so terrible about it, I offered to quit school and get a job myself. Of course, she wouldn't hear of it.

"You're so close to graduation, Rose. Don't be stupid."

"Well, how are we going to manage, Mommy?" I asked. "Bills are raining down around us like hail."

"We'll get by, somehow," she said. "Other people who suffer similar tragedies do, don't they?" she asked. It sounded too much like another of Daddy's promises floating in a bubble. I didn't reply, so her worrying continued.

At first she didn't tell me about her desperate pleas to her father, how she had belittled herself, and had accepted his nasty descriptions of her and of Daddy just to see if she could get him to advance her some money. In the end he relented and sent a check for a thousand dollars, calling it charity and saying since he would give this much to the Salvation Army, he would give this much to us. But he left it pretty clear that Mommy shouldn't ask him for another nickel. He told her he thought struggling, suffering, would be the best way for her to understand fully what a mess she had made with her life by not listening to him. It was more important for him to be right than generous and loving. When she finally broke down and told me all of it, she was shattered.

"I used to love him," she moaned as if that had been something of an accomplishment.

"Doesn't everyone love their fathers?" I asked.

"No," she said with her lips twisting and writhing with her pain. "There are some fathers you just can't love, for they don't want your love. They see showing emotion as weakness. I can't even remember him kissing me, whether it was good night, good-bye or on my birthday."

I decided Daddy had been correct about people like that: just cut them away as you would cut away so much swamp grass and keep your boat surging forward.

After the funeral and the period of bereavement, I returned to school. The night before I told Mommy that I had decided I was going to pretend Daddy wasn't gone. He was just on some sales trip. I was doing what he always did when he was faced with unpleasant events and problems, I decided. I was ignoring death. She became angry as soon as I finished telling her.

"I won't let you," she said. "You're not going to fall into the same traps I fell into, traps he set with his promises and his happy-go-lucky style. I let him mesmerize me, bedazzle and beguile me until I became too much like him. Look what it's gotten me!" she cried, her arms out. She turned to the mirror. "I'm old beyond my years because of all this worry and trouble.

"No, Rose. No. Your father is dead and gone. You must accept the truth, accept reality, and not live in some make-believe world as he did, and as I permitted myself to live in as well. Now we have to find ways to make the best of our lives without him.

"I'm sure wherever he is, he's belittling what happened to him and telling other souls to forget it. He's telling them they can't do anything about it, so just say, 'Whatever' and play your harp. He's probably looking for ways to move on to another heaven or hell for that matter, trying to get himself thrown out," she said. She smiled, but she was crying real tears, too.

I hugged her and promised not to ignore reality anymore. She forced me to confront it dramatically that night by helping her box all of his things, most of which she had decided to donate to charity.

"If we only made enough money to use it as a write-off," she muttered.

I hated folding his clothes and stuffing them in cartons. The scent of his cologne was still on most of them, and when the aroma entered my nostrils, it stirred pictures of him in my mind and the sound of his voice in my ears. I worked with Mommy, but I cried and sobbed, especially when I felt him twirling my hair and heard him reciting, "Your eyes are two diamonds. Your hair is spun gold. Your lips are rubies and your skin comes from pearls. My sweet Rose."

Closing the cartons was another way to say, "Good-bye, Daddy. Good-bye."

When we were nearly finished with the clothes in the closet, Mommy found a manila envelope under two boxes of old shoes in the far corner. She opened it and pulled out an eight by ten black and white photograph of a young woman. There was nothing written on the photograph or on the back of it and nothing else in the envelope.

"Who's this?" she wondered aloud, and I looked at the picture with her.

"You don't know?"

She shook her head.

The picture was of a woman who looked to be in her twenties. I couldn't tell the color of her hair, but it was either light brown or blond. She had a very pretty face with a button nose and sweet, full lips. There was a slight cleft in her chin. She had her hair cut and styled with strands sweeping up about her jawbone and she had high cheek bones with a smooth forehead. She looked very happy, as happy as someone who had found some great contentment in her life. There was that peacefulness in her eyes.

"She's no relative of mine, and I don't believe she's a relative of his," Mommy mused aloud. "Of course, she might be a cousin I never met, but why wouldn't he have ever shown me her picture?"

In the background we could just make out what looked like a large plantation house, a Greek revival with the grand pillars and style that were characteristic of some of the wealthier estates around Atlanta.

"Well," Mommy concluded with a deep sigh, "it doesn't surprise me that he never showed me the picture. Just another thing he didn't think mattered, I suppose."

She put it aside and we finished the work. I thought about the picture before I went to sleep and then I shrugged it off just the way Mommy had, thinking of Daddy's favorite word, "Whatever."

Barry Burton had called and visited me during the bereavement period, and he was there to greet me at my locker when I returned to school in the morning.

"Before you stumble on the gossip," he told me, "I want you to be prepared."

"What gossip?"

"There's talk your father deliberately killed himself, committed suicide."

I felt the hot tears of fury and pain forming under my lids. What right did anyone have making up such stories about him and why did they care anyway? Were they all so desperate for gossip? Or was it just the girls who despised me for being more attractive than they were? All these little jealousies were like termites eating away the foundation of any friendships in this place, I thought. I hated them all.

"If anyone does dare to say that in front of me . . ."

"Someone *will* do it just to get you upset, I'm sure," he warned. I could tell from his tone that he more than anticipated it. It hit me as sharply as a rock in the forehead when I gazed into his eyes.

"It's Paula, isn't it?" I asked.

He nodded.

"Why?"

He shrugged.

"She's been telling people about how it was when she went over to your house to pick you up that night, things she supposedly felt or heard."

"That's all a lie!"

He looked down.

"I think," he said softly, "that Ed was more interested in you than he was in her, and she learned that after we left them together. It didn't sit well with her. Remember English class and Shakespeare . . . 'Hell hath no fury like a woman scorned.' "

"This isn't English class and I don't care what Shakespeare or anyone else wrote. It's me and my family that's being scorned."

Was being attractive a curse or a blessing? Would I never have a close girlfriend because of that?

"I don't know where she got the idea that I cared for Ed Wiley anyway. If he has a crush on me, that's not my fault. I never encouraged him, Barry."

He smiled.

"I'm glad," he said. "Don't worry about it. Ignore her as best you can."

"Whatever," I said.

"Pardon?"

"Nothing. I've got to get to class."

"Right."

I know he stayed at my side as much as he could that day in hopes of preventing any problems, as well as because he really wanted to be with me. As it turned out, Paula was only a cowardly whisperer. She didn't have the courage to say anything aloud, especially anywhere near me, but I could tell from the way many of the students she had spoken to were looking at me and whispering that she had been spewing her verbal poison all around me. I was the one who eventually had to confront her, and confront her I did at the end of the day.

I walked up to her quickly as she was leaving the building and I scooped my arm under hers, pulling her to the side. She was so shocked she could barely resist. I knew she was athletic and more physical than I was, but I was driven by such rage, I think I could have broken her into pieces. She knew it, too, and didn't challenge me.

"I know you've been saying things about my family and my father, Paula. If you do it again, I'll rip out your tongue," I said so calmly, my eyes so fixed on hers, she could barely breathe.

She started to stutter an excuse and I put my hand flatly on her chest.

"Don't do it again," I said, digging the nail of my forefinger into her enough to make her back up. Then I walked away from her, my heart probably pounding louder and harder than hers.

Barry had seen me take her aside. He was waiting in his car to drive me home. After I got in, I told him what I had done and said and he laughed.

"You carried out a preventive strike. Good work," he

told me. "You're going to be all right, Rose. You're going to be just fine."

After we pulled into my driveway, he gave me a quick kiss before I got out of his car.

"I'll call you later," he promised. "Maybe we can do something this weekend, huh?"

"Maybe," I said.

Somewhere very deep inside me, I sensed that grief would thin out no matter how thick and terrible it had been. I would never forget Daddy of course, but in time, he would grow distant. It would be as if we had let go of each other's hands and he had drifted back, back into the shadows, back into the vault of my memory.

Spirited by my return to normal life, I was hoping Mommy would be somewhat revived in spirit when I entered the house. Soon our lives would start to resemble some of what they had been, but the moment I set eyes on her, I knew it wasn't so, not yet.

"What's wrong, Mommy?" I asked. She was sitting on the sofa staring at a dark, mute television set.

"Mr. Weinberg hired someone else for the position at his insurance agency. He said he had made the decision before your father died or he would have given it to me. He looked sincere, even sick about it, but I don't want to be hired out of charity. I want to be hired because people believe I'm qualified.

"Now what?" she asked the dark television set. "I've got to search for something I'm suitable for, and what am I experienced to do? Work in a fast-food restaurant, find a counter-girl job in a department store? They pay bare minimum wages. We can't survive on that."

She turned to me, her eyes filled with rage as well as self-pity.

"When you get married, Rose, don't put all your faith and hope in your husband. I should have developed some skill, some talent, some means of being truly independent. Who would have expected I would have to start over like some teenager at this point in my life?" she moaned.

"I should just quit school and get a job, Mommy. I can finish my high school diploma later."

"No," she said. She pulled herself up and sucked back her tears of remorse. "I've got an appointment at social services. We're entitled to some money and if we have to . . ."

I didn't want to hear the word welfare, but it lingered on her lips. I could practically see its formation.

"I'll at least look for a weekend job, Mommy. Please."

She sighed and shook her head.

"Where's your father when I need him to say his famous 'Whatever' now?"

She rose with great effort and started out.

"I'll start fixing something for dinner. Go do your homework or call a girlfriend and jabber on the phone, Rose. I don't want to see you lose your chance to live, too," she added and shuffled off.

What a sad sight she made. It left a lump of lead in my chest. I had to swallow hard to keep the tears back. Daddy had let us down so badly. Even the memory of his smile was losing its shine for me.

But I had no idea how much it would.

Not until the door buzzer sounded an hour later.

I was on my way down to set the table and see what else I could do to help Mommy, so I went right to the door and opened it. A stylish woman who looked to be in her late forties or early fifties stood there. She wore a navy blue three-button suit and had her reddish-blond hair done in a square cut with the front ends at a slant. She wore medium high heels and looked to be about five feet four or five. Her aquamarine eyes scanned me so intensely, I felt as if I was under a spotlight. She didn't smile, but her eyes were filled with interest and curiosity. Although I was absolutely sure I had never seen her before, there was something vaguely familiar about her. It came to me before I spoke. She had the same slight cleft in her chin as did the mysterious woman in the photo Mommy had found in the closet when we were packing Daddy's things for charity.

"Am I correct in assuming that this is the home of Charles Wallace?" she asked in perfectly shaped consonants and vowels, despite her thick Georgian accent.

"Yes," I replied. I looked past her and saw the late-model black town car with a chauffeur in our driveway. He sat with perfect posture, staring stiffly ahead like a manikin.

"I would like to see Mrs. Wallace," she said.

"Who's there, Rose?" Mommy called from the kitchen.

"My name is Charlotte Alden Curtis," the elegant woman told me.

I stepped back and she entered. She looked at our hallway, the walls, the ceiling as if she was deciding if anything was contaminated.

"There's someone here to see you, Mommy," I called back.

"You are the daughter," the woman said, nodding. "Yes," she added as she confirmed something in her mind after studying me a bit longer. "His daughter."

Mommy came out of the kitchen, wiping her hands on a dishtowel.

"Who is it?" she asked as she approached us.

"My name is Charlotte Alden Curtis, Mrs. Wallace," she said and looked like she expected that would mean something to Mommy.

"Oh," Mommy said, looking to me to see if I knew any more. I shook my head slightly. "Well, how can I help you?" Mommy asked.

"I have come here to tell you exactly how you can help me, Mrs. Wallace," Charlotte Alden Curtis said. "May we sit and talk someplace? I am not accustomed to holding court in a hallway."

Mommy just stared at her a moment and then snapped her head to the right, realizing the woman was waiting for a reply.

"Oh, yes, of course. Right this way," Mommy said, leading her to our living room. She nodded at the sofa where I had left a magazine and I hurried ahead to get it and pick up the glass of lemonade I had left on the center table. "Please," Mommy said nodding at the chair across from the sofa.

Charlotte Alden Curtis considered it as if she might turn down the suggestion and then sat slowly, leaning back and looking up at us. I realized we were both gaping. Mommy nudged me and we both sat on the settee.

"What is this about?" Mommy quickly inquired.

"Your husband," Charlotte replied with gunshot speed.

"My husband? Oh." Mommy's body relaxed in a slight slump. "Does he owe you money?"

Charlotte Alden Curtis lifted her eyebrows and pressed her shapely lips together so firmly, her otherwise narrow cheeks bubbled.

"I am hardly a bill collector," she said. "Are you accustomed to bill collectors in designer clothes?"

"Well, who are you? What do you want?" Mommy demanded somewhat more firmly.

"I am Angelica Alden's older sister, and what I want is justice, not money," she answered. "It has taken me some time to locate y'all. Your husband moved you people so often, apparently. Of course, I understand why.

"My nephew Evan is something of a computer wiz these days. The computer is actually a godsend when it comes to Evan. He's confined to a wheelchair as a result of a spinal deformity that affected his legs. It was Evan who finally tracked y'all after I pleaded with him to do so. He never wanted to find your husband. I'm sure he could have done it way before this," she added. She paused and looked around the living room with the same expression of utter contempt.

"I understand he's dead," she added.

"My husband passed away recently, yes," Mommy said. "Why did you want to locate him if it has nothing to do with money?"

"Passed away," Charlotte muttered instead of answering. "He passed away some time ago, as far as I am concerned."

"What is it you want, Miss—or is it Mrs. Curtis?" Mommy asked, her voice now ringing with annoyance as well as impatience.

"It's Mrs. Curtis. I am a widow. I lost my husband ten years ago. Congestive heart failure. He was pounds and pounds overweight, a heavy smoker and drinker, and stubborn as the proverbial mule. He had other self-destructive habits as well, but I won't get into that now.

"Suffice it to say he left me well-to-do, wealthy

enough to care for my wayward sister and her child all these years. My sister and I raised her boy. You can just imagine what a burden that has been. It's hard enough to raise teenagers these days," she said, looking at me, "much less a teenager with special needs."

Mommy said nothing. She and I just stared and waited.

"A little over a year ago, my sister Angelica passed away, too. She was in a brutal car accident, a head-on collision caused by a drunken redneck who still walks the earth and, I am sure, still overindulges himself in every way possible. One of those nephews of a judge with some influence. You know how those things can be," she added.

"Her death had a very heavy impact on Evan, of course, but an even heavier one on me."

Mommy nodded in sympathy, but still waited tensely to understand the point of this visit.

"Well, what exactly can we do for you, Mrs. Curtis? At the moment we can barely do enough for ourselves," Mommy said.

"I know just how true that is. What I would like, what I'm proposing, is that you and your daughter come live with me and help me take care of Evan," Charlotte Alden Curtis finally said.

Mommy smiled with confusion.

"Pardon me?"

"I can't bear the burden any longer and I shouldn't have to bear it alone," Charlotte continued. "It's aging me faster than I would like, to say the least."

"I'm sorry for you, Mrs. Curtis. However . . ."

"I know you're in financial turmoil, Mrs. Wallace. Once I learned where y'all had gone this time, I had

my attorneys make inquiries. You can't keep up the
rent even for a house like this," she added, looking
about our home as if it was nothing more than a
tent.

"That might be true," Mommy said, her indignation
rising like mercury in a thermometer, "however, I am not
in the habit of having strangers come to my home to
make demands on us just because we're in a temporary
crisis."

"Temporary," Charlotte said, smiling and shaking her
head. "Why delude yourself, Mrs. Wallace? Unless you
find a daddy for Rose here, you'll always be in a monetary crisis. You have no work skills, no significant record
of employment, and I don't believe you are the type who
wants to do menial labor. You're still an attractive and
relatively young woman, as I am. You shouldn't be burdened with the responsibility of providing the basic
necessities of life for yourself and your daughter. You
have a lot of good living to do, beautiful things to enjoy.
Just as I do."

Mommy started to speak, but stopped and looked at
me. I shook my head again.

Mommy shook hers and started to laugh.

"Really, Mrs. Curtis, I do feel sorry for you, but why
should we even entertain the idea of moving in with you
to help you care for a disabled child? I have no experience with that sort of thing, either, and Rose certainly
doesn't. I must say, Mrs. Curtis, your searching for us
and coming here to make such a request makes no sense
to me and . . ."

"It will," Charlotte said confidently.

"Really? Why?"

"Evan is your husband's child," she replied coolly.

The words seemed to bounce off me, but Mommy looked as if all the air had gone out of her lungs. She turned as white as rice.

"What did you say?"

"I said, Evan is your husband's child, your daughter's half-brother," she added, looking at me.

Mommy started to shake her head. Charlotte opened her pocketbook and took out two envelopes.

"This first one contains a letter your husband wrote to my poor sister, making pathetic excuses for himself and his behavior with her and offering to pay for her to have an abortion. That offer came too late, not that Angelica would have agreed to do it. She was a helpless romantic. You'll recognize his handwriting and his signature, I'm sure.

"This second letter also contains a check, an even more pathetic attempt to buy off his guilt, I suppose. It's for a thousand dollars."

Daddy's bonus, I thought as she handed both envelopes to Mommy. She took them, but she looked like she didn't have the strength to hold them. I watched her take out the letter from the first one and read it. She put it down and looked at the second and at the check.

"Well?"

Mommy's eyes looked frozen over.

"Mommy?" I said. She handed me the letters and the check and I read it all quickly, my heart feeling as if it had stopped altogether and evaporated. My chest felt that empty, that hollow.

"I don't know what to say, Mrs. Curtis. You can see that this is all a very big surprise to me," Mommy managed.

"Well, I would hope so. I don't know how any woman

could live with a man knowing he had seduced a young, impressionable woman, made her pregnant, and then deserted her, especially after she gave birth to an imperfect child, his child, who needs such special care.

"In the early years, I paid for all the nursing and the rehabilitation and the tutors. Angelica lived for the longest time under the illusion that your husband would eventually come to her assistance and to the aid of his own child. He had her believing they would live happily ever after.

"It broke her heart to see how he avoided her as much as possible, sometimes never contacting her at all for months and months. The foolish girl actually prevented herself from finding new and substantial relationships with other men, more responsible and decent men, because your husband kept her on the edge of her chair with his 'very soon now' sort of lies.

"Well, she's gone and there's just the two of us, the poor child and myself, and frankly, I am not ready to live like some nun, sacrificing all of the finer things in life. As you can see, I am still young enough to enjoy the fruits of my husband's fortune.

"Now that you are destitute, it makes absolute sense for you to come to my home and help me care for Evan. I have a sizable fortune, a large old plantation house just outside of Atlanta. I have servants, of course, but the boy needs more than a maid and an occasional nurse's visit. He needs family."

"Family?" Mommy asked, a smile of incredulity on her face.

"Well, other than myself, some cousins on my side, and your husband's relatives, your daughter is the only immediate family he has.

"Frankly, Mrs. Wallace, I do believe you have some responsibility here."

"I do?"

"Your husband bears the guilt. If your husband runs up a monetary debt, you are still responsible for it as well, aren't you? His death doesn't forgive all that. Certainly a child is at least as valuable and as important as some money."

Mommy's mouth opened and closed. She shook her head.

"As I see this," Charlotte said, gazing around the living room, "I'm offering you a way out of this disastrous mess your husband has left you."

"You want me to become a mother to your sister's child?" Mommy finally was able to ask.

"And your husband's child and your own child's half-brother," Charlotte replied. She pulled herself up. "In point of fact, my dear, you have more reason to be a surrogate mother to him than I have."

Mommy sat back.

"Why don't we plan on your visiting tomorrow? I'll send my car for you. Perhaps when you see where you would live and what you would enjoy, you'll lose any hesitation."

She rose and looked at me.

"Evan would so much enjoy having someone his own age around him. He's had minimal contact with other teenagers, and that's why he's so tied to his computer. You could do a great deal for him, my dear. You could help repair the terrible injury your father visited upon my family and my poor dead sister. Shall we say about ten A.M.?" she asked Mommy.

Mommy looked incapable of replying.

"My mother and I will discuss all this, Mrs. Curtis," I said. "It's all quite a shock."

"Yes, but imagine the shocks I've experienced," she retorted and started out. I rose to follow her to the door. After she opened it, she turned back to me.

"No one knows about this disgrace and no one needs to know. As far as the inquiring public goes, you and your mother will be hired to help me manage. Should you refuse, I would have to speak with my attorneys to determine what course of action would best benefit poor Evan."

"What's that supposed to mean?" I asked.

"There is paternal responsibility."

"We have nothing, Mrs. Curtis. You know that already," I said sharply.

"Yes, I know. I suppose I would have to find some sort of institutionalized setting for Evan. Another burden of suffering piled on his poor soul, and all because your father turned his charms on my poor sister. Remember your Bible, my dear. The sins of the father are visited on the heads of his children."

She turned and stepped out.

"Someone will call you tonight to confirm the pickup tomorrow morning," she concluded and walked to her waiting car.

I watched her vehicle drive off, the sight of it lingering like a vivid new nightmare.

4

The Mansion

Mommy was still sitting exactly where we had left her, the same dumbfounded expression on her face. After a moment she turned to me.

"Do you believe all that?" She looked down at the letters in her hand and the check. "How could he have done this? How could he have kept such a dark secret? Did he treat this with the same nonchalance he treated everything else in our lives? Did he not expect that it would come back at him someday?"

I lowered myself to a chair and stared at the floor. Like a tickle that turned into a scratch, a horrible gnawing thought made its way to the top of my thoughts. Slowly, I raised my eyes to Mommy.

"Some people think Daddy might have deliberately killed himself, Mommy. Do you think this makes it more likely to be true?"

The idea dawned on her, too, but when it came to her, it was more like a slap in the face.

She shook her head, but she started to cry. I leaped from my chair to embrace her and the two of us sat there on the settee, rocking each other, tears streaking down both our faces. Finally, she took a deep breath and sat back.

"What does that woman really want?" she asked me.

"I don't know, Mommy."

She thought a moment.

"She did look very rich," she said, and gazed with haunted eyes at our small, dark, and tired living room. "Maybe we should see what it's really all about."

"You mean, go there?"

"Why not?" Mommy asked, rising. "When you're at the end of your rope and dangling, you look kindly on any hand reaching out to hold you up, Rose. Any hand," she concluded and returned to the kitchen.

Neither of us had much of an appetite, but we both ate mechanically so the other would. Every once in a while, Mommy would choke back a sob and shake her head while she muttered about Daddy.

"I almost do feel sorrier for that poor dead girl than I do for myself. I can see how she could easily be charmed and persuaded by your father. He enjoyed spreading his illusions and dreams. He was the Pied Piper of Fantasyland, leading us all down the road to popped bubbles."

She thought a moment, and then jumped up from the table and went upstairs. Moments later she returned with that black and white photograph she had found in the closet and put it on the table. We both stared down at the young woman again, Mommy nodding.

"This must be Angelica. I can see the resemblances to Charlotte, can't you?"

I had to admit I could.

"Why did he keep her picture in our house?" she wondered aloud.

She shook her head at my blank stare.

"You don't have to say it. I can see it in your face. Why should I look for logic in a man who never paid attention to logic?" She took a deep breath and gazed at the picture again. "I'm not going to look for ways to deny it, to pretend it didn't happen, Rose."

Just then, as if some great power was listening in on our conversation and arranging for everything to happen, the phone rang. Mommy went to it and I listened.

"Yes," she said, "we will be ready." She nodded as she listened and then she hung up. "The car will be here at ten," she said. "We might as well learn all of it. You'll have to miss a day of school, Rose."

"Okay, Mommy."

It saddened me, but when I looked down at the photograph, it seemed as if the girl in the picture was smiling more.

When Barry called me later that evening, I was tempted to tell him about it all, but my embarrassment and my fears that it would fan the fires of nasty gossip, especially regarding the cause of Daddy's death, kept me from uttering a word of truth. I told him I would go to the movies with him on Friday, but not to be concerned about my being absent tomorrow. I said I had some important family business that needed to be attended to and left it at that.

"I'll miss you," he said. It added the touch of warmth I desperately needed to keep the chill from my cringing heart.

The town car was there promptly at ten the next morning. There was only the driver waiting. He was a tall, dark man with military-style posture. He introduced himself simply as Ames and opened the doors for Mommy and me. We got in and moments later, we were headed toward Atlanta.

"It's really only about thirty minutes from here," he explained. "If you'd like any candy, ma'am, there's some in a dish behind you."

"No, thank you," Mommy said.

He was quiet the remainder of the journey until we were approaching the driveway of the Curtis mansion.

"We're here," he announced.

Two sprawling great oak trees stood like sentinels at the scrolled cast-iron gate, which was fastened to two columns of stone. It opened before us and we drove on to see a truly magnificent two-story house with four Doric pillars, a full height entry porch, and elaborate cornices. Mommy looked at me with amazement in her eyes.

"Is this a house or a museum?" she muttered.

The grounds spread out around the house for what looked like miles. I saw two men trimming bushes and another riding a lawn mower. In the distance a line of trees formed a solid wall of green under the blue horizon. I had seen houses and land like this before, of course, but I had never known anyone who actually lived in such a home.

The driver brought us to the front steps. We got out slowly, both of us so busy filling our eyes with the sights and the immensity of the estate, neither of us saw the front door open.

A short, plump woman wearing a white apron and a blue maid's uniform waited. We started up the stairway. Instinctively I moved closer to Mommy.

"Right this way, please," the maid said, and we entered behind her.

"A museum," Mommy whispered again.

Before us was a curved stairway with a shiny, thick mahogany balustrade; on the walls were large oil paintings of beautiful country settings, lakes, and meadows, all done in vibrant colors, many, it seemed, by the same artist. Vases on marble-topped tables and glass cases filled with expensive-looking figurines, crystals, and the like lined the hallway, the floor of which was Italian marble.

"Please wait here," the maid said, showing us into a sitting room with elegant gold-trimmed velvet curtains over the windows, a plush white rug, and oversized pieces of furniture including what looked like a brass statue of an Egyptian queen. The room was so large, I thought we could put most of our present house in it. "Mrs. Curtis will be here in a moment. Would you like anything to drink—a cold lemonade, juice, soda?"

"Lemonade," Mommy said.

"Yes," I added.

"Very good," the maid said and left us.

Mommy strolled around the immense room looking at the artifacts, the paintings, and the antique furnishing.

"A woman who owns all this could *hire* a family for the boy," Mommy declared. "Why would she need us?"

"Because hired help is not family," we heard from behind us and turned to see Charlotte Alden Curtis enter.

She looked as elegant and stylish as the day before, albeit a little younger in a cream-colored pantsuit. Gold earrings dangled from her lobes. She wore a gold necklace and watch that looked bejeweled enough for the queen of Saudi Arabia.

"I'm very happy you decided to come. It was a wise decision for yourself and your daughter," she told Mommy.

"We came to see what this was all about, Mrs. Curtis. It doesn't mean we've agreed to anything."

"Let's agree on one thing immediately: that you'll stop calling me Mrs. Curtis and I'll stop calling you Mrs. Wallace. My name is Charlotte and I'm not much older than you are, Monica—a month, matter of fact. Please," she said, indicating the sofa. She sat across from us.

The maid brought in the lemonades, asked her if she wanted anything, which she didn't, and then quickly left.

"This one, Nancy Sue, has been with me for three years, a record of sorts for a household servant these days. Things," she said with a great sigh, "are not what they were. You have to work harder to find the quality of help my parents and my husband's parents once enjoyed. The grand style is still out there, but it takes more work to attain it."

Grand style? We were simply hoping to survive and she was talking about the quality of servants.

"Let me begin by telling you that I have already spoken with the headmistress of the school I would have Rose attend here. She assures me she would make Rose's transition easy, accommodating her needs and helping her to adjust rapidly."

That's right, I thought. *I would have to leave school, and right at the end of only the first quarter of my senior year!* I turned sharply to Mommy.

"That would be a major problem," she said.

"Oh, no, no, believe me, it won't. If need be, the school would provide a special tutor just to help her adjust. We'll arrange for it no matter what it should cost. I'm sure it won't be any sort of obstacle."

"The work isn't everything. She's made friends, become . . ."

"Friends?" Charlotte pulled herself up and turned to me. "You can certainly keep any friends, any real friends you've made, but imagine being able to invite them here as compared to where you are now," she said with naked arrogance.

"I don't have many friends," I admitted. I thought about the nasty rumors being spread about Daddy and what I had to face when I returned. "Not many at all."

She smiled.

"You will here, my dear, I'm sure. You are an exceptionally attractive young lady. Boys will flock to you as bears to honey, but I bet you know that already."

I started to protest how that wasn't really my biggest concern, but she rose to end the topic.

"Let me show you the house," she suggested. "I am rather proud of it. It's an authentic Greek revival."

She started out and we followed down the hallway to a large dining room with a table that seated twenty. There was a second, more informal sitting room, an office that looked unused, and of course, the large kitchen.

When we stepped into the hall again, I heard Charlotte say, "Good," under her breath and I turned to look to my right.

Evan had wheeled himself out of his room. Mommy and I gazed at him. He had Daddy's shade of hair, and it was down around his shoulders. The bangs were too long, so that he had to part the strands to prevent them obstructing his vision. He wore a pair of jeans and a T-shirt that said Evan Dot Com, something he took off his computer, and a pair of leather slippers with no socks.

"I'm happy you've decided to come out to meet everyone, Evan," Charlotte said. "This is your sister, Rose, and her mother, Monica."

He stared at us a moment, and then he turned the chair sharply and wheeled himself back into his room without a word.

Charlotte groaned.

"Oh, dear. You can see what it's like. He can be so difficult, withdrawn. I try so hard to teach him common courtesies, but he has gotten so he is far more comfortable in the society of computers and machines than he is in the company of people. The poor boy avoids all human contact. That's what I am hoping you will correct, dear," she said to me. "He hasn't a single friend. Oh, he has all those names he talks to over the computer, but that's hardly being in any sort of society."

"How is his health?" Mommy asked.

"Aside from his problem with his legs, he is a healthy young man. He doesn't get out long enough to catch anything," she added as if that was something to regret. "I have to have the barber come here when he will permit it and then he won't let the man do much more than snip an inch or so here and there, and you should see what it's like to get him to go to the dentist or to his doctor. The only thing that gets him excited is shopping at one of those electronic stores, and he doesn't do that very much anymore either, because he's able to do it all over the computer. Sometimes, I think he is turning into a computer."

She sighed again.

"Please," she said, "follow me."

She led us up the stairs to show us what would be our rooms.

The room she said would be Mommy's had a queen-sized cherry four-poster bed, a sitting area with a fireplace and a television set in a matching wood cabinet. The room had its own bathroom. There were two large windows facing south with pretty flower-patterned curtains. The floor was a rich maple wood with an area rug. The room looked warm, comfortable, and very inviting. Charlotte pointed out all the closet space.

When Mommy said she had hardly enough to fill half of it, Charlotte replied, "Well, you will be buying more clothes, Monica. I want you to be very stylish and in fashion. My hope is you and I will become good friends and go to many social affairs together. You'll be the sister I've lost," she said. "I'm looking forward to that," she added with such sincerity, Mommy had to look at me with surprise. I didn't know what to say or do to react.

"Let's look at Rose's room," Charlotte quickly continued.

The room she declared would be mine was right across from Mommy's and just as large, also with its own bathroom and small sitting area with a television set on a stand. There was a queen-sized light oak bed with what looked like handmade quilts. Above it was a ceiling fan, and there were two large windows with curtains that matched the quilts. The area rug was somewhat larger. This, too, looked very warm and comfortable.

"You can have your own phone, of course," Charlotte told me. "I'll have it set up with your private number."

What could I say? The room was easily twice, if not three times, the size of my present room, and I didn't have my own bathroom like I would here.

"This was my sister's room," she added. She turned to me to see my reaction.

I felt a quickened heartbeat and looked at the room again.

"Of course, all of her things are gone. I gave most of it

away and stored some of her personal things in the attic.

"There are two more guest bedrooms and the master bedroom up here and a guest bedroom downstairs," she said. "As you can see, plenty of room, too much for just little old me and poor crippled Evan now."

Mommy looked at me again and then turned to her.

"What is it you expect from us exactly, Charlotte? You have a maid who cooks your meals and cleans your home. You have a chauffeur. You have all you need to look after you and the house. I understand why you want a companion for Evan, but what would I do?"

Charlotte nodded and sat on the chair to the right of the bed. Her face softened, her eyes warming.

"That's all true, Monica, but when I leave here, I can't help feeling I'm deserting him. This is such a big house. It can feel so empty sometimes, so cold. With you and Rose here, too, there will be so much added warmth. I am hoping it will eventually bring Evan out and what my poor dead sister wanted so much for him will finally take place. Does that help you understand? Doesn't it make sense?"

Nodding slowly, Mommy looked around the room and at me, her mind obviously reeling with indecision, confusion.

"I am simply trying to get some good from all this tragedy and unhappiness," Charlotte said, seeing the same thing in Mommy's face. "Why should y'all continue to suffer? Why should Evan? Why should I when I have all this at my fingertips, more than I need?"

Mommy's head seemed to nod on its own and keep nodding.

"Let us talk about it, Charlotte," she offered.

"Oh, yes, dear," she replied with excitement. "Stay

here. I'll see about lunch for all of us. Maybe Rose can entice poor Evan to come out and eat with people instead of a computer monitor," she said, rising quickly. "Feel free to look all around while I make the arrangements," she said and left us.

"I'm absolutely overwhelmed," Mommy said, reaching out to steady herself on the bedpost. "My head is spinning. Look at this place. It's like a five-star hotel. These rooms are so large and beautiful and the grounds . . . and you would attend a better school and she wants to buy me clothes . . ."

She paused and looked at me.

"What do you think, Rose?"

"I'm just as overwhelmed, Mommy. I don't know what to say. I don't want you getting sick with worry about our financial situation, a financial situation Daddy left us. I can also see how Charlotte is right and how she seems to need us. In a very twisted and strange way, this good thing is Daddy's doing, too."

Mommy nodded.

"Yes. I'll do it if you will," she said quickly. "I'm not so proud as to cause us to miss a chance to escape our misery and put so much of a burden on you."

I looked around at what would instantly become my new world, my new life. I couldn't stop my heart from pounding in anticipation, but what was it anticipating? Good things or bad?

"Let's look at all the rest of it," Mommy said suddenly, so filled with such excitement and joy, she shed the lines of worry and sorrow instantly.

Already she was looking younger, happier.

Charlotte Alden Curtis was right. She was either an angel of mercy.

Or an angel of temptation leading us to a deeper fall into unhappiness.

Mommy and I wandered through the house looking at the pictures of the Curtis and Alden families. We both lingered over pictures of Angelica. There were very few pictures of Evan, and in these he was always looking away or down and never smiling. I picked up the one on the grand piano and looked more closely at his face. It was only natural I suppose for me to look for resemblances to Daddy and to myself. I thought he definitely had Daddy's nose and jaw as well as his hair. In the pictures where I could have some view of his eyes, I thought they were his mother's eyes, and he did have his mother's slightly cleft chin.

Charlotte had her maid set up a small buffet lunch for us on the patio that was on the west side of the house and therefore soaked in warm sun. Soft blue umbrellas shaded the rolls, meats, and salads that were placed on the tables.

"Why don't you go to Evan," Charlotte asked me, "introduce yourself, and see if you can get him to join us for lunch?"

"I can't just go to his room," I said.

"Of course you can, dear. I want y'all to feel this house is your house immediately. Go on," she urged. "He won't bite. The worst thing he'll do is what he does often to me. He'll ignore you, pretend you're not there."

I looked at Mommy. She smiled some encouragement and I shrugged and started toward Evan's room. What a strange feeling came from realizing I was about to meet my brother for the first time. We shared the same father. We had similarities in our looks. Did that mean we might think alike, feel things the same way?

And what did he think of our father now? Did he hate him for what he had done to his mother, for helping to create him and then deserting him? Would his anger toward our father spread to me? Would he resent me and hate me no matter what I said or did?

I was actually trembling a bit when I approached the door to his room and knocked. I heard nothing, and thought perhaps I had knocked too softly, so I did it again much sharper, harder. Still, he didn't say come in or ask who it was. My third set of knocks actually opened the door. It wasn't closed tightly at all. It swung in and I looked at his room.

I hadn't been in many boys' rooms, but this certainly didn't look like any I would imagine. The walls were bare. There weren't any posters of sports heroes or movie and television stars or rock singers. The room itself resembled a cold, aseptic hospital room. There was a special bed made up with stark white sheets and pillow cases bounded by railings. Around the room were all sorts of therapeutic equipment.

At first I didn't think Evan was in the room, but when the door finished opening, I saw him staring at a computer monitor. He was also wearing headphones, which explained why he didn't hear my knocking. I saw that there was a microphone attached to the headphones and he was talking softly to someone. I thought I shouldn't interrupt him, but something told him I was in the doorway. Perhaps it was the shadow that came from the light behind me or maybe I was reflected in the glare of his computer screen. Whatever it was, he turned suddenly and looked at me, practically stabbing me with his furious eyes.

"I'm sorry," I began. "I knocked and then knocked again and your door just opened."

He said something into the microphone and slowly took off the headphones, placing it all in his lap.

"She tells me you're my sister," he said. His voice was deeper than I had expected and not unlike Daddy's. "My half-sister," he added.

"It seems to be so," I replied.

"She's trying to make it sound like half is better than none," he said. "That's not always true. Half a glass of cyanide isn't better than none; half a headache isn't better than none."

"I'm hardly poison and I don't think I give people headaches," I retorted. "Look, this is just as much a surprise for me and my mother as it is for you, believe me. More so," I added after a beat, "because, according to Charlotte, you've known about us for some time."

He stared, his eyes so unlike Daddy's. They were definitely his mother's eyes entirely—a deep blue, sapphire, but so penetrating, searching, and unmoving.

"I don't see why you and I have to suffer because of what others have done," I suggested.

His eyes brightened and softened.

"Oh, and how do I stop suffering?" he asked with a bit of an impish smile. "The best doctors haven't come up with an answer. Can you?"

"I'm not talking about that."

"What?" He was wheeling toward me. "What's that?"

"Your unfortunate condition," I said, nodding at him in the chair.

"Unfortunate condition. Yes, that's a good way to put it. Thank you. I used to call myself crippled."

" 'If you accept misery, you will be miserable,' Daddy used to say."

"Daddy? Daddy," he muttered. "You'll have to tell me

about Daddy," he added, spitting the word like some profanity.

"I will," I said defiantly. "I'll tell you lots of things if you let me, but first you have to want me to. I'm not coming here begging you to be friends. I'd like to be friends, but if you don't want me to be your friend . . ."

"It's up to me. I know. She's always saying things are up to me—as if I really had any control of anything," he complained.

"You do when it comes to our relationship."

He stared and then smiled.

"What's your real name?"

"That's my name."

"Rose? That's on your birth certificate?"

"Yes."

"What were they going to call the next child, Daffodil?"

"Very funny," I said. "Look, I'm hungry. There's a nice lunch out there. Do you want to have some lunch with me and talk sensibly, or do you want to shut yourself up in here and try to make us feel terrible, too?"

"That's a tough one," he said. He looked back at his computer. "I may have to go on a search engine to find the answer."

"Yes, well, when you do, come on out and join me," I said and started to turn away.

"Okay," he said.

"Okay?"

"Okay, I'm coming. Lead the way, *Rosie*."

"I'm glad my name amuses you," I said and we started down the hallway, him wheeling himself alongside me. "I can push you, if you like," I said.

"Thanks, but this is all the exercise I'm getting today. My therapist isn't coming today."

"What were you doing on the computer? Who were you talking to?"

"I was in a chat room with other shut-ins. I created the club. It's called Invalids Anonymous. We compare notes and depress each other."

"Doesn't sound like fun."

"We just got started. We'll find a way to have fun yet."

We reached the patio doors. Charlotte looked up. She and Mommy were seated at a table, talking and eating.

"Well, isn't this nice," she said.

"Yes," Evan said, "one big happy family."

He looked up at me with a half smile on his face, waiting for my reaction. In that split second, I saw the pain and the loneliness as well as the impishness in his eyes. He wasn't just crippled with a bone deformity. He was all twisted emotionally, full of anger and self-pity.

And yet I thought he was actually a very good-looking boy. He had the best of Daddy's features and his mother's. If some sparks of joy could light some happiness in those eyes, he would be very attractive, I concluded.

He seemed to be challenging me with his recalcitrant stare, daring me to do something that would help him, daring me to really be his sister, to be sincere and care about him. He looked like he expected me to flee, to turn away in disgust, but I didn't.

I smiled at him.

"This is my mother, Monica," I said. "She and my father named me Rose."

His eyes softened and filled with some humor.

"Hello, Evan," Mommy said.

He said hello politely.

"Can I get you a plate of food, Evan?" Charlotte asked him.

"No," he said sharply. He looked up at me. "I'd rather have Rose do it. By any other name, she'd smell as sweet."

Okay, I thought. *I'll play, too.*

"Too bad you don't," I threw down at him.

He seemed to wince, and then he laughed. The sound of it must have been alien to Charlotte. She dropped her mouth in amazement, and then looked at Mommy as I pushed Evan toward the food.

"I do believe this was meant to be," she said.

I would soon learn that what she meant by this and what we would interpret it to mean were two entirely different things.

5

Evan

After lunch, Evan allowed me to push him down the paths that wove through the gardens, ponds, and grounds around and behind the grand house. He said he wanted to show me his favorite places, but I sensed he wanted to get away from his aunt and Mommy to talk to me. I soon learned that Charlotte wasn't exaggerating when she characterized Evan as an introverted fifteen-year-old boy who had chained himself to his computer and who had minimal contact with the physical world around him. He reminded me of the allegory of Plato's Cave, one of the dialogues in Plato's *The Republic,* which my English teacher, Mr. Madeo, had made me read as an extra assignment just a few weeks ago.

In the allegory, people were living in an underground cave and chained so they could only look at the wall ahead of them. Above and behind them a fire burned so that everything that moved between the fire and them was thrown on the wall in the form of shadows. All they knew as real were the shadows and the echoes of sounds they heard and thought came from those shadows.

As Evan talked and described some of the things he did on his computer, the people he met and had gotten to know only over the Internet, I thought to myself that he was living in a cave—an electronic one, but still, a cave. His only friends were people he heard over his earphones and saw on his computer monitor. He traveled through the monitor and knew about exotic lands and people, but he had never really left the grounds of this estate. The only flowers he smelled or touched were the ones he could experience from his wheelchair trips down these paths. His world was populated solely by nurses, doctors, and other medical people, as well as a few servants and his tutor, Mrs. Skulnik, a fifty-eight-year-old retired math teacher who he said had a face like an old sock, so full of wrinkles it would take a tear two months to travel down to her chin.

"And she smells," he said, "like sour milk. I've told my aunt that I don't want her, but she says it's difficult to find someone else. I know she's not even trying.

"Maybe I don't need a tutor anyway," he suddenly thought aloud and looked up at me. "Maybe now that you're moving in, you can be my tutor and I'll just take the high school equivalency exam."

"It's not definite that we're moving in, Evan."

"I meant, if you do."

"I don't know if I can do that, Evan. I don't know if it's even legal," I said. "Doesn't the tutor have to be a licensed teacher?"

"Right," he snapped, looking down quickly. "It was a stupid idea. Forget it."

"I didn't say it was stupid, Evan."

He stopped talking. I could see how quickly he could be discouraged. Fooling around with him at lunch, meeting his challenges and quips with my own, had, strangely enough, gotten him to relax enough with me so that he was willing to talk with me and be with me privately. From the way his eyes traveled over my face, searching for sincerity, I could feel how difficult it was for him to place his trust in anyone. No wonder it was easier and far more comfortable for him to deal with people through a computer. There was so much less danger of being disappointed. If someone displeased you, you simply clicked the mouse and sent them into electronic oblivion.

"You wouldn't have the time for me, anyway," he finally said. "Once you started school here, you'd make lots of friends and wouldn't want to be tied down to some invalid, even the president of Invalids Anonymous."

"That's not true," I protested.

"Right. You just wouldn't be able to wait every day to rush home to help me with schoolwork. The truth is, you're probably the most popular girl in your school."

"The truth is, Evan, I don't have all that many friends at the school I'm at now," I revealed.

He looked up at me.

"Sure."

I stopped pushing his chair and walked around to the front so he would have to face me.

"For your information, Evan, I can count on the fingers of one hand the girls I care to talk to at school. Mommy, Daddy, and I have moved so many times, I never had a chance to make meaningful relationships. I can't even remember most of the other kids I knew. Their faces are like one big blur to me. It just so happens, our present address is the longest I can remember occupying, and it's not even a full two years!"

His self-pity dissolved as that look of interest and some trust seeped into his eyes again, warming them.

"I saw just how many places you've lived in. Why did you move so much?"

I looked off at the trees and folded my arms under my breasts.

"I used to think it was just because Daddy got bored easily or didn't care about important things as much as he should have, but after we learned about . . ."

"Me? The tragic accident of my birth?" he asked, the corners of his mouth turning down.

"I don't think of you as a tragic accident, Evan. Look, I expect I'll get to know you better, and maybe I won't like you. Maybe you're too bitter, so bitter that I won't be able to help," I said. "But from what I can see and what I've heard so far, you seem to be very intelligent. When I said I wasn't sure I could help you as your tutor, I was thinking to myself that you've already taught yourself so much, you probably know more than I do even though I'm two years older than you.

"Anyway," I continued, "yes, when we heard about you and your mother, both Mommy and I began to think that Daddy moved so much to avoid being pinned down by his added responsibilities. He was like that, I suppose," I said.

Evan's face softened further, making him look more like a little boy to me.

"I pretended I wasn't interested in him whenever Aunt Charlotte talked about him, but I would like to know more about him," he said. "I know I should hate him more than I could hate anyone, but I can't help wondering about him."

"I couldn't help loving him. I still love him. He was

probably the most charming man I'll ever meet, but I can't deny being hurt and disappointed by what he's done, for Mommy as much as for myself. Maybe more than for myself," I added.

Evan stared at me and then, after a deep breath, said, "The reason I thought you wouldn't care to spend so much time with me is I thought you were so pretty, you surely had a string of boyfriends calling on you and would if you came here to live as well."

"Well, thank you, but I don't have a string of boyfriends."

"You won a beauty contest, didn't you?" he asked.

"No, I didn't win. I was first runner-up. Wait a minute," I said with my hands on my hips. "How did you know about that?"

"Aunt Charlotte told me. She had a detective."

"A detective? I thought she just had some attorneys doing some inquiries. A real detective?"

"Philip Marlowe himself," Evan joked. "I don't know, some retired policeman, I think. That must have been some beautiful girl to beat you."

"I'm not that beautiful, Evan."

"Can we promise each other that we won't lie to each other about the obvious at least, Rose? I'm crippled and you're pretty enough to be in the movies and that's that."

It was my turn to smile.

"She was related to the owner of the company," I revealed.

He laughed.

"I knew it. Don't you have at least one boyfriend, someone you like?"

"I'm seeing someone nice at the moment, yes," I admitted. "I'd like you to meet him."

He studied me for a moment and then looked down.

"No, you wouldn't," he said. "You're just being nice. You probably don't want anyone to know about me," he added, reverting to that bitterness. "There's no reason why you'd want anyone to know we're related."

"That's not true."

"My aunt promised your mother she'd keep it all secret. She told me."

"Well, it's embarrassing for her."

"And for you," he punched at me. "I'm just an embarrassment for everyone."

He spun his chair around and started pushing himself back toward the house.

I watched him for a moment and then shot forward and stopped him by putting my hands on his arms and leaning into him.

"Just a moment," I ordered.

"Let go. I got to get back to my room," he said. He glared at me, his eyes burning with anger and tears. He tried to thrust me aside, but I clung to his arms, weighing him and his wheelchair down so he couldn't move.

"No. You're going to stay here and listen. I'm not someone you can click off like you click people off on your computer."

"What?"

His face turned crimson with rage right down to his neck. I was sure his tantrums and explosions of anger always got him what he wanted, but my feet were planted firmly.

"You're not going anywhere until you promise to stop this. I certainly don't want to move in here and live with you if you're going to be like this all the time."

"Like what?"

"Like Mr. Self-pity."

I released my grip and stood up straight before him.

"Okay, we won't lie to each other about the obvious. You're right. This is not a lucky break for you and most people are not crippled and in a wheelchair, but you'd be surprised at how many people are crippled in other ways. For one thing, you're more intelligent than most people your age. I can see that immediately. You could probably do something wonderful with your life because of that and because of other talents you have that you don't even know about yourself.

"Most people who walk easily won't do something wonderful with their lives. I don't know if I'll do anything worth spit, but I'm not going to moan and groan about it. I'm going to make the best of what I have."

His eyebrows lifted.

"Really?"

"Yes, really. Daddy didn't do a good thing with your mother and you, I know, but he had a philosophy that helped him get by and often helped me face disappointments, too."

"And what exactly was this brilliant philosophy?" Evan asked, sitting back in his chair and folding his arms across his chest.

"He used to say there was no sense in worrying about things you have no control over." I smiled.

"What's so funny about that?" he asked.

"When I was a very little girl and something would bother me, he would always come into my room to stop me from crying or sulking."

"Terrific. Lucky you."

"One day," I continued, ignoring his sarcasm, "he brought a beautiful little wooden box in with him. It's this big," I said, holding my hands about a foot apart, "and it has that face of tragedy engraved on it on one side, and the face of happiness on the other . . . you know, what the Greeks used."

"You mean masks, not faces, and they originated with the Dionysian cult," he said.

I smiled at him.

"I bet you're a walking encyclopedia."

"Walking?"

"I mean . . ."

"I know," he said quickly. "Aunt Charlotte calls me Mr. Computer Head, so I had this T-shirt made up: Evan Dot Com. I ordered it over the Internet. It's where I do all my shopping now. But forget that. Tell me about the box," he said impatiently, like a child who didn't want to have a fairy tale end.

"Daddy said whenever something bad happened or something sad, I should write it down on a slip of paper and put it in the box and then turn the box so the happy face, the mask of comedy," I corrected, "is turned to me, and that would help me forget about it."

He nodded slowly. I expected some new sarcasm any moment, but he looked thoughtful.

"When you come here to live, if you actually do, be sure to bring the box along," he said. "I'll have lots to put in it," he added and wheeled himself forward. I watched him for a moment and then walked slowly after him, thinking that maybe we were more alike than either of us really knew or, more importantly, wanted to admit.

"Well, I see you two have been getting along like two sweet hummingbirds. That's wonderful," Charlotte cried as we returned to the patio.

"Yes, everything's going to be just peachy-keen from now on, Aunt Charlotte," Evan said and continued to wheel himself past Mommy and Charlotte and into the house.

Mommy looked at me quizzically. I tilted my head a bit and smiled back at her with a slight shrug of my shoulders. She looked very anxious.

"Why don't I let you two talk a bit?" Charlotte said, looking from me to Mommy. "I have to make some social phone calls. I'm on so many committees these days."

She rose and went into the house, and I sat at the table watching the maid clear the food and dishes away.

"What do you think of all this, honey?" Mommy asked.

"I don't know, Mommy. It's certainly beautiful here."

"And look at what would be our rooms, and there are servants and no more money worries. She wants to take me shopping the day after tomorrow," Mommy continued excitedly. "She says I must have what she calls 'decent clothes' to wear because she does a great deal of socializing and I must be part of all that now. I must say, my head is whirling. Parties, dinners, dances, trips to Atlanta to the theater, and she will pay for everything. Such generosity."

"Did she indicate any more specifically what she expects from you, Mommy?" I asked suspiciously.

Mommy shook her head.

"Just to be here, to help create a feeling of family, to help her cope, I suppose. It doesn't sound very difficult. She's looking for a companion, someone her own age, I think."

"Why would a woman with all this need to draft a companion, Mommy?"

"I don't know all the answers, Rose, but should we look a gift horse in the mouth?" she asked.

"I guess not."

"Did you get along with Evan?"

"He's a very sensitive and angry person," I said.

"Who needs someone like you," Mommy insisted. I could see Charlotte had done a wonderful sales job, not that she needed all that many different ways to persuade. The house, the grounds, all of it was enough for anyone to give up her life without a second thought.

"Maybe," I said cautiously.

"So shall we say yes, Rose?" Mommy asked me.

I took a deep breath. We were going to move again. Even Daddy's death didn't stop that now. Mommy looked so excited about it, so enthusiastic. How could I even think of putting up any obstacles at this terrible time in her life?

I nodded.

"Okay, Mommy," I said. "Let's move in."

She clapped her hands and then reached out to hug me.

Charlotte must have been watching us from inside that patio door because she was out just as we embraced.

"Does that mean yes?" she asked Mommy.

"It does," Mommy said.

Charlotte smiled.

"Welcome then, you two. My home is now yours as well." She turned to me and added, "Evan will be so pleased. Come upstairs, Monica. I must show you this new outfit I bought at Saks last week. I think we're almost the same size," she added.

"Her closet is like a department store. She has clothing with the tags still hanging off," Mommy whispered,

and then she leaped to her feet and started toward her.
Just before she entered the house she looked back at me
and beamed a smile as she raised her arms.

"We're due for a little luck," she called back to me
and disappeared.

I looked out over the grounds toward the shadows in
the forest.

A little luck, yes, but is it good luck or bad? I wondered.

Time keeps all the secrets buried under weeks and
days, hours and minutes, and we poor unfortunate souls
have to pluck them away second by second, searching for
our discoveries, our great moments of pleasure and happiness, and our great moments of terrible disappointments and sadness, I thought.

How soon would we know what secrets awaited us
here? I felt confident there would be more than one.

Mommy was so eager to go home and start our packing, she was downstairs and ready to leave as soon as
possible. Charlotte offered to hire people to help, but
Mommy explained that we had so little of real value to
bring with us, it wasn't necessary.

"We'll donate our pathetic furniture to the Salvation
Army," she told Charlotte. "Not a piece of it would
belong here anyway."

Pathetic? I thought. Once it was special to us; once
we were happy about the house we had rented and the
furnishing we were able to manage. Now, that was all to
be discarded like so many of our recent memories. I
knew if Mommy could, she would wipe her mind clear
like some magic slate. She would be like Daddy was and
think, *Forget the past. Concentrate only on the here and*

now. How sad it was that we had very little to cling to, to bring with us.

Even our photo albums, full of pictures from so many different places, so many homes, looked more like a travelogue than a family history.

"I'm happy about that," Charlotte told Mommy and then looked at me as well to add, "You're both starting a new life, Rose. Let everything be fresh. We're going to take you shopping for new clothes, too, and new shoes to match. Don't even bring an old toothbrush. I have new ones in your bathroom cabinets."

Mommy laughed and the two of them walked out arm in arm as if they were already old, dear friends.

"I'll say good-bye to Evan," I shouted after them.

"Oh, yes, do that, and be sure to tell him you'll be back tomorrow."

"Tomorrow, but that's so quick, Mommy. I have school and I have to . . ."

"Charlotte has arranged it all, Rose. You're enrolled in the school here already, remember? The administration is getting your transcripts in the morning."

"How did . . ." I didn't finish the question. Mommy had already turned away. I finished it in my thoughts, however. *How did she know we would accept and come here for sure?*

It put a cold but electric feeling through my veins and made my heart thump for a few moments. Were we so desperate and forlorn that anyone could come along and hold our destinies in the wind like kites and watch us be blown from one place to another? I could feel it. Whatever little control we had of ourselves was drifting away.

Daddy had done a great deal more than he had ever

dreamed when he had his love affair with Angelica and a child with her, I thought.

Evan's door was open this time, but he was back where I had found him previously, at his computer.

"Hi," I said. He wasn't wearing earphones. "I guess it's happening. We're actually moving in tomorrow," I said. He kept working as if he hadn't heard me. "Did you hear what I said, Evan?"

"Yes, but I knew that was going to happen," he replied, still working the keyboard and looking at the monitor.

"How did . . ."

"Wait. There," he said and turned. I heard the printer going. "It's coming out." He nodded at the printer, which was on the table to his right. I walked in and waited by it, watching as the picture began emerging. I felt the heat building in my neck and face as it was forming. Finally, it was done, and I picked it up.

It was a picture of Daddy, me, Evan, Mommy, and his mother Angelica, all together.

"How did you do this?"

"It's not hard," he said. "I had pictures of everyone and scanned them in together to make that. There it is, the big happy family."

It gave me the chills.

"Where did you get this picture of Daddy?"

"Aunt Charlotte found it in my mother's things. I got your picture and your mother's from the file Aunt Charlotte's detective made.

"I was going to put Aunt Charlotte in there, too, sort of in the background like some puppeteer or something. What do you think? Should I?"

I stared at him.

He smiled.

"Come here, watch this," he said, and began working again. He brought up a picture of Charlotte, cut off her head and pasted on the body of a small gorilla. I laughed and then he put her head on the body of a naked, buxom woman.

"Evan!"

"It's magic. I can turn anyone into anything. Look what I did for you," he said and clicked something that was already completed.

It came up on the screen. He had taken the photo of Sheila Stone from the newspaper story of the Miss Lewisville Foundry Beauty Contest and substituted me with the crown on my head.

"See how easy it is to right the wrongs?"

I laughed, and he clicked again and brought up a picture of himself riding a horse, and then one with him running in an Olympic race.

"I wish that was real, Evan," I said softly.

He smiled at me.

"It is real. This is make-believe," he said, indicating his wheelchair.

Daddy would agree, I thought. *Daddy would love this.*

"You've got your own magic box," I said softly, gazing at his computer monitor.

"Exactly," he said, smiling, and I wondered if I really would help him or harm him by doing what Charlotte had hoped I would do: bring him out of this room and away from his own world.

6

—❦—

A New Life

Mommy attacked our home with a vengeance. It was as if she was getting back at all the bad luck and hard times she had ever suffered after marrying Daddy. Anything that in the slightest way provided a painful or unpleasant memory was eagerly dropped into the garbage cans, no matter what its monetary value. She did the same with things I had thought were important reminders of her relationship with Daddy.

I was really surprised at how she sifted through her wardrobe, selecting so many dresses, blouses, pants, and even shoes to give away. None of it was worn-out or faded. When I questioned her, she turned to me and said, "You heard Charlotte. What point would there be in bringing these clothes to that house? They're so out of style, she wouldn't want me to wear them anyway. And besides," she added like a little girl just before Christmas, "she's buying me a whole new wardrobe. You heard her."

"Maybe she was just exaggerating, Mommy."

She thought a moment and then shook her head, first slowly and then vigorously as she convinced herself more and more.

"No, no, Rose, she wants us there too much and she doesn't want us to be unhappy and leave. No. For the first time, what little old me wants is going to be important."

She then advised me to do the same thing: scrutinize my clothing and pack in boxes whatever was too old or out of style.

"You'll give it away along with all my stuff," she told me, but I didn't listen.

Something inside told me to beware of being too beholden to Charlotte Alden Curtis. Maybe it was the manner in which Evan spoke of her and showed what he really thought of her. His sarcastic remarks about her seemed sharper to me than they were about anyone or anything else, and when he looked at her, he always seemed to narrow his eyes with suspicion and distrust. I realized of course that it could just be his way. He had first looked at me in a similar fashion. Still, I wasn't as optimistic about the move as Mommy was. In the back of my mind, I saw it as just another pit stop on the way to some other destination Fate had already determined for us.

While I was packing, Barry called, and it occurred to me how strange and curious my sudden departure from our school would seem to all the other students. Paula would surely use it as confirmation of her theories and justification for her rumors. *But what difference does all that make to me now anyway?* I thought. *I will be gone from here forever.*

Barry was stunned at the suddenness of our moving. I

explained how it was an opportunity for us that we couldn't afford to pass up and how it provided a solution to our financial dilemma. Mommy and I had concocted a cover story for our instant move, a story she was using with the landlord as well. According to Mommy, Mrs. Curtis was an old friend of my daddy's family and needed someone to help her with the care of her invalid nephew since the unfortunate death of his mother. It was a fiction based on some truth, which made Mommy more comfortable about our lies.

"Oh, sure," Barry said. "I can understand all that. Actually, you're not that far away anyhow. Can I come out to take you to dinner Saturday?"

"I'd like that," I said and promised to call and give him my own phone number as soon as it had been established.

I was very happy that he wouldn't give up on me so easily. We talked a little longer. He asked questions about Evan and Charlotte, but I was able to simply say I didn't know enough about it all yet. It bothered me to have to throw up a wall of deceit between us. I was more comfortable and at ease with Barry than I had been with any other boy and I liked him very much.

Daddy's exploits had shown me what deception could do to a relationship. It made every word uttered and every kiss given seem like just so much smoke. If someone didn't know himself where his heart belonged, how could you ever trust his promises or his claims of love? How similar had Daddy's words of love with Angelica been to the words of love he pressed with his lips into Mommy's ear? Did all men practice one set of romantic and cherished utterances on every woman they met and wanted? Without trust there could be no love, I decided, and understood why Evan had so dark a vision for himself. He surely believed he would be without love his whole life.

Could I change that? Did I want even to try? Was I the right person for the task anyway? At the moment, still recovering from what Daddy had done to us, I was one of those crippled people I had described to Evan. How could I convince him to open his heart to anyone? How could I promise him rainbows? I was still under the dark clouds myself.

It was very difficult falling asleep for the last time in this house. Butterflies circled themselves in my stomach every time I thought about what we were committing ourselves to do. To me it looked like Charlotte Alden Curtis was using us, as if we were some sort of Band-Aid to cover the rips and tears in the fabric of her own tattered family life. It was surely like asking the blind to lead the blind, I thought. Mommy wasn't really strong enough to be anyone's crutch. She had trouble standing on her own two feet.

When I did finally fall asleep, I tossed and turned so much, I found the blanket wrapped so tightly around my legs in the morning it was as if I was trying to tie myself down to keep myself from rising and going through with the move.

Mommy was up at the blink of sunlight through the veil of clouds that were daubed over the pale blue morning sky. I heard her bustling about, making final checks of drawers and closets and then marching up and down the hallway and stairs, deliberately making more noise than usual so I would get up and join her. Finally, she called to me.

"Don't forget Charlotte is sending the car at ten, Rose. We want to be ready!"

Ready? Would we ever be ready for this? I wondered, but rose, showered, and dressed in jeans and one of Daddy's old flannel shirts he had given me months ago.

"Why didn't you throw out that shirt?" Mommy asked the moment she set eyes on me. "You don't want to go to a house like that wearing some old, smelly shirt, Rose."

"It's not smelly, Mommy, and I don't expect we'll have to dress up every day, all day, just because it's a mansion."

"Well, I've decided to do something about myself," Mommy explained as she poured her coffee and sat at the table. "I'm going to get rid of this haggard, old-lady look, do what Charlotte suggested and get an up-to-date hairstyle, take more care with my makeup, and dress nicely all the time. I want to look like I belong in that house.

"She's really not any more attractive than I am, is she?"

"No, she's not, Mommy."

"But she looks like she is because of the way she dresses and how she takes care of herself. Your father had me thinking those things didn't matter much. He was happy keeping me locked up in this house. That's why he was never very enthusiastic about any jobs I had.

"Now," she added, her lips tightening, "we know why."

Despite all Daddy had done, I couldn't get myself to harden my heart against him. He was dead and gone, but his smile lingered on my eyes and his laughter still echoed in my ears. He must have loved us. He must have, I told myself.

Charlotte's chauffeur Ames helped us load the car. Mommy had arranged for the landlord to take possession of most of the good furniture and even the kitchenware in lieu of our rental obligations. We were really leaving the house with as little as possible, which was just what Mommy, and apparently Charlotte Alden Curtis, wanted. I had the most and Mommy didn't stop complaining about it.

When we arrived at the Curtis mansion, Ames and Nancy Sue brought in most of our things and put away what belonged in each of our rooms. Nancy Sue began to hang up Mommy's clothes first and then came in to do mine. Mommy was so excited and pleased about that.

"I never had a maid, even when I lived with my parents," she told me in a loud whisper. "Imagine having someone care for your clothes and clean your bathroom, making sure you have all that you require. I can get used to this fast. I surely can," she declared.

She did look like a little girl who had been brought to a toy store and told she could have whatever she wanted.

"I made your hair appointment," I heard Charlotte tell her in the hallway soon afterward. "Two o'clock."

"Today!" Mommy exclaimed.

"Why wait?" Charlotte replied, and Mommy squealed with delight.

I came out just as Charlotte was telling her where they were going to go to lunch first.

"I think you should wear my Donna Karan suit. Come try it on," she urged.

Mommy flashed a bright smile at me and raised her eyebrows.

"Are you settling in nicely?" Charlotte asked me.

"Yes," I said.

"Whatever you need, just tell Nancy Sue. Tomorrow morning, Ames will drive you to school. Everything is all set there. It will be like you've always attended."

"I doubt that," I said. "I've been a new student in enough schools to tell you it's never easy."

"This time it will be," Charlotte assured me. "I'm a rather big contributor to the fund."

Fund? What fund? I wondered.

"Isn't that wonderful?" Mommy pressed on.

"We'll see," I said cautiously.

"Relax, enjoy the house today, and get to know Evan better," Charlotte said. "At the moment his tutor is with him, but she leaves in less than an hour. Oh, your phone is already connected."

"Isn't that wonderful?" Mommy asked me. I had to admit, it did overwhelm me.

"Come along, Monica. We've got a lot to do," Charlotte insisted before I could utter another word.

"I'm right behind you," Mommy cried, and the two of them went off.

I stood there for a moment, listening to them giggling like teenage girls. Was I wrong in being so hesitant and doubtful? A part of me was happy for the way in which Charlotte Alden Curtis had wiped the gray stains of depression off Mommy's eyes and replaced them with a childlike glee, but a part of me still remained very nervous. I was like someone waiting for that famous second shoe to drop. I didn't know where or how it would drop, but it would. I was sure.

Maybe I was just envious, just wishing I could be like that, too.

I decided I would take Charlotte's advice and relax and enjoy the house. I took more time in the library, impressed with all the books, the leather-bound editions of the classics and the collections of old magazines. The family room had a wide-screen television set and a state-of-the-art sound system, and a beautiful dark hickory-wood pool table.

In the kitchen Nancy Sue was preparing lunch for me and for Evan. Instead of asking me what I liked, she was going to set out a variety of luncheon meats, breads, and cheeses. It seemed like wasted effort and even wasted food, but when I commented about it, she told me it was what Mrs. Curtis ordered. From the tone of Nancy Sue's voice, I understood that when Charlotte spoke, it was gospel.

The pale blue sky had become more vibrantly blue with every passing hour, and the thin veil of clouds had drifted west. We were having another one of those unusually warm days for this time of the year. I strolled along the same path I had followed with Evan the day before until, this time, I reached an oak tree. I was drawn to the trunk when I spotted what looked like carving. It turned out to be Evan's initials and what I guessed were his mother's initials. I really hadn't thought much about his relationship with his mother and how deeply he must have suffered her loss. He had said so little about her yesterday. Were they close? How did she treat him? What had she told him about Daddy? I probably had as many questions for him as he had for me.

When I turned to start back to the house, I saw him out on the patio watching me.

"I've got to get fresh air as soon as my tutor leaves," he explained when I approached. "I actually tried spraying some of my mother's old perfume around the room before she comes, but it doesn't seem powerful enough to overcome the stink."

I laughed.

"Why don't you just tell her?"

"So she goes complaining about me to my aunt Charlotte? No thanks. I'm tired of hearing how ungrateful I can be. I see you were looking at my tree. It was planted just about the time I was born."

"Then those are definitely your initials?"

"And my mother's. She used to bring me out there for a picnic. She'd set out a blanket and play the radio or her CDs and we'd look at the clouds and describe what they suggested to us. Often, we both fell asleep. Aunt Charlotte said we brought ants back into the house in our clothing or in the blanket."

"What would your mother say to that?"

"Nothing really. She had a way of just looking at her and smiling a smile that said, 'Don't be silly, Charlotte.' It was enough to shut her up."

"I imagine you miss her a great deal."

He stared at me a moment, his eyes glassing over.

"As much as you miss our daddy, if not more," he finally said. "Did you bring the magic box?"

"Yes," I replied, smiling.

"Good. Put this in it for me," he said and held out his hand with a slip of paper between his thumb and forefinger. I took it.

"What is it?"

"A disappointment," he replied.

"Can I look?"

"You probably would anyway."

"I would not. It's your personal disappointment. I'm not the sort of person who . . ."

"Okay, okay. Look already and spare me the speeches."

I unfolded it and read the word, *Arlene.*

"Arlene? That's your disappointment?"

He shrugged.

"She was my cyber girlfriend until late yesterday, when she decided to break up and go into a private chat room with someone else."

I shook my head, a confused smile on my face.

"It's how I go out on a date," he explained. "We talk to each other in a private chat room. She and I got along really well and had some good times. I guess I wasn't sexy enough."

"Sexy enough? How can you be sexy on the computer?"

He smiled.

"You'll see. One of these days."

"Lunch," Nancy Sue announced from the doorway.

"Good. Now that I drove Mrs. Skulnik out of my nose, I'm hungry," he said and started to wheel himself into the house.

I hurried to catch up, wondering what he was talking about when he talked about cyber dates.

He asked me so many questions at lunch, I was barely able to chew my food and swallow. Mostly, he wanted to know what my school experiences were like. When I began in a new school, did I always gravitate toward a certain clique of friends? What kind of people did I like?

And what about my classes? Was there a great deal of flirting always going on behind the teacher's back? How many school dances had I attended? Did I have a boyfriend I regretted losing so much that I was actually in physical pain? Was I ever on a team or a cheerleader or in a play and what was that like? On and on it went, making me feel he was truly like someone who had just arrived from another planet.

"I can't imagine really learning in such a setting," he finally said after hearing some of my school experiences. "There's so much to draw away your attention. Did you ever go to an all girls' school?" he asked quickly. "Without members of the opposite sex present, it might be easier. Well?"

He was so impatient for my responses, he couldn't wait for me to start to talk.

"No, Evan."

"I can't imagine not being related to you and being in a class with you," he suddenly said, but he said it like a scientist evaluating data. "I'd be looking at you all the time and never concentrating."

I smiled, even though he had made it sound like cold analysis.

"You're going to give me a big head, Evan. There were always prettier girls in my classes."

"I doubt that. I've never been in school like you, but I've seen plenty of girls."

"Oh?"

"There's this personal dating service on the Internet where the girls put up pictures of themselves and describe themselves. Then boys send them their pictures and descriptions and they communicate for a while to see if it might work into anything. I've done it plenty of times. Of course, I substitute pictures so they never see me like this," he said, indicating the wheelchair.

"What's to keep anyone from doing the same?"

"Nothing, if that's all they want to do. But if they actually want to meet someday, they better show the truth, don't you think?"

I nodded.

"I have no illusions about it. The chat is as far as I'll be able to go."

"You never wanted to meet this Arlene?"

"No," he said quickly. "Maybe she dumped me because she found out the truth about me. Besides, I'm not talking about her anymore, remember. She's going into your magic box," he reminded me.

I laughed and nodded.

"Right."

"What about that boy you're seeing? Does he know you've actually moved?"

"Yes, and he's coming to take me to dinner on Saturday. You'll meet him. His name is Barry Burton."

"Great alliteration."

"Pardon?"

"You know, B and B? The repetition of consonants?"

"Oh. I bet you have one of those very high IQs, don't you?"

"Off the charts," he said smugly.

"What do you want to do, to be, Evan?"

He thought a moment.

"I guess I'll become a brain surgeon. What they'll do is make a platform by the operating table and I'll wheel up on it and lean over the patient's head."

I stared at him coldly.

"I don't know," he said in a softer tone. "I like to write. I've been working on a play."

"Really? Can I read it?"

"No," he said quickly.

"Why not?"

"It's nowhere near ready and it's not any good. It's just a dumb idea."

"Why don't you let me be the judge of that?"

"Oh? And you are a critic?"

"No, but I've been in plays, as I told you, and I would be honest."

He stared a moment and then he shrugged.

"Maybe I'll show it to you later."

"I'd like that," I said.

After lunch we went outside and I got him to talk a little more about his mother. I listened, practically holding my breath for fear he would stop.

"Sometimes—often, I should say—I felt she was more like the child and I was more like the parent. She was so trusting and always saw the best in everyone, even Aunt Charlotte. She had a beautiful laugh, musical, and she sang to me all the time. 'I'll be your legs, Evan,' she told me. 'Forever and ever if need be, so don't feel sorry for yourself.'

"She never thought she would die before me, I know. She thought I was so fragile I would surely pass away one day, just evaporate or something, and she would be at my side.

"When I was young, she was overprotective, afraid I would catch every little germ. The doctors kept assuring her that aside from my, what did you call it, unfortunate situation? Aside from that, I was relatively as healthy as any other person my age. Of course, I don't have the athletic abilities. I tried building up my arms and my chest, but she was always worried I was doing too much and after a while I stopped doing that.

"She liked it when I read to her. We read a lot of poetry together and we even read plays together and performed out there by the tree. She did a great Juliet, but I was a lousy Romeo.

"Aunt Charlotte complained, telling her she was dot-ing on me too much and sacrificing herself too much. She told her she should be out socializing with young men, finding someone. She could have easily, I suppose. She was beautiful, as beautiful as you," he added.

"She looks beautiful in every picture I've seen of her," I said softly.

"Yeah. Aunt Charlotte was always after her to get out, mix with people. I think she was hoping my mother would find a man, marry, and take me away so she wouldn't have to deal with all this. Poor Aunt Charlotte got stuck with me. She would send her out to meet some blind date she had arranged through one of her society friends sometimes. She would harp on it and badger her so much, my mother would finally agree.

"What kind of a date was it where she had to go meet the guy somewhere anyway, huh?" he demanded, his eyes beginning to burn with hot tears. "Why couldn't he just come here and pick her up? Don't people go out on dates like that anymore?" he asked me. "Maybe Aunt Charlotte was afraid they would see me and be frightened off.

"It was the same sort of thing the night she was killed," he said. "Why did she have to go out that night?"

He wiped a fugitive tear from his cheek quickly.

"I'll write it on a piece of paper for the magic box," he said, and took a deep breath. "But I don't think there's enough magic even in that box."

He smiled.

"I keep her alive in my own magic box, but she's alive in so many ways. See those rose bushes over there?"

I looked and nodded.

"She planted those bushes. They're her roses and when they come up, they remind me of her. I think of

them as waiting for her to prune them, nurture them.
Sometimes, I see a shadow move or hear a footstep in the
hallway and expect her to come walking into my room,
her smile beaming at me, her voice light and full of
laughter.

"You think of me as full of self-pity, but it was difficult to be that way with my mother. She just refused to
let gray skies over our heads. If anything made us sad
even for an instant, we were to close our eyes and think
of blue. 'There!' she would cry, 'It's beautiful now. Isn't
it, Evan?'

"I felt obligated to make her happy and agree. You
know what I mean?"

"Yes," I said. "Daddy was like that."

"Mm. Maybe that's what drew them together. I wonder what *their* first date was like," he thought aloud and
then looked down at his hands in his lap, lowering his
head like some flag of defeat.

"I'd like to see how someone goes on a date over the
Internet," I said to help move him from his terrible sorrow.

He raised his eyes to me quickly.

"Really?"

"I don't know as much as other people my age do
about computers. I started the course this year, but I've
got a lot to learn yet."

"It's easy," he said. "Aunt Charlotte thinks it's rocket
science, but she doesn't even know how to work the
microwave oven. She's never had to do much for herself.
I'll show you most of it in a few hours," he promised,
permitting excitement to enter his voice.

"I'd like that, Evan. Thanks."

He smiled coyly.

"What?" I asked.

"I'll show you one of my computer dates, but you've got to share your date, too. You've got to tell me about it, okay?"

"Sure," I said.

It seemed innocent enough.

But I didn't know what he meant, how much he really wanted from me. Despite all his electronic relationships and connections, he was really very lonely. It showed in his shadowed eyes.

And then I thought, maybe Charlotte wasn't so wrong. Maybe she expected I would fill in some of the empty places that Evan's mother once occupied for him. It wasn't a bad thing to want for him, I thought. Perhaps she did care about him and feel terribly sorry for him. Who could blame her for bringing us into her home if that was truly the reason? It made me feel bad for doubting her or distrusting her.

But then I thought again about the lesson in the allegory of Plato's Cave: Things are not always what they seem to be. Wait, wait for the last bit of darkness and shadow to fall victim to the light, and then look again, think again, feel again.

Then you will know what is true and what is not.

7

—❦—

Heart of the Angel

I had no idea how much time I had spent in Evan's room watching him work his computer and learning about it. I couldn't help but be fascinated by the exchanges going on between the boys and girls he and I watched in the so-called dating room.

"I used to date this girl, too," he told me. "Her screen name is Dreamluv. She didn't change her dating room password so I can eavesdrop."

He looked at me and smiled.

"I think she wants me to listen in. It's her way of teasing me. She thinks it bothers me, I guess. I blew her off two days ago," he said.

"How old is she?"

"She says she's seventeen, but from her vocabulary and responses, I'd say she's more like twelve, wouldn't you?"

"I can't believe this," I remarked when I saw that the conversation between Dreamluv and her supposed new boyfriend Spunky was rapidly becoming raunchy and quite vulgar. They began to tell each other things to do to themselves and then report the results.

"Disgusting!" I cried, and Evan clicked them off instantly.

"Now you've seen cyber sex," he remarked with a casual shrug.

"I don't want to see it. It makes me sick to my stomach."

"For most of these people," he said, nearly in a whisper so that I had to struggle to hear him, "it's all they have. They're either too shy or they think they're too ugly to meet people face to face. Some of them are in my Invalids Anonymous organization. I'm sorry if it upset you."

Before I could respond, I heard Mommy's and Charlotte's voices echoing down the hallway. The sounds of their laughter and their shoes clicking over the tile floors brought my eyes to the clock.

"They're back! Look what time it is. We've been here for hours, Evan."

He shrugged.

"Sometimes I'm here all day. I even have lunch brought to me, and occasionally dinner."

"I'd better see what Mommy's done. Thanks for showing your computer to me."

I went out to greet Mommy and see what her hair was like now and stopped dead when I saw. She had a hairdo that was practically a carbon copy of Charlotte's. She was wearing Charlotte's designer outfit and her makeup was different too: a far brighter shade of lipstick, and more vivid rouge and eyeliner. She had an armful of boxes, and there were more boxes at her feet.

"Oh, Rose, come quickly and help me with some of this," she cried.

"What is all that and what have you done to your hair, Mommy?"

"Don't you like it?" she asked, turning to model her coiffure.

"I took her to my personal beautician," Charlotte said, "who treated her with lots of tender loving care."

She stood off to the side gloating at her new creation like a Doctor Frankenstein.

"Well?" Mommy asked, waiting for my response.

"We brought your mother into the twenty-first century," Charlotte bragged.

"It's not you, Mommy," I said, and Mommy's smile wilted quickly. "You're wearing too much makeup, too," I complained. "It's gross."

Charlotte laughed.

"Really, dear, your mother was made up by a cosmetic expert at the department store."

"I don't care. It's too much for her," I insisted. "You look . . . cheap," I said.

"Oh, my," Charlotte said, bringing her hand to the base of her throat.

"That's enough, Rose," Mommy snapped at me. "Help me with these packages. We're taking it all up to my room."

I gathered what I could.

"Where's Evan?" Charlotte asked.

"At his computer," I said.

"Really?" She grimaced like someone who had bitten into a rotten hard-boiled egg. "I was hoping you might draw him away from all that," Charlotte said and shifted her eyes quickly toward Mommy, whose eyes turned nervous with fear that I had somehow let her down.

"We did spend almost an hour and a half outside talking," I said.

"Good. A little more every day and maybe you'll get him to become social and normal."

"He is normal," I insisted. "He's just in a great deal of pain."

"Not according to his doctors and nurses," Charlotte bounced back at me.

"I'm not talking about that kind of pain. I'm talking about the pain in his heart," I said.

"Oh, well, perhaps you can help him forget that," she continued. "It's why I wanted y'all here, you know," she added, the timbre in her voice colder, more formal.

"Of course she will," Mommy quickly said. "Won't you, Rose?"

"I don't know, Mommy," I said honestly.

"Well, I do," Charlotte said. "You will. We will lift the gloom and doom out of this house and bring it back to its glorious days when the halls were filled with laughter, the rooms were stuffed with wonderful, good-looking people and music and the clinking of champagne glasses, or we will die trying, won't we, Monica?"

Mommy smiled and laughed.

"Yes, Charlotte, oh, yes."

"We met some nice people at lunch, didn't we?"

"Yes," Mommy said. "We did."

"Especially that Grover Fleming," Charlotte said, her voice full of teasing. "He nearly wore lines in your face with the intensity of his looks. I've never seen him so infatuated with anyone. And he's a catch, worth *millions!*" she emphasized.

"He was very nice," Mommy admitted. Her eyes looked as dream filled as a teenager's.

"And don't forget we've been invited to dinner in Atlanta this weekend," Charlotte continued.

"Dinner?" I asked. "But how . . . who?"

"Friends of Charlotte's," Mommy said.

"Grover will be there," Charlotte added.

"I'll tell you all about it later," Mommy said. "Let's take all this up now, please," she insisted and started up the stairway.

I glanced back at Charlotte. Her look of cold satisfaction put a stick of ice on the back of my neck.

As soon as we entered Mommy's room, she began to unpack her things to show me one outfit after another, matching shoes, new blouses, belts, even some expensive-looking costume jewelry.

"The saleswoman said I looked ten years younger in this," she told me when she held up a burgundy pantsuit.

"When I looked at the price, I nearly fainted, but Charlotte didn't blink an eyelash. Take a guess at how much she spent on me today. Go on. Take a guess."

"I don't care, Mommy. This is . . . sick."

"Sick? Why?"

"Why would she do all this for you and spend so much money on you?"

"We've been all through that, Rose," Mommy said, dropping the outfit onto her bed and reaching for hangers. "It's a trade-off. I don't feel a bit guilty or strange about any of it either. We'll earn our keep here, I'm sure. You've already started becoming friends with Evan and helping him, haven't you?"

"I'm not doing it to earn my keep, Mommy. He is my half-brother, isn't he?"

"Charlotte's told me so much about him, how introverted he really is and how much it troubles her," she continued as if I had not spoken. "You know he's never gone to a movie? He doesn't want to go for rides or go into the city. She has to pull teeth to get him to get new clothes and shoes. He doesn't care what he wears, and look at his hair! She's considered having him drugged and then having a stylist sneak in and do him one night."

"Brilliant. That's sure to bring him out," I said and plopped into the French Provincial chair in her sitting area.

Mommy paid little or no attention to me. Her eyes were fixed on each outfit as she hung it up and described how she had looked in it when she had put it on in the store.

"The other salespeople came around to remark how nicely everything fit me," she continued. "I had my own little fan club for part of the afternoon, just the way you did that day I bought you your outfits for the beauty contest, remember?"

"They do that only to get you to buy things, Mommy," I said.

"Now, Rose, they knew we were going to buy things. They didn't have to do anything. Charlotte's well-known in these stores. The way they cater to her, jump and drop everything they're doing when she appears . . . it took my breath away to see such devotion."

"It's not devotion. It's servitude. They're beholden to her for what she spends there."

"It's the same thing in the end, isn't it, Rose? Who would you rather be, the salesgirl or Charlotte?"

"Never Charlotte," I insisted.

Mommy laughed at me as if I was saying the silliest things. I found myself getting more and more infuriated. I could see from the way she paused to gaze at herself in her vanity mirror every other minute that she was infatuated with her new look.

"Why did you let them cut your hair like that, Mommy?"

"When did I ever have the money or the chance to be in style, Rose? Why, I could see the difference the moment we walked out of that salon. Men on the street were pausing to look my way. Even men in automobiles turned toward us. It's been a long time since I turned a man's eyes to me like that. I've been living in a cocoon your father wove around me all these years. Who had time or the inclination to be beautiful before this, or even care?

"This," she said, pausing and holding one of her new dresses against her bosom as she gazed about the room, "is like a miracle. To get a second chance at life at my age."

"You're not that old, Mommy."

"You're as old as you feel," she countered, "and when I was living back in that . . . that life, I felt old. Suddenly, it's as if I have sipped from the fountain of youth."

She closed her eyes and then she opened them on me.

"You'll see. You'll begin to enjoy all this, too. Wait until you attend that school tomorrow and make friends with boys and girls from well-established families. You won't complain about the gossip and the jealousies."

"That's ridiculous, Mommy," I said, scrunching my face in amazement. "There's probably twice as much."

"Nonsense. When you have all this, you don't feel

threatened and you don't have to tear someone else down to make yourself feel good. Why, they'll all appreciate you more, Rose. You'll see."

She continued putting her new things away. She seemed like some stranger to me, saying things, having ideas I had never heard from her lips before. I didn't know whether to be more frightened or angry.

"What's this dinner you're going to this weekend?"

"A dinner at one of the fanciest hotels in Atlanta where there's an orchestra playing while you eat. See why I needed better clothing?"

"Barry's coming to take me out to dinner Saturday," I said.

She stopped putting away her clothes and turned to me.

"Really, dear, don't you think you should shed the past? You'll meet far nicer and finer boys tomorrow, and I'm sure before the week's out, you'll be asked on a date. You don't want to have to refuse someone from here because you've failed to cut the ties to that other place, now do you?"

Tears came to my eyes, tears of definite anger and disappointment. I took a deep breath and stood.

"Yes, I do," I said. "I don't measure people by their bank accounts, and when I meet someone as nice as Barry I don't turn him away in hopes that I'll meet someone who lives in a mansion, Mommy."

"You'll learn," she said, shaking her head and darkening her eyes with pity. "I was hoping our lives, my mistakes would have been enough to drive it home by now, but hopefully, you'll learn."

"That's a lesson I'd rather skip, Mommy. You used to say that real love is true wealth."

"That's something poor people tell themselves to make themselves feel better, Rose. Love," she said, shaking her head. "It's a soap bubble, full of rainbow colors, but as soon as you touch it, it pops and you have nothing but some illusion to remember.

"I'd rather remember all this," she said, nodding at the walls as if they were made of gold. "You'll see."

She thought a moment and then she laughed.

"Did I show you the necklace and earrings? They're made of that material that resembles diamonds. You can't tell the difference. It's called Diamond Air, Cubic Zirconia."

"Really, Mommy," I said. "Someone who has the wealth and background you're raving about would surely be smart enough to know the difference," I said.

She considered what I said and then shrugged.

"Well then, he'll decide to buy me the real thing, won't he?"

She laughed and turned back to her closet. I sat there a moment staring at her and then got up and left. She didn't even know I had.

I wasn't comfortable being driven to school by a chauffeur, but Charlotte insisted and Mommy was like her cheering section, urging me to agree to each and every suggestion concerning me that Charlotte made. At breakfast, she even had the audacity to suggest I cut my hair more like theirs, too.

"Then we'll all look alike," I said.

"What of it?" Charlotte asked, her eyes blinking with innocence.

"One size doesn't fit all when it comes to things like that. I'm me. You're you. Mommy's . . ."

"Mommy," Charlotte said. She looked at her and Mommy turned away. There was a time, only hours ago, it seemed, when that would have brought pride to her eyes, not shame and embarrassment. "Can't you call her Monica?"

"What? She's my mother. Why do I have to call her Monica?" I asked.

"Calling her Mommy just makes her sound . . . older," she insisted. "At least do it in front of any guests we have," she requested.

Again, I looked at Mommy to see if she would disagree, but she was silent and threw me a small smile.

"Is that what you would like me to do, Mommy?"

"I don't see why it's such a world-shattering thing," Charlotte pursued.

"You don't have a daughter or a son," I said sharply. "You're not a mother."

"Rose," Mommy chastised, shifting her gaze at Charlotte.

"That's all right, Monica," Charlotte said in her sweet Southern voice. "Rose happens to be correct."

She turned back to me, her eyes narrowing.

"No, I'm not a mother, dear." She laughed a cold, mechanical laugh. "But after seeing what most mothers, and fathers, I should add, put up with these days, I can't say I feel deprived and disappointed. Modern children are so unappreciative. They think everything is coming to them just because they were brought into this world. They almost want to punish their parents for having the nerve to conceive them. You know what I'm talking about, don't you, Monica? We were discussing it yesterday in the car after we saw that poor woman being nagged to death by her spoiled daughter at Tiffany's."

"Yes," Mommy said quickly.

I turned to her sharply.

"Fine," I said. "From now on, I'll call you Monica, Monica. I'd better get on my way. I don't want to be late for my first day in my new, wonderful school. Am I dressed stylishly enough?"

"Oh, don't worry about that," Charlotte said with a small laugh that brought curiosity to my face.

"Go on, dear," Mommy said. "I'm sure you have a lot to do."

"Of course she does," Charlotte said.

I marched out of the dining room and almost fell over Evan who was sitting back in his wheelchair just outside the door. He smiled at me.

"Aunt Charlotte getting under your skin?" he asked.

"Like a tick," I said, and he laughed.

"I came out to wish you good luck today," he said. "I can't wait to hear all about it."

"Thanks," I said. I felt like fanning my face and imagined smoke pouring out of my ears. He wheeled along beside me as I walked to the door.

"Wait," he said when I opened the door and started to close it behind me. He wheeled out onto the portico. "I like watching you walk."

"What?" I started to smile.

"You have such perfect posture and you glide along as if you're always on some runway modeling clothes or something."

"You're embarrassing me. You just haven't seen that many girls, Evan."

"I've seen enough," he said, his eyes fixed firmly and full of conviction. "On television, over the computer, out there," he said, nodding at the road in front of the estate.

"I've seen enough to know you're someone special, Rose. Don't let any rich, spoiled girl at school make you feel inferior. None of them can hold a candle to the fire you have," he added. He spun on his chair and wheeled himself back into the house with two swift motions, as if he had dared say something and wanted to flee from my reaction.

The door closed.

I smiled to myself and suddenly became very conscious of the way I walked down the steps to the waiting automobile.

"Good morning, Miss," Ames said.

"Good morning, Ames. It's a beautiful day, isn't it?" I asked, gazing at the sky and the magnificent grounds for the first time this morning.

"Rather," he said and closed my door for me. Moments later, I was being driven to my new school and wondering what else lay ahead on this highway full of surprises.

The school certainly turned out to be one of them. Charlotte had never said it was a parochial school called Heart of the Angel. Of course, I had never attended a parochial school either. When Ames pulled up in front of the building, I sat in the car and stared at the front steps and the statues of the angels on both sides of the main entrance, which was two wide, tall glass doors above which were the words HEART OF THE ANGEL embossed in granite.

Dozens of students were heading up the stairs. The girls all wore white blouses and blue skirts and the boys were in dark slacks, white shirts, and black ties. None of the boys had very long hair. Most looked like military-style haircuts.

"Miss?" Ames asked after he had opened the door for me and waited a few long moments for me to step out.

"I didn't know this was a religious school," I said as I emerged.

Ames looked at the building as if he hadn't thought about that either.

"One and one is two wherever it's taught," he muttered. "I'll be out here at three-thirty," he added and closed the door.

I watched him drive off and then hesitantly started up the stairs. Because I wasn't in uniform, I attracted attention. The moment I entered the lobby of the building, however, a short, very slim girl with a tight mouth and small, dark eyes approached me with her right hand extended. All of her features were small, nearly childlike. My hand was not big, but hers looked lost within my closed fingers.

"Hi," she said, "I'm Carol Way English, your big sister."

"Big sister?"

The idea that this diminutive girl was anyone's big sister seemed amusing.

"It means I'm going to help you get oriented quickly. First," she said, attempting to be perfect in speech and manners, "we'll go to the office and get your class assignments, and then we'll go to Mrs. Watson's and she'll fit you with your uniform."

She looked down.

"You're supposed to wear black shoes. Weren't you told?"

"I wasn't told anything," I said.

"Pardon me?"

"I didn't know I was going to a religious school," I said.

She looked skeptical, her smile hinging the corners of her small mouth, stretching her lips and widening the nostrils of her too perfect nose. I suspected cosmetic surgery.

She laughed as if I had said something very funny and shook her head.

"Just follow me. Your name is Rose?"

"Yes."

"You don't exactly have rose-colored hair."

"I wasn't named after my hair. My father liked the name. He thought it was cheerful. Roses usually bring people happiness. He liked to quote that line from Shakespeare about a rose by any other name smelling as sweet."

"You're kidding?" she said, shaking her head, and then continued down the hallway to the bank of offices.

I was rushed along, given my schedule, a building map, school rules, and a letter from the guidance counselor about how to behave in class so as to get the most out of your lessons and how to do your homework. Don't sit in front of the television set when doing your homework. Get a good night's sleep so you'll be alert every day. *Does anyone really read this?* I wondered.

I was fitted for a uniform, but I didn't see why size even mattered. The blouse I was to wear looked two sizes too big on me and the ankle length skirt wrapped like a blanket around my hips. Again I was told to come in black shoes the next day. I think if Mrs. Watson could, she would have dyed the shoes I was wearing. She made me feel as if I had dressed obscenely.

The classes were much smaller than any I had

attended in my previous schools. The students seemed more afraid to be caught misbehaving. Teachers merely had to look angry or disapproving, and whoever was causing even the slightest disturbance became an obedient, polite, and attentive student. Carol Way English had quickly explained to me that students here could be asked to leave and their parents would lose the tuition money.

Before I was brought to my first class, I had to meet with Sister Howell, whose welcome to my new school consisted entirely of a review of the rules that she made sound like the Ten Commandments. When she smiled at the end of her lecture, it was like stamping a smile on the outside of an envelope. She flashed it and then quickly returned her face to that stern look.

The speed with which I was entered, dressed, warned, and delivered to my first class made my head spin. My teachers were all very nice and concerned, however, and each took some class time to review where I was in my studies and what I needed to do in order to catch up.

Carol Way English introduced me to all my teachers and to other students, never failing to explain, "Her father named her after a flower that brings happiness." Her eyes filled with laughter when she added, "By any other name, she would smell as sweet." Some of the other students laughed, too, but most looked downright bored. At lunch and during the few minutes we had to move from one classroom to another, I was interrogated like some prisoner of war. Everyone wanted to know where I was from, where I now lived, and what my parents did. There was very little reaction or interest until I let it be known that my father had recently died in an accident.

My best class of the day turned out to be my last class, physical education—not that I was any sort of female jock. We were given uniforms for that, too. The teacher, Miss Anderson, had just begun a unit in dance. She was teaching everyone the swing, and it was great fun. The warm-up exercises were, she explained, the same used by professional dancers, ballerinas included. I had not had any sort of dance instruction, of course. Anything I knew, I had picked up on my own.

Miss Anderson asked me to come to her office as soon as I was dressed. She was my youngest teacher, probably not more than in her mid- to late twenties, tall with long legs. She had a softness in her light-blue eyes that put me at ease immediately. I liked her smile. It was the kind that made you feel comfortable, welcome. So many of the teachers I had in my previous schools, and in this one, seemed in a defensive posture, just waiting for their students to misbehave or not pay attention or care about their subjects. There was always tension.

Miss Anderson, who let it be known that her first name was Julie, even though I was not to call her that in school, looked like she really enjoyed her work from the start of the class to the end. She had patches of tiny light brown freckles on the crests of her cheeks and naturally bright orange lips. She kept her reddish-brown hair short, but it had been cut with some style and kept a bit wavy.

"You have a lot of natural rhythm," she told me almost immediately. "Have you had some formal dance instruction?"

"No," I said, almost laughing at the idea.

"I did," she said. "For a long time, I thought I was actually going to be a professional dancer. I was even in some shows, but I didn't have the temperament for that sort of life, I guess. What do you want to be?" she asked. No one else had, not even the headmistress.

"I don't know. I thought about modeling," I said. It was funny. I didn't know her at all, but just her way, her sincerity, put me at ease enough to tell her what I hadn't told anyone else: my fantasy.

"You could do that," she said without the least bit of discouragement. "I've always wanted to do a unit in interpretive dance, but I've been afraid to try. I've helped the drama teacher sometimes when he needed some dancing in his musicals and I do our spring variety show. I still keep my finger in the dream," she added. "If you want, stop by after school one day and we'll try some things," she said.

I nodded even though I didn't know what she meant or what I would do.

It was a good finish to my first day, however. All day long I vowed to burst into the house when Ames drove me back, and start screaming at Charlotte and even Mommy. How dare they put me in a parochial school without telling me? My meeting with Miss Anderson had a calming effect. I wasn't as furious when I entered the house.

Mommy and Charlotte were on the patio drinking from what looked like martini glasses. I heard Mommy's laughter first.

"Hi, Rose. How was your first day at the new school?" she asked immediately. I saw from the blush in her cheeks that she had already drunk more than one of whatever it was in that glass.

"It's a parochial school," I replied, finding myself angrier about her drinking than the deception.

"So? You'll get a better education," Charlotte said.

"Why didn't you tell me?"

She shook her head.

"I didn't see why that was important. You don't have to become a nun, just listen to what they say and your teachers tell you," she said. "Most of the substantial people I know around here want their children in Heart of the Angel, if they're not already in it."

"Did you know about this, Mommy?" I asked. "I mean, Monica?"

I could see from the expression on her face that she had.

"Why didn't you tell me?"

"I didn't want you to have any preconceived bad feelings," she recited.

I glanced at Charlotte, sensing those were her words she had planted on Mommy's tongue.

"We never kept secrets from each other before," I said.

"It wasn't a secret, really," Charlotte said.

"I was talking to Monica," I said. I looked at Mommy. Her eyes shifted away guiltily.

Charlotte's slow smile lit up her dark eyes with a sinister glow.

"If you don't want to go there, we'll enroll you in the public school, but you'll be in crowded classes and you'll get an inferior education. My goodness, you don't have all that much longer to go before you graduate, Rose," she continued. "Any other girl would be grateful."

"I'm not worried. I know I'll survive," I said, "but my mother and I don't keep things from each other, or hadn't before now."

"I'm sorry, Rose," Mommy said.

Charlotte started to speak, but I quickly snapped, "I'm sorry, too."

Then I turned and walked back into the house.

Moments later, I heard their laughter again and the clink of glasses.

The way it resounded in my heart, it was as if they had clinked them against my bones.

8

—※—

Barry

"**D**id you know I was being sent to a parochial school?" I asked Evan when I went to see him after I had spoken to Mommy and Charlotte.

"Sure," he said. "Why, didn't you?"

"No."

I sat on his bed. He was at his computer, but had stopped whatever he was doing and wheeled toward me.

"What was it like?" he asked, and I described the building, the teachers, and some of the students. I guess I really sounded happy about Miss Anderson and her excitement about dancing.

"I told you there was something magical in the way you moved," he declared. "It doesn't surprise me that she saw it, too, after only an hour. Maybe you should really think about becoming a professional dancer."

"I don't know. Right now, I feel like I'm in some sort of limbo and can't imagine what I'll be doing next week, much less the rest of my life."

"You look very upset," Evan said.

I revealed how disappointed and angry I was at Mommy for not confiding in me.

"Your aunt is a bad influence," I complained. "My mother would never have done such a thing before we came here."

He didn't laugh. He nodded, thoughtful.

"She's tenacious, like a bulldog until she gets what she wants. I tried to help my mother. She was good at ignoring her when she could, but she was no match for Aunt Charlotte's persistence. My mother was too nice to argue or disagree and she always believed Aunt Charlotte had her best interests and mine at heart anyway.

"I've gotten so her words just float over me. I know it drives her mad. Try to ignore her. Do what you want anyway," he advised.

He asked about the schoolwork and I described some of what I had to do to catch up. It amazed me how much he knew about my senior class subjects and he had all sorts of suggestions and helpful places to research on the Internet.

In the days and weeks that followed, I often did my homework with him. We would listen to music he downloaded over the computer and do my math and science problems. With his skills I had the world's best libraries practically at my fingertips—or his, I should say.

Barry came on Saturday to take me to dinner, as he had promised. We had spoken on the phone a number of times during the week. I could tell from the way he held back when I asked that I had been a topic of discussion at school for a while. What he didn't tell me until we met was how many arguments he had had and the trouble he had gotten himself into defending me.

Mommy and Charlotte had left for Atlanta before
Barry's arrival on Saturday. Evan was very nervous about
meeting him. On Friday, he told me not to bother bringing him to his room for an introduction.

"He's not here to see me," he said, "and I'll only present a problem for you. How do you explain me and all?
Why bother coming up with anything? Just go out and
have a good time," he said, but I wouldn't hear of it.

"Barry's very nice, Evan. You'll see," I said, but he
was so nervous about it that he kept his door closed on
Saturday and pretended to be asleep when the hour of
Barry's arrival drew closer.

I was happier to see Barry than I realized I would be.
It was as though he brought with him all the good memories I had from the one place we had been for the
longest time, a place I could call home. When he drove
up, I ran out to embrace him. He kissed me on the cheek,
but I held onto him and he looked into my eyes, smiled,
and then kissed me again softly on the lips.

"Hi," he said, happy with my big greeting. "It's good
to see you, Rose. You look great."

He pulled back and drank in the house and the
grounds.

"Wow!" he said. "A lot different from where you were
last, huh?"

"A lot different in a lot of ways. C'mon," I said, grabbing his hand and leading him up the stairs and into the
house. Of course, he was impressed with the size of the
rooms and the elegant rich furnishings, the art and the
statues. I quickly explained that my mother had gone to
Atlanta with Charlotte.

"But I want you to meet Charlotte's nephew," I said,
"before we go out to dinner."

I had told him about Evan's handicap, but I had emphasized how intelligent he was and how expert on the computer. When we went down to his room, the door was still shut tight. I knocked, waited, and called to him.

"Evan. Barry would like to meet you."

He didn't respond.

"Maybe you shouldn't push it," Barry suggested softly.

I knocked again and waited.

"He's still asleep, I guess," I said. Barry nodded. I glanced back at the shut door, disappointed.

Barry had done his research of the area and knew where to go for dinner. Once we got to the restaurant and sat at our table, I never stopped talking. He listened attentively, nodding and smiling occasionally. When I realized I had barely begun to eat, I stopped talking and he laughed.

"I'm sorry," I said. "I probably ruptured your eardrums."

"No. I loved listening to you. I think the dancing you're doing sounds very exciting. By the way, I don't know if I'd told you I applied to NYU early admissions, but I did, and I've been accepted."

"Oh Barry, that's wonderful. Congratulations. You're still thinking of becoming a lawyer?"

"Yes, but I'm thinking I want to be involved in prosecution, maybe become a U.S. attorney someday."

"You'll be whatever you want, I'm sure."

"So will you," he countered. "I couldn't imagine anyone saying no to you, Rose."

I smiled. I was almost too excited to eat. The food was delicious, but my stomach felt as if I had just gotten off a roller coaster. In the last week I had hit so many peaks and valleys emotionally, I wasn't surprised.

Barry talked about some of the other kids I had been somewhat friendly with, excluding Paula, of course. Every time I brought up her name, he tried to change the subject. Finally, he told me about some of the arguments he had had and the fight he had gotten into with Ed Wiley, which had resulted in his being in detention for a week.

"Oh, no. You were such good friends. I hate to be the cause of anything like that."

"You weren't. It was all Paula's fault. Let's just talk about good things from now on, Rose," he said quickly, letting me believe there were even more gruesome and ugly details.

After dinner we rode back to the house slowly. I could sense he was prolonging his time with me. I didn't want him to leave either. I suggested he come in and maybe we would find Evan up. We didn't. His door remained shut and when I knocked again, we got the same silent response. It wasn't that late yet, so we went into the family room and started watching some television, sitting beside each other on the long settee.

We began to kiss, small, exploratory kisses, our lips grazing our faces, his moving over my eyes, my nose, and always finding their way back to mine. I turned into him and moaned softly.

He chanted my name as if it was a prayer, and he told me how much he had missed me and longed to see me. His hands moved up from my waist to my shoulders and then over my breasts. It felt good to be loved, to be wanted, to be needed. I said nothing when he reached back and shut off the lamp beside us. Only the glow of the television screen cast any illumination over us. It was a warm light, making his face glow. When he undid the buttons of my blouse and slipped it off my shoulders, he brought his lips down to follow the lines of my neck to my shoulders and kissed me again while he took my blouse off completely. I could feel him fumbling with my bra clip and reached back to undo it myself. He nudged it away with the tip of his nose and began to kiss my breasts.

Excitement within me spiraled out, reaching every part of my body, right down to my toes. I had no idea how far we would go. I toyed with complete abandon and he went further and further, moving his hands up my legs, over my thighs, until he made my heart nearly leap out of my chest.

"We'd better stop," I whispered in his ear, even though I didn't want to stop. I almost wished he would ignore me, but he was too sweet and loving not to listen. He held me tightly, waiting for his own breathing to calm.

"My heart's pounding like some sledgehammer," he said.

"I'm afraid they'll come home and walk in on us, Barry."

"No, you're right," he said. "Of course."

"I don't want you to be upset," I said and kissed him. He kissed me back.

"When you go beyond a certain point, it's like trying to stop a car on ice," he muttered. He kissed my breasts again and held me just as tightly. "It's hard to just stop," he said, not moving away. "Maybe if we do it slowly, like easing out of quicksand."

"You think I'm quicksand?"

"I wouldn't mind if you were pulling me down and into you, Rose," he said.

I smiled and kissed him. He moved down, his lips traveling over my breasts again to my stomach and to my skirt, which was still undone. I pressed my hands against his ears and felt myself being pulled along as he went further and further until I gasped.

"Please," I said with barely a breath.

"All right. I'm sorry. I want you so much," he said.

We lay next to each other, waiting for our blood to settle, like water that had reached its boiling point. All we could hear was the sound of our own deep breathing. Then, I heard something in the hallway and moved quickly to get my bra back on and my blouse.

"Are they here?" he asked nervously. He reached over to turn the lamp on.

We both listened. Except for the very low murmur of the television, it was silent again. I rose slowly and went to the door. I thought I heard the squeaking sound of Evan's wheelchair and then the nearly silent closing of his door. My heart pounded. Had he seen us?

"Rose? Anyone there?"

"No," I said.

"Maybe I should get going," Barry said, coming up beside me. He kissed me on the cheek and I leaned back into him while he held me, kissed my hair, and whispered, "I really like you, Rose. I like you a lot."

"I'm glad, Barry," I said. I turned to him and we kissed again. Then we walked to the front door.

We stood outside looking up at the starry night sky. There was no moon but the stars seemed closer, their illumination washing the world in a silvery glow that turned the trees into sentinels manning the walls of our castle, keeping all the sadness and worry away from us, securing our dreams. It was magical.

"I'll call you tomorrow," Barry promised.

"Good."

He kissed me again and then he left, letting his hand slide slowly through mine. I kept mine extended as if the warmth and the feel of his remained, even though he was already down the stairs. He paused at his car, waved again, and got in. I watched him drive off. Then I embraced myself and went back into the house.

I stood in the foyer and listened. The television was still on, but I didn't see or hear Evan. I returned to the family room, straightened out the settee, and then turned off the set. Before I went upstairs, I walked quietly toward Evan's room. I noticed that his door was slightly ajar and there was some light behind it, a flickering glow.

"Evan?" I said at the door. He didn't reply. I nudged it open a bit more and gazed in. At first what I saw seemed so strange, I thought I was imagining it. He was at his computer, wearing his headphones—and nothing else. For a moment I couldn't breathe. I stepped back, closed the door as quietly as I could, and fled up the corridor, up the stairs, and into my room.

Whatever he was doing, I thought, I had no right to spy on him and certainly no right to judge him. I pushed the images out of my mind, quickly replacing them with images of Barry and sounds of his voice, his words, our wonderful lovemaking.

I had wanted to be as intimate as possible with him, but I didn't want him thinking that if I was that intimate with him so quickly, I might be the same with other boys. It has to be special; it's important that it's special. It won't have the same meaning and significance if it isn't, I thought.

But I was certain in my heart that we would be complete lovers soon. I fell asleep dreaming of that and the wonder of what just the thought of it did to the way I saw and felt about everything around me. It was as if all my senses had been heightened and my blood made richer. The tips of my fingers and toes tingled with expectation. I moaned softly to myself, hugged my pillow, and pressed my cheek to the soft fluffiness, anxious to travel quickly through the dark doors of sleep into the wonder of my fantasies.

Just before dawn, I woke with a start. It felt like someone had nudged my shoulder with his or her forefinger. I sat up and listened. The house was dead quiet, but I thought about Mommy. What time did they return? I had not heard a sound. Was I in that deep of a sleep? Too curious to fall back to sleep, I rose, put on my robe, and quietly made my way out and to Mommy's room. The door was shut, but I opened it very quietly and peered in at her bed. There was enough light pouring through the window to see it outlined and to clearly see that she was not in it, that she had not been in it.

My heart did a flip. Where was she? I closed the door and listened and then returned to my bedroom, but I was unable to fall asleep. I lay there listening for someone. I finally heard the maid moving about downstairs, so I rose, washed, and dressed as quickly as I could. When I descended, she was preparing the breakfast table.

"Good morning, Nancy Sue," I said, trying to hide my anxiety.

"Morning, Miss."

"Have you spoken with Mrs. Curtis already?" I asked.

She looked at me as if I had asked her if she had been to the moon.

"No, Miss."

"I just wondered," I said. I went outside and walked to the garage where I saw the car. If the car was back, where was Mommy?

I went in and to Evan's room, knocking on his door.

"Evan? Are you up yet?"

"Yes," he said and opened the door. He was dressed and in his wheelchair. "I thought I'd come out for breakfast today. Did you have a good time last night?"

"Yes, Evan. Why wouldn't you answer when I knocked? I wanted you to meet Barry and he really did want to meet you very much."

"I wasn't in the mood for company," he said quickly and wheeled himself into the hallway. "Did you have breakfast already?"

"No."

"Good. You can tell me about your evening, if you want," he said.

"Wait."

He paused and looked at me, puzzled by my tone.

"My mother," I said.

"What about her?"

"She's not back. The car is back, but she isn't."

"Oh." He smiled and looked up as if he could see through the ceiling. "Auntie Charlotte's work, I'm sure," he said.

"What do you mean?"

He started to wheel himself toward the dining room. I followed quickly.

"Evan? What did you mean?"

"I told you how she was always trying to fix my mother up with someone, arranging dates. Maybe she thinks she's Cupid," he said and turned sharply into the dinning room. "Good morning, Nancy Sue. I'm starving today. How about some eggs and grits?"

"Very good, Master Evan."

"Just call me Evan, Nancy Sue. I've asked you a hundred times. I'm past being a master this or that," he lectured. She looked more amused than upset and left to prepare his food.

"What are you saying, Evan?" I demanded.

He shrugged.

"She went to a party where my aunt Charlotte introduced her to some fine gentlemen or gentleman, and you say she's not back. It's not rocket science, Rose."

"My mother isn't like that," I said, shaking my head.

"My mother wasn't either," he said. "But here I am." He gazed out the window. "Here I am."

More frightened than furious, I spun on my heels and marched down the hallway and up the stairs. I went to Charlotte's closed door and knocked. I heard her groan so I knocked again.

"What is it?" she cried.

I opened the door and stepped into her bedroom. She was still in bed, the comforter drawn to her chin. With the netting over her hair and her pale face peering over the blanket at me, she looked like some sort of space creature.

"What is it? Something happen to Evan?"

"No. Where's my mother?"

"Oh," she said. She struggled to get herself into a sitting position and reached for a glass of water before responding. "She's not in her room?"

"No."

She smiled.

"She'll be back soon, I suppose," she replied.

"What do you mean? What happened to her?"

"Nothing she didn't want to happen to her, I expect. She and Grover enjoyed each other's company far more than even I had anticipated. She accepted an invitation to see his family's Atlanta apartment and they left the party. I waited for them to return, but," she said with a smile, "she didn't."

"Are you saying my mother spent the night with a man she has just met?"

"Your mother is a grown woman, Rose. Don't you think you're being a bit overly dramatic about this? She's still a young woman. Let her enjoy what's left of her youth and beauty.

"What she or any woman in her state doesn't need is an anchor tied to her legs in the form of a neurotic daughter."

"I'm not a neurotic daughter!"

"Good. Then all will be well. Would you please ask Nancy Sue to bring me some black coffee and some ice water? Thank you," she said, lowering herself back under her comforter. She closed her eyes to indicate that the conversation was at an absolute end.

I stared at her, fuming, and then left, closing the door a bit too hard, for I heard her groan in dismay.

Mommy didn't return until late in the afternoon. Evan and I were out on the rear patio. I was reading and talking about *Hamlet* with him because it was a play my class had already done and I had to read and understand quickly. He had gone on the Internet and printed out some very helpful study guides, and he had read the play himself. His understanding of the language and the metaphors amazed me. Sometimes when he spoke or explained something I had missed, he sounded like my teacher at school. I told him so. I could see he was proud and enjoyed the compliment.

"You see, Evan. You do have a lot to offer people. You've got to stop living like a hermit, an electronic hermit with your computer as your only window to the world. You've got to interact with people, too."

"People disappoint me too often," he said.

"So? You'll meet other people who won't."

He stared at me for a moment and then nodded.

"Tell me about our father," he requested. "I mean, really tell me everything. I want to know the silliest, smallest details about him."

"Okay," I said. Despite it all, I loved talking about Daddy. I closed my eyes and brought up the visions of him I most cherished. I described his gestures, his smile, the cologne he wore, his funny expressions, some of the impulsive things he had done and would do. I went on and on and when I gazed at Evan, I saw a soft smile on his lips.

"The way you make him sound, I can almost understand why my mother became involved with a married man. He was a snake-charmer. I guess, if I had met him, I would have been forced to like him myself, even though I wouldn't approve of him."

"I think so, Evan."

"Thanks," he said and sat back. That was when we heard Mommy's laughter and voice.

He looked at me sharply.

"Don't make her feel like a sinner," he warned. "I did that to my mother sometimes, and I've always regretted it."

"I just want to know exactly what's going on here," I said, jumping up.

I heard all the conversation coming from the living room and hurried to it, where I found Charlotte sitting across from Mommy and a tall, dark-haired man with a mustache like Clark Gable, a strong square chin, high cheekbones, and a dazzling pair of the most beautiful hazel eyes I had ever seen. He was long-legged and trim and wore a dark blue blazer and a pair of light blue slacks with blue boat shoes.

"This must be Rose," he said before I could speak.

"Yes, it is," Mommy said. "Hi, honey. I'd like you to meet Mr. Fleming."

"Please, call me Grover," he said, rising. He extended his hand. I glanced at it and at Mommy and then shook it, letting go so quickly anyone would have thought his was full of thorns. Charlotte was beaming from her chair.

"Hello," I said, forcing the word through my tight throat.

Nancy Sue entered with a tray, carrying three glasses of champagne.

"Ah, wonderful," Grover declared. He handed Mommy hers and I saw by the way she looked up at him that she was lost in his eyes. It made my heart deflate like a balloon. Charlotte took hers.

"Thank you, Nancy Sue. Rose, would you like anything?" she asked sweetly enough to make my stomach churn.

"No, thank you," I said quickly.

"How was your date, honey?" Mommy asked.

"Very nice," I said. "I tried to wait up for you."

"Where's Evan?" Charlotte quickly asked.

"On the patio. We were studying *Hamlet* together."

"Ah, to be or not to be . . . for me, there is no longer a question," Grover declared, his eyes on Mommy, who looked like an adoring teenager. He tapped her glass with his.

"Why don't you see if you can talk poor Evan into going to a movie this afternoon?" Charlotte suggested. She turned to Grover. "The child either has his nose in a book or his eyes glued to a computer screen. He doesn't get out of the house."

"Oh?" He turned to me and smiled. "If anyone can get him out, I'll bet it's you, Rose," he said and laughed a tight, small laugh that made my nerves tremble. Mommy looked like she enjoyed every breath he took.

Couldn't she see how smooth he was? He slid around the room with his eyes, his gestures, and his smile like some eel, titillating both Charlotte and Mommy. He used his good looks well, with confidence, even arrogance.

"Don't worry about us," Charlotte continued. "We're going to a dinner party."

"Another dinner party?" I blurted, looking at Mommy.

"Yes," she said, exploding with excitement. "Isn't it wonderful?"

I looked at Grover, whose eyes were on me, darker, more expectant and analytical, waiting for my reaction. Charlotte was her usual smug self.

"I don't know, Monica," I said with words sharp enough to cut ears, "is it?"

I turned and left the room. Charlotte and Grover's laughter felt like small rocks thrown at my back. Evan took one look at me when I returned to the patio and simply said, "Uh-oh."

I didn't respond. I kept marching off the patio and down the path, my head down, my heart thumping.

Evan wheeled himself behind me and caught up when

I reached his tree. He didn't speak. He watched me sulk for a few long moments.

"I like being with you," I finally said, "and I wanted to get to know you very much, but I think living here is a big mistake."

"It's hard, I guess, to see your mother with some other man. You keep thinking about your father. I didn't have that problem," he added, "but I didn't like her being with anyone anyway. I guess I had the old Oedipus complex, huh?"

"I don't mind her finding someone else. I don't want her pining away in some attic, dying like an old, frustrated widow," I said sharply. "That's not it, but . . ."

"But what?"

"I don't know." I shook my head. I didn't know exactly. I looked down at him. His eyes were intense, glued to my face.

"There's something not right."

He smiled.

"Something's rotten in the state of Denmark," he said, quoting one of the lines from *Hamlet* we had just discussed.

"Exactly," I said. I looked back at the house. "Exactly."

9

Dancing

In the months that followed, Mommy's social life continued to grow. There were strings of days when we didn't even see each other, and if there were some dead spots, some days or nights when it appeared there were no dinners to attend, no shows to see, no art galleries and openings to appear at, Charlotte always managed to come up with something for them to do, some additional shopping, some elaborate lunch. She bought Mommy more clothes, more costume jewelry, more shoes. They traded outfits. They became almost inseparable.

Maybe out of anger or out of frustration and nervousness, I devoted myself to my studies and to the dance lessons Miss Anderson conducted. Soon, it was just the two of us remaining after school. She told me she was a frustrated choreographer and loved the idea that she now had a student with whom or on whom she could experiment. Her idol was Bob Fosse. She had videotapes of his work that we watched together. When she explained and demonstrated something and I tried it, she was always pleased.

"You've got something, Rose," she said. "You pick all of it up so easily, and you've got the looks and the legs. Think seriously about this," she advised.

Evan was very supportive and very excited for me. He decided we should create a dance studio and had Nancy Sue and Ames clear everything out of the guest bedroom down the hall from his room. He even ordered some large wall mirrors to be installed. Charlotte didn't oppose it or even acknowledge it with much more than a simple, "How delightful, Rose. You're getting him interested in something other than himself and his dreary computer."

When Mommy learned about it, she recited almost the exact words, but she rarely stopped by to see me practice. Evan would spend hours with me, sitting in his wheelchair and watching me go through the warm-up exercises and routines.

"Doesn't all this repetition bore you, Evan?" I asked him. He shook his head vigorously.

"No. It's like I'm moving through you, with you. You're my legs. I love it," he declared.

That made me feel good about it, and soon I was able to forget that he was there, that his eyes were fixed on every muscle movement clearly visible in my tights.

Barry returned every Saturday he could to take me to a movie or to dinner, sometimes just to enjoy a picnic on the grounds, but he still hadn't met Charlotte, nor had Mommy been around when he had arrived. Their weekends were always filled with social activities in and around Atlanta.

Finally, Evan consented to meet him. I couldn't help being nervous for both of them, but to my delight, Barry knew more about computers than I had anticipated. Once their conversation turned to that, they were both at it around Evan's computer and I felt like a third wheel on my own date. They took great delight in showing each other different Internet sites and showing each other shortcuts.

"Excuse me," I said, "but weren't we talking about going to the movies tonight after we had something quick to eat? What are we supposed to eat, a health bar?" I asked with my hands on my hips, nodding at the clock.

"Oh," Barry said. "Sorry."

I laughed.

"It's all right. I just started to feel lonely," I said, and they both laughed, after which Evan immediately looked guilty for stealing Barry away.

"Sorry," he said, too.

"There's nothing for you to apologize for, Evan. Why don't you come out with us?" I suggested.

It put such terror in his eyes, he couldn't respond for a moment. He looked at Barry and at me and started to shake his head.

"I know your wheelchair folds up and goes in the car trunk, so don't use that as an excuse," I warned.

"Sure," Barry said. "Come along with us. You'll love this movie."

"I can't. I . . ."

"Have a date on the Internet?" I punched at him. He turned crimson. "I'm sorry," I said quickly. "I didn't mean . . ."

"No, no, it's all right. I did promise to chat with someone, but . . ."

"You'll come along?" Barry asked.

Evan looked at me.

"Please come, Evan," I pleaded, and he took a breath and nodded.

"Okay."

"Great."

"I've got to prepare a bit," he said.

"We'll wait for you in the living room," I said and Barry and I left him.

"Thanks for doing that, Barry," I said.

"He's great. No problem," Barry told me, and I kissed him.

It turned out to be a wonderful evening. Evan's interest and excitement in everything we did and saw made both Barry and me feel good. It was almost like taking a child out and watching him experience things you took for granted.

When we came home, I made us all hot chocolate with whipped cream and we sat around and talked about the movie for a while. Then Evan, looking at me first, excused himself, thanking Barry, and wheeled to his room to let us have some time together. Barry stayed later than ever. I was concerned for him, but he insisted. When we began to kiss, I took his hand and stood up, leading him out of the living room, up the stairs, and into my bedroom.

"The ice is a lot more slippery in here, Rose," he said when I sat on my bed and still held his hand. "Stopping might be impossible."

"I'm not afraid," I said. "I'd slide anywhere with you."

He laughed and knelt down before me, putting his head on my lap while I stroked his hair.

"You're trembling," I said, feeling it.

"In anticipation," he replied.

He stood up slowly, leaned over to kiss me, and we started to make love.

"You're so beautiful, Rose," he said, "but you're so casual and down to earth, you make me feel comfortable. People say beauty is only skin-deep, but it's not true with you. Yours is inside and out. I can't imagine caring for anyone more than I care for you. I love you so much, it makes my heart ache and stops me cold wherever I am and whatever I'm doing. I must look stupid with this silly smile on my face, seeing your face before me no matter who or what is in front of me."

"I hope you look stupid forever and ever then," I said. He laughed and held me for a moment before bringing his lips to mine and then slowly, in graceful motions, helping me take off my clothing and taking off his. "I came prepared," he whispered. "Just in case we found ourselves on the ice."

"Slide," I urged him.

Daddy used to say that if you build something up too much, no matter how wonderful it is, you'll be disappointed.

"Keep a lid on your expectations, Rose. Take things slowly, enjoy the surprises."

I tried so hard not to expect bells ringing or feel myself floating on clouds, all the things I read in books. This was my reality, my entrance into womanhood. Anyone could have sex anytime, but to have it with love was what I was longing for and hoping would happen. It was the only dream I permitted, the one expectation I would not deny myself.

And it was all that I had imagined it would be. We were gentle with each other and loving. We did feel connected, a part of each other in a deeper way. It seemed to

me we tasted each other's very souls, and when it was
over, we held onto each other to prolong the moment and
put it forever and ever indelibly on the very face of our
hearts.

When Barry and I stepped out of my bedroom, we
walked right into Charlotte coming up the stairs. She
paused, a wide, salacious smile on her face. Mommy was
not with her.

"Is this your boyfriend from the past?" she asked.

Barry looked nervously at me.

"No. He's my boyfriend from the present. Barry
Burton, this is Charlotte Alden Curtis."

"Hello," Barry said.

"Is Rose giving you a tour of the house?"

She laughed and continued up the stairs.

"Don't wait up for your mother," she said as she
passed me.

I felt the blood rush into my face and quickly continued down the stairs. Without a word, I walked out of the
house.

"What did she mean?" Barry asked.

"My mother is enjoying the social life Charlotte has
found for her. She seems to take pleasure in my uneasi-
ness about it," I said, firing a hot look back at the doorway.

"Will you be all right?"

"Yes," I said. "Don't worry, Barry."

He nodded and then kissed me good night. I watched
him leave and looked toward the darkness that closed in
around his car, wondering where Mommy would be
spending the night tonight and what would become of us.

All the next day, Mommy's behavior and new

lifestyle gnawed at me. At dance practice, Miss Anderson immediately saw something was bothering me.

"You're missing beats, Rose," she said. We were rehearsing for the spring variety show. I was going to do an interpretive dance she had choreographed. "Something wrong?"

At first I shook my head and just started dancing again. Then I stopped and started to cry. It was as if my tears had control of me. I couldn't stop them and I couldn't stop shaking.

Miss Anderson put her arm around me and led me to the chair.

"Can I help you?" she asked.

I swallowed the heavy throat lump and took a deep breath.

"No," I said. "It's not something anyone can help, I guess."

"Try me," she pleaded.

I told her about Mommy and how she had changed so much. She listened with a look of concern, nodding occasionally with understanding.

"Maybe you don't realize how lost she was after your father's passing, Rose. She had to find a way out of her pain, too."

"She's just so changed," I moaned.

"Great events change you sometimes," Miss Anderson said. She went on to tell me how she had been a very shy girl most of her life. She revealed that she had an older sister who had died from Hodgkin's disease.

"She was beautiful and bright and well on her way to becoming a dancer, too. She was like you, born with natural rhythm, graceful, with the ability to touch people's hearts and souls through her dancing. When she died, it broke my mother and father's hearts. I felt an obligation to fill her shoes and smothered my shyness. I had to wash the gloom out of their eyes. Great events change you," she repeated.

"I guess," I said, wiping my cheeks.

"Your mother will be fine," she said. "Give her a chance. She won't forget who you are and who she is to you, I'm sure."

I nodded and smiled.

"Thanks."

"I can't have my star being sad unless it's part of the dance," she declared, and I laughed. "Ready?"

"Yes."

I was back at it and much better. During the months that followed, I continued to practice at home for Evan and, occasionally, when Barry arrived early on the weekends, I danced for him as well. They were a great audience, boosting my confidence with their clapping and howling.

Evan went out with us more often, sometimes just for a ride, sometimes to eat and go to a movie. We took him shopping at the mall as well, where he and Barry pondered over new computer software products. Often, I would be sitting outside the store, waiting for them. Beside me on the benches were husbands who had brought their wives and were patiently waiting as well. It made me laugh to see the expressions on their faces when they realized I was the one waiting for my boyfriend and my half-brother to shop until they dropped and not the other way around.

The spring variety show was coming upon us fast, and with every passing day, every new morning that I woke and realized how close we were, my heart increased the speed of its beat. It got so I was almost frozen in my bed, afraid to start my day at school. I saw my name up on the posters in the hallways, heard my teachers talking among themselves. They were all telling me how much they were looking forward to my performance. Miss Anderson wasn't sparing any adjectives describing me, it seemed. I begged her not to blow me up so high in everyone's eyes.

"I'll never meet their expectations," I cried.

"They'd have to be total clods," she replied. "Stop worrying. You can't help being who and what you are, Rose. I can feel it," she declared with such drama, I was mesmerized. "Stopping it would be like trying to hold back the sun."

Her words took my breath away and filled me with exaltation. Soon I was eating, breathing, sleeping dance. I would wake up in the morning exhausted and imagined that I had gotten up and dance-walked instead of sleep-walked.

I don't know how many times I reminded Mommy about the upcoming performance, but I was terrified she wouldn't show up because she would have some social obligation or another. She was still seeing Grover Fleming. Every time she mentioned his name to me, I held my breath, anticipating her telling me he had proposed or something, but that didn't come, and I began to wonder if Miss Anderson wasn't right, after all. Mommy was just trying to find herself again and wasn't making any new lifelong commitments.

Finally, the Saturday of the variety show arrived. Barry and I had convinced Evan to go shopping for a new suit. Barry said he would come early in the morning to take him. I pleaded with Evan to do it, claiming it would help me keep my mind off my performance and help me to be less nervous. He had access to credit cards and funds. He was nervous about it, but he truly enjoyed the day with us. Barry helped him try on the clothes and I sat and passed judgment on how he looked. He was so shy and embarrassed, his face was like a red rose most of the time, but in the end, I could see the pleasure in his eyes when he held his packages in his lap. He even agreed to have his hair styled and shortened.

"My two escorts," I declared when we returned to the house that day.

"Your two big fans, you mean," Barry cried.

The three of us laughed. We carried our merriment with us into the house, all three of us ravenously hungry from excitement more than anything, I suppose. However, the moment we entered the house, I could sense that something was different. For one thing, when Nancy Sue saw me, she shifted her eyes away quickly. Even Ames gazed at me longer and then moved along as if he was uncomfortable in my presence.

"You two go ahead," I said to Barry and Evan. "I'll join you in a minute. I want to talk to my mother," I said and hurried up the stairs to her bedroom. The car was still in the garage and Ames was here, so I knew she hadn't left for any social affair with Charlotte. *She better not be planning to do so,* I thought.

The door was closed. I knocked, waited, knocked and called to her.

Charlotte stepped out of her bedroom. She was wearing one of her Armani tuxedo suits.

"Oh, Rose honey, you were gone so long," she said with her usual syrupy sweetness. "Monica waited and waited as long as she could."

"What? What do you mean, waited? Waited why?"

"To say good-bye, of course," she declared with a wide, gleeful smile.

"Good-bye?" I shook my head. "No. Tonight's the variety show. She didn't go off to one of her social events tonight. No," I insisted and opened the door to find Mommy and prove Charlotte wrong.

Not only wasn't she there, but there was a new sense of emptiness to the room itself. I saw one of the closet doors was nearly half open, revealing naked hangers. The top of her vanity table was cleared. Gone was all her makeup.

I spun around. Charlotte stood in the doorway, gloating.

"Where is she?"

"A wonderful thing has happened," Charlotte said. "Grover has asked her to be with him. They've gone off together."

"Be with him? I don't understand. What does that mean? Marry him?"

"Well, marriage wasn't specifically mentioned," she said. She scrunched her nose. "People today often just run off and live together. It's less intimidating." She pealed off a laugh and turned.

"When is she coming back? Didn't she leave a letter, a note for me?"

"Oh, yes," she said, turning at the top of the stairs. "She did mention a note or something. I think she said she would leave it on your bed. I'm sorry I can't come to your performance tonight, but there's an event for the mayor of Atlanta that I just must attend. Break a leg," she added. It was the traditional good wish for a performer, but in her case, I thought she meant it literally.

She started down the stairway, and I rushed into my room. There was a small envelope on my pillow. I seized it and ripped the envelope impatiently.

Dear Rose,

Please forgive me for not attending your dance recital tonight, but a wonderful thing has happened. Grover has asked me to be with him, to be his special lady. We're off to vacation in Hilton Head, South Carolina. It's sort of a test to see how we'll do around each other night and day. I know we'll do well. I know this seems impulsive, but I remember how your father enjoyed being impulsive. There's something to be said for it. I feel like a young girl again. I feel the sun will shine forever on my face.

Charlotte has promised to look after you and any of your needs. She's really been a great friend to me and she will be to you, I'm sure. She's happy about what you've done for Evan and so am I.

I'll call you as soon as I stop to take a breath. Be happy for me.

Love,
Monica

My fingers weakened and the letter floated out of my hand to the floor. I felt so hollow inside. My muscular new legs lost all their strength and I sank as well. Lying there, I sobbed and sobbed until it hurt.

Because I took so long to meet Barry and Evan, Barry came up to see what was wrong and found me lying on the floor, my eyes closed, my hand now clutching Mommy's note.

"Rose!" he cried, rushing to my side. "What's wrong?"

I sat up slowly and wiped my cheeks. Then I just handed him the note. He read it quickly and looked at me.

"You had no idea this was going to happen today?"

"No," I said. "I always had an aching fear, but I didn't think it was going to happen this fast. And today of all days!"

"I'm sorry," he said, looking at the note. "I know it's hard for you," he added, "but you can't let this spoil your performance, Rose. You've worked too hard."

"How could she do this?"

"I'll be there for you and so will Evan, and we'll clap enough for four people," he promised, to bring a smile back to my dreary face.

I didn't smile but I rose and we went down to have something to eat. Evan took one look at me and knew immediately something very serious had happened. I told him and he, too, told me how sorry he was but how important it was for me not to get myself so depressed that I would ruin my performance.

"The show must go on!" he cried. He and Barry did their best to cheer me up. They clowned around and made jokes, Barry imitating me warming up and Evan pretending he was a stern dance instructor shouting orders.

As the clock ticked closer to the hour at which I would have to prepare myself, I began to understand the concept of stage fright. I wasn't sure I would actually be able to get up and go, much less dance in front of hundreds of people.

"I'm going up to take my bath," I told them. "I need some time alone," I whispered to Barry.

"No problem, Rose. I'll help Evan get himself dressed. We men have to work on ourselves, too," he added in a deliberately loud voice.

I filled the tub and lit a candle. While I soaked, I listened to some soft music and tried to keep myself calm. I couldn't help thinking about Daddy and how carefree he had been about everything in his life. He seemed a man who shrugged off tension and pressure as easily as a duck shook off water. *Didn't I inherit any of that?* I wondered.

Maybe it all caught up with him, I thought. As hard as it was to face, maybe all the pressure and tension he had locked up in some secret place in his heart overflowed finally and he exploded. Maybe he did take his own life.

I could hear him at my side, reciting, "Your eyes are two diamonds. Your hair is spun gold. Your lips are rubies and your skin comes from pearls. My Rose petal."

"Oh, Daddy," I moaned. "Oh, Daddy, I need you now. I've always needed you. Sinner or not, you were my Daddy," I whispered and swallowed back my tears.

Somehow the forces that drive anyone to achieve, to go forward and try to accomplish something significant in his or her life, took over inside me. I fixed my hair and my makeup, dressed, and went down at the appropriate hour. Both Barry and Evan were waiting patiently, both looking very handsome and trying not to look nervous for me.

"You're both very handsome," I said.

"You," Evan said before Barry could get the words out, "look fantastic."

"Ditto," Barry said.

He helped get Evan into his car and we were off, my heart no longer pounding. It was more like a snail that had pulled itself into a shell, the beat so low, I had to put my hand over my breast to see if I was still alive.

The size of the audience made it impossible for me to swallow. I thought I would simply faint at the feet of all these elegantly dressed adults and my classmates. This was surely a super critical audience, rich people who had been to one professional performance after another, I thought, and nearly turned and ran from the auditorium.

Barry took charge of Evan, wheeling him to a place in front of the stage while I went backstage to meet Miss Anderson.

"I can't do this," were the first words out of my mouth.

She looked at me askance, smiled, shook her head, and put her arm around my shoulders to walk me away from the others.

"Do you think I would ask you to do something I knew you couldn't do, Rose?"

"That audience . . ."

"Will be blown away. You'll see," she promised. "What's the worst that can happen anyway?"

"I'll fall on my face," I said.

She shrugged.

"So you'll pick yourself up and start over while I come out and do a two-step."

That brought a smile to my lips.

"I know you're going to do well. When it's over, I'll have a surprise for you," she said.

"What?"

"If I tell you, it won't be a surprise, now will it? Just go get into your costume and do your warm-up exercises. We're starting the show. You're number five."

She squeezed my hand and left me so she could tend to the others.

Something happened when I walked out and into the spotlight. I wouldn't think about it until much later, when I was alone and after all the applause had long died down, even its echo in my ears. Alone and quiet, I would first realize and remember how Miss Anderson had hugged me when I came off and into the stage wing, how my classmates in the show had gathered around me to congratulate me, some of them so impressed they just wanted to touch me. I would first realize and remember all the people, strangers who came up to me after the show to make a special point of complimenting me. Later I would hear, "You were fantastic. You were wonderful. You were so good you brought me to tears." It was as if all the words, all the accolades had been frozen, put on pause just outside my ears, and then later, when I had a chance to reflect, they were released to flow through my ears.

I couldn't forget Barry's and Evan's faces, however. They were both beaming so brightly, I thought they could light up the whole school. Barry kissed me and Evan reached up to take my hand. I hugged him, too.

"Your mother's a fool for not being here," Evan whispered.

When I had first stepped into the wings about to go onstage, I had thought about Mommy and wished she was out there. I had even imagined her surprising me and showing up. After the performance, she would come rushing backstage to throw her arms around me and cry with happy tears. She would say, "I woke up halfway to Hilton Head and realized I couldn't miss this and am I ever so glad I did."

It was one of those soap-bubble fantasies. Of course, it popped and was gone. She wasn't there.

As soon as I had changed and come out to meet Barry and Evan, Miss Anderson reappeared with a man at her side. He was tall and very elegant looking, but very slim with dark, thin lips and strong dark eyes.

"Rose, I'd like you to meet someone," Miss Anderson said. "He's an old friend of mine."

"Not so old," the man said quickly.

"A good friend of mine," she corrected. "Edmond Senetsky."

"Hi," I said. I was looking for Barry and Evan and gazed past him.

I saw him smile and glance at Miss Anderson.

"I'm not as impressive as I imagined," he told her.

"I didn't tell her anything about you," she explained to him.

He raised his eyebrows.

"Oh?"

"I didn't want to make her any more nervous than she was."

"She didn't seem very nervous to me," he said.

I looked more attentively at him. Who was he?

"Rose, Edmond is a theatrical agent, but more important, he is the son of Madame Senetsky, who runs the famous Senetsky School of Performing Arts in New York. He was visiting one of his clients in Atlanta and I asked him to stop in tonight to see you."

"Oh," I said. *What does this mean?* I wondered.

"I didn't tell you about him because I didn't want you to have any disappointments."

"Very diplomatic of you, Julie," he told her. "You knew I wasn't going to be disappointed."

"I hoped you weren't."

"I trust your eye for talent almost as much as I do my own," he said. I thought he sounded terribly arrogant. He turned to me.

"I think—no, I *know* my mother would want you to attend her school. You'll remind her of herself," he added with a smile. "She was a dancer as well as an actress. She had classical training, the same sort you'll get in her school."

"I'll get?"

Miss Anderson smiled.

"My mother permits me to choose one student a year for her. It's taken years and years of proving myself to get her to do that," he said.

"You think I should go to her school?" I asked.

"Precisely."

"But . . ."

"We'll talk about it later, honey. I know you have people waiting for you."

"It's nice to have met you," I said to Edmond.

"Yes, well, if you're smart, and lucky, you'll meet me again," he said.

I thought that was quite odd and quite egotistical, but I didn't say another word. I hurried to join Barry and Evan and bask in the glow of my great success with the two people I loved the most in the world, hoping I wouldn't cry when I thought about Mommy.

Epilogue

━━⟋⟍⟋━━

In the end I suppose there was more than one reason I decided to go to Madame Senetsky's School of Performing Arts in New York City. I was upset because it was almost a week after the variety show performance before Mommy called me. There was a letdown after the show anyway. All the preparation, practice, dedication had reached a peak. Miss Anderson and I still danced after school, but it wasn't the same, and there was a heavy cloud of depression hovering over me from morning until night. Every time the phone rang, I waited to hear my mother's voice, but I didn't, and I began to wonder if I ever would.

Finally, I did.

"Rose sweetheart, how are you?" Mommy cried.

"I'm all right," I said.

"Tell me about your little show. Was it as successful as you hoped?"

"Yes, Mommy."

"I wish I could have been there. I should have been there," she added, a dark note in her voice that cracked at the end of her sentence.

"Mommy? Are you all right?"

She was silent.

"What's wrong?"

"Oh, Rose, I've been a stupid schoolgirl, it seems," she said, her voice so choked it was only a whisper.

"I don't understand."

"Grover left me this morning. And it was embarrassing, too. He didn't pay the hotel bill."

"What? Why?"

"He got up earlier than I did, and when I went looking for him, I was given a note he had left at the desk. He said he had made a mistake thinking he could be with only one woman. He said he didn't want to hurt me any more, so it was best he just leave."

"Why haven't you come home?"

"I'm too embarrassed. I had to sell some of my jewelry to pay the bill here."

"I'll pack and come to you, Mommy. Tell me where to come."

"No, honey, no. You're in a safe place with your brother. Stay there. I'll work things out for myself."

"Have you called Charlotte?"

"Not yet."

"Well, call her. She'll send you money."

"I will. I want to spend some time alone, thinking about my life. I might try to get some work for a while. I'm not Blanche DuBois in *A Streetcar Named Desire*—I don't want to depend on the kindness of strangers anymore. I'll be all right. Then I'll come back and we'll figure out what to do."

It was then that I told her about the Senetsky school and what had happened. She was very happy for me.

"Oh, you should do it, Rose. Do it."

"I don't know yet," I said. "There's money involved."

"We'll find a way. Do it," she pleaded.

"Mommy, I can't do anything until I know you'll be all right."

"I'll be all right if you will," she promised, "and you will if you have something to achieve. I'll call you in a day or so. I promise. I've been such a selfish, self-absorbed fool and neglected you, Rose. I'm so sorry."

"Mommy . . ."

"Get yourself in that school. Do it," she said before hanging up.

Evan knew how much I was waiting for her call. He was in the hallway, watching for me. We went into his room and I told him what had happened. He looked very suspicious.

"She's telling me the truth, Evan. Why are your eyes so full of doubt?"

"Remember 'something is rotten in the state of Denmark'?" he said cryptically.

"Yes."

I had no idea what he meant.

"There's something you should know," he said. "I never told you because I didn't want you feeling worse or angrier at your . . . our father. The night my mother was killed by that drunken driver, she was going to rendezvous with our father. My aunt Charlotte made her go. I overheard their conversation. She wanted her to blackmail him, make his life miserable. I don't think she was going to do that, but I know my aunt Charlotte. When my mother was killed, she felt cheated."

"What does this have to do with what happened to my mother?" I asked.

"Maybe nothing," he said. "I don't know."

He thought a moment and then he said, "Just follow me."

He wheeled out and I followed him to the office. He went to the desk and opened a drawer to take out a checkbook.

"What are you doing?" I asked. He didn't reply. He turned the pages and then he looked up.

"Just as I suspected," he said. "I guess I always had it in the back of my mind, but your mother and Grover seemed so happy together, I didn't want to even suggest such a thing and make you worry more."

"What are you talking about, Evan?"

I came up beside him and he pointed to the record of checks paid. Charlotte had been giving Grover Fleming money.

"I sort of knew that he was one of those Southern gentlemen with a rich name and no bank account," Evan said. "There was a time when he tried to court my mother, but Aunt Charlotte discouraged it. I never liked him much."

"I wish you had told me," I said.

He nodded.

"I wish I had, too."

"Well," we heard, and looked up to see Charlotte in the doorway. "And what do we have here?"

Evan closed the checkbook and backed away from the desk.

"Why did you do this?" I asked.

"Do what?" She entered the office, with a big, sweet, innocent smile on her face.

"Be the devil and tempt my mother into the abyss of self-indulgence," I said.

"My, my, such dramatic words. Evan, you didn't give them to her, did you?"

"She does pretty well for herself, Aunt Charlotte," he said.

"Yes, I suppose she does."

"Why? Why did you arrange for Grover to hurt her like this? Why did you really bring us here?"

Anger deepened the lines in her face and turned her eyes into orbs of darkness and hate.

"Your father destroyed my sister's life. Everything that's happening now is just."

"You're a sick, evil woman," I charged.

"Really? I'm sick and evil?" She smiled and moved closer. "Did I bring this poor child into the world without a father, a child who needs more attention and love than most children? Did I try to buy off my guilt with an occasional check in the mail and keep a poor, innocent girl strung along on promise after promise, lie after lie?"

"But why punish them, Aunt Charlotte?" Evan asked for me.

"She knows. I told her when I first met her," Charlotte said. "The sins of the father are visited on the head of the child."

"You didn't get to punish him, so you decided to punish them?"

"Justice for you and your mother," she told him.

"You never really knew my mother, knew your own sister. She would hate you for what you've done, hate you almost as much as I do now!" he said.

Her cruel smile of victory turned into a sneer.

"Your mother was always too weak and too trusting.

That's why she suffered. There are only two kinds of people in the world, Evan, the strong and the weak. I chose to be the strong. Sometimes, the choice is already made for you," she added, looking down at him. "You should be grateful you have me to protect you."

"Like a rabbit's grateful to a snake."

She laughed again.

Then she looked at me sternly.

"I won't blame you if you decide to leave and join your mother wherever she is."

"She's not leaving to join her mother. She's going to a prominent school for the performing arts," Evan said firmly.

"Whatever," Charlotte replied. "I have a dinner date with Grover. I must get myself ready," she said, then turned and left us.

"She's right," I said, my eyes burning with tears of self-pity and tears of anger. "There are only two kinds of people."

"So you be one of the strong. Succeed. Succeed for both of us, Rose."

"How can I do it, Evan? I don't have the money."

"Yes, you do," he said. "I'm going to give it to you and she can't do anything about it."

I started to shake my head.

"You're my hope, too, now," he said. "Help me get out of this chair, out of this . . . prison, by being a successful dancer. I'll be there with you whenever I can," he promised.

He reached up for me and I knelt down and hugged him. We held onto each other, tied by blood, tied by dreams, tied by hope and love.

*   *   *

He was able to give me the money. He had funds Aunt Charlotte didn't even know about. He had taken some of his trust fund and played the stock market over the Internet, and he had easy access to the money. The very next day Miss Anderson was able to tell Edmond I would attend his mother's school.

A week later, Mommy called to tell me she had landed a decent job in Atlanta. She was going to work for a local television station. When she had learned what Charlotte had done, she would have nothing more to do with her. She came to my high school graduation and she, Evan, Barry, and I went out to celebrate. Afterward, before she left to return to Atlanta, we had some time together. We sat and had coffee on the patio of a little café.

"I really don't have anyone but myself to blame for what Charlotte did," she told me. "I let myself believe in fairy tales."

"You were very vulnerable, Mommy, and she took advantage of that."

"There's a sign on the wall in the offices where I'm working now. It reads, IF YOU ACT LIKE SHEEP, THEY'LL ACT LIKE WOLVES. Your Daddy used to say that. The trouble is," she added with a thin, little laugh, "we women need to be sheep sometimes. We need to be devoured by a good wolf once in a while."

"Never, Mommy. We never need that."

She shrugged.

"I've never been strong. But you're different, Rose. I'm not worried for you. You're going to make something of yourself. I'm so proud of you."

"I'm worried about you, Mommy."

"Don't," she ordered. "I'll be fine. There's got to be a

real prince out there for me somewhere. Someone has the glass slipper that will fit my foot and magically turn me into a princess."

Who's better off? I wondered. People who have no fantasies, no dreams, or those who can't seem to shake them off, who walk about with a hopeful smile and eagerly turn themselves to the sound of any soft voice, any jeweled promise?

We said good-bye and hugged and held each other and promised to stay in very close touch, even when I lived and studied dance in New York. When she walked away, I couldn't help feeling she was the daughter now. I was the mature one. It filled my heart with such fear for her.

Actually, it was harder saying good-bye to Evan. He and Barry were the only people I cared about besides Mommy. I knew I would be able to see Barry in New York since he was attending NYU, but once I left, I had no idea when I would see Evan again. Travel was not going to be easy for him.

On a beautiful afternoon with clouds so white they looked made out of milk, Evan and I said good-bye by his tree.

"Will you be all right here, Evan, living with her still?"

"It doesn't matter. It hasn't up until now. She has her life and I have mine. We have little to do with each other really."

"I don't like the thought that you'll be locked up in your computer world again, never getting out."

"Oh, I'm going to get out more. Don't worry about that. And I'm hoping you'll be on a computer, too, and we can e-mail each other and stuff. We'll talk on the phone and, when you're ready, I'll even come to New

York. Don't worry about me now, Rose. Your coming here was the best thing that ever happened to me. Aunt Charlotte doesn't understand. She thinks she got some sort of revenge, but she did me a great favor."

"Me too," I said quickly.

"She's not strong. She's trapped in her own arrogance and conceit. One day she'll wake up and look at herself in the mirror and see only a sour old lady. She'll spend her days in her private hell, believe me."

"You're so wise for someone your age, Evan. I wish I was as wise as you."

"I've had a lot of time to think, study, meditate, I guess. It's made me twice my age, probably. I'm not happy about it. I wish I'd had a normal childhood, too.

"I wish I was out here again, a little boy, holding my mother's hand," he continued, "listening to her read me fairy tales, playing games like deciding what this cloud looks like or that. Pretending instead of analyzing, imagining instead of thinking. You gave me some of that back, Rose."

"Whatever I gave you was only half of what you gave me."

"That figures. I'm your half-brother," he said, joking.

"You're my whole brother. You'll always be," I said with firmness. I kissed him. "You want to come out front to say good-bye for now? Mommy will be here any moment to get me," I said.

He shook his head.

"No. Just walk off, Rose. I'll stay here a while. I've got things to say to the birds, the trees, the clouds. I just want to feel the sun on my face."

I smiled, pressed his hand one more time, and walked away.

I looked back once.

He was sitting upright, looking out at the trees in the distance and holding his head as if his mother was with him, pressing hers to his, and beginning a wonderful new fairy tale.

I could almost hear her voice.

"Once upon a time . . ."

Honey

Prologue

—⚬—

During the spring of my seventeenth year, I learned a shocking truth about my family. It turned my blood so cold, I thought I would freeze in place, become a statue like Lot's wife in the Bible.

Neither my mother nor my father wanted me to ever know that there were such dark secrets buried in our family vaults, secrets that deserved to be buried forever and ever.

Daddy once said, "As soon as we're born, we're given private burdens to carry, burdens we simply inherit. Sometimes those are the burdens no one but you can carry for yourself, no matter how much someone loves you and cherishes you, Honey.

"In fact, the truth is, the more you love someone, the more you want to keep him or her from ever knowing the deepest, darkest secrets in your heart."

"Why, Daddy?" I asked.

He smiled.

"We all want to be perfect for the one we love."

That meant no stains, no dark evil, nothing that would bring shame and disgrace along with my name. I knew that.

I also would soon know why it was impossible.

1

—‹‹‹m›››—

Never Say Good-bye

In the spring of my senior year in high school, my uncle Peter was killed when his airplane crashed in the field he was crop dusting. A witness said the engine just choked and died on him. He was only thirty-five years old, and he had been my first pretend boyfriend. He had taken me flying at least a dozen times in his plane, each time more fun and exciting than the time before. When he performed his aerial acrobatics with me in the passenger seat beside him, I screamed at the top of my lungs. I screamed with a smile on my face, the way most people do when they have just gone over a particularly steep peak of tracks on the roller coaster at the Castle Rock Fun Park, which was only a few miles east of Columbus. Uncle Peter had taken me there, too.

He was my father's younger brother, but the five years between them seemed like a gap of centuries when it came to comparing their personalities. Daddy was often almost as serious and religious as Grandad

Forman. Both were what anyone would call workaholics on our corn farm, actually Grandad's five-hundred-acre corn farm, which also had chickens and cows, mainly for our own consumption of eggs and milk. Grandad sold the remainder to some local markets.

Everything still belonged to Grandad, which was something he never let any of us forget, especially my step-uncle Simon, who lived in a makeshift room over the cow barn. Grandad Forman claimed that way Simon would be close to his work. One of his chores every day was milking and caring for the milk cows. He was the son of Grandad's first wife, Tess, who had lost her first husband, Clayton, when his truck turned over on the interstate and was hit by a tractor trailer. Clayton worked for Grandad at the time.

Simon had just been born when Tess married Grandad, but Grandad always regarded him as if he were an illegitimate child, working him hard and treating him like he was outside the family, treating him like the village idiot.

There were only very rare times when all of us, my uncle Peter, my father and mother, and my step-uncle Simon would be around Grandad's dark oak dining room table, reciting grace and enjoying a meal and an evening together. However, when we were, it was easy to see the vast differences among everyone.

Mommy was tall with a shapely figure, often kept well-hidden under her loosely fitted garments. She didn't wear any makeup and never went to a beauty parlor. Her rich, dark brown hair was usually kept pinned up. On special occasions, I helped her wave a French knot. Mommy wasn't born here. She had come from Russia when she was in her late teen years, accompanied by her aunt, Ethel, who was a relative of Grandad Forman's through marriage.

Simon was the biggest of the men in our family. His father had been a very big man, six foot five and nearly three hundred pounds. Simon had grown very quickly—too quickly, according to Grandad Forman, who claimed Uncle Simon's body drained too much from his brain in the process. Always taller than anyone his age, Simon was large, towering, and lanky, awkward for almost anything but heavy manual labor, which only made him more massive and stronger. When I was very little, I rode on his shoulders, clutching his hair like the reins of a horse.

Simon never did well in school. Grandad claimed the teachers told him Simon was barely a shade or two above mentally retarded. I never believed that to be true. I knew in my heart he simply would rather be outside and couldn't keep his eyes from the classroom windows, mesmerized by the flight of a bird or even the mad circling of insects.

Simon was only twelve when Grandad Forman moved him into the barn and more or less forced him to leave public school. Besides his farm chores, Simon's only other real interest was his beautiful flower garden. Even Grandad Forman was forced to admit Simon had a magical green thumb when it came to nourishing the beauty he could garner from a seed. My mother and I were often the happy recipients of a mixed bouquet of redolent fresh flowers, to place in vases in our rooms or throughout the house. It amazed both of us how something so delicate could come from someone so hulking.

Anyone would look small beside Simon, but Uncle

Peter was barely five foot nine and slim to the verge of being called thin. He had as big an appetite as my daddy or even as Simon at times, but he was always moving, joking, singing, or dancing. His body tossed off fattening foods and weight like someone tossing heavy items out of a boat to keep it from sinking. He had long, flaxen hair, green eyes, and a smile that could beam good feelings across our biggest cornfield. He cheered up everyone he met, excluding Grandad, who ordinarily viewed a smile and a laugh as a possible crack in the spiritual wall that kept the devil at bay.

Sometimes, for fun at dinner—when Uncle Simon was permitted to eat with us—Uncle Peter would challenge him to an arm wrestle and put his graceful, almost feminine fingers into the cavern of Uncle Simon's bear-claw palm. Uncle Simon would smile at Uncle Peter's great effort to move his arm back a tenth of an inch. Once, he even put both his hands in one of Uncle Simon's and then he got up and threw his whole body into the effort, while Uncle Simon sat there as unmoving as a giant boulder, staring up at him in wonder the way an elephant might wonder at a mouse trying to push it away. Daddy and Mommy laughed. Grandad Forman called him an idiot and ordered them both to stop their tomfoolery at his dinner table, but not as gruffly as he ordered me or Daddy or even Mommy when he wanted us to perform some chore or obey some command.

I always felt Grandad Forman was less severe on Uncle Peter. If Grandad had any soft or kind bones in his body, he turned them only on him, favoring him as much or as best he could favor anyone. From the pictures I saw of her, Uncle Peter did look more like his mother than he did Grandad, and I wondered if that was what Grandad saw in him whenever he looked at him. His and Daddy's mother was Tess's sister, Jennie, whom Grandad married a year after Tess's death from breast cancer. Simon was only three and needed a mother, but after a little more than eight years of marriage, Grandad lost Jennie, too.

According to everything I've ever heard about her, my grandma Jennie was a sweet, kind, and loving woman who treated Uncle Simon well, too well for Grandad's liking. It wasn't until after she had died of a heart attack that he moved Simon out of the house and into the barn. According to Uncle Peter, and even Daddy, she wouldn't have tolerated it, even though everyone who knew my grandmother said she was too meek and servile in every other way and permitted Grandad to work her to death. She was often seen beside him in the fields, despite a full day of house cleaning and cooking.

However, Grandad Forman had a religious philosophy that prevented him from ever taking responsibility for anything that had happened to his family or anyone else with whom he might have come into contact. He believed bad things happened to people as a result of their own evil thoughts, evil deeds. God, he preached, punishes us on earth and rewards us on earth. If something terrible happens to someone we all thought was a good person, we must understand that we didn't know what was in his or her heart and in his or her past. God sees all. Grandad was so vehement about this that he often made me feel God was spying on me every moment of the day, and if I should stray so much as an iota from the Good Book or the Commandments, I would be struck down with the speed of a bolt of lightning.

Consequently, Grandad Forman did not cry at funerals, and when the horrible news about Uncle Peter was brought to our house, Grandad absorbed and accepted it, lowered his head, and went out to work in the field just as he had planned.

Mommy was nearly inconsolable. I believe she loved Uncle Peter almost as much as she loved Daddy, almost as much as I loved him. We cried and held each other. Daddy went off to mourn privately, I know. Uncle Simon raged like a wild beast in his barn. We could hear the metal tools being flung against the walls, and then he marched out and took hold of a good size sapling he had planted seven years before and put all of his sorrow into a gigantic effort to lift it, roots and all, out of the earth, which he did.

"Lunatic," Grandad said when he saw what he had done. "God will punish him for that."

That evening I sat on the porch steps and stared up at the stars. I had no appetite at dinner and couldn't pronounce a syllable of grace. I wasn't in the mood to thank God for anything, least of all food, but Grandad thought wasting food was one of the worst sins anyone could commit, so I forced myself to swallow, practically without chewing. Mommy, who cooked and cleaned and kept house for him as well as for Daddy and me, choked back her tears, but sniffled too often for Grandad's liking. He chastised her: "It's God's will, and His will be done. So stop your confounded sobbing at dinner."

I looked to Daddy to see if he would speak up in her defense, but he stared forward, muted by his sorrow. Unlike Uncle Peter, Daddy was a quiet man, strong and compassionate in his own way, but always, it seemed to me, caught in Grandad's shadow. Grandad Forman was still a powerful man, even in his early seventies. He was about six foot three himself, but walked with

stooped shoulders. He reminded me of a closed fist—
tight, powerful, even lethal. He had a thick bull neck,
was broad-shouldered with long, muscular arms and a
small pouch of a stomach. His skin was always dark
from working outdoors, and he always had a two- or
three-day wire-brush beard because he didn't waste
razor blades.

Once, he must have been fairly good-looking. Daddy
had inherited his straight nose, dark, brooding eyes, and
firm lips, but Daddy was slimmer in build, with well-pro-
portioned shoulders. From the pictures we had of
Grandma Jennie, I thought he had inherited her best
qualities, too. Despite his quiet manner and his dedication to work, Daddy was nowhere near as hard as
Grandad.

"Life's got to go on," Grandad declared, lecturing to
Mommy. "It's God's gift, and we don't turn our backs on
it."

Almost for spite, to show us he practiced what he
preached, he ate with just as much vigor and appetite as
he had ever done, and looked to us to do the same.

I was glad when I could get away from him.

On my tenth birthday, Uncle Peter had bought me a
Stradivarius violin. It was very expensive, and Grandad
Forman complained for days about the "waste of so
much money." But I had taken some lessons at school,
and talked about how I had enjoyed playing a violin.

"That's what we need around here," Uncle Peter had
decided, "some good music. Honey's just the one to
make it for us."

He even paid for my private lessons. My teacher,
Clarence Wengrow, claimed I had a natural inclination
for it, and early on recommended I think seriously about

attending a school of performing arts somewhere. Grandad Forman thought that was pure nonsense, and would actually become angry if we discussed anything about my music at dinner, slapping the table so hard he would make the dishes dance. Uncle Peter tried to get him to appreciate music, but Grandad had a strict puritanical view of it as it being another vehicle upon which the devil rode into our hearts and souls. It took us away from hard work and prayer, and that was always dangerous.

Grandad could go on and on like a hell-and-damnation preacher. Daddy would sit with his head bowed, his eyes closed, like someone just trying to wait out some pain. Most of the time Mommy ignored Grandad, but Uncle Peter always wore a soft smile, as if he found his father quaint, amusing.

I couldn't get Uncle Peter's smile out of my eyes that first night of his death. I heard his laughter and heard him call my name. He loved teasing me about it. Mommy had named me Honey because of my naturally light-brown complexion and the honey color of my hair and my eyes. I understood Grandad Forman immediately let it be known that he didn't think it was proper, but Mommy was able to put up a strong wall of resistence and brush off his tirade of threats and commands.

Uncle Peter would sing, "We've got Honey. We've got sugar, but Honey is the sweet one for me."

He would laugh and throw his arm around my shoulders and kiss the top of my hair, pretending he had just swallowed the most delicious tablespoon of honey in the world.

How could someone with so much life and love in him be snuffed out like a candle in seconds? I wondered.

Why would God let this happen? Could Grandad Forman be right? It made no sense to me. I wouldn't accept it. I would never permit myself to think the smallest bad thing about Uncle Peter. He had no secret evil, in his heart or otherwise. It was all simply a galactic mistake, a gross error. God had made a wrong decision or failed to catch it in time. However, I knew if I so much as suggested such a thing in front of Grandad, he would fly into a hurricane of rage.

"Oh, dear God," I prayed, "surely You can right the wrong, correct the error. Turn us back a day and make this day disappear forever," I begged.

Then I picked up my violin and played. My music flowed out into the night. It was an unusually warm spring, so we could enjoy an occasionally tepid evening when the approaching summer let it be known it was nearly at our doorstep.

Suddenly I saw a large shadow move near Uncle Simon's garden, and quickly realized it was he. I stopped playing and went to him. He was sitting on the ground like an Indian at a council meeting, his legs around a flower he had just planted. I could smell the freshly turned earth.

"What's that, Uncle Simon?" I asked.

"For Peter," he said. "He likes these. Snapdragon," he said.

"That's nice, Uncle Simon."

He nodded and pressed the earth around the tiny plant affectionately with his immense fingers, so full of strength and yet so full of gentle kindness and love, too, especially for his precious flowers, his children.

"Play your violin," he said. "Flowers like to hear the music, too."

I knew he often talked to his flowers, which was something that Grandad pointed out as evidence of his being a simpleton. He was the simpleton, not Uncle Simon, as far as I was concerned.

I smiled, knelt beside Uncle Simon, and began to play.

Uncle Peter will always be part of my music, I thought. *I'll always see his smile.*

As long as I played, he lived.

I would play forever.

And we would never say good-bye.

Maybe that was God's way of saying He was sorry, too.

2

Uncle Simon

We lived in a turn-of-the-century two-story structure with a wraparound porch and nearly fifteen rooms. It was typical of many of the farmhouses in our region of Ohio, houses that were expanded as families grew and their needs increased. The floors were all hardwood. Some rooms had area rugs worn so thin anyone could see the grain of the slats beneath them. Grandad believed in keeping things until they literally fell apart. To replace something merely to change a style or a color was wasteful and therefore sinful. He expected the same sort of sacrifices from his possessions as he did from his family.

All of the art in the house was simple and inexpensive. Most wall mountings consisted of pictures of relatives in dark maple oval frames, all of them captured without smiles on their faces. Daddy explained that, once, people didn't believe in smiling for photographs.

"They thought it wasn't serious and made them look silly if they smiled."

There wasn't one picture of Grandad Forman smiling. Most of the ancestors looked like they suffered from hemorrhoids, I thought, and told Daddy so. He roared with laughter, but warned me never to say such a thing in front of Grandad.

The remainder of our wall hangings consisted of dried flowers pressed under glass, some simple watercolors of country scenes, and lace designs made by Grandad's mother and sisters, all of whom were now gone.

The appliances in the house, including the refrigerator, were nearly twenty years old. Everything had to be repaired as much as possible, even if in the end the repairs would cost more than a replacement. It was true that Grandad was very handy and able to fix most of his machinery himself. He believed the less dependent a man was on anyone, the stronger he was, and the better able he was to live a righteous life. Too many moral compromises were made to satisfy other people, he said.

Mommy wasn't ashamed of what she could do in the house. She kept it very clean and whatever could shine, did shine, but she was too ashamed of the age and the tired look of our furniture to want to invite anyone to our home. I couldn't remember a time when she or Daddy had asked friends to dinner, and we never had a house party.

On occasion my music teacher, Mr. Wengrow, was asked to stay to dinner. He appreciated Mommy's good cooking, but it was easy to see he wasn't fond of sitting across from Grandad, who made negative remarks about his profession. He called it frivolous, and insisted that any activity that wasted our time made us more susceptible to evil. He defined a wasteful activity as anything that didn't provide something useful to touch.

"Music touches our hearts and our minds, our very souls, if you like," Mr. Wengrow suggested softly. I thought that was a beautiful way to put it, but Grandad's reply was simply, "Nonsense and more nonsense."

To Grandad's credit, everything on our farm—the barns, the henhouse, the fields, the equipment—was kept in sparkling clean shape. Dirt, rust, grime, and grease were all treated like symptoms of disease. As soon as I was old enough to bear any responsibility and complete any chore on my own, I was given work. Mommy and I bore all the responsibility for the house itself, but Grandad Forman had me out in the fields bailing hay, helping with the planting and the harvesting, cleaning equipment, picking eggs and feeding chickens as well as cleaning out the henhouses. Often, when the work was really too hard for me, Uncle Simon would instantly be at my side, completing it quickly. I had the feeling he was always watching me, watching over me.

One consequence of having all these chores was the difficulty, if not impossibility of participating in after-school activities along with other students my age. Mommy complained about that, and I think because of her complaints, Grandad restrained his criticism of my violin lessons. At least I had that, thanks to Uncle Peter, who on occasion would stand up to Grandad and argue, which was something Daddy just never would do.

But I never thought Daddy was simply a good son honoring and respecting his father. As I grew older, I became more and more curious about Daddy's relationship with Grandad Forman. I sensed there was something beyond the biblical commandment to honor your parents. There was something else between them, some deep family secret that kept Daddy's eyes from ever turning furious and intent on Grandad, no matter what he said or did to him or to Mommy and me. Rarely did either he or Grandad raise their voices against each other. Grandad's voice was raised in his glaring eyes rather than his clicking tongue, and Daddy choked back any resistance, disapproval, or complaint.

He seemed to go at his work with a fury built out of a need to channel all his unhappiness into something that would please Grandad and, at the same time, give himself some respite, some form of release from the tension that loomed continuously over us all, that darkened our skies, and that kept the shadows on our windows and made us all speak in whispers.

In the evening, when all my chores were done and all my homework, too, I would practice my violin. My room faced the barn, and I could often see Uncle Simon sitting by his open window, listening to me play. He had no television set, nor did he have a radio. For Uncle Simon, watching television in our house was equivalent to my going to a movie in town. Mommy asked him over often, but when he came, if he ever came, he came meekly, moving in tentative steps, waiting for Grandad to bark at him, telling him he should be getting an early night to prepare for the morning's work. Sometimes he did drive him out, but if Mommy protested enough, Grandad backed down and went off muttering to smoke his pipe.

Daddy enjoyed Uncle Simon's company, even if it was only to talk about the farm, the crops, and Uncle Simon's flowers. They also talked about animals and the migrating birds. Daddy knew how close Uncle Simon had been to Uncle Peter. After Uncle Peter's death, Daddy did seem to make more of an effort to spend time with Uncle Simon.

Because Uncle Simon was not usually invited to eat with us, I was to bring him his hot supper.

If Mommy could have her way, Uncle Simon would be invited to eat with us every night, but Grandad complained about how he stank and said it ruined his appetite.

"What do you expect, Pa?" Mommy countered, her Russian accent still quite heavy even after all these years. "He doesn't have a decent place to bathe or shower. That outdoor shower you constructed isn't much, and it's cold water!"

"You don't need to spend hours wasting water. Keeping it cold makes him move faster and waste less," Grandad said.

"You have hot water, don't you?" Mommy fired back at him. Sometimes she showed great courage, and when she did, Grandad always looked for ways to weasel out of the argument, rather than take a fixed position and stubbornly defend it.

"I don't use much of it," he bragged.

"But you have that choice," she continued.

"I won't waste any more time talking nonsense," Grandad proclaimed, and left the room. The upshot was that Uncle Simon was still not welcome on a continual basis, and I was still bringing him his hot food.

I didn't mind doing it, especially after Uncle Peter's death. I, like Daddy, wanted to do what I could to keep the wolf of loneliness away from Uncle Simon's door. The little bit of mirth we had in our lives was gone for him as much as it was for me, I thought.

Most of the time he was waiting for me at the barn door, but occasionally, I brought it up to his makeshift living quarters, furnished with an old, light maplewood table with only two chairs, a bed, and a dresser. Grandad had wired the room so Uncle Simon had a standing lamp and a table lamp. There was a rug Mommy had given him and a pretty worn easy chair, its arms torn in places.

I know it embarrassed him to have me come up the stairs with his food. He'd hurry to stop me at the door, if he could. I offered to sit with him while he ate, but he always told me no. I'd better get back and help my mother or practice my violin.

"Don't know why you send the child over there anyway," Grandad would tell Mommy. "Just leave it on the porch and let him come fetch it. He'll turn her stomach with his pigsty ways."

"Put it out like food for a dog, Grandad? Is that a Christian way to treat so hard a working man?"

Grandad pretended he didn't hear her.

I never paid all that much attention to what Uncle Simon smelled like anyway. All of the odors on the farm seemed to comingle. Mommy practically bathed herself in her cologne before she went shopping with Daddy, and she bathed twice a day, despite Grandad Forman's groaning about wasted water.

"This farm has submersible wells," he lectured. "They could run bone-dry on us one day. Waste not, want not."

"Cleanliness is next to godliness," Mommy fired back at him. Their duels using biblical quotes, quotes from psalms as swords, were sometimes amusing to watch. I knew Mommy enjoyed beating him at his own game. She was always telling him to do unto others as he would have others do unto him. His retort was something like, "That's what I'd expect them to do to me and they're right to do it. Don't forget, an eye for an eye."

To which Mommy would shake her head and say, "And soon we'll all be blind."

Grandad would wave his hand as if he was chasing away gnats and walk off, his head down, his long arms swinging in rhythm to his plodding gait.

When did he ever laugh? When did he ever feel happy or good about himself? Why was he so worried about sinning and going to hell?

Maybe he thought he was already in hell. It wasn't to be very long before I would understand why.

3

—⁓—

Tears on My Pillow

Uncle Peter's death remained vivid and depressing, a burden I could not easily unload. Sometimes, I would just stop doing my homework and start crying. Sometimes, I woke up in the middle of the night and pressed my face to my pillow to stifle the tears. My throat ached from holding down my grief. No matter how clear the day, how blue the sky, it looked gray and overcast to me. I spent my free time walking alone, my hands in the pockets of my jeans, my head down. It was even difficult to play the violin, because when I did, it made me think of him and I made mistakes. Mr. Wengrow abruptly ended my first lesson after Uncle Peter's death and told me I was just not ready to return to my daily life. He was sympathetic and told me grief, especially grief over someone very dear to you, becomes a part of who and what you are and is not easily put aside.

"Give yourself a little more time," he advised.

I didn't want him to leave. I was caught between my

great sorrow and great guilt, feeling I was letting down Uncle Peter and his memory. Both Daddy and Mommy were very concerned. They both knew that, except for when I had to eat with Grandad, I barely touched my food. Even the simplest of my farm chores became nearly impossible. Uncle Simon was everywhere, covering for me so that Grandad Forman wouldn't complain. Many times I found my work had already been done before I arrived to do it. I knew it wasn't fair. Uncle Simon had more to do than most people, even for someone as big and powerful as he was.

The few friends I had at school began to avoid me. I knew why. I knew I was too depressing to them, and there was just so much time they wanted to give my period of mourning. They wanted to talk about their flirtations, their music and television programs, and here I was staring at the lunch table in dark silence, not listening to what they were saying and not caring.

I didn't watch television or listen to music and had no interest in going to the movies or on trips with anyone who asked, so they stopped asking. I felt like a balloon that had broken loose and was drifting in the wind aimlessly, carried in whatever direction the breeze was going, and slowly sinking into darkness.

Finally, one night when I had wandered off after dinner, Daddy came out to find me. I had gone down to the pond and sat on the small dock, my feet dangling only an inch or so from the inky water. Around me, the peepers were conducting a choral symphony, punctuated occasionally with a splash when a bullfrog leapt into the water. Because of the way the stars danced on the water and the solitude here, the pond was one of Uncle Peter's and my favorite places.

"Hey," I heard Daddy say, and turned in surprise to

see him walking toward me. "Why aren't you doing homework or practicing your violin?" he asked when he was beside me.

"I have it all done, Daddy. I did it in study session today."

"Okay, but I've gotten used to hearing that violin," he said.

I looked out at the dark water.

"Uncle Peter would be pretty upset, after all he did to get you started," Daddy said softly. "I told you I was going to continue paying for your lessons."

"I know." I choked back my tears.

Daddy then did something he had never done before. He sat next to me on the dock, keeping his feet just above the water, too. For a long moment neither of us spoke. The silence seemed to engulf us like a warm blanket. I imagined his arm around my shoulders, just the way Uncle Peter would embrace me occasionally and laugh or try to cheer me up.

"I miss him a great deal, too," Daddy said. "Every time I hear someone laugh, I turn to see if Peter is coming through a door or over the field toward me. I warned him about doing that crop dusting, but he was so carefree about everything in his life. He just refused to see danger or evil anywhere. He was too pure a spirit."

"I know," I said. A fugitive tear started to run down my left cheek. I flicked it off quickly, the way I might flick off a fly.

"However, the last thing Peter would want is for all of us to stop living, too, Honey. You know that, right?"

I nodded.

"It just hurts too much, Daddy. I can't be anything like Grandad and I don't want to be," I said defiantly.

He was silent and then he nodded.

"No, I don't want you to be like him, either," he admitted.

"I don't think he really loves any of us," I continued.

"I guess he does in his own way, Honey."

I shook my head.

"You don't accept terrible things happening to people you love as easily as he does."

"You don't know how he mourns or when. He does, in his own way," Daddy insisted. "It doesn't do any good to dislike him. It doesn't bring Peter back. Did you ever hear Peter speak against him?"

"Not in so many words," I admitted. "But he didn't approve of him," I insisted.

"I think he felt sorry for him. That's the last thing Grandad wants, however," Daddy warned, "anyone feeling sorry for him."

Why not? I wondered. What was so terrible about people showing you sympathy?

We were both quiet again. Then Daddy reached out and put his arm around my shoulders.

"I don't want to see you so unhappy so long, and your mother is very worried about you, Honey," he said.

"Did she send you out?"

"No, I'm here because I'm just as worried," he told me.

I relaxed and let my head fall against his shoulder.

"What all this does, Daddy, is make me afraid of ever loving anyone else. It's like what happened when we lost Kasey Lady."

I was referring to our beautiful golden retriever, who had eaten some rat poison Grandad set out for rodents in the henhouse.

"Mm," Daddy said. He loved that dog, too.

"After we buried her, Mommy told you she never wanted to have another animal. She couldn't take the pain of loss."

"She'll change her mind one of these days, or the first time she sets eyes on another cute puppy.

"People lose people all the time, Honey. You can't stop it and you can't stop yourself from loving someone. It isn't like turning the lights on and off. It has its own life, its own power, and sweeps over you."

"Is that what happened to you, Daddy? Is that why you and Mommy got married?" I asked.

He was quiet and then he laughed.

"No," he said. "Hardly."

"What do you mean?"

"Our situation was somewhat reversed. We got married first and then fell in love," he revealed.

I pulled back and looked up at him.

"I don't understand. How do you do that?"

"Well, after your grandmother Jennie had died, Grandad Forman decided we needed a woman on the farm. He wasn't going to remarry. He said he was too old and God didn't mean for him to have a wife, but I wasn't exactly burning up the world with my romantic skills. Matter of fact, I hadn't had a girlfriend since the tenth grade, and she got married to someone else a day after graduation.

"Oh, I had a date here and there, or what you would roughly call a date, I guess, meeting someone at a dance or at the movies, but nothing ever became anything. Peter was seeing lots of women, but he was too free a soul to give any woman the sense she'd be important enough to be his wife forever and ever. He liked what he called 'playing the field.'

"There were many nights when he and Grandad went at it, Grandad ridiculing and criticizing Peter's lifestyle, even calling him sinful and warning him that God would not look kindly on him."

"I'm sure he believes Uncle Peter's death was because of that, doesn't he?" I asked quickly.

Daddy looked away.

"Maybe."

After a moment, he turned back to me.

"Anyway, it was clear that the obligation to bring a woman into our lives fell on my shoulders."

He paused and tossed a pebble into the lake.

"You know your mother came here when she was only just nineteen."

"With her aunt, yes," I said.

"Well, Grandad was impatient with my failure to just go out and find a wife, so he contacted Mommy's aunt Ethel, who brought your mother to America to marry me."

"What are you saying, Daddy? You mean, she knew she was coming here to marry you, even though she had never seen you before?"

He nodded.

"And Grandad arranged it?"

"Yes."

"But why would Mommy do that?"

"Things were hard for her where she lived in Russia, and this was an opportunity to escape it."

He laughed.

"I'll never forget the way we were introduced. Your grandad said, 'Here's your wife. The wedding will be tomorrow.'"

"But why did you do it? I mean, I know Mommy is

very pretty and all, but she was still a stranger. How can you marry someone without knowing anything about her?"

"When I first saw your mother that day, I actually felt sorrier for her than I had been feeling for myself. No one looked more helpless, more lost, more terrified of tomorrow. I couldn't even utter the word no.

"And then I looked into her eyes, past the fear, past the terror, and I saw something that warmed my heart. I don't know if that qualifies as love at first sight, but I thought I could make her feel good, and I hoped she could do the same for me.

"In time, we grew closer and closer. Maybe we didn't have the sort of romantic start people see in movies and read in books, but what we have is strong. We've become tied to each other in deep ways. I don't think she could stop herself from loving me any more than I could stop myself from loving her.

"If that could happen to me, it will surely happen to you, Honey. Don't worry about it. Love will find its way into your heart, and it will be more comfortable there because of what your uncle Peter gave you and taught you."

"I hope so, Daddy."

"I know so," he said. He smiled at me and stood up. "How about you come home and practice that violin?"

"Okay, Daddy," I said, and rose. He reached for my hand.

"Look at you," he said, "with calluses on your palms from your farm chores. I bet that alone scares away most of the boys today. You're too tough for them."

I laughed.

"I haven't held hands with any lately," I said.

"Never mind, you will," he said.

I couldn't remember the two of us having a more warm and wonderful conversation. It did help me regain my composure, and that night, I played the violin better than I had for weeks. When I looked out the window, I saw Uncle Simon had come to his. I couldn't see the expression on his face, only his big body was silhouetted in the frame, but I knew that he was wearing a smile. I could feel it even across the yard.

I never stopped mourning the death of Uncle Peter, but in the days that followed my quiet conversation with Daddy at the pond, I felt myself emerging from the darkness and looking forward to the light. I began to talk more at school, cared more about my appearance, and practiced my violin with greater determination. Mr. Wengrow was very pleased with my progress and told me so.

One day he made a surprising proposal.

"I have another student I tutor. He's a pianist, and I think it might be of great benefit to you both if you practiced some music together. I don't know if it's possible, but I would suggest you come to my home to do so. I have a piano there. What do you think of the idea?

"Actually," he said before I could respond, "the two of you are my most exciting and promising students. I would want to give you both extra help and not charge you for it. I wouldn't be in this work if I didn't have a passion for it and I didn't get great satisfaction out of finding students like yourself and Chandler," he added.

"Chandler? You don't mean Chandler Maxwell?" I asked.

Chandler Maxwell was a very wealthy boy in my

class whom everyone considered to be the poster boy for being stuck-up. Except for some geeky younger boys who seemed to idolize him, he had no friends whatsoever. He came to school in a shirt and tie, with his hair trimmed almost military style and his slacks perfectly creased. There wasn't a single school activity that appeared to interest him. He didn't belong to any team, any group, any club. Everyone had the feeling he was looking down on their efforts, and everyone wondered why he didn't attend some expensive private school anyway.

Apparently, his father, who was president of one of the local banks, didn't believe in sending him to a private school. He had succeeded with a public school education and his son should do the same was the philosophy he preached to anyone who asked.

Most of us knew Chandler played piano. There were times when he played it at school, and the choral teacher and the band instructor both tried to get him to participate in their concerts, but he steadfastly refused, simply shaking his head with a smirk that suggested he thought their suggestion was ridiculous.

Naturally, the other boys mocked him, teased him, even tried to get him to fight, but he never did. If I could say anything on his behalf it was that he had remarkable self-control and the ability to ignore anyone and anything that displeased him.

He was not bad-looking, either. There were occasions when I stared at him and his eyes met mine, but he always made me feel guilty, made me feel as if I had stolen a look at a forbidden subject. I know I turned crimson and shifted my eyes away guiltily, and then chastised myself for being so interested, even for an instant. I wanted to hate him and despise him as much as all my friends did, but something kept me from doing that, something kept me stealing glances.

"Yes," Mr. Wengrow said. "Chandler Maxwell. I've already discussed the possibility with him and he is willing, especially after I described your talent."

"Maybe he won't think I'm so talented once he hears me play," I said.

"Chandler respects my opinion on such matters, Honey. He wouldn't be working with me otherwise, believe me. He's a very opinionated and an extraordinarily self-confident young man. Personally, I think he has musical genius."

I raised my eyebrows. I knew Chandler was a good student, but not within the top ten students in my class. He was in all of my classes—including my language class, even though I suspected he didn't have any interest in taking Spanish. He always looked so bored, but took it because there was a language requirement. Whenever he was asked to pronounce or recite something, he did it so softly Mrs. Howard had to ask him to repeat it, and eventually would give up on him.

"I don't know," I said.

The idea was intriguing, but at the same time frightening. What if he made fun of me? I knew how sarcastic he could be. Most of the boys who jeered him didn't even understand his comebacks and how degrading and nasty they were. When that happened, I could see the self-satisfaction in his eyes. If he caught me looking at him, he tightened his lips and narrowed his eyes with suspicion, as if he was afraid I might expose him.

"Well, would you like me to speak to your mother

about it?" Mr. Wengrow asked. "Because of her background, she has a real appreciation for good music."

"I don't know," I repeated.

"Well, let me mention it and then you and your family can discuss it. I suppose there would be some consideration about getting you to my home and back."

"I have my license," I said quickly. "I've been driving since I was ten, actually. On the farm, I mean. I'm sure I could use my daddy's pickup."

I realized I was solving problems enthusiastically. I did want to do this.

"Fine. We'll talk about it in more detail next time I come," he said.

Before he left, he did talk to Mommy and Daddy. Grandad was present, but made no comments, unless we counted his grunt.

"It sounds like a good opportunity," Mommy told me later that night. "Mr. Wengrow's so excited about it, he says he won't charge for the added time. What do you think, Honey?"

"I guess I could try to see how it goes," I offered.

Daddy looked pleased and nodded.

They were both so nervous about my moods and emotions these days that anything that promised to bring me some pleasure was desirable.

"Then we'll tell him it's fine with us," Mommy said.

"I'll need the pickup, I think," I told Daddy. "I wouldn't want you to have to drive me."

"You can use the pickup, but you had better clean it up before you get in it," Mommy said. "You don't want to walk into someone's home smelling like a farm girl."

"What's wrong with that?" we heard Grandad call from the living room. He was listening through the walls.

"Nothing a good shampoo and bath won't cure," Mommy retorted.

Daddy actually laughed loud enough for Grandad to hear.

It brought a smile to my face.

Uncle Peter wouldn't have laughed much louder, I thought. He's still with us.

4

---※---

The Lesson

Needless to say, I was very nervous the first night I drove over to Mr. Wengrow's house. I rushed through dinner, which brought me looks of displeasure from Grandad Forman's piercing, reprimanding eyes, and then I went upstairs to my room and agonized over what I should wear.

Should it be one of my better dresses or skirts, or should I just wear what I wore to school? Was I making too much of all this? Would I be overdoing it, pumping up Chandler's already exaggerated ego? What if I dressed nicely but he pulled a complete switch and came in a pair of jeans and a T-shirt, showing me how little he thought of the occasion? Wouldn't I feel the fool?

And then what about my hair? Should I have washed it? Was brushing it and spraying it enough? How much makeup should I put on? Just lipstick, or a little rouge? I kept smelling myself, terrified that I would bring the farm odors along with me. Chandler would surely say something unpleasant about that. I was positive I overdid my cologne.

Finally, I settled on just a little touch of lipstick, no rouge, and my dark blue skirt and light blue short-sleeve blouse. I put on a pair of sandals, took one last glimpse of myself in the mirror, and hurried downstairs, not realizing until I was at the bottom that I had forgotten my violin.

Mumbling complaints about myself to myself, I hurried back upstairs to fetch it and then took a deep breath, calmed myself, and walked slowly down the stairs. Mommy came out to tell me to drive carefully.

"Come right home afterward, Honey," Daddy called from behind her.

When I stepped out of the house, I saw that Uncle Simon had washed the truck. He was just wiping off the windshield, and stepped away as I approached.

"I told your daddy I would do it," he said before I could ask or say a word.

"Thank you, Uncle Simon."

"I checked the air in the tires and the oil, too," he added. "Everything's fine."

"I'm only going about four miles, Uncle Simon," I said, smiling. "It's not more than a ten-minute ride," I added.

"Most accidents happen close to home," he said. I realized everyone was nervous about everyone else since Uncle Peter's accident.

"I'll be careful," I promised, opening the truck door, putting in my violin, and turning back to him. He stood there, nodding.

"Thank you, Uncle Simon," I said again, and got on tiptoe to give him a quick kiss on his cheek. Even in the darkness, I could see his face bloom like one of his red roses. His eyes brightened.

I got into the truck, waved, and drove off, taking a hard bounce on the rise in the driveway Grandad never cared to have fixed because it reminded us that "life was full of bumps to avoid or tolerate."

Moments later, I was on the highway. My heart sped up with my anticipated arrival at Mr. Wengrow's. When I pulled into his driveway, I realized I would have to park next to Chandler's beautiful late-model black Mercedes. I pulled as far from it as I could.

Mr. Wengrow lived in a modest one-story Queen Anne, set back on close to an acre of land. He was a bachelor who had lived with his parents. His mother had passed away first and his father had died just last year. During the day he taught music at a private elementary school.

Mr. Wengrow greeted me in a dark brown sports jacket, an open shirt, and a pair of brown slacks and shoes. I was glad to see he wasn't dressed any more formally than usual.

There was a very small vestibule on entry with a mirror on the right. The frame of the mirror had hooks for jackets and beneath it was a small, dark oak table with a flower-patterned vase. It had nothing in it, and I regretted not asking Uncle Simon for some flowers to bring.

"Right on time," he said smiling. "Chandler was a little early. He likes to spend more time warming up," he explained, raising his voice over the sound of the piano, which seemed to get louder.

He led me to the living room on the left. It had modest, colonial furnishings with a large dark brown oval rug. The grand piano was prominent, actually too large for the room, which was well-lit by a ceiling fixture and two standing lamps, as well as the small lamp on the piano. Mr. Wengrow had set up my music stand to the right, with its clipped light already on and waiting for my sheet music.

Chandler was dressed like he dressed for school, a tie and slacks. He didn't look up or stop playing when I entered. Both Mr. Wengrow and I watched him for a few moments and then Mr. Wengrow nodded toward my stand. I took my violin out of its case and stepped up. Chandler finally lifted his fingers from the keys and turned to me.

"I didn't know you were taking private lessons," he said.

I wanted to say, *How would you know? You never say two words to me at school,* but instead, I nodded and said, "Mr. Wengrow just told me about you, too."

"Oh?" He looked at our teacher.

"Don't you two see each other at school?" he asked innocently. "I just assumed . . ."

I looked at Chandler.

"We see each other," he said, his eyes softening and becoming impish, I thought. "But we've never exchanged résumés," he added.

"Well, now you both know. Shall we begin?" Mr. Wengrow said, and started to outline what he hoped to accomplish.

Almost immediately I made one mistake after another, and sounded like a first-year student. I became even more flustered because of that and made more mistakes.

"Take your time," Mr. Wengrow kept saying.

Every time we had to stop, Chandler lifted his fingers

off the keys but held them hovering there and stared ahead. He said nothing encouraging. Finally, he stood up.

"Why don't you work with her for a few minutes solo, Mr. Wengrow? I have to make a phone call anyway," he added and, without waiting for a response, walked out of the room.

I felt like bursting into tears.

"I'm sorry," I said.

"It's all right. Every time you do something different, you'll have some butterflies. With time and experience, you'll find ways to overcome it, I'm sure. Let's go back and do this one more time," he urged patiently.

After a while I did feel myself calm down. When Chandler returned, he glanced at me quickly but took his place at the piano and waited for Mr. Wengrow's instructions. We played on and I did better and better, so much better, in fact, that Chandler started to glance at me, his eyes revealing appreciation.

"Good," Mr. Wengrow muttered, nodding. "Good. That's it. Good. Well, Chandler," he said stepping back when we ended, "was I right about Miss Forman or not?"

"You were very much right," Chandler said, glancing at me and then standing.

"Shall we say same time, same night next week?" Mr. Wengrow asked.

"It's fine with my schedule," Chandler said.

"Honey?"

"What? Oh, yes," I said.

"Good night, Mr. Wengrow," Chandler said, and started out. I put my violin away quickly.

"You both have the makings of fine musicians, Honey," Mr. Wengrow said. "I have high hopes."

"Thank you," I said. I heard the front door open and close.

He has as much personality as a dead snail, I thought. I felt stupid now even worrying about what I wore, what I looked like. I almost wished I had smelled like a cow when I arrived. *He needs something sharp stinging his nostrils,* I concluded. I never knew a boy could stir such rage in me without saying a word.

Mr. Wengrow followed me to the door to say good night. I thanked him and left, my head down as I walked.

"Watch your step," I heard, and looked up quickly to see Chandler waiting at his car, leaning against it, his arms folded.

"You drove that truck?" he asked, nodding at it.

"It didn't drive me," I replied.

He smiled and nodded.

"I know your farm. My father's bank carries the mortgage."

I knew his father was a bank president, of course, but I had no idea where Grandad Forman had his business affairs. I didn't reply. I went to the truck, opened the door, and put the violin on the seat.

"You are good," he said, stepping closer to me. "I trusted Mr. Wengrow not to waste my time, but he sometimes exaggerates to make the parents of his students feel good about their so-called prodigies."

"My parents don't think I'm a prodigy. Is that what yours think you are?" I shot back at him. "Is that why you play the piano?"

He shrugged.

"I don't know. Maybe. I play because it pleases me and seems to please people who hear me do it. Why do you play the violin?" he countered.

I thought a moment.

"An uncle of mine once said I don't play it."

"Huh?"

"He said, 'It plays you.' "

"It plays you?"

"Exactly," I said, getting into the truck and looking out the window at him. "If you can find a way to understand that, you might find a way to understand yourself."

"Who says I don't understand myself?"

"No one. Who else can know if you do or not but you?"

I started the engine. He drew closer.

"What are you, full of riddles?"

"Not any more or less than anyone else, I suppose. I enjoyed playing my violin with your accompaniment, Chandler. You don't play the piano. It plays you," I said, smiling, and put the truck in reverse.

I backed out of the driveway and took one last look at him. He was still standing there, watching me. I waved and then drove off, my heart thumping so hard, I thought I would have a rush of blood to my head and pass out.

He has beautiful eyes, I admitted to myself. He didn't turn them to me as much as I would have liked, but on the other hand, if he looked at me too much, I would probably have a harder time concentrating on my music. Still, it was nice to think of them now. It brought a smile to my face, and that smile remained there like a soft impression in newly fallen snow.

"You look like you had a good time," Daddy said when I entered the house. He and Mommy were in the kitchen, talking. Grandad had fallen asleep in his chair in front of the television set. He was snoring at a volume that was almost as loud as the program.

"What? Oh. Yes, it was very good, Daddy."

"I'm glad," he said. "Maybe you really should think of a career in music."

"Maybe," I said, and went up to my room.

I sat at my vanity table and stared at my image in the mirror, wondering if I was at all attractive. Was my nose too small, my lips too thin, my eyes too close together?

I stood up and began to undress, gazing at myself as I stripped down to bare skin. I had a figure people called perky, cute. Would I ever be beautiful? It seemed to me that boys didn't take cute girls seriously enough, only the girls who were beautiful. I'd always look too young. When I once voiced such a complaint, Mommy told me to just wait twenty years, I'd love being considered too young then; but who wanted to wait so long to be happy about herself? Not me. I wanted to be happy about myself now.

I realized I was standing nude in front of my mirror and judging my breasts, my curves, and my waist. Was this sinful? Would I be punished for my vanity? Grandad would certainly say so, I thought, and I almost expected to hear a boom of thunder and see the sizzle of God's displeasure light up my bedroom windows.

I heard the phone ring and a moment later Mommy called up to me.

"There's a phone call for you, Honey."

"Me?" I scooped up my robe and hurriedly put it on as I went to the foot of the stairs. Mommy was standing at the bottom. "Who is it?"

"Chandler Maxwell. He sounds so formal." Mommy shook her head and laughed. "He sounds more like one of your teachers than a classmate."

"Yes, he does," I said, laughing to myself. *What could he*

want? I wondered. Did he get angry at me for teasing him? Is he calling to tell me he won't attend another lesson?

We had one phone, situated in the hallway. Grandad didn't see any need for another and certainly didn't see a need for me to have my own phone, so there wasn't that much privacy for anyone who received a call—not that I received very many.

"Hello," I said. Mommy walked back into the kitchen.

"I'm sorry to bother you so late."

"It's not that late."

"Yes, well, for many people it might be," he insisted.

"Well, what is it?"

"I have tickets to the production of *Porgy and Bess* at the convention center. It's light opera."

"I know what it is," I said.

"It probably won't be that good, but my father gets these tickets because of the bank, and I was wondering if you would like to go. It's this coming Saturday night. I know that's giving you very short notice," he added before I could respond, "so I won't be upset if you can't go. I just thought you might enjoy the music. We have so little of it in our community and—"

"Yes," I said to stop him from going on and on.

"Yes?"

"Yes, I'd like to go. Thank you."

"Oh, well, good. I'll see you in school and give you more detail."

"That's fine. Thank you."

"Maybe . . ."

He hesitated. I waited a moment and then said, "Yes?"

"Maybe, if you're able to, you could, I mean, I could take you for something to eat first."

"Oh. Sure. I guess," I said.

"Fine. I'll give you more detail in school," he repeated.

"Okay."

"Well, then, good night. See you very soon, I hope," he said.

"I'll see you in school tomorrow, Chandler," I reminded him, laughing to myself. I didn't think anyone could be more nervous and shy than I was. I now suspected that most of what people interpreted as his arrogance was just his shyness.

"Right. See you then," he said and hung up.

"What was that all about?" Mommy asked from the kitchen doorway.

"Chandler Maxwell's father gets tickets to shows and he wanted to know if I'd like to go see *Porgy and Bess* Saturday night. I said yes. Is that all right?"

"That's very nice," Mommy said. Daddy came up beside her.

"He wants to take me to dinner first," I added.

"Well, that's a full-blown date. Sounds like something special," Daddy kidded.

"She could use something new to wear," Mommy told him. He nodded.

"I don't have to buy something new," I said.

"Your mother wants you to so she can help you pick it out," Daddy said, smiling at her.

"But . . ."

"He's right," Mommy said, stepping forward to take my hand and smile. "There's a point in every mother's life when she starts to relive her own youth through her children, especially a daughter."

I smiled. It wasn't something she and I had done very often.

"Okay," I said. Then I ran up the stairs, my heavy footsteps waking Grandad, who called out to ask what was going on in his house? It sounded like the roof was caving in. Couldn't we walk softer?

Not tonight, I thought. Not tonight, Grandad. I was so excited, I didn't think I would fall asleep. I got into my nightgown and under the covers, anxious for the night to pass and the morning to bring me to school.

I reached over and turned off the light on my nightstand, throwing the room into darkness.

Outside, the moon had just gone over the west side of the house. Like a giant yellow spotlight, it lit up the barn and my step-uncle Simon's window. He was sitting there, looking toward mine.

And I realized I had left it wide open while I had been studying my naked body. Had he been there that whole time? I was too old now to leave my window open like this, I thought, and went over to draw the shade.

After all, I told myself, *Chandler Maxwell had called me for a date.* I would buy something new and beautiful and I would fix my hair and study how beautiful women in magazines did their makeup. Men would start to notice me. It would be as if I had just been discovered standing there or walking or sitting at a table.

Who is that? they would surely wonder. Every smile, every look of appreciation would be like hands clapping.

Emerging from childhood, a woman is surely reborn. It's almost as if a light goes on inside us and the glow from it brightens the stage and opens the curtain. When that happens, one way or another, all of us live off the applause.

5

—❦—

A New Song Begins

I used to think that I was exceptionally shy. If a boy stopped to speak to me or showed me any attention, I could feel the heat rise to my face immediately, and just knowing my skin was starting to glow like the inside of a toaster made me even shier. I had to shift my eyes away and always spoke quickly, giving whoever it was the impression I wanted to get away from him as fast as I could. It wasn't my intention, but I could understand why someone would think that.

When I arrived at school the following day, I looked forward to seeing Chandler. His locker was halfway down the hall from mine, and pretty soon I saw him arrive. He glanced my way, but to my surprise, he returned his attention to his locker, took out what he needed, closed it, and walked on as if he and I had never met. For a moment I was so stunned I had to question my own sanity. Did we speak on the phone and did he invite me to dinner and a show? Or was that a dream?

I hurried to homeroom, now even more curious and more eager to speak with him. He sat two rows left of me. When I entered, I looked at him, but he had his face in one of his textbooks as usual, not bothering to look up when the teacher spoke or when the announcements came over the public-address system. Our teacher asked everyone to take his or her seat. Roll was taken and then the bell for our first class rang. I deliberately moved slowly so Chandler and I would be side by side as we were leaving the room.

"Hi," I said as soon as he was beside me.

"Hi," he replied; he gazed about nervously for a moment and then sped up and walked away, swinging the briefcase he carried, which looked like a lawyer's attaché case and was the object of many jokes.

I just stood there, amazed, as other students moved by, some knocking into me because my feet were planted in cement.

"You all right?" Karen Jacobs asked me.

"What? Oh. Yes," I said and started to walk to class. She tagged along.

Karen was a mousy-looking girl with big though dull brown eyes, whose life was apparently so boring she fed off everyone else's sadness as well as happiness. Almost ninety percent of what she said to anyone daily was in the form of a question. Sometimes I thought she resembled a squirrel, hoarding information, tidbits, anecdotes about other people, like acorns; and sometimes, I thought she was more like a parasite, existing solely off the life of her hosts, which in this case was anyone who cared to share his or her revelations.

"I saw you say something to Chandler Maxwell. What did you say?"

"I said hi."

"Why?"

"Why not?" I fired back at her. She looked confused and lagged a step or two behind me.

During my first-period class, however, I sensed her nearly constant study of my every glance and gesture. Maybe she had some sort of built-in radar for these sort of things. Whatever she had, she homed in on my interest in Chandler and made us the subject of her study for the day. I knew she was eager for gossip she could use to ingratiate herself with some of the other students, especially the girls in our class who made no effort to hide their dislike of her.

As it turned out, this was exactly what Chandler was trying to avoid. Between periods one and two, as we were moving through the corridor, he swooped up beside me and said, "Here."

He had a slip of paper in his hand. For a moment I didn't know what he wanted. He repeated, "Here," and I took the paper. The moment I did, he walked away. When I paused to open the note, Karen moved closer. I felt her approaching and I shoved the paper into my math text.

"Didn't Chandler Maxwell just hand you something?" she asked me.

I turned to her.

"Yes."

"What was it, something secret between you?"

I was annoyed, but for some reason, I decided to lie.

"I dropped some notes when I left English literature just now, and he picked them up and gave them to me. Why didn't you say something about it?"

"I didn't see you drop anything," she insisted.

"How could you miss it?" I countered. "You've been watching me like a hawk."

"I have not," she protested, but fell back as if I had just slapped her face.

I knew she was just waiting for me to take out the note in my next class, so I deliberately pretended no interest. I don't know why it was so important to me to be surreptitious, but it was obviously important to Chandler, so I maintained the same very low profile.

It wasn't until I had time to go to the girls' room that I took out the note and read it. It was, as he promised, details about Saturday night: what time he would pick me up, where he would take me for dinner, what time the show started and ended, and what time I could expect to be home. He hadn't even signed it or anything. I was disappointed, but I was more angry. How could he be so impersonal and so insensitive? Was I the first girl he had ever taken on a date? Maybe he didn't know how to behave.

That did give me reason to pause. Maybe I was his first real date, too. Why did I assume that he had taken other girls out? No one ever spoke about it. If anyone would know, it would certainly be Karen Jacobs, and I never heard her pass any gossip along concerning him.

I was hoping he would be friendlier at lunch. Chandler usually sat with some computer heads in the rear of the cafeteria. I was ahead of him in the line and deliberately found an empty table, anticipating his joining me; but he didn't. He went to his usual place and, moments later, some of the girls in my class, including Karen, sat at my table. I could see from the looks on their faces that Karen had begun to spread a story. I decided she was going to be the editor of the *National Enquirer* one day.

"Is something going on between you and Chandler Maxwell?" Susie Weaver asked me almost immediately. She was a very attractive red-haired girl who was already dating college boys and had an air of sophistication about her that made her the target of every other girl's envy. All of us, including me, hung on her every comment and pronouncement as if it were relationship gospel. Her seal of approval on a boy someone was seeing was sought after and appreciated, and when she condemned someone, everyone joined the bandwagon and found faults where none really existed.

"Why?" I replied, which was a mistake. I should have either vehemently denied it, if I wanted to deny it, or owned up to it and defended it.

Her lips softened and spread like two strips of butter on a frying pan.

"How long have you been sneaking around with him?" she followed.

The other girls smiled, and Karen looked so self-satisfied, I felt like smearing my piece of pizza over her pudgy blah face.

"I haven't been sneaking around with him or anyone else," I said.

"Really?" Susie looked at the others. She wore a look of achievement, the expression of some investigator who had just exposed the criminal. The others nodded. "You don't have to be ashamed. Unless you and Chandler are doing something pretty kinky," Susie added, and started eating.

"I'm not ashamed. There's nothing like that going on!"

"Or embarrassed."

"I'm not!" I practically screamed.

"Do you go to his place, or do you take him into your barn with the cows?"

"Stop it!"

"Sensitive, isn't she?" Susie asked the others. All eyes were on me.

I took a deep breath, calming myself.

"Chandler and I are taking private music lessons together, if you have to know," I finally confessed. "We have the same teacher, and he's having us practice duets, me on the violin and Chandler on the piano."

"So, you admit you're making music together," Susie said, and the whole table roared and giggled with laughter. "I hope you're on key and in rhythm."

Their laughter was louder.

"Does he say please first and thank you afterward?" Janice Handley asked. She was Susie's alter ego, her gofer, ready to jump at her beck and call.

There was more laughter.

My face turned white before it turned scarlet. I glanced back at Chandler. He was looking my way now, an expression of concern and disgust on his face.

"Come on," Susie said in a mock-friendly tone of voice, "tell us about it. You can trust us. We're all your friends."

"Some friends," I said. I glared at Karen. "Are you satisfied? Think they like you any more than they did before school started today?"

I rose, picked up my tray, and left the table, their laughter roaring like a waterfall behind me. I sat out the remainder of my lunch hour in a stall in the girls' room. Two of the girls who had been at the table came in, and I heard them talking and laughing about me and Chandler.

What interested me was their conclusion that he and I were made for each other. Somehow, because I was unable to participate in after-school activities and did so little with them and the others, they interpreted it to mean I was just as snobby.

As I was entering Spanish class, Chandler caught up with me.

"Don't take the school bus home," he said. "I'll take you. Just wait at your locker."

He spoke quickly, like someone giving very secret information about an impending rebellion, and then took his seat and ignored me the rest of the period. Every once in a while, I saw some of my classmates looking my way, whispering and then laughing to themselves.

It was as if my eyes were washed with a good dose of reality and opened wider. Susie Weaver wasn't as sophisticated as I had thought. None of them were. Maybe they were out there, doing things I never did: drinking, smoking, hanging out late into the night, being sexually active, but that didn't make them sophisticated. They suddenly all looked like immature people dressed in adult clothes. Most of them were just as insecure as I was, if not more so, and what they did was mock me or someone else in order to cover up the truth about themselves.

I used to feel terrible about not having loads of friends, not being invited to parties, not dating regularly, not being Miss Popularity, and being thought of as a prude, too religious, too moral, but now I felt relieved, even lucky. What I felt terrible about missing looked more than simply insignificant. It looked foolish, wasteful. Maybe there was too much Grandad in me, but I wasn't feeling sorry about it.

I guess I really was an outsider, a loner of sorts. I

guess Chandler and I did appear made for each other. I hurried to my locker after class and waited eagerly for him. He deliberately lingered until most of the school had left. When that bell ending the day rang, it was often like a stampede. Anyone watching outside would think we had all just been released from doing hard time in a state penitentiary.

"What happened in the lunch room?" he asked me as soon as he approached.

I told him how Karen Jacobs had seen him pass me the note and then had made a big thing of it with the others who enjoyed teasing me.

"What did they say?"

"Stupid stuff," I replied. "I wouldn't honor it by repeating a word."

He nodded.

"That was why I didn't bother you all day. I was afraid of something like that. I know I'm the source of amusement for many of these yahoos."

I laughed at his reference to *Gulliver's Travels,* which we had been studying in English—yahoos were human creatures who were dirtier and more stupid than talking horses.

"I just thought what you and I did wasn't any of their business," he continued. "I thought—no, correction, I *knew* they would pick on you if you had anything to do with me."

"You didn't have to worry about me," I said, my eyes narrowing with angry determination. "They don't bother me. I can take care of myself."

He nodded.

"I wasn't worrying about that. I was worrying that you would . . ."

"What?"

"Get driven away and change your mind," he admitted. He looked back so he could avoid my eyes.

"I'm not that easily influenced, Chandler. I'm not going to go out with someone or not go out with someone because of what *they* think. I have a mind of my own," I insisted. "You should have known that."

He looked at me and nodded.

"I do now," he said, and then we both laughed. It felt good. It felt as if I had been holding in some happiness the whole day and it was ready to explode.

"I'll take you home," he said, and we left the building.

He kept his car so well, it looked new. The leather smelled wonderful and felt soft to the touch. He had a built-in CD player and a telephone, too. I was very impressed, but I didn't want to seem like someone who had never been off the farm.

"It happened to me once before," he said after a few minutes of driving.

"What?"

"Something like this. I was in the tenth grade. You probably don't remember, but I was going with Audra Lothrop for a week or so. Her friends really made fun of her and turned her against me. I decided most of the girls in this school are lollipops."

"Lollipops?"

"Shiny, sweet, and insubstantial," he recited. "You're the first girl I've spent any time with who is focused on something other than her hairdo."

"That's not true, Chandler. They're not all like that."

He shrugged.

"It hasn't been important to me to make friends with

any of them," he said, but he sounded like someone trying to convince himself of something he really didn't believe in his own heart. "How come you don't have someone steady?"

"Too occupied with my family and my work, I guess. My uncle Peter used to be my escort. He took me everywhere."

"That's the one who was killed recently?"

"Yes."

He nodded.

"Makes you want to stay home and pull the covers over your head," he muttered.

"Yes, exactly."

"Music gets you out. It gets me out, too," he admitted. "That's why I thought you were different from the lollipops. I have a confession to make," he declared.

"What?"

"I noticed you long before Mr. Wengrow suggested we practice together. I pretended I didn't, but I did."

He was quiet, and so was I. He had revealed more than I expected someone like him would already.

"Maybe we'll find more to get us out," I said.

He turned and smiled at me.

When we turned up my driveway, I tried too late to warn him about Grandad Forman's bump. Both our heads nearly hit the ceiling of the car.

"Sorry," I said. "I forgot."

"It's all right. I think. Are my eyes still where they were before I made the turn?"

"Yes," I said, laughing.

When we stopped, Uncle Simon stepped out of the barn and looked our way.

"Wow, he's big."

"He's a very gentle man, Chandler. All those beautiful flowers you see are his doing."

"I guess that's what brings him out."

"Exactly. We all have something."

"You have more," he said. "I'm looking forward to Saturday night."

"Thanks for the ride home. Bye," I said, closing the door.

I watched him back up, turn around, and leave. When I looked at the barn, Uncle Simon was gone, but standing on the porch and looking down at me was Grandad. He looked angry.

"What?" I asked.

"You should be in the henhouse."

"Not this soon, Grandad. I wouldn't have been home this early if I had taken the bus."

"You watch yourself," he warned. He looked in Chandler's direction. "The devil has a pleasing face."

Anyone or anything that does is the devil to you, I wanted to tell him, but I didn't.

Instead, I lowered my head and walked into the house, away from the fear and the threat that came from his distrusting eyes.

I knew what his trouble was, I thought.

He has nothing to bring him out of the darkness. His only companions were the shadows that lingered in the corners of our home.

I wasn't at all like him. Rather, I hoped and prayed I wasn't. His blood flowed through Daddy's veins and mine, but Grandma Jennie's and Mommy's surely overpowered it.

Or else I would face each dawn with just as much distrust and just as much dreadful expectation.

When he lay his head down for the final sleep, he would finally come out of his darkness only to enter another. That was what loomed ahead for him.

I thought about what Daddy had said about Uncle Peter and Grandad, how Uncle Peter felt more pity for him than he did anger toward him.

He might not like it, but I pitied him, too. Even without Daddy's having told me, I just knew it was better not to let him know.

6

~~m~~

Transformation

I couldn't remember when I was as impatient with the clock as I was waiting for the days to pass until Saturday. Even filling my time with farm chores, homework, and violin practice didn't make those hands move any faster. Chandler was no longer avoiding me at school. The hens had their reason to cackle, but we both avoided them. I learned how to keep my eyes in tunnel vision, something at which Chandler had become expert.

"Why did you lie about you and Chandler?" Karen Jacobs came forward to ask me at the first opportunity. "You were ashamed after all, weren't you?"

"I'm only ashamed of you, Karen. You're so frustrated, you're pathetic," I shot back. Her mouth fell open wide enough to attract flies.

Later, when I told Chandler, he burst into a roar of laughter that drew everyone's attention to us. We were beginning to enjoy our notoriety.

After school on Friday, Daddy took Mommy and me

to the mall, where she helped me find a new dress and matching shoes. While we were there, I bought Uncle Simon his birthday present. He was going to be forty-five on Sunday. Mommy had decided to make him dinner and a cake, and had thrown down the gauntlet as soon as Grandad began to utter some opposition. She announced it at dinner Thursday night.

"Making a big thing out of a grown man's birthday is heathen," Grandad started.

"We're going to have a nice party nevertheless," Mommy flared.

I never saw her fill so quickly with what Daddy half-humorously referred to as her Russian fury. The veins in her neck rose against her skin, her shoulders lifted, her hands pressed down on the table, and her eyes looked like they were on springs and would come popping out to shoot across the table at Grandad's face.

Whenever she flew into a high rage, Mommy never turned crimson as much as she developed these two milk-white spots at the corners of her lips. She spoke slowly, taking great care with her words the way someone just practicing the language might. In any case, whatever Grandad Forman saw in her at Thursday night's dinner was enough to close the door quickly on his objections. He shook his head and returned his attention to his food.

Mommy's body slowly receded, losing the swollen shoulders and neck. She threw me a confident smile of satisfaction and talked about her cake. She was planning on making Uncle Simon's favorite: strawberry shortcake.

At the mall I found him a beautiful new set of gardening tools, and then a card specially designed for an uncle. I never called him anything else and never viewed him as a step-uncle, even after I was old enough to understand what that meant. To me he was as much a part of our family as Uncle Peter had been. Love bound us closer than blood.

It had been some time since Mommy and I had gone shopping together. By watching television, she had seen the changes in fashion, but it was still a bit shocking and curious to her. I ended up choosing a round-neck sleeveless shell top in all-over paisley print with shades of fuchsia, burgundy, and black. To wear with it I bought a stretchy, pull-on, knee-length skirt with one-inch ruffle at the hem. To complete the outfit, I chose platform shoes that had crocheted uppers with stretch elastic ankle straps and a ridged sole. Daddy joined us just as I was trying the outfit on, and when I looked back at him standing beside Mommy, I saw an expression of pride on both their faces.

"You look very nice," Daddy said. "Makes you look older."

"Makes her look her age," Mommy corrected. "She's no longer a tomboy farmhand. She's my young lady."

"Mine, too," Daddy said.

"Grandad's not going to like this. He's always saying women are practically naked these days," I said.

"Don't you worry about him," Mommy said, a little of that fury coming back into her eyes. "It's not his business."

She threw Daddy a look, but he turned his eyes away and then said he would bring the car around and meet us at the mall's main entrance.

My heart was thumping with joy and excitement as Mommy and I walked out with my packages piled in my arms. I couldn't help wondering what Chandler would say when he first saw me. Most of my clothing, especially the clothes I wore to school, was so plain and unflattering.

"We'll fix your hair nice, too," Mommy decided.

I smiled to myself, imagining what most of the other girls my age would say or think if their mothers suggested such a thing. I had no fear about Mommy cutting, brushing, and styling my hair for me. Without any sort of formal education, she had come from Russia carrying an unofficial, unwritten degree from the school of common sense and everyday skills. Her grandmothers and her mother had taught her how to cook, create and mend clothes, clean any kind of surface, provide first aid and generally make do with so much less than we had now. They taught her all this before she was ten years old.

What's more, Mommy didn't need Grandad Forman looking over her shoulder to be sure she didn't waste a morsel of food. She knew how to turn leftovers into a fresh new meal. I knew the mothers of my classmates would criticize and ridicule her for being a slave in her own home or something, so I rarely, if ever, bragged about her abilities.

Once, when I had an English assignment to write an essay about someone I considered heroic, I wrote about Mommy. It was before I knew she had come here specifically to marry Daddy without ever having met him. Still, I had often wondered and thought about the courage it had to have taken for someone so young to enter an entirely different world, where people spoke a different language, had different customs and styles, and whole new ways of living. I knew she had come with very little in her possession. What sort of faith in herself did that demand?

Today, my classmates and their mothers moaned and groaned about an hour or so delay at an airport or a traffic jam on a major highway. Girls my age, who were only a year or so younger than Mommy when she had arrived here, thought the world was coming to an end if their CD players broke. The stories they heard about their own grand- and great-grandparents were akin to fables and science fiction. I knew if I told them about Mommy they would look at me as even more of an outsider, weird.

I told them next to nothing.

On Friday night, Mommy worked on my hairdo. She surprised me by having had Daddy buy some recent fashion magazines, so she could study some of the current styles.

"I used to do my mother's hair," she explained after I had washed mine and sat at her small vanity table with a towel over my shoulders. "She handed me a brush when I was no more than five and I would spend hours stroking her hair while she sang or did some needlework. Her hair was the color of dark almonds and she had hazel eyes with tiny green specks. I wondered if I could ever be as beautiful.

"I used to think we would remain forever as we were. I would be forever five and she would be forever a young woman who, when she strolled through our village, wearing that angelic soft smile on her lips, captured the imaginations of every man who saw her, no matter what age. Wives glared angrily at their husbands. I saw it all, walking beside her, holding her hand. I felt like a princess with the queen."

She laughed.

"Why do you laugh, Mommy?"

"Me, thinking I was a princess. We were so poor. My

father was a cobbler. He worked very hard to put food on the table. We made use of every crumb, believe me."

"Why did you have to leave Russia, Mommy?" I asked.

"For years my father lived with an imperfect heart. He had a valve problem that, here in America, could be repaired, but we had no money for such a medical procedure. When he died, my mother struggled by taking in other people's wash, mending, doing housework. I was working side by side with her. She aged so quickly it broke my heart."

She stopped working on my hair and stared at herself in the mirror, but I knew she was looking back at a stream of memories instead.

"When I was sixteen, she collapsed one day and was taken to hospital. They said she had to have her gallbladder removed. It was a botched operation in a hospital with poor sanitary conditions. A staph infection was what finally sucked the life out of her. I had to watch the health and beauty drain away every day. It was almost as if . . . as if she was evaporating, disappearing right before my eyes.

"One of the last things she said to me was 'Get away from here whenever you can, whatever way you can.'

"I went to live with my aunt."

She took a deep breath.

"The rest you know."

"No, I don't, Mommy. I never knew you came here deliberately to marry Daddy without ever seeing him. How could you do that?"

She smiled.

"Well, I did see a picture of him, but it was a poor picture of a man standing next to a tractor. I thought a man who works with the earth, who makes things grow, has to have a respect for life. I saw kindness in his eyes when we first met, and kindness, my darling daughter, is a rare jewel where I come from, believe me.

"When you look at a young man with whom you think you might become romantic, search for that. Search for a love of living things. You want someone strong, but strong doesn't mean cruel, doesn't mean ruthless. You don't want a conqueror. You want a strong arm around you, yes, but you want soft eyes. You want someone who doesn't love you as a thing possessed, but someone who possesses him."

"How did you get so wise, Mommy?" I asked. I was looking at her in the mirror.

"Pain," she replied. "Unfortunately, that can be the best teacher. But what good is it all if I can't pass the wisdom on to you, my darling daughter? I know your generation is fond of ignoring, even ridiculing their parents and grandparents. I suppose every younger generation is guilty of some of that, but those of you who don't, who take in some of it at least, are far ahead of the others.

"But enough of this serious talk. You're going on a nice date. Let's make you beautiful."

"Can I be beautiful, Mommy?"

"Of course you can. Look at you. You have a face that makes the angels jealous and this hair . . . it's so rich a miser would choke with envy. I could sell these strands we cut," she kidded. "I should put them in little plastic bags and set up a roadside stand."

I laughed and looked at myself with wonder. Afterward, I thought my mother was truly an artist. When she had finished cutting, blow-drying, and styling my hair, it took my breath away. My whole look had changed. I thought I had suddenly been thrust onto that stage of sophistication I believed belonged only to girls like Susie Weaver. It was as if Mommy had waved a magic wand over my head and turned me from the farm girl with calluses on her hands into Cinderella, ready to go to the ball with her prince.

Would some ugly demon take joy in striking the clock at midnight and turn me back, or would Mommy's magic be too strong even for the evil that Grandad saw looming everywhere in the world around us?

He didn't see me until I sat down for dinner. Before that, I brought Uncle Simon his hot plate. He wasn't waiting at the barn door, so I called to him and started up the stairs. He was sitting under his lamp, trimming a bonsai tree. It was something in which he had just recently become immersed. Mommy had raved so much about his first attempt, he went on to a second and now a third. Grandad thought they were simply silly things, but I saw the way he stared at the two Uncle Simon had given Mommy. He stole looks when he thought no one noticed, but I did, and it brought a smile to my face. If he caught me watching him, he would mutter some ridicule about them again.

"That's beautiful, Uncle Simon," I said. He'd been so intent, it made him jump in his seat.

When he set eyes on me, his mouth opened a little and he just stared. I put his tray on his table.

"What is that one?" I asked.

"What? Oh. It's an incense cedar. Smells good. Here," he said, holding it toward me. I sniffed.

"Yes," I said with delight.

"You look different," he said.

"Mommy did my hair. I'm going to a show tomorrow night with my friend Chandler."

"Oh." He looked at his bonsai plant and then at me. "This will be yours," he said. "When it's finished."

"Thanks!"

"It needs music," he warned.

I laughed.

"Okay, Uncle Simon."

"Watching you grow up is the same as watching a flower blossom," he said. He didn't smile or have an impish gleam in his eyes, as some men might when they said such a thing. It was a simple statement from his heart, and it brought tears to my eyes.

"Thank you," I said.

He looked at his food.

"I'd better get back to the house. Grandad hates waiting for anyone when he's ready to eat."

Uncle Simon nodded. I glanced back at him as I left to descend the stairs. He was gazing at me with such a different expression, almost as if he wasn't completely sure I was who I claimed to be, almost as if he wondered if he had seen an apparition.

It's only me, Uncle Simon, I thought. *It's really only me.*

Grandad's reaction was just about what I had expected. He took one look at me and turned to Mommy to declare that I looked like a cheap girl of the streets with my hair cut and styled this way.

"What do you know about such women?" Mommy snapped back at him.

Grandad actually turned a shade darker than beet red.

"I know what I know," he stammered.

"Well, you don't know what is in style and what is not," Mommy said simply and shrugged.

Daddy's lips softened as his eyes turned to her with appreciation.

Grandad looked from one to the other and then at me. He lifted his thick right forefinger.

"Remember. There is no peace, saith the Lord, unto the wicked."

"Beware, old man," Mommy shot back at him, her eyes blazing. "He without sin cast the first stone."

She and Grandad fixed their eyes on each other in such a lock, it took my breath away. I felt an icy hand on my back as the clock ticked.

Then Grandad looked down at his food and Mommy continued serving dinner.

It was the quietest meal I could remember. My ears were filled with the pounding of my heart.

I felt as if I had opened another door in the mansion filled with mysteries when I stepped out of childhood into a woman's world. I had changed right before everyone's eyes.

And soon I would see that they had changed, too.

7

⬿

The Wages of Sin

We had no door chimes, no buzzer, only a stem of cast iron with a small ball of iron welded to it to drop against a metal plate. Grandad Forman made it himself. With so few visitors to our home, no one lobbied him to improve upon it. Waiting for Chandler's arrival, I was so nervous it felt like a small army of ants were parading up from my stomach to march around my drum-pounding heart. I debated going downstairs early and sitting by the front window, watching for his car coming up the drive, and then I thought that would look tacky or make me seem too anxious.

Instead, I remained in my room, staring at myself in the mirror, fidgeting with my hair, my clothes, alternating holding my breath with taking deep breaths, and listening hard for the sound of that metal doorknocker reverberating through our hallway. Grandad and Daddy were still out in the west field with Uncle Simon.

Mommy was downstairs working on their dinner. I looked at the clock and remembered one of Mommy's favorite expressions: "A watched pot never boils." The hands of the clock indeed looked like they hadn't moved since my last glimpse.

"You're being foolish, Honey," I told myself. "You're acting like a child. It's just a date, just dinner and a show."

Just dinner and a show!

I've never been taken by a boy in my school to dinner and a show, I thought. What was this restaurant he was going to take me to? Would it be some fancy place, where all the other patrons would take one look at me and know I had never been there or anywhere like it before? Would they whisper and smile and laugh at the "girl just off the farm"? And then would they watch my every move to see if I knew which fork to use, did I talk with my mouth open or keep both elbows on the table? Would I eat too much or too little?

Would they laugh at my clothes, my hair, my makeup? Would they know Chandler Maxwell's family and wonder what Chandler was doing with someone so unsophisticated? Would I see all this ridicule in their faces and simply burst out in tears and run from the table?

It was easier milking cows or shoveling chicken manure, I thought.

The metal clang echoing through the house made my heart stop and start. It sounded again, and Mommy called up to me.

"Should I get it for you, Honey?"

"I'm coming," I cried and jumped up. I bounced down

the stairs. Mommy came out of the kitchen and stood in the hallway, looking toward the front door. I opened it quickly and stepped back.

Chandler was dressed in a dark blue suit and tie. He looked even more nervous than I was, and for a long moment, neither of us spoke. We just contemplated each other.

"Oh," he said, and brought up a corsage he was holding in his right hand, just behind his leg. "This is for you."

I took it in my hands gently, so gently anyone would have thought it was a newly laid egg.

"Thank you," I said.

Mommy came forward.

"Hello," she said. "You look very handsome," she added.

"Thank you. Honey looks terrific," Chandler said.

"Oh, this is my mother," I leaped to say.

Mommy glanced at me with a laugh on her lips and extended her hand to Chandler.

"How do you do," she said.

"I'm Chandler Maxwell. Pleased to meet you, Mrs. Forman," Chandler said.

"What a beautiful corsage," Mommy said.

I started to fumble with it.

"Here, let me help you do that," Mommy said and fixed it properly. She stepped back. "Very nice. Well, I hope you two have an enjoyable time."

"Thank you," Chandler said. He glanced at me and I stepped forward, walking out with him.

He hurried ahead to open the door for me.

"Thank you," I said and got in.

I looked back at the house. Mommy was in the living

room window just between the curtains, peering out at us. I could see the soft smile on her face. Chandler moved around to the driver's side, got in quickly, and started the engine.

"You really do look terrific," he said as we pulled away and down the drive.

"Thank you. Remember the bump!" I cried, and he hit his brake and slowed to go over it.

His laughter broke the film of cellophane we had wrapped around ourselves. I could feel my body relax.

"I hope you like Christopher's. It's close to the theater, so I thought that would be a good choice. You ever been there?" he asked.

"No," I said.

The truth was I had never even heard of it. The only restaurants I had ever gone to were places Uncle Peter had taken me, and they were all more or less restaurant chains, never anything fancy or expensive. Grandad thought eating out was close to a cardinal sin because of the cost.

"It's pretty good. They have a French chef, who's part owner, so he makes a great effort. It's one of my parents' favorite places."

"Oh. Will they be there tonight?" I asked quickly. The thought of that put a dagger of cold fear through my heart.

"No. They have a dinner party at Congressman Lynch's home. That's why my father gave me the tickets. The congressman is in the midst of his big reelection campaign, so he continues to court big political contributions," Chandler added with a smirk. "My mother really enjoys all that glitter. My father has to keep up appearances and mingle. There is a lot of politics involved at the bank. Actually," Chandler said, "there's a lot of politics in practically everything my parents do."

The world he comes from, I thought, *is so different from mine, I would almost feel like Mommy had felt coming from Russia, if I was ever introduced to it.*

"My father says your grandfather's farm is one of the most successful family-run farms in our community," Chandler said. "I didn't get to look around much, but it does look like it's in great shape. I know it's very hard work."

"Very," I said.

"You don't want to become a farmer's wife then, huh?"

"No," I said emphatically and with such conviction, he laughed.

"So, you better practice that violin and get yourself into a good school. Or marry someone very rich," he added.

"If I marry anyone, it won't be because of what he has in his bank account," I replied.

Chandler threw me a look of skepticism.

"I mean that," I said.

"Okay," he said.

When we pulled up to the front of the restaurant, there were young men there to valet park Chandler's car. One of them rushed to open my door, and then another was at the restaurant door to open that for us. I took a deep breath and stepped in alongside Chandler. He approached the hostess, who immediately recognized him and called him, "Mr. Maxwell." She escorted us to our table, a corner booth.

"This is a little more private than the other tables," Chandler explained when we were seated. "I don't like feeling I'm in a fish bowl, do you?"

"Oh, no," I said. He had no idea how grateful I was, being seated where fewer people could observe us.

"I can't get us any wine," he said apologetically.

"That's all right."

The only wine I had ever drunk was a homemade elderberry on Christmas, but I wasn't going to tell him that.

The waiter greeted us, again obviously familiar with Chandler. He handed us the menus, which to my surprise had everything in French. I started to declare my inability to read it, when Chandler turned the page and I saw it was all translated.

"I recommend the duck," Chandler said.

I stared in disbelief at the prices. Everything was à la carte. The only thing they gave us was a platter of bread.

"This is very expensive," I said.

Chandler leaned forward again to whisper.

"I've got my mother's charge card. No problem. Order whatever you want, even caviar, if you want."

"Oh, no," I said quickly. The caviar was more than a hundred dollars itself. "I'll have the duck."

"Good. Me, too," he said, and ordered that for us, and two of what I thought were ridiculously priced salads as well as a large bottle of French water. He told the waiter we were going to a show and the waiter promised to get us served quickly.

I glanced around at some of the other people. The restaurant was only about a quarter filled. Chandler explained that it was early. The people here were probably all going to the show, too. Everyone was well-dressed, the women in fancy gowns, the men in suits, even tuxedos. I began to worry that I was very under-dressed. I didn't have any of the glittering jewelry all the

other women had. Chandler misunderstood my looking
at everyone with such interest.

"Don't worry," he said confidently, "none of the lollipops are here." He leaned forward and smiled. "It's like
flying above bad weather. That's what money does for
you."

"Not everyone with less money is bad weather,
Chandler," I said.

He shrugged.

"No, not everyone, but enough of them."

"I don't have lots of money," I said.

"Yes," he said, nodding and looking at me firmly, his
eyes becoming small and intent as they often did, "but
you will, Honey. You will."

"How do you know that?" I asked, smiling.

"I know. I have a built-in wealth detector."

I started to laugh.

"I do!" he insisted.

We were served our salads and talked about the music
we were practicing.

"Mr. Wengrow's a bit eccentric," Chandler said, "but
I respect his music skills. I've learned a great deal since
I've been with him, and he's big enough to admit that he
will bring me, and now you, to a point where we'll have
to go on to someone more knowledgeable and experienced to improve any more. My parents wanted me to
have someone else as a tutor, someone one of their
friends had used, but I refused. They thought because
Mr. Wengrow was charging far less that he wasn't as
good."

"He's the only teacher I've had."

"And look at what wonders he's doing with you,"
Chandler said quickly.

"Do you really believe that, Chandler?"

"I'm not in the habit of saying things I don't believe," he replied.

I smiled at him, this time not so displeased with his arrogant tone.

The waiter arrived with our main dishes and we began to eat.

I was impressed with the duck, and had to admit that I had only eaten wild duck my mother had prepared.

"We still have time for dessert," Chandler said, checking his watch. "What about a crème brûlée?" he suggested. "They really make a great one here."

I had never had one before, of course, and didn't even know what was in it.

"I guess," I said.

When it came and I took a taste, I was unable to hide my pleasure and surprise.

"First time you had that?" he asked.

"Yes. It's so delicious," I declared, and he laughed.

"I knew it would be fun being with you," he said. "I'm glad you said yes."

"I am, too."

I was able to glance at the bill. Grandad Forman would have exploded at the table, I thought. He would yell that he could buy another cow for that.

When we arrived at the theater, there were valets to park the car there, too. I was surprised and pleased at our seats. They were practically on the stage. Contrary to what Chandler suspected, the show was wonderful. Afterward we both raved about the leads and the quality of the music.

All the way back to the farm, we talked incessantly, leaping in on each other's momentary pauses as if we were terrified of silence. As we approached the driveway, Chandler slowed down to nearly a crawl.

"I'm sorry," he said. "I should have asked you if you wanted to go somewhere else first."

"That's all right. I couldn't eat anything else," I said.

"Your big uncle going to be waiting at the door?" he asked.

"He might be," I said, laughing.

Chandler brought the car to an abrupt stop.

"Then I better kiss you good night right here," he said and leaned over to kiss me. It was a quick kiss, almost a snap of lips. He knew how disappointing it was even without my saying anything. "Not too good, huh?"

"Let's say you're better at playing the piano."

He laughed, hesitated, and came toward me again. This time the kiss was longer and hard enough to start my heart tapping and bring a warmth up my body. He held himself close.

"You're the prettiest, nicest girl in the school, Honey. I've got to thank Mr. Wengrow."

"He might not understand why," I said, and Chandler laughed.

"No, he might not." He sat back. "Sure you don't want to go somewhere else?"

I looked up the driveway. I knew Mommy and Daddy were waiting up for me, and Uncle Simon was most probably sitting by his window, too.

"Not tonight," I said. "But I had a great time. I really did. Thank you," I said.

"Okay," he said, his voice dripping with disappointment. He started up the driveway. "Bump away," he cried, and we laughed as we went over Grandad's hump in the road.

I didn't see Uncle Simon anywhere when we pulled up. His room looked dark, too. I did see a curtain move in the living room.

"Looks quiet here," Chandler said. "I could have gotten away with a good night kiss after all."

"It's not too late," I said.

He smiled in the dim pool of light coming off our single, naked porch bulb. Then he slid closer to me, put his arm around my shoulder, and brought his lips to mine again, stronger, longer, full of passion.

"Just takes practice," I said. "Like the piano."

He laughed loudly.

"I really like you, Honey. You don't beat around the bush or pretend to be someone you're not. You're fun to be with. I mean it."

"I'm glad," I said and started to open the car door. He got out quickly and ran around to finish opening it for me.

"Miss Forman," he said with a mock bow. "We hope you enjoyed yourself tonight."

"Indeed I did, sir."

He walked me to the front steps, said good night again, and got back into his car. I watched him back away and then I waved to him, and he waved back and started down the driveway.

"You let that boy touch your body sinfully?" I heard, and spun around to see Grandad step out of a deep shadow to the right of the front porch.

"Grandad, you frightened me."

"Remember, the wages of sin is death. Remember."

"I didn't sin," I flared. "I didn't do anything wrong."

"I saw you," he said, stepping into the perimeter of the light. "I saw you in the car."

"It's not a sin to kiss someone good night, Grandad."

"One thing leads to another," he said. He pointed his finger at me. "God knows what lust lies in your heart. You'll bring His wrath upon us all," he declared.

"I will not," I said. "That's a silly thing to say."

"You were too close with Peter," he suddenly said. It took my breath away.

"What? What's that supposed to mean?"

"I watched the two of you. The Lord saw what was in both your hearts and struck him down."

"That's a horrible thing to say, Grandad. How can you say such a horrible thing? You're terrible! I hate you for saying something as terrible as that."

"Don't be insolent," he threatened and took a step toward me.

"Leave her be," we heard. I turned to see Uncle Simon coming out of the barn.

"Go on with you," Grandad said, waving at him.

The front door opened and Mommy stepped out. She took one look at Grandad, another at me, and then at Uncle Simon.

"What's going on out here?" she demanded.

Instead of replying, I put my head down and ran up the stairs, past her and into the house. Daddy was in the hallway, a look of surprise on his face, too.

"Honey?"

I shook my head, the tears flying off my cheeks, and charged up the stairs into my room and slammed the door shut.

Thank God Chandler had driven away when he had.

I didn't put on the light in my room. I simply threw myself on my bed and pressed my face into the pillow. Grandad's horrible words circled me like insistent mosquitos, biting and stinging. How could he harbor such ugly thoughts in his mind? How could he turn something that had been gentle and kind, loving and beautiful, into the most detestable and ugly ogre of smut and filth? He made me feel dirty inside and out. I shook my body as if to throw off the stains.

What had he been doing all those years while I was growing up and Uncle Peter was at my side, taking my hand, showing me wonderful things in nature, swinging me about, hugging me, kissing me, and lavishing gifts on me? Was he hiding somewhere in the shadows, watching us, forming these disgusting thoughts? The day Uncle Peter was killed, did he actually look at me and think I was somewhat responsible?

I started to sob when I heard my door open and close softly. I stopped, took a breath, and turned. Mommy was standing there, her back against the door. The moonlight illuminated her face. For a moment it looked like a mask, her eyes were so dark and deep.

"What did he say to you, Honey?" she asked softly.

I scrubbed the tears out of my eyes with my fists and sat up, taking a breath before speaking, not knowing if I could even form the words in my mouth.

"He said I was too close with Uncle Peter and because of that God struck him down."

Mommy said something in Russian under her breath.

"He's a sick, twisted old man. You must not pay any attention to him."

"I can't look at him," I said.

Mommy came over and sat beside me. She patted my hand and stroked my hair.

"Did you have a good time with Chandler?"

"Yes, a wonderful time. He spent a lot of money on dinner, too."

She laughed.

"When I was a young girl, my mother used to tell me to find a man who is frugal, who won't waste a ruble on you because, in the end, you'll have security."

"Chandler's family is very rich, Mommy. They can waste money and still have security."

She laughed again.

"Why is Grandad Forman so mean? Why would he say such a thing to me now?"

"He's coming to the end of his life and looking back on his own sins," she said. "He's trying to win back God's sympathies. He thinks he's Job from the Bible. He likes suffering because he thinks it gives him a chance to show God how faithful he is."

"What sins are in his past? He lives like a monk or something," I said.

"No man is perfect, especially not your grandfather. Forget what he said. He's like some creature eating out its own heart. I won't let him say anything like that to you again," she vowed.

"How can you stop him, Mommy? He owns everything. He never stops reminding us."

"He owns nothing," she said and stood up. "Go to sleep thinking about the nice things that happened tonight. Tell yourself your grandfather wasn't even there."

"I thought Uncle Simon was going to get into a fight with him. I was so frightened."

"I know. Don't think about it," she repeated. She walked to the door.

"Practice your violin, Honey. Do well in school. I'll

tell you what my mother told me. Find a way to leave this place," she added, then opened the door and left me sitting in the darkness, wondering what she had not said.

In my heart I knew it would come; it would come soon.

8

Making Beautiful Music

Despite his constant Bible-thumping and hell and damnation speeches, Grandad Forman was not a church-going man. In fact, he was highly critical of organized religion, calling it just another exploitation and therefore another playground for the devil. Mommy chastised him for this, especially on Sunday when she, Daddy, and I would get dressed up and go to church. Uncle Simon was too shy about meeting people and being out in public, and Mommy never pressured him, but she and Grandad often argued about his refusal to attend the Lord's house of worship.

"I don't need no preacher to tell me what God wants of me and what He don't," Grandad insisted.

"You need to bow your head in the house of the Lord more than any of us," Mommy threw back at him.

Their eyes locked and Grandad left the room or walked away, mumbling to himself. He did spend his early Sunday time alone, reading his Bible, the pages of which were worn so thin, the edges were torn and yellow. From the time I was a little girl on, I was always fascinated by the way he gripped it in his hand, holding it tightly between his thumb and fingers as he would the handle of a hatchet or a hammer, sometimes waving it at one of us, especially Uncle Simon. When he did, Grandad's eyes were always brightened, luminous and shiny, resembling stones in a brook. After seeing Star Wars, I had a dream in which I saw a ray of light come out of Grandad's Bible, which he wielded like a sword over us all, even Uncle Simon.

Every Sunday, after I returned from church and changed into my jeans, I would hurry out to help Uncle Simon weed his garden and tend to his plants. This Sunday I was very excited because I was going to give him his birthday present. Mommy had already told him about our special dinner, after which we would have his birthday cake. I found him on his knees, working around a patch of ginger lilies. Everything I knew about flowers, I knew because of Uncle Simon.

It was a particularly beautiful late spring day with a breeze as gentle as a soft kiss caressing my face. Against the western sky, I saw a string of clouds so thin they looked like strips of gauze. A flock of geese in their perfect V-formation were making their way farther north. *What a wonderful day for a birthday,* I thought.

As I approached Uncle Simon, I could hear him muttering lovingly to his flowers. It brought a smile to my face. As if he had known where my uncle Simon was this morning, the minister had preached about a respect for life and how that gave us a deeper appreciation of ourselves, our own souls, and God's precious gifts.

"Happy birthday, Uncle Simon," I said, and he turned

quickly and looked up at me, his bushy eyebrows lifting like two sleeping caterpillars. He looked from me to the gift box in my hands, and then wiped his hands on the sides of his jeans and stood up.

"What's that?" he asked.

"Your birthday present." I thrust it toward him. "From me, Mommy, and Daddy," I said. I wasn't going to include Grandad, not only because he didn't contribute to it, but because he ridiculed birthdays.

Uncle Simon took the box so gently in his large hands, I smiled.

"It's nothing breakable," I said.

He stood there, gazing down at it, looking overwhelmed by the fancy wrap.

"Open it," I urged, anxious to see his reaction to the gift.

He looked at me and nodded. He tried taking the paper off carefully, but it tore and he looked disappointed in himself. Then he opened the box and gazed at the new garden tools.

"Ooooh," he said, stretching his expression of pleasure as if he was peering down at some of the world's most precious jewels. "Good. Thank you, Honey."

I smiled and stepped forward, lifting myself on my toes to kiss him on the cheek.

"Happy birthday, Uncle Simon."

He nodded and took out the tools, turning them around and inspecting each more closely.

"They're almost too pretty to use," he said. He gazed at his old, rusted, crudely made ones as if he was about to say a final good-bye to an old, dear friend.

"It'll make your flowers happier," I said.

He smiled.

"Yes, it might," he agreed and turned to scrape away some weeds.

I got down beside him and we worked in silence for a while. His garden was growing so well and was so large now, people came around to see it and offer to buy flowers from him. He cherished every plant so much, he was at first reluctant to give any up, but Mommy convinced him by telling him he was giving the flowers added life through the pleasure and enjoyment others took in them. He would have done most anything Mommy asked him to do anyway, I thought.

When Grandad Forman saw that he was beginning to make some significant money with his flowers, he told Uncle Simon he had to give him a percentage for the use of the land. Uncle Simon would have given him all of it, but Mommy stood between them like a broker and negotiated Grandad down to ten percent. She found out what a fair price was for each of the flowers, too. Recently, Daddy had brought up the idea of making a regular nursery, investing in a greenhouse.

"It would be a profitable side business," he declared.

"I can't see putting any real money behind him," Grandad said.

"Why not?" Mommy challenged. "Has he ever failed to do something you asked him to do? Has he ever neglected his chores?"

"He's got the brain of a child," Grandad insisted.

Mommy straightened her shoulders and gazed down at him with eyes so full of fire and strength, both Daddy and I were mesmerized.

"The wolf also shall dwell with the lamb, and the leopard shall lie down with the kid; and the calf and the young lion and the fatling together; and a little child shall lead them," she recited.

"You don't have to quote Scripture to me," Grandad cried, the lines in his face deepening as he stretched his lips in anger. His leather-tan skin looked as stiff as the crust of stale bread.

"Seems I do from the things you say. And," she added softly, "things you do."

He looked at her and then looked away.

"Do what you want," he muttered, "but not with any money of mine."

It was still a secret, but Daddy was seriously looking into the greenhouse idea.

"Who taught you how to grow flowers so well, Uncle Simon?" I asked him as I worked with him.

He paused and looked toward the house as if he actually saw someone standing there.

"Your grandma," he said. "I worked with her in her garden. It was the only place and time she had any peace," he added, a shaft of embittered light passing through his dark eyes. He dug a little more aggressively for a moment, and then his body relaxed and he went back to his calm manner.

I watched him, admiring how he drifted into a rhythm, how he and his work seemed to flow together, his face full of pleasure and contentment, and I thought about what Uncle Peter had said about me and my violin.

The flowers play Uncle Simon, I thought. They nurture him. They rip the weeds away from him. They turn his face to the sunlight and the rain.

That evening, looking as clean and well-dressed as he could, he came to the house. Daddy gave him another present: his favorite aftershave lotion, which had a flowery scent. Mommy had prepared a turkey dinner with all the trimmings. It was as good as our Thanksgiving. Grandad Forman muttered about the cost of such a meal just for a grown man's birthday, but ate vigorously nevertheless. Then Mommy brought out the cake.

"I couldn't put all the candles on the cake, Simon," Mommy explained, "so I just lit the one to represent them all."

He laughed and blew it out. We all sang "Happy Birthday." Grandad almost moved his lips, but shook his head as if to deny his own inclinations. Afterward, we sat in the living room and I played my violin for Uncle Simon. As usual, I became lost in my melodies, feeling as though the violin was a part of me, as if my very being flowed into it and out in the form of music.

Toward the end of my little concert, I opened my eyes and looked at them all. What surprised and even put a titter of anxiety in my heart was the way Grandad Forman was looking at me. Gone from his face was any expression of disdain or disapproval. For a moment he looked like any warm and loving grandparent might, sitting there and listening to his grandchild perform. It confused me, but I was sure I saw something deeper in him. I wanted to call it love, but I was afraid to think that. Toward the end, I caught the way he glanced at Mommy and how that changed his expression, restoring his cold, impersonal manner.

"Time to go to sleep," he declared after Mommy, Daddy, and Uncle Simon gave me their applause. He rose and walked out of the room.

"Thank you," Uncle Simon said.

"Many more birthdays, Simon," Mommy told him and gave him a hug and a kiss.

Daddy patted him on the shoulder.

I walked out with him and stood on the front porch, watching him cross the yard toward the barn. Daddy came out and stood beside me.

"How can this be enough for him, Daddy?" I asked. "How can he really be happy?"

"I guess it's a matter of finding your own way, making peace with that part of yourself that's usually demanding more, that lusts after things others have and makes you discontented with what you have," Daddy said.

"You make it sound bad to want more, Daddy. Isn't it good to be ambitious?"

"Sure, but when it keeps you looking over at the next field, you never enjoy what you've accomplished, what you've grown on your own. That's too much ambition, I guess."

"How do you know when it's too much, when you should stop?" I asked.

He shook his head.

"It's different for everyone, Honey. Something inside you has to cry out, enough!"

"Has that happened to you?"

He smiled at me and put his arm around my shoulders.

"Yes," he said, "and now, I can watch you go for it."

"Like Uncle Simon watches his flowers emerge from the seeds he planted?"

"Yes."

"And like Grandad watched you and Uncle Peter?"

"Something like that," Daddy said, but his arm lost its tightness and his eyes shifted away. It was as if he was suddenly searching the shadows for signs of one of Grandad's demons.

"I better get to bed," he told me. "We've got work to do tomorrow."

He left me on the porch, looking into the darkness and then up at Uncle Simon's room. The light went out there, too, and I suddenly felt a chill. I don't know where it came from. There was barely a breeze and the night was warm.

It came from inside me, I concluded.

It came from the sense of some terrible secret still looming above me, masked, disguised, hidden behind the eyes of those who loved me and those who knew and were stirred by the same wintry feeling creeping in and over all our smiles and all our laughter, and even into our dreams.

The following week, Chandler and I officially became an item at our school. We were together everywhere we could be together. The joy we were taking in each other's company quickly became apparent, and soon I detected the looks of envy in the eyes of girls who were still searching for someone. I also noticed that Chandler was far less defensive with and suspicious of other students. The relaxation that was evident in his face took form in the way he dressed as well. He started coming to school in far less formal clothing; his hair wasn't as plastered and stiff, and he was joking and laughing with other students more often than before.

"We took a vote," Susie Weaver told me after lunch on Friday, "and decided you've been a good influence on Chandler Maxwell. He's almost a human being now."

"Thank you so much for your compliments," I said with a cold smile. "It is a coincidence."

"What? Why?"

"Chandler and I were wondering when you were going to become a human being," I replied, and left her with her mouth open wide enough to attract a whole hive of bees.

That afternoon Chandler asked me to go to a movie with him. He thought we should go have something to eat first, too, but said it wouldn't be any fancy restaurant.

"Let's just have a pizza or something," he suggested. "To celebrate our continued musical success."

We had pleased Mr. Wengrow at our duet lessons on Wednesday night. Chandler had come to the house to pick me up and take me there. I saw the look of both pleasure and surprise in Mr. Wengrow's face.

All he said about it was, "I'm happy you're both getting along so well. It shows in your work."

We exchanged conspiratorial smiles and worked with new enthusiasm.

"I know that Chandler is all set as far as his continuing education goes," Mr. Wengrow said at the end of our session, while I was putting my violin in its case, "but you're still not decided, is that correct?"

"No," I said. "My parents and I talked about my attending the community college and living at home."

"There's no music program there that will add to your ability and talent in any significant way," he said quickly. "I don't mean to interfere, but I think you've got what it takes to get into a prestigious school for the performing arts. I'll speak with your parents, of course, but I wanted to talk to you about it first."

I looked at Chandler, who shrugged and smiled.

"What school? Where?"

"I have a good friend who is actually the accountant for a theatrical agent. I would like to contact him to see if he would do me a favor and get an audition arranged for you."

"Oh," I said. "Where?"

"New York City," Mr. Wengrow said.

"New York City!"

All I could think of was Grandad Forman's ravings about the twin cities of iniquity being Los Angeles and New York. He called them both cities built by Satan, and loved to point his finger at the television screen whenever some horrible crime or event was reported occurring in either of them.

"There!" he would cry. "See what I mean?"

"If you're going to do anything significant in the arts, you should be in New York City," Mr. Wengrow said.

I shook my head.

"I don't think my parents would like that, Mr. Wengrow."

"I'll have a word with them," he said. "Don't worry. I'll get them to understand."

Chandler was going to the Boston University School of Arts. His father was an alumnus of BU and a heavy contributor, not that Chandler couldn't get in on his own ability.

"Mr. Wengrow's right," he told me afterward. "You'll smother to death here. You've got to get out and into the big wide world."

It made me very nervous to think about it, so I didn't, and up until the following weekend, Mr. Wengrow had not spoken about it with my parents. If he had, he might have been very discouraged and not mentioned the discussion to me at all, I thought.

On Friday, Chandler drove up to take me to the movies. I had put on a mustard-colored light sweater and a pair of jeans with a pair of high-heel sneakers I had managed to get Mommy to buy me, despite how silly she thought they looked. She couldn't understand why they were the rage. I had my hair tied in a ponytail.

"You look like Debbie Reynolds in one of those old movies," Chandler declared as soon as he saw me come bounding down the front steps. "I love it."

"Thank you."

He was wearing a black mock turtleneck shirt, which brought out the dark color in his eyes. I thought he looked very sexy, and practically leaped into the car to sit beside him. I couldn't remember when I had been happier.

As we started away, Grandad came out of nowhere onto the driveway and stood in the wash of Chandler's car headlights. His gray hair looked like it was on fire, his eyes blazing at us. Chandler hit the brake pedal and I gasped.

"Who's that?" he cried.

"My grandad," I said.

"Well, what's he doing?"

Grandad simply stood there in our way, staring at us. Suddenly he raised his right hand, and I saw he was holding his sacred old Bible. He held it up like some potential victim of a vampire would hold up a cross in a horror movie, and then he stepped to the side and disappeared into the shadows.

Chandler turned to me, amazed.

"What was that all about?"

"Just drive," I said, choking back my tears. Chandler stared at me. "Drive, Chandler, please."

"Sure," he said and accelerated, taking the bump too hard.

I curled up into a ball. I was filled with a mixture of anger and fear. No matter how Mommy stood up to him, I couldn't help but be intimidated by his accusing eyes. Memories of him coming into my room when I was a little girl abounded. I saw him standing over my bed, chanting his prayers, reciting his biblical quotes, giving me warnings about hell, sin, and damnation that I was still too young to understand. What I did understand was there was some sort of danger awaiting me should I do anything defiant.

"What was that in his hand?" Chandler finally asked. "Honey?"

I took a deep breath and emerged slowly, like a clam opening its shell.

"His Bible," I said.

"Bible? Why was he holding it up?"

"To remind me that the wages of sin is death," I said in a tired, defeated voice.

"Sin? What sin?"

"The sin he thinks I'm about to commit," I said.

Chandler was very quiet. Then he looked at me, shook his head and smiled.

"The movie is only rated PG-13."

I looked at him, and then we both laughed. It felt like balm on a wound. He reached out to touch my hand, and I slid closer to him.

"I've got to admit, he scared me," Chandler said. "I couldn't imagine who or what he was, jumping out into the drive like that."

"Let's not talk about it anymore," I begged.

"Okay," he said, eagerly agreeing.

At the pizza restaurant, we talked about some of the other students at school, our classes, and Mr. Wengrow.

Chandler's theory was that because he had no children, he put fatherly concern into us and saw himself as a surrogate father, giving us guidance.

"Sometimes, I feel like he cares more about me than my own father," Chandler admitted. "I mean, my dad wants me to succeed and all, but he doesn't have the same interest in my music or faith in what I can do with it. He's always talking to me about becoming a lawyer or going to medical school, as if nothing else has any reason to be. I get the distinct feeling he's paying for my lessons just to humor me, almost like putting up with a nuisance."

"What about your mother?" I asked.

"She usually goes along with anything he says. She's busy at being busy."

"What's that mean?" I asked, smiling.

"She makes work for herself. No one appreciates the fax machine as much as my mother. She lives off the papers that all the organizations, volunteers, and people send her, and then she spends hours filing, organizing meaningless things. She's content as long as her name is on every possible list of patrons and committee lists, whether she actually does anything for the cause or not.

"It's like she lives in a castle built out of cards, or invitations to charity functions, I should say. She's turned it into her own cottage industry."

He sounded so bitter about it.

"You're upset about all that?"

He stared at his piece of pizza for a moment and then shook his head.

"Sometimes, I wish I was a charity instead of a son. I'd get more attention. What about your parents? Do they care about your music?"

I told him about Uncle Peter and how Daddy had become more and more committed to my playing.

"They should let you go to a good school then," he said. "I hope Mr. Wengrow can convince them. You have something, Honey. You can be someone."

"So can you," I said quickly.

"I don't know. Maybe."

"Why maybe?"

"I don't have as much passion as you do. I'm good, technically very good, I know, but there's one other thing that makes the difference, and you have it," he said, his eyes fixed on my face. "I envy you for that."

"You've got it, too," I insisted.

He smiled.

"Maybe if I keep hanging around with you, it will rub off or I'll catch it, like a cold," he said. "Of course, we have to get closer and closer before that might happen."

"That's okay with me."

We stared at each other. I felt my heart begin to pound, the warm glow rise from just under my breasts, up my neck, and into my face.

"We can go to a different movie tonight," he said.

"What do you mean?"

"My parents are out for the evening. I have a great DVD collection. You ever see a DVD movie?"

"I don't even know what it is."

"You've got to see it," he said excitedly. "I have about fifty movies. You can choose any one you want. You'll think you're in the movie theater. Okay?"

He waved to the waitress for our check.

I felt as though I had stepped into the ocean and was being pulled out to sea with the outgoing tide. There was no way to resist. It was best to simply relax and go along.

*   *   *

Chandler's house was a large, stone-wall-clad Tudor with a circular driveway set on a grand track of prime land just outside our small city. From the well-trimmed hedges and bushes to the immaculate sidewalk and rich dark oak front doors, his house looked elegant enough to be the home of a governor. I was awed by the size of the entryway, the marble floors, and elaborate chandeliers. All of the furniture looked brand-new and expensive.

"C'mon," he said eagerly after we had entered. He took my hand and rushed me along past the large dining room, in which I glimpsed the longest table I had ever seen, dressed with place settings and silver dishes as if a gala evening was about to commence.

He brought me to what he called their media room. There was a television set so big it nearly rivaled some of the smaller-screen movie theaters.

"Dad's always competing with his friends when it comes to state-of-the-art equipment," he explained. "Wait until you hear the sound system."

He opened a dark mahogany wood closet to reveal a collection of movies that looked like it contained anything and everything ever made.

"Choose," he commanded.

I shook my head.

"I don't know where to begin."

"Whatever you want," he said. "Don't worry about the ratings either," he said, winking.

I glanced at him and then at the titles. I really didn't know which one to pick.

"You choose," I said.

"Okay. This is one of my favorites," he said. "Sit on the settee," he added, nodding toward it.

I sat and waited for him to get it started. Everything was on a remote, even the room's lights. He dimmed them and sat beside me. The movie began, and it was everything he had described. I did feel as if we were in a theater.

"Incredible, huh?"

"Yes," I said.

"We can even have popcorn, if you want."

"I'm still stuffed with pizza."

"Me, too. Want to drink something? Anything?" he said impishly.

"I'm fine," I said.

He nodded and we sat back to watch the movie. I felt his arm move around my shoulders and then his hand against my side, pulling me closer to him. His lips were on my cheek, soon moving up to kiss my hair.

"We're not going to see much of this movie if you do that," I said. When I turned to him, he was only an inch or so from me.

His response was to kiss me on the lips and hold me tighter.

"Pretend we're in an old drive-in movie," he whispered.

"I've never been in one," I said.

"Me neither, but we can pretend, can't we?"

"I don't know."

"I do," he said. He kissed me again, moving his lips down to my neck. "I really like you, Honey. No one makes me feel as comfortable and happy as you do."

I said nothing. His words, his warm touch, the power of his eyes were quickly sweeping away any tenseness I had. I felt myself soften in his arms and wanted to kiss him as hard and as passionately as he was kissing me. When his hand grazed my breast, I tightened.

"It's all right," he said. "If you like me as much as I like you, it's all right."

My heart was pounding. The tingle that traveled up and down my spine and swirled in around my heart was delightful, warm, welcome. His fingers went under my sweater and moved quickly up to my breast. When he touched me, he brought his lips down on mine harder. His tongue moved between my lips. We were sliding down on the leather settee and he was moving over me. He had lifted the edge of my bra cup and touched my naked breast. It seemed like thunder in my head, my blood was rushing so fast around my body.

"I think I love you, Honey. I can't imagine liking someone as much as I like you without it being love," he continued, whispering in my ear.

"Like the serpent whispered into Eve's ear," I heard Grandad say.

Chandler's right hand moved down behind my shoulder and under my sweater. His fingers and palm traveled like a hungry spider up to my bra clip, which he squeezed and undid so quickly, I barely had a chance to shake my head. My bra lifted and a moment later, his left hand was over my breast. I was breathing so hard and fast, I thought I would faint.

There were feelings being born everywhere along my legs and in the pit of my stomach, feelings I had tempted and taunted in dreams. My own rush of pleasure was sweeping over me like the wave I imagined myself caught in earlier. I could feel the great struggle going on inside me, the battle between the forces that wanted me to push him away and jump up and the forces that wanted me to soften, relax, fall back, and invite him to go further and further.

"You do love me, too, don't you, Honey? Don't you?"

he pleaded, lifting my sweater so he could bring his lips to my breasts.

I opened my eyes. I wanted to say yes. I wanted to speak, but I suddenly imagined Grandad standing there looking down at us, nodding. He extended his arm to put his Bible on Chandler's back, and I screamed.

Frightened by my cry, Chandler pulled himself away. The image of Grandad evaporated instantly, popping like a bubble.

"What's wrong?" Chandler asked.

I caught my breath and sat up.

"I'm sorry," I said. "I couldn't . . ."

Chandler slumped against the settee.

"Don't you like me enough, Honey?"

"Yes, I just . . . couldn't, Chandler."

"Why not?"

"I couldn't," I repeated and fixed my bra. "I'm sorry," I said.

"Me, too," he said, looking petulant and crabby. "We probably should have just gone to the movie theater."

"I said I was sorry, Chandler."

"When you wanted to come here, I thought you wanted to be with me."

"I do," I insisted.

"Right."

"I've never done this before," I confessed. He looked at me, and then at the floor. "I thought you knew that, too."

"I'm not exactly Don Juan myself," he said. "What I felt, what I hoped, was that when the right girl came along, a girl who thought I was the right guy," he added, turning back to me, "we'd trust each other enough to . . . to love each other."

I felt tears coming to my eyes.

"I trust you and I *want* to love you," I said. "But . . ."

"But?"

"You didn't just sit at your piano and start playing Mozart's Concerto in A Major, did you?"

He stared at me a moment.

"It's not something you need to practice to get right. At least, I don't think of it that way," he said.

"But it's not something to rush into, either. It's not practice. It's building a relationship, learning to care and care for each other until you both feel ready for all of it," I said. "Too many girls I know don't think it's anything special anymore. Am I wrong?"

"No," he said. He smiled. "Okay," he said. "I'm sorry."

I sat back, and we both turned to the movie once again.

But out of the corner of my eye, I looked to the doorway. I searched every shadow.

I was looking for Grandad.

9

—✦—

The Pond

Chandler and I enjoyed the remainder of the movie and then sat and talked for nearly an hour afterward. We had just started out when the front door opened and his parents came in, quite unaware that Chandler had brought anyone to their home. I knew that was true because they were arguing quite vehemently as they entered, his father complaining about his mother's ridiculous infatuation with the Ivers, who he said were perfect examples of the nouveau riche, people who had inherited money and had no class.

"This," he declared before either of them glanced our way, "is a perfect example of why clothes do *not* make the man. An oaf in a tuxedo is still an oaf, and I'm surprised that you, of all people, can't see that, Amanda."

"I am not infatuated with anyone. I'm merely . . . oh," Chandler's mother moaned, grimacing so emphatically she made her face look like a rubber mask, stretching her lips and widening her eyes when she saw the two of us standing there, listening to them.

She was otherwise an attractive woman, stately, her black hair perfectly cut and styled. She wore a thin wrap with fur cuffs and a collar, and diamond earrings hung in gold leaves glittered under the hallway chandelier's light. When she turned and her wrap opened, I saw the biggest diamond pendant I had ever seen in real life, lying softly just above her cleavage, prominently displayed in her deep V-neck satin gown.

Chandler's father was dressed in a tuxedo with a vibrantly red silk scarf over his shoulders. I guess dapper was the proper word for him. I saw the great resemblance between Chandler and him, especially around their eyes and their mouths. However, Chandler's nose was smaller and straighter, and I thought he had a stronger chin. They were about the same height.

"What's this?" he asked, a look of annoyance disrupting his face. It was as if Chandler had brought home a prostitute or something. At least, that was the way he made me feel when he fixed his critical eyes on me.

"Dad," Chandler said, not losing a bit of his cool, calm demeanor, "Mom, I'd like you to meet Honey Forman, the girl I told you about, the one who plays the violin and practices with me once a week," he added, obviously annoyed it was taking both of them so long to recall my name and who I was. "At Mr. Wengrow's house? Remember?"

"Oh," his mother said, jumping as if someone had touched her behind with one of Grandad's cattle prods. "Yes, of course." She scrunched her nose and wrinkled the area around her eyes as she peered at me. "You two weren't practicing your music now, were you?"

"I doubt that," his father said, giving her a look that practically shouted "stupid."

"Oh," his mother said again. "Then what . . ."

"I brought Honey here to see our new television system and watch a movie on it," Chandler explained.

"New television system?"

"He's talking about the DVD player, new wide-screen television set, and the surround sound system I recently had installed, Amanda," his father said.

"Oh." She looked very confused.

"I wonder why it doesn't surprise me that you've forgotten about it," his father said.

"Well, you know I don't watch very much television these days, Dalton."

"Right."

"We were just on our way out," Chandler said. "I'm taking Honey home."

"Forman. Right, yes. Your grandfather is Abraham Forman, the Forman farm," Chandler's father said, as if he was giving me the information for the first time. "It's one of the more successful family-run farms these days," he told Chandler's mother. "It's an immaculate property, a jewel in our community," he added. "The farmer is still a large part of the backbone of this country," he lectured.

"How nice," Chandler's mother said. "I'm sorry I can't stand here and chat, but I must get out of these clothes and relax, Chandler. We didn't have an enjoyable evening," she said, "and I'd just like to forget about it as quickly as I can. Nice to have met you . . ." She looked at Chandler. "I'm sorry, did you say her name was Honey or did you call her honey?"

"That's my name, Mrs. Maxwell," I said.

"Is it? How . . . different. Well, nice to have met you anyway," she said and walked toward the stairs.

Chandler moved quickly to open the front door for me. He and his father exchanged angry looks, and we started out.

"Good night, Mr. Maxwell," I said. "It was nice to meet you, too."

Chandler closed the door sharply behind us before his father could reply.

"Sorry about their being so stuffy," he said as we walked to his car.

"I guess they were just taken by surprise," I said.

He nodded, but after we started away, he said it wasn't just their being surprised.

"I wish I could blame it on that, but I'm afraid my parents are somewhat snobby. They both come from wealthy families and rarely have gone anywhere in their lives that wasn't first class. All their friends are just like them," he continued. "I'm like you, Honey. I need to get away, too. Especially from that," he tagged on.

"What are you looking for, Chandler?" I asked him, wondering what he meant by "like you."

How could I not wonder how he and I were alike? The worlds we came from were so vastly different. Most of the young people our age would and even did envy him for what he had already. I remembered Daddy's comments about people who were always looking beyond their own fields of achievement, their own accomplishments, yearning to have what someone else had. Was Chandler one of them? Would he ever be happy?

He was quiet for a long moment. Then he smiled to himself and turned to me.

"Remember that night after our first duet practice, when you told me if I understood how the piano plays me, I'd understand myself, and I countered by saying who says I don't understand myself?"

"Yes," I said.

"Well, I was just being a big shot, Honey. I don't know who I am. I think I'm on the bottom of the list when it comes to that. I mean, I should have no problem with identity. My parents put our name out there prominently. Everyone knows who I am but me.

"Parents take it for granted that because you have inherited their name and because you walk in the long, wide shadows they cast, you'll be just another example of who they are and what they are. My parents can't even begin to imagine me not being happy with the things that make them happy.

"Somehow, parents take it personal if you claim your own identity, set out to be different. They see it as a rejection of them, but it's not that. It's a search for your own self-meaning.

"That's what I have to discover and that's why I have to get away."

He grimaced.

"Sorry," he said. "I didn't mean to get so deep and lay all this heavy stuff on you."

"No, I'm glad you did."

"Really? Most girls would just think me very boring, I'm sure," he said.

"You're hardly that, Chandler."

He smiled.

"I am without you," he said.

He reached for my hand and I snuggled closer to him. We were silent, moving along, the headlights of his car plowing a path through the darkness for us, both of us wondering what really lay ahead.

He drove very slowly up our driveway, probably expecting Grandad to pop out at us from some dark shadow again. I was half-expecting something like that myself. To both our reliefs, there was no one around. It was quiet and dark. Uncle Simon's light was off and so were most of the lights in my house.

"I had a good time, Honey," Chandler said. "I hope you did, too," he added, a worried look in his eyes.

"I did," I said convincingly enough to bring a smile back to his face.

"I'll call you tomorrow, if that's all right."

"Yes, I'd like that," I said. He edged toward me and I met him halfway to kiss him good night. Then I got out, closed the car door softly, and ran into the house. There was just a small lamp on in the hallway. I tiptoed up the stairs. They creaked like tattletales, and when I reached the landing, Mommy stepped to her bedroom doorway.

"Have fun, Honey?" she asked. She was in her night-gown, her hair down around her shoulders.

"Yes."

"Good. Okay, sleep well. We have a big day on the farm tomorrow," she said to explain why they were all asleep already.

Besides our usual chores, there was the planting of the north field, and I knew that Daddy and Grandad had some repair work to do on the grain combine, the machine we used to harvest our corn in the fall.

"Good night, Mommy," I said and entered my room.

My mind was so heavily occupied with all that had happened on my date with Chandler that I didn't see what was on my bed until I actually had gone to the bath-

room, put on my nightgown, and reached for the blanket
to turn it back and crawl under.

There, prominently before me, was Grandad's old
Bible with a faded blue ribbon inserted in the pages to
mark a place. For a moment I stood there frozen, almost
too afraid to touch it. Grandad had once told me the story
of a sinful woman who, when she attended Communion
at her church, choked to death on a wafer.

"When a soiled soul confronts something holy, the
Lord's retribution is mighty and dreadful," he said.

I thought about calling Mommy to show her what he
had done, but I was afraid. What if something terrible
happened to her because I made her lift the Bible off my
bed? Was I a fool to believe in such things? Despite what
I thought of him and his ways, Grandad Forman was so
confident, so sure that he knew what God wanted of us.

To illustrate his confidence, he often pointed to his
success as a farmer.

"God rewards me for my devotion," he claimed.
"Everything I have, everything I do is dependent upon
nature, solidly in the palm of God's very hand. He could
wipe me out in an instant," he said, snapping his fingers
right before my eyes.

I felt my heart jump in my chest when he did that.

As a result of all that, whenever Grandad looked at
me, I would think God Himself was looking at me
through Grandad's eyes. Sometimes I fled from them,
avoided him, afraid that he could actually read my
thoughts and know I had dreamed wicked things. All the
days of my youth, he seemed to hover over me and
around me more than he did anyone else in our family.
Why? What did he know about me that I, myself, didn't
know? It used to terrify me and still did a little. Was there

something dark and evil inside me? Was I what Grandad Forman called, "prime feed for hungry Satan"?

Standing up to him once, Mommy recited Scripture in defiance of his dreadful threats and promises.

"Though I speak with the tongues of men and of angels, and have not charity, I am become as sounding brass, or a tinkling cymbal," she told him, backing him off.

Surely, she was right. Merciful God would not hurt me for anything I had done without knowing why it was sinful, I thought, and I picked up the Bible, intending to put it aside, but I couldn't help being drawn to the pages Grandad obviously had marked for me to read before I went to sleep.

He had marked First Corinthians, 5:11: *But now I have written unto you not to keep company, if any man that is called a brother be a fornicator, or covetous, or an idolater, or a railer or a drunkard, or an extortioner; with such a one, no, not to eat . . . put away from among yourselves that wicked person.*

What did he mean? Did he mean Chandler? Did he mean me, myself?

How dare he make such an accusation? He had never even met Chandler, how could he condemn us without knowing what was truly in our hearts?

I felt like heaving his Bible and his threats out the window, and actually walked toward it to do just that, but when I started to open the window, I stopped. I couldn't put the blame on the Good Book, and it was sacrilegious to treat it like some garbage. Feeling trapped, I grew furious, went to my desk, and ripped a sheet of paper from my notebook. Using a black Magic Marker so it would be large and prominent, I wrote one of Mommy's

favorite retorts: *Judge not that ye be not judged,* and then
I taped it to the cover of Grandad's old Bible.

I went to his room and placed it at the foot of his door
so it would be the first thing he saw when he rose in the
morning. I felt good about it, but I couldn't help trembling. Mommy was the one who stood up to him the best
of all of us, certainly not me.

But someday soon I'd like to know why I was his
favorite target for his hell and damnation speeches.
Why did he see the face of a sinner in me? What had I
ever done to give him such thoughts and fears? How
could he ever think such dreadfully disgusting thoughts
about Uncle Peter and me? It gnawed at my insides like
some ache that would never go away. I vowed I would
know the answers.

Yet, I was almost as afraid of the answers as I was of
the questions themselves.

Saturday was the long and difficult day it had
promised to be. By the time I rose and went down to
breakfast, Daddy and Grandad were long in the fields
with Uncle Simon. I looked at Mommy to see if Grandad
had said anything about his Bible and what I had taped
onto it. I expected he would rail about my defiance and
lack of remorse or something, but Mommy's talk was
only about how hard Daddy was going to work and how
she wished Grandad would agree to hire another man, at
least during planting and especially during harvesting.

"Simon does the work of two, maybe even three ordinary men, but your father hates to see him take on so
much and do so much of what is his. Your grandad is a
different story. The man feeds off his defiance and stubbornness. It fuels him and gives him the strength and

energy of a man half his age. Say what you will about
Abraham Forman, you have to give the devil his due,"
Mommy rattled on.

"I'll get out there and help," I said.

"You shouldn't be out there under this sun. Women
and girls your age work like that back from where I
came, but they quickly grew old beyond their years. I
don't like your hands getting too tough and hard. It will
hurt your violin playing, Honey."

I looked up with surprise. She had always admired
and encouraged my playing, but she didn't speak of it as
anything I would definitely do with my future.

"You really think that's important, Mommy?"

She paused in her work and turned to me, wiping her
hands on a dish towel.

"Your father and I have had a talk with Mr. Wengrow.
That man thinks a great deal of you and your talent. He
did from the start. I have a mother's pride, of course, but
he's a musician, a teacher, and he thinks you have what it
takes to make a life with your violin. He wants us to let
you try out for a school in New York City."

"I know," I said.

"Your father's worried about it, but I'm not."

"How come?" I asked.

She sat at the table and reached for my hand to hold.

"You are not much younger than I was when I set out
for America with Aunt Ethel," she said. "We arrived in
New York City first, and all the traffic and the people,
the tall buildings, hustle and bustle was frightening,
but," she said with a small smile on her lips, "exciting,
too. I had lived my whole life in a small country village.
I thought I had landed on another planet, and don't forget, our English was not so good then, but we had some

cousins who helped us and then we came here to Ohio to live.

"You have lived all your life in a rural world, too, but you have had the advantage of being in big cities and seeing what it's really like on television and in your movies. It won't be as strange to you, and you're a good girl, Honey. You'll always do the right thing, I'm sure. I'm not worried," she emphasized. "If it's right for you, you'll be right for it."

"I don't know if I am, Mommy. I don't know if I'm really as good as Mr. Wengrow thinks."

"Well, we'll find out," she said, patting my hand and rising. "What will be will be."

"Daddy agreed then?"

"Daddy agreed," she said. Her smile faded quickly. "Don't expect any encouragement from your grandfather. He'll be reciting prayers for the dead as soon as you set out."

"Why does he think so little of me, Mommy? Why does he *expect* me to be a sinner?" I asked her.

She shook her head.

"It's his way with everyone," she said and continued her work.

"No, it's not, Mommy. You know it's not. He's always been on me, lecturing, warning, trying to frighten me into being a good girl. Why?" I pursued.

"It's his way," she repeated, this time with her back to me.

I told her what he had done the night before with his Bible and what I had done in return. She listened, her eyes growing smaller and darker.

Then she nodded.

"I thought he was quieter this morning and had that

mad gleam in his eyes, like someone who had seen Satan himself stroll through the house."

"I'm afraid of him," I admitted.

She stared at me and nodded again.

"It's good that you'll leave this place," she said with such vehemence, I lost my breath for a moment.

"But why, Mommy? Why do you say it like that?"

"I just do."

"Why is Grandad so stern with me?"

"Because he's a sinner himself," she blurted.

"I don't understand, Mommy. How is he, of all people, a sinner? Because he won't go to church?"

"No."

"Then why, Mommy?"

"Leave it be, Honey. Go on, play your violin. Practice," she ordered and once again turned her back on me.

It left me cold, even colder than I had felt when I had seen Grandad's Bible on my bed.

Chandler phoned mid-afternoon and asked me if he could come by.

"I have something I want to give you," he said.

"What?"

"If I tell you, it won't be a surprise."

I laughed and told him to come. Then I told Mommy. Daddy, Uncle Simon, and Grandad were still out in the fields. I waited outside for Chandler, who arrived even sooner than I had anticipated. He stepped out of his car and handed me a gift-wrapped box.

"What is this? Why did you buy me something? It's not my birthday or anything," I said.

"I don't need a reason to buy you something," he

insisted. He looked so intense, so determined, I nodded.

"What is it?" I sat on the front steps and undid the ribbon, then tore away the paper and opened the box. There was a pile of sheet music within, all for the violin.

"Chandler, this is a lot. It must have cost a lot, too," I said, thumbing through the pieces. I estimated well over two hundred dollars worth.

"It's all Bartok," he said. "You've got An Evening in the Village, First and Second Sonata, First Rhapsody, Hungarian folk tunes, and Romanian folk dances. I was thinking about your audition and what you should prepare for it. I suggest the First Sonata and something from the Romanian folk dances. Anyone would get a good view of your ability from that."

"Thank you, Chandler," I said. "It's a wonderful gift and you brought it at the right time. My parents are going to let me try. Mr. Wengrow convinced them."

"I knew he would," Chandler said.

"Well, you knew more than I did." I embraced the box of music and stood up. "Thank you," I repeated and kissed him on the cheek.

Just as I did, Grandad, Daddy, and Uncle Simon came around the barn. My heart stopped and started. Daddy waved, but after a moment's hard stare, Grandad turned and went into the barn, with Uncle Simon trailing behind him.

"Come inside," I said. "I'll put this away and we'll go for a walk."

Chandler said hello to Mommy, who made conversation with him while I put away the gift of music. Then we left the house and I took him toward the pond.

"This is my favorite place here," I said. "I used to spend time with my uncle Peter here."

Chandler nodded, gazing around.

"Very peaceful, pretty."

"Sometimes I sit on the dock and dip my naked feet in the water. Minnows swim around my toes."

"Let's do it," Chandler said, and sat to take off his shoes and socks. I laughed and did the same.

"Wow, that's a lot colder than I expected," he cried when his feet hit the water. "I think my ankles are going to turn blue. How come it's not bothering you?"

"I guess I'm just used to it," I said with a shrug.

"All I've ever been in is a heated pool."

He closed his eyes to endure it, then finally surrendered and brought his feet out, curling his legs so he could rub his ankles. I laughed and helped, rubbing the chill out vigorously.

"You must have steel flowing through your veins to enjoy that," he said.

"Feeling better?"

"Yes, thanks."

"It's refreshing. It wakes you up," I said.

"I was awake, thank you!"

I brought my feet completely out and he rubbed mine, too.

"In some countries, we'd have to get married now," he said. "Touching someone's naked feet is very intimate."

We looked into each other's eyes, locked in the warm flow of our gazes. I knew he wanted to kiss me and I wanted him to kiss me. I spun around and lowered myself to his lap, the move taking him by delightful surprise. He laughed, moved to make me comfortable, and began to stroke my hair.

"You grew up in a very beautiful place, Honey. I'm jealous. I wish I had a place like this to run to when I

wanted to be by myself, instead of just closing my bedroom door or putting on my headphones and turning up
the music. It's all in you: the water, the fresh smell of
wild grass and wildflowers, the sunlight. It gives you
your glow, makes you blossom."

"Funny you say that. Uncle Simon thinks of me like
he does his precious flowers."

"He's right."

He touched my lips and I kissed the tip of his fingers.
He smiled, lowered my head gently from his thigh to the
floor of the dock and spread out beside me so we were
face to face. Then he kissed the tip of my nose.

"I might come to you someday," he said, "and remind
you I've touched your naked feet. Then I might ask you
to marry me, Honey."

"I don't know if I'll ever get married."

"Sure you will. If anyone might not, it's me," he said.
"I haven't had good examples. My parents aren't exactly
poster children for the institution. But," he continued,
running his finger down the side of my face and under
my chin, "with you, I'm sure it would be very different.
You're real.

"Although," he added, "sometimes I think you're too
good to be true and you really are just a dream. The only
way I'm sure is when I do this," he said, and leaned forward to kiss me.

I closed my eyes. I felt the warm breeze and smelled
the fresh water and the scent of wildflowers. I breathed
deeply, filling myself with such happiness and pleasure
as his lips lingered on mine, and then I opened my eyes
and gasped.

Grandad was standing over us, gazing down, his eyes
blazing, a machete in his hand.

For a second Chandler didn't realize Grandad was there and looked confused by my expression. Then he turned on his back, looked up at Grandad, and practically leaped to his feet in a single move.

"Sinners," Grandad accused, waving the machete at Chandler. "And on my land. You'll turn it into Sodom and Gomorrah, just as I was told you would," he fired at me. His eyes widened. "The prophecies, the prophecies!"

"We didn't do anything wrong, Mr. Forman," Chandler began to protest. "We were just . . ."

"Fornicator. Get thee away, Satan," Grandad ordered, raising the machete again. Chandler's eyes nearly popped. He backed up, looking confused and frightened. I got to my feet and scooped up our shoes and socks. I took his arm and marched him off the dock.

"Don't look back at him. Just keep walking," I said.

"He's crazy. Wow! He was going to kill me, I think. Would he swing that at me, really? Is he coming after us?"

"Just keep walking," I muttered, the tears choking my throat.

Grandad was shouting biblical phrases at us.

"I'm sorry, Chandler. I didn't think he would come sneaking around after us. I thought they were working on the grain combine."

"What's wrong with him?"

"He's afraid of going to hell," I said, gazing back. He looked like a mad prophet raging against the heavens, his arms lifted, that machete pointed in our direction.

"He should be locked up somewhere. He's dangerous."

Daddy and Uncle Simon had just parted and Daddy was stepping onto the porch when we appeared, hurrying from the path to the pond toward Chandler's car. Both he and Uncle Simon turned to watch us a moment.

"Why are you guys walking barefoot? Something wrong, Honey?" Daddy asked when we drew closer.

"Grandad," I said.

"What did he do?"

"He frightened us and accused us of things," I said. "And he waved his machete at Chandler."

"He did what?"

Daddy and Uncle Simon looked toward the pond.

"I'd better get going," Chandler said, reaching for his car door handle. He didn't pause to put on his shoes and socks first. "I'll call you. Or, maybe you call me when you can," he added. He looked absolutely terrified. I couldn't blame him.

"I'm sorry," I said. He nodded, started the engine, and drove off quickly, forgetting the bump again.

I looked up at Daddy.

"He's horrible," I cried. "I don't care if he is your father and my grandfather. He's just horrible. I hate him!" I shouted and ran up the steps, past Daddy and into the house, not looking back.

Inside, I burst into tears.

"Honey!" Mommy shouted after me as I charged up the stairs. "Why are you barefoot? What's wrong?"

"Grandad!" I cried. "I wish he was dead!"

Such was the mad old man's influence and effect on me all my life that I immediately regretted saying such a thing. I bit down on my lip so hard, I could taste the blood. If God was nearby, waiting to swoop down on me for being an evil person, He would surely do so now, I thought.

Shivering and wishing I could crawl inside myself

and hide, I threw myself on my bed, embraced myself, and closed my eyes, waiting for the sound of thunder even on a day like this.

All that followed was silence and the slow ticking down of my racing heart until I drifted into a welcome sleep.

10

—⁓—

Sins of the Father

When I awoke, I was greeted with a funereal silence. Mommy had let me sleep and it was well into the early evening. Through my window I could see the last vestiges of daylight were clinging to the horizon like the hands of a drowning person hoping to be pulled back up. The yellow shafts of thin light against the inky sky resembled fingers, reaching, searching for help.

I sat up, scrubbed my face with my dry hands and sighed so deeply, I thought I would crack my spine. I listened again for any sounds, but I didn't even hear the drone of the television set or anyone's footsteps or muffled voice. For an additional few moments I sat there, resurrecting the terrible moments at the pond. I saw Chandler's expression of terror and shock again and again. Surely, he would not want to have a thing to do with me now. He must believe I came from madness.

I rose and went downstairs slowly, still listening for someone. I found Mommy sitting on the front porch in her rocking chair. She had a knitted shawl wrapped around herself and her eyes were closed.

"Mommy?" I said, and she sat up.

"How are you, Honey? Hungry?"

"No. What's going on? Where's Daddy and Grandad?"

"Daddy and Grandad had a very bad argument after what happened," she began. "I thought they would come to blows. Actually, I thought Grandad would swing that machete at him. Your uncle Simon stepped between them and just stood there like a wall, and they stopped.

"It calmed down. They ate some dinner and then went out to work on the grain combine. That's where the two of them are. Simon went up to his room. He's got a bad cold, probably from having only cold water to bathe in and sleeping in that dank, dark place."

"Did he get his dinner?"

"I brought it to him," she said. "Why don't you have something to eat now, Honey?"

"I was so embarrassed, Mommy," I moaned. "Chandler will probably have nothing to do with me now."

"Oh, I'm sure he will," she said.

"You weren't there. It was terrible. I was never so frightened myself."

"I know. Let me make you something to eat," she insisted, rising. "At least some hot soup."

She put her arm around me and we went inside.

After I ate a little, I picked up my violin and began to play. More and more lately, I was finding it helped me express my innermost feelings. The music always revealed what was truly going on within the caverns of my heart. I didn't play that long, but when I gazed out my window, I saw Uncle Simon had been sitting by his, listening. He had a light on, and he looked different because his head was slumped. I supposed he had fallen asleep. I waited to see if he would wake and wave good night, but he didn't, so I put away my violin.

I was feeling very, very tired myself. The emotional drain was deeper than I had imagined. Maybe I was just very depressed, but almost before I let my head fall back on the pillow, my eyes closed, and the next thing I knew, the light of morning was brightening my room.

The house was quiet. When I glanced at my clock, I saw it was well after nine. We usually left for church between eight and eight-thirty. I rose, washed, and dressed as quickly as I could. When I descended the stairs, I found Mommy had left a note for me on the refrigerator door.

> *Daddy and I decided to let you sleep this morning. There's pancake batter in a bowl in the refrigerator. Eat a good breakfast. We'll see you after church.*

I wondered where Grandad was. I was certainly not in the mood for any of his hell and damnation speeches and had made up my mind that if he started on me and Chandler, I would either walk away or tell him to mind his own business. My indignation fueled my courage and fired up my anger. I marched around the kitchen, slamming pans and silverware harder than necessary. I needed noise. The silence made it feel as if the world was closing in on me.

I ate deliberately, chewing hard, swallowing and digging my fork into my pancakes as if I had to kill each one before I could eat it. All the while I had my eyes fixed on that doorway, anticipating my grandad's entrance, but he did not come. Winding down, I finished eating and washed and put away my dishes, the pancake skillet, and silverware. By the time everything was cleared away and cleaned, I heard Daddy's truck pull up in front of the house. I stepped out to greet them.

"Morning, Honey," Daddy called.

"Did you make yourself some breakfast, dear?" Mommy asked immediately.

"Yes," I said. "Sorry I slept so late."

"That's all right. We were glad you got whatever rest you needed, dear," Mommy said.

She looked very pretty and fresh this morning, and I thought Daddy was very handsome in his sports jacket, tie, and slacks. Mommy paused to kiss me on the forehead. Then her eyes got small and dark.

"He bother you any this morning?"

"I haven't seen or heard him."

"Grandad's up in the west field, probably," Daddy said. "There's a wooded place there he's used on Sunday as his private church for years."

I knew the place. Because Grandad Forman put such a holy stamp on it and because it was his private place, I stayed away from it.

"He's been troubling," Mommy told Daddy. "And I don't mean just the incident yesterday with Honey and Chandler, Isaac. There's a new madness in him. When he came at you yesterday, I thought he would swing that machete for sure," Mommy said. "He's mumbling to himself and talking to the shadows more than ever. It's not good."

Daddy nodded and gazed toward the west field.

"I know," he said. "He and I worked together as usual afterward, but he would barely speak to me and kept reciting phrases from the Bible. It gave me the creeps the way he turned his head when he spoke, as if some invisible person was there beside him."

"It's troublesome. Very troublesome, Isaac," Mommy emphasized.

"I'll try to talk to him some more and get him calmed down," Daddy promised. "He should be back soon."

"I haven't seen Uncle Simon this morning either," I said.

"Oh, Simon's still quite under the weather today, Honey. He's been developing a bad chest cold and I told him to make sure he rests himself well," Daddy said.

"Did he have his breakfast?"

"I brought him some hot oatmeal before we left for church," Mommy said. "Well, I guess I'll go change into something more ordinary."

"Me, too," Daddy said.

I looked at the barn. It was so rare for Uncle Simon to be under the weather and incapacitated. I thought he was invincible. If he was sick enough to stay in his claustrophobic room, it had to be serious.

"Maybe Uncle Simon should see a doctor and have some medicine," I said.

"You know how he is about that," Mommy replied. "I'll make him some chicken soup for lunch."

She and Daddy went inside. I stood there thinking awhile and then I went in and fetched my violin and the box of music Chandler had bought for me.

"I'm going over to see Uncle Simon," I shouted to Mommy and Daddy, who were still changing clothes.

I went to the barn and then up the stairway to Uncle

Simon's room. He didn't reply when I knocked on his door, so I opened it and peered in. He was in bed. I thought he was asleep, but as soon as I started to back out and close the door, his eyes opened.

"Honey," he said, followed with a flow of coughs. "Something the matter?"

"No, Uncle Simon. I was just coming over to practice my violin and see if you needed anything."

"Oh," he said. He wiped strands of hair off his forehead and propped himself up. He wasn't wearing any shirt, and there was a patch of redness at the center of his chest.

"Do you have a fever?" I asked him.

"No," he said, shaking his head vigorously. He coughed again.

"That doesn't sound good, Uncle Simon."

"It's nothing," he insisted.

"Mommy's making you some chicken soup, but if you don't feel better soon, you should go to a doctor," I said firmly.

He nodded, but with no real conviction.

"You're going to play the violin for me?" he asked, finally showing some light and excitement in his eyes.

"I wanted to start on some of the music my friend Chandler Maxwell gave me yesterday. I'm going to audition for a special school in New York City," I explained.

His eyes widened with amazement.

"New York City?"

"Uh-huh."

I took my violin out of its case and pulled one of his two chairs up closer to the bed. Then I sat, opened the box of music, and sifted through the sheets, deciding to start with Bartok's First Sonata.

"I'm just learning this," I explained.

He nodded, looking fascinated. It warmed my heart to see how I was cheering him up and helping him feel better already. He propped himself up a little more and waited. I tuned up and warmed up and then I started on the music. Every time I stopped to start again, he nodded enthusiastically.

"I really shouldn't do this without Mr. Wengrow. It's hard judging yourself."

I started again and I played for quite a while before stopping. When I glanced at him, I saw that he had closed his eyes. The music appeared to have soothed him, but his face was very flushed. I set the violin down, and he looked at me with some surprise.

"You look like you've got a high fever, Uncle Simon," I said.

I went to him and put my lips to his forehead. It was the way Mommy always tested for a fever.

I had barely done so when Grandad's cry made me jump and turn quickly toward the doorway where he stood, clutching his Bible. I hadn't heard him come up the stairs.

"Jezebel!" he screamed. "Get away from him."

"He's sick, Grandad."

Grandad nodded and smiled so coldly it sent a chill across the room and into my heart.

"Yes, he's sick," he said. "Sick with the strain of evil that's in you both. You'll bring down the Lord's vengeance on me! Whore!" he cried.

Tears flowed so quickly and freely from my eyes, I couldn't flick them away fast enough.

Suddenly Uncle Simon rose from his bed, and to my shock, he was naked. He waved his mallet of a fist at Grandad.

"Get out of here with your garbage talk," he roared. It felt like a crash of thunder.

Grandad stared wide-eyed, as if he was looking at the Angel of Death. He pointed at him.

"Sinner!" he shouted, turned, and fled.

Uncle Simon quickly realized he was uncovered and seized the blanket to wrap around himself.

"You better go," he said.

My heart was pounding a hole through my chest and back. I shivered and trembled, gathering my music, putting my violin back into its case.

"I'll tell Mommy what happened," I promised. "You didn't do anything wrong."

Uncle Simon was back under the blanket, his eyes shut, his thumb and fingers pressing on his temples.

"You need a doctor," I insisted and hurried out, never so frightened. I checked the yard for signs of Grandad and then rushed to the house.

Mommy was in the kitchen working on her chicken soup when I burst in. For a moment, I couldn't speak. She looked at me, saw how upset I was, and dropped the knife she was using to cut up a carrot. It clattered on the floor.

"What's wrong?"

"Grandad . . . Uncle Simon," I blurted. "It was a terrible scene!"

Daddy heard the commotion and hurried down the stairs.

"What happened?"

As quickly as I could get out the words, I described what had occurred, how just as I had innocently checked on Uncle Simon's temperature, Grandad appeared in the doorway and called me names. Without saying Uncle

Simon was naked, I told how he had jumped up and threatened to bash Grandad with his fist. I spoke so quickly, it turned my throat into a tunnel with sandpaper walls. Mommy had to give me a glass of water to finish

"Isaac," Mommy said. "It's come to pass. I feel it. I know it."

"I'll get out there," he said. He went for his boots.

"Be careful," she cried after him.

"What's come to pass?" I asked.

Mommy shook her head and sat hard on a chair, lowering her forehead to her propped hand.

"Mommy?"

She shook her head and sighed. Just as she lifted it to speak, we heard the most ghastly, animal scream. The look in Mommy's face matched my own terror.

"Isaac," she cried and the two of us ran out of the house.

The shouting was coming from the area behind the barn where Uncle Simon had his wonderful garden. Mommy reached for my hand as the two of us ran across the yard. When we turned the corner of the barn, we saw Uncle Simon. He was barefoot, wearing only jeans and holding a scythe in the air, poised to bring it down on Grandad, who was sprawled on the ground.

Flowers everywhere had been slashed with that scythe. The garden was decimated. Daddy was on the sidelines, his hand extended toward Uncle Simon, who stood like a pillar of rage over my grandfather.

"Don't do it, Simon," Daddy pleaded. "You can't do it."

Uncle Simon's arms shook with the effort to hold back and the effort to sweep down. There was no doubt in my mind that he had the power to slice Grandad in half.

"Simon!" Mommy shouted. She let go of my hand. "Isaac, tell him. Tell him!" she commanded Daddy. He looked at her, then at me, and then he stepped closer.

"Simon, he's your father," he said. "He's your real father."

Uncle Simon looked at Daddy and then down at Grandad, who had his arm extended up to try to ward off the deadly blow when it came. He clutched his Bible in his hand as if it would act as a shield.

Uncle Simon shook his head.

"Yes," Daddy said. "It's true, Simon. It's true. Tell him!" he shouted at Grandad.

To me it seemed as if the air had stopped moving around us and we were frozen in time. Nothing moved, not a bird, not a rabbit. The whole world was holding its breath.

Grandad shook his head.

"I don't confess to him," he cried. "I don't confess to him."

"Simon," Mommy said in a softer tone. "Isaac is telling you the truth. You can't do this. We'll make it all right. Please, Simon."

I was crying and shaking so much, I couldn't have spoken if I had wanted to. Uncle Simon gazed down at Grandad a moment and then he tossed away the scythe and marched toward his flowers, kneeling down to repair whatever he could.

Grandad Forman rose slowly. He looked from Daddy to Mommy to me and shook his head, backing away. He pointed at me.

"It's in the blood," he said. "My sins are carried in the blood."

"No!" Mommy shouted back at him. "Your sins were

born and will die with you, not with us. Go make your own peace and leave us be," she ordered.

He turned and stumbled away, clutching his chest with one hand, his Bible with the other. After a few steps, he paused to look back at us. He was mumbling to himself and looked insane, his hair flying up every which way.

"Go into the house, Dad," Daddy shouted at him.

Grandad shook his head and then walked faster, almost running toward the west field as if he had to flee. We saw him stumble and fall and then get up and hurry along, gazing back at us until he was nearly gone from sight.

"I'd better go after him," Daddy said.

"Leave him, Isaac. We've got to get Simon to bed," Mommy said, stepping toward him. She put her hand on Uncle Simon's shoulder. "Go back to bed, Simon. You need rest before you get very, very sick. Isaac and Honey will repair what can be repaired for you."

"She's right, Simon," Daddy said. "Go on back to bed."

Simon stared at his mutilated garden, two large tears flowing from his eyes.

"I'll fix whatever can be fixed, Uncle Simon," I promised, tears falling from my chin as well.

"You'll plant again, Simon," Mommy said. "Go on."

Daddy put his hand under Uncle Simon's arm, more to urge him up than to lift him. He rose, slowly, looking after Grandad, not so much with hate and anger in his face now as much as confusion.

"I won't let him be my father," he said.

Mommy smiled.

"I don't blame you," she said.

Uncle Simon shook his head. He looked at the

destroyed garden and then toward the direction Grandad
had fled.

"Can't be," he said. "Can't be."

He let Daddy guide him away.

"Wait," Mommy called after them. Daddy turned to
her. "Don't take him back to that barn. Take him to
Peter's room in the house," she ordered.

Daddy smiled and nodded.

"C'mon, Simon. It's time you came home," Daddy
told him.

Mommy put her arm around me. I had finally stopped
shaking and had swallowed down the lump that had
closed my throat. My tears felt frozen over my eyes.

"You all right, Honey?"

"Yes." I looked over the devastated garden. "I'll fix
whatever I can."

"Okay. I'll go finish making the soup and give him
something for his fever." She looked after Grandad
Forman. "If that lunatic comes back, come into the house
to tell me."

"You weren't telling the truth, Mommy, were you?
You made that up about Grandad being Uncle Simon's
real father just so he wouldn't hurt him, right?"

"No, Honey, it *is* the truth. Your grandmother Jennie
told your father about it years ago. Her sister Tessie and her
first husband worked for Grandad, and Grandad committed
a sinful act with her. She became pregnant, and soon after,
her husband was killed. He died never knowing, which was
a good thing, I suppose. Grandad then married Tess, but
Simon was a living reminder of his sin, so he treated him
badly and eventually, after Jennie's death, tried to keep him
out of his mind by moving him out of the house.

"After Jennie died, the sin was a heavier weight on his

conscience, I suppose. He believed God was punishing him again by taking her. He became even more crazed with his biblical visions.

"Her sister Jennie didn't want to marry him, but he forced her to by describing Tess as a seductress and making Jennie feel a responsibility to Simon. She was a good woman and she cared lovingly for Simon, Peter, and your father, but that didn't stop Grandad from seeing his demons in all of us."

"And so Grandad thought I would be a sinner because he had been? That's why he's always been all over me with his threats of hell and damnation?"

"Yes, but you must not let any of that affect you, Honey. It's his private madness and his own guilt that makes him think most of the crazy things he declares and does.

"For a long time, your daddy felt sorry for him. He tried always to be a dutiful son, to help him live with himself, to recover. He was too good a son, if you ask me."

"Did Uncle Peter know all this, too?"

"Not according to your father, no. Your grandmother never told him. He was different—a lighter spirit—and she didn't want to put any burden on him that would change him. He was her favorite, but Daddy didn't mind that. In a way, they were both protecting Peter."

"Poor Uncle Simon, though. Why was he tortured for his father's sins, left in the dark alone?"

Mommy smiled.

"I've always felt he was better off living without the knowledge and being estranged from your grandfather. In his way, I think Simon has found some contentment," she added, looking at the broken flowers.

"And now Grandad has even destroyed that," I said mournfully.

"It will be repaired, and if I know Simon, it will be better and bigger. Daddy is definitely going ahead with that greenhouse idea, too."

"Good."

"I better get inside and help with Simon. I'm sorry all this came out this way, Honey, but I never doubted that some day it would. It festered on your grandfather's soul and leaked poison into his heart for a long time. Maybe he can find some peace now as well."

I nodded.

"Don't ever think something is wrong with you or you have a strain of evil in you because of him. His sins live and die with him," Mommy assured me.

She kissed me, squeezed me to her, and then walked toward the house.

I turned to what looked like a battlefield and began to repair what little could be restored.

Maybe it was the effect of being in Uncle Peter's room. Uncle Simon had loved him so much. Or maybe it was Mommy's wonderful homemade soup. Maybe it was a good dose of aspirin, or maybe it was a combination of everything, but Uncle Simon relaxed, his face looked far less flushed, and he fell into a comfortable sleep very soon afterward.

"We'll move him back into the house permanently," Daddy vowed.

"I think if he still has a high fever, we should take him to see Dr. Spalding tomorrow," Mommy said.

"I'll try," Daddy told her. "He might not want to be blood-related to Dad, but he shares some of his stubbornness. That's for sure."

Mommy laughed.

Could we find a way to mend all this? I wondered. How I loved the both of them for their eternal optimism, for the way they bore down and gritted their teeth no matter what difficulties arose. I hoped and prayed I had their perseverance. I knew if I intended to go forward with a career in music and entertainment, I would surely need it. Rejection and defeats would be all over the road to any sort of success.

The day went on. I kept hoping to hear from Chandler, but he didn't call, and I wasn't up to calling him just yet. I had worked in the garden for nearly an hour, fixing what I could, and then I came in, showered, and joined Mommy and Daddy in the kitchen, where they were just getting ready to have a late lunch.

"It's been hours, Isaac," she told him. "I guess you'll have to see what's become of him."

Daddy nodded.

"Should I come with you, Daddy?" I asked him.

"No, it's not necessary," he said.

"Maybe she should, Isaac," Mommy said. The worry in his eyes made him reconsider.

"Okay, sure," he said. "He's probably still up in the west field."

"Hopefully, coming to his senses," Mommy said.

Daddy nodded, and he and I left.

"Was it true that Uncle Peter never knew any of this, Daddy?" I asked as we walked over the field.

"Sometimes I felt he did, that he knew instinctively. He never asked any questions or made any statements, and I never brought it up with him. Peter was Grandad's only window on happiness and light. I couldn't find it in my heart to close that window. You remember how Grandad would chastise him but do it relatively gently. I never saw him take a strap to him or ever strike him.

"I suppose Peter was some sort of salvation, some sort of redemption to him."

"But Daddy, Grandad accused me of doing sordid things with Uncle Peter."

"Only after Peter's death. Whatever hope or strain of kindness lingered in my father died with Peter that day, and of course, Grandad assumed it was God's way of imposing additional punishment. He blamed himself. He blamed you. He blamed us all. It's as though he believes we're all infected with the disease of his own sins.

"I know you hate him for what he did to Uncle Simon's garden and the things he's been saying to you, but you don't hate him half as much as he hates himself, Honey. Just remember that if you can, and maybe you can find some part of yourself that will forgive him and sympathize. It will make you feel better, believe me," Daddy said.

I nodded, my eyes filling as I realized, perhaps for the first time, how wise and kind he really was.

"I will, Daddy," I promised. "I will."

"I know you will, Honey. The one thing Grandad's failed to realize is you are his salvation. You are his redemption. You're the promise every rainbow leaves behind for us."

He embraced me and we walked like that until we saw the patch of forest ahead of us.

"I don't see him there," Daddy said, shading his eyes with his right hand.

I didn't either.

"Maybe he went home a different way, or maybe he went somewhere else."

"Maybe," he said, but his eyes continued to be narrow and suspicious as we continued toward the woods.

We were only about a hundred yards from it when Daddy stopped and seized my hand.

"What?" I asked and gazed ahead. Slowly, I could discern Grandad sprawled on his back.

"I see him. He's asleep. Let's not frighten him," Daddy said. We walked slowly, quietly.

"Dad," my daddy called softly. He raised his voice and called again.

Grandad Forman did not respond. I could see he had his Bible on his chest and both his hands over it.

"Dad!"

Daddy hurried into the patch of woods. I lingered a dozen feet back and watched as Daddy knelt down beside Grandad and shook him. Then he put his fingers on Grandad's neck and searched for a pulse. After a moment he lowered his head.

"Daddy?"

He lifted his head and looked at me.

"What's wrong with him?"

Daddy shook his head.

"Go back to the house, Honey, and tell Mommy your grandad's gone. He's found his peace."

11

~~~

Heart Song

Grandad Forman's funeral wasn't a big one. Most of the friends and acquaintances he had were either dead or too sick and weak to attend. Chandler's father attended, and Chandler accompanied him. His mother didn't. There were a few other business people there and some friends of Daddy's and Mommy's. I didn't think Uncle Simon would want to go, but he surprised me.

He also surprised Mommy and Daddy by agreeing to go see a doctor. Dr. Spalding put him on an antibiotic that had an almost immediate effect. His fever diminished and, although his cough lingered, it was far less severe, so he would have no problem attending the services. He had only one set of nice clothes. Mommy pressed his jacket and pants and Daddy found him a black tie to wear and tied it for him. Mommy even shined and polished Uncle Simon's one and only pair of dress shoes.

It was a simple church service, but it was Daddy's idea

that I add to it by playing my violin. As I played, I tried to remember only the good things about Grandad: the pride he took in his work and the success of the farm, his physical strength at his age, and the rare but precious moments when he looked softer, gazing almost lovingly at me.

I saw how proud and happy it made Mommy as I played, and when I looked at Chandler, I saw a glow in his face that warmed my cold, dark heart. I smiled inside and eagerly greeted him at the end of the service.

"I'm sorry I haven't called you," he told me. "I thought first that I might have had something to do with all this."

"You didn't and neither did I, Chandler."

"When are you coming back to school?"

"Tomorrow," I said, and then hurried to join Mommy, Daddy, and Uncle Simon for our trip to the cemetery. Grandad's first wife Tess was buried beside her first husband. Grandad was to be laid beside my grandmother Jennie.

"I'm not so sure she's happy about that," Mommy whispered.

We smiled secretly through our eyes, and we held hands while the final words were spoken over the coffin and Grandad was lowered into the earth from which he had made his living and did love. No one was more willing to become dust unto dust, I thought.

I joined Uncle Simon, who had gone to visit his mother's grave. He was just standing there, staring at the tombstone as if he could see her face in the granite. I knew that from time to time Daddy drove him here to plant flowers.

"She died before I could hear her speak. I don't remember her at all," he said mournfully.

"She's inside you, Uncle Simon. You carry her in your heart."

He nodded and took my hand. We stood there for a moment longer and then joined the others.

The four of us drove back to the farm in relative silence, all of us reliving our own memories and dealing in our own way with the reality that death to someone close to us brings.

I was so happy to return to school the following day. I couldn't get enough homework or be bored in any class. I bathed in the noise and the chatter in the hallways and cafeteria. I even welcomed the envy and green eyes of some of my classmates when they saw how closely Chandler and I kept to each other. Anyone could see there was something special going on by the way our eyes lingered on each other's faces.

My lessons with Mr. Wengrow became more intense. He was very pleased with the music Chandler had bought for me and agreed with the choices for my audition. I practiced obsessively. I looked forward to our joint lessons and I saw how Chandler made Mr. Wengrow concentrate far more on me than on him.

Almost nightly now I would play for Uncle Simon, Mommy, and Daddy in the living room. The music that had once been kept closed in to avoid Grandad's criticism and dire predictions of evil was set free, flowing through the house and over the grounds. As the weather improved and evenings became warmer, I would play outside at night. I would even bring my violin along and play while Daddy and Uncle Simon worked in the fields sometimes. My instrument and I were inseparable. Extra help was hired and they all looked at me and listened with amazement, hearing this kind of music while they worked.

"I wouldn't be surprised if she's sleeping with that violin beside her," Daddy kidded.

"It's not too far from me at any time," I said.

Chandler and I went out both Friday and Saturday nights now, and there were weekends when he visited with us and watched television and then took walks with me. We sat at the pond often. He claimed the water was warming and he could stand dipping his feet in as long as I could.

One night in late May, a particularly warm one, we decided to go swimming. It was an impulsive and exciting decision, because we were going to skinny-dip. I brought out two large towels for us, and under a moonless sky with many stars throwing down a silvery rain of light, we undressed with our backs to each other and then waded in and dove down, crying out in both pleasure and shock. We embraced and kissed, feeling our naked bodies touch in the water. He kissed my breasts and held me as we listened to the symphony around us: the peepers, the frogs, an owl inserting its inquisitive "Who? Who? Who?"

Afterward, wrapped in the towels, we held each other and kissed again. We came the closest to doing the most intimate act of love. Despite burying my childhood fears and driving the demons from our lives after Grandad's passing, I couldn't stop imagining his face glowing in the darkness, his eyes like the tips of candlelight, watching us.

I buried my face in Chandler's chest and made him stop. He held me tightly.

"Not yet," I said. "Not here."

"Okay. I love you, though, Honey. I don't want to do this with anyone else."

"Me neither," I admitted.

I knew that it would be wonderful, but I couldn't help being afraid that, once we did it, once the mystery and the longing was gone, we might lose interest in each other. Chandler continually promised that would never be, but I was afraid of promises. The sun always promised the flowers it would be there for them, but gray days came and so did long, hard rains, washing away the soil. A promise is just a hope, I thought, and a hope is a plan, a dream for the future. It needs much more to make it work, to make it grow. It needs the same tender loving care Uncle Simon gave his seedlings and his plants.

Were we ready to make such a commitment to each other? I wondered. *What would happen to us once we were separated by great distance?*

It made me hesitate, and hope that my hesitation wouldn't discourage Chandler too much and give him doubts about my love for him and his own love for me. Meanwhile, the music continued to bind us, to weave itself around and through us, sewing us together in ways other people couldn't even imagine. Sometimes, I had the feeling we were making love through our music, touching each other very intimately. Mr. Wengrow seemed to feel it, too, and often looked embarrassed by just being there between us, near us.

"I've given you both all that I have," he finally decided. "It's time for you to go out and grow with people far more equipped than I am."

He learned that there was just one more opening at the Senetsky School, and I would be competing with three other prime candidates for it. I was scheduled to audition early in the afternoon on the first Saturday in June. Daddy and Mommy were going to fly to New York with me the day before. I thought it would be a very expensive gamble, and then I wondered how we would pay for my tuition if I should be fortunate enough to be selected. Daddy surprised me with a revelation.

"Your grandad was truly one of the most successful farmers in Ohio, Honey. He wasn't exactly a miser, but he was pretty frugal, as you know. He didn't live or run this farm as if it was successful. He ran everything as if we were on the verge of bankruptcy.

"The truth is, I never knew exactly how much money he had, we had. He liked keeping me in the dark about it, I guess. After the funeral, we met with Mr. Ruderman, Grandad's accountant, and learned about the trust funds.

"The truth is," Daddy said, flashing a smile at Mommy, who was smiling already, "we're probably richer than your boyfriend's family. So don't worry about the money. Worry about the music!"

I did as he suggested, honing my skill with the violin. Getting into this school, winning approval from someone outside of my circle of family and friends had become paramount. It would truly give me the wings I needed to fly off and become whatever I was capable of becoming. The adventure, the risk, all the excitement filled my days and nights with tons of impatience.

Finally, the day came. We were packed and ready to drive to the airport. Just before we left, I went over to say good-bye to Uncle Simon. He was organizing his new flower beds, planning his nursery.

"We're ready to go," I announced. "I'm so nervous, I can barely walk."

He looked at me, and then he bent down and picked up what looked at first like just an ordinary washcloth.

"This is for you," he said, and I carefully opened the fold to see a tiny white carnation.

"It's a flower famous for bringing good luck," he said.

Uncle Simon knew all the symbolism for all his flowers. How Grandad could have ever believed him to be ignorant was beyond my understanding. It was what he had expected because of the sin, I thought, but how unfair and how untrue.

"Thank you, Uncle Simon. I'll keep it close to me," I said. "I'll press it between the pages of my music."

He smiled and I stood on my toes to kiss him good-bye.

He seized my hand unexpectedly as I turned to leave. I looked back at him.

"When you make your music," he said, "think of my flowers. Think you're playing for them."

"I will. Oh, I will, Uncle Simon. Forever."

I ran to join Mommy and Daddy and soon after we drove to the airport.

All three of us were like children entering a toy store when we landed in New York and were driven into the city. It was dark by then and the lights were overwhelming. It was one thing to see it in movies and on television, but a far different and deeper experience to actually be there, to be gazing up at skyscrapers, to see the bridges lit, to hear and see the traffic and the endless stream of people.

Our hotel suite was comfortable—and high enough up to give us a breathtaking view of Manhattan. We were all too excited to fall asleep and watched television almost until midnight. My appointment at the theater in which I was to audition wasn't until eleven. Daddy had planned it out so we would fly back on an early afternoon flight. I trembled, wondering if we would fly back with hope or defeat in our eyes.

We had breakfast and then the hotel doorman called us a taxi. None of us said very much. We sat and looked out the taxi windows, gaping at everything. Actually, I was looking through everything, not really seeing the people and the stores anymore. I was too nervous and afraid. My heart was pounding so hard, I was sure I wouldn't have the strength to lift the violin into position.

Mommy squeezed my hand and smiled confidence into me.

"You'll do your best, Honey," she said. "That's all you can do. After that, whatever is to be will be. When I came here as a young woman, I had to have faith in destiny. I had to believe that what was going to be was good. After you do all you can, there is nothing left but to watch and wait and accept. You must learn how to accept."

"To bend and not break," I repeated. It was one of Daddy's old sayings.

She nodded.

"Exactly."

We arrived at the theater and entered with almost as much curiosity as trepidation. It was an empty theater. There was no one in the lobby to greet us. For a few moments, we stood around. Daddy checked his watch.

"They did say eleven, right?"

"It's on this letter," Mommy emphasized, holding it up. He had read it a number of times anyway.

Suddenly a door to our right burst open and a tall, thin, dark-haired woman emerged, her heels clicking on the tile floor of the small lobby.

"Hello," she said. "You're Honey Forman, I assume?" she asked, holding a paper in her right hand. She had

large brown eyes and a sharp nose. Her lips were pencil-
thin and curled a bit up in the corners after she spoke.

"Yes," I said.

"We're running a little late. Just proceed to the stage.
There is a music stand on it for you. Start your pieces as
quickly as possible," she added.

"I'm Honey's mother and this is her father," Mommy
said pointedly.

The tall woman widened her eyes and nodded.

"Yes," she said. "I'm Laura Fairchild, Madam
Senetsky's personal assistant. Please," she added, mov-
ing to the door. She looked and acted more nervous than
I was.

Mommy looked at me, shrugged as if the woman was
beyond help, which brought a smile to my lips, and then
nodded for us to go forward.

The theater was pitch dark except for the wide spotlight on the stage, which bathed the music stand in
light. When our eyes got used to the dark seats, I could
make out someone sitting in the rear. It was a woman
with her hair pinned up, wearing something very dark
and sitting so still, I wondered if she was real or a
manikin.

Laura Fairchild gestured toward the stage.

"Please," she said. "We must get started."

Daddy and Mommy took seats and I hurried to the
stage. I opened my case and took out my violin and my
music. First, I set the music on the stand. My hands were
trembling so badly a sheet fell, and I watched it float to
the stage floor. I knew I looked amateurish and awkward
scooping it up and placing it on the stand, but I couldn't
help it. When I placed it there, I saw it had been the sheet
over Uncle Simon's little white carnation. The sight of it

had an amazing, calming effect on me. I felt myself relax, grow more confident.

After my warm-up, I took a deep breath, remembered all that Mr. Wengrow had emphasized about my posture and demeanor, and began. It was a slow start for me. I wasn't into it as well as I knew I could be. The setting, the rush-rush had chilled my enthusiasm. But suddenly, when I looked out at that dark theater, I envisioned Uncle Simon's flowers. The front row was filled with babies breath, birds of paradise sat beside pink and white carnations. Daisies looked over the heads of forget-me-nots, and on the aisles were blue, yellow, purple, and white irises. Jasmine was scattered throughout.

I could feel the smile spread over my face and fill my heart with joy. I played on, soon flowing into my music, feeling myself soar with the melody.

When I was finished, I couldn't believe how exhausted I felt. The effort had drained me of all my energy, it seemed. For a moment, I couldn't breathe.

"Thank you," I heard Laura Fairchild shout.

Immediately after that, I heard the doors to the theater open and close. Daddy was down at the foot of the stage to help me.

"That was wonderful, Honey," he said. "I never heard you play better."

"If she doesn't want you, she's a fool," Mommy declared before I could say a word of self-criticism.

I laughed to myself. How lucky I was to have parents like these, I thought.

Mommy was angry about the way we were treated. She complained almost all the way home, bringing it up repeatedly.

"Why couldn't the woman introduce herself properly? Why couldn't someone say something encouraging or even something discouraging, for that matter? What sort of a school is this anyway? I want to speak to Mr. Wengrow first chance I get," she said.

"Don't blame him for anything. He was only trying to help her," Daddy cautioned.

Mommy pressed her lips together and shook her head.

"New Yorkers," she muttered. "How rude. Maybe you shouldn't think of it anyway."

I understood she was simply trying to prepare me for a great disappointment. It was loving concern, like putting a bandage on before you even hurt yourself, but I didn't want to be one of those people who turned bitter and turned on their own dreams. I wouldn't be like the famous fox in the fox and the grapes fable, the one who couldn't reach the grapes and so declared them sour anyway.

There was nothing sour about having an opportunity in New York City. I would always dream of it, even if it was beyond my reach.

The days seemed to fall away quickly until graduation. All of my fellow students, including the ones who put on the biggest faces of bravado, bragging how far they were getting away from this "dull and boring place," suddenly started to look more like soldiers about to enter battle. Now their faces were full of anxiety, trepidation, and worry. The jokes, the songs, the pounding of the breast and defiance drifted out of our conversations.

The great clock was ticking. It would soon bong the hour when we would be cut away from the big boats that had protected and carried us so far. We would be out there, drifting on our own, making our own course, and either crashing on the rocks, into the obstacles, or sailing faster into the success that awaited us. Not knowing made cowards of us all, put the child back into our faces, the tension back into our eyes, lowered our voices, quickened our smiles, sped our tender hearts.

For Chandler and me, there was an added reality. Time wasn't just ticking on our childhood, it was ticking on our budding romance. He was scheduled to leave for an early orientation and had decided to start with some summer courses. Despite all of our urgent and firm pronouncements of love for each other, we couldn't help but wonder and be anxious about the days of separation, the great distances between us, the direction our new lives would take. It shadowed our every move, every word, every phone call, every embrace and kiss.

On the Thursday before graduation ceremonies, the phone rang just before noon. Mommy answered and called me with a cry that at first frightened me. What new terrible event had occurred? My first thought ran to Chandler and his family, but Mommy wasn't looking gloomy when I bounced down the stairs and turned to her and the phone.

"It's Mr. Wengrow," she said breathlessly. "You've been accepted. He wants to congratulate you."

She held the receiver toward me. For a moment I couldn't move. It was as if I was being handed the torch to carry for so many people, the torch to bring them out of the darkness and into the light Mommy had wished and prayed for so many times.

She shook it impatiently.

I lunged forward, took it, and brought it to my ear.

"Mr. Wengrow?"

"Congratulations, Honey. You beat out some of the country's best. Madame Senetsky was very impressed with you. I hope you understand what a wonderful opportunity this is. Well more than ninety percent of her graduates go on to successful careers and those who don't, don't because of some personal failing, not because of her schooling. You'll be receiving a packet of information in an overnight delivery. I'm very proud of you and proud to have been part of your success. Don't forget me when you become rich and famous," he kidded.

"Oh, I won't, Mr. Wengrow. Thank you. Thank you so much," I cried.

Tears were streaming down my face so hard, I could fill a dry well.

Mommy hugged me and then we went out and hurried to the west field to tell Daddy and Uncle Simon.

"We'll celebrate. All of us. We'll go to a fancy restaurant tonight!" Daddy cried. "We'll spend so much money, Grandad will spin in his grave. Twice!"

Uncle Simon laughed. They both hugged me and I hurried back to call Chandler. He came driving over soon afterward and we went to what had become our favorite place down by the pond.

"I'm very happy for you, Honey. I knew this would happen. I just knew it."

"I didn't. I thought I was not going to get it. They were so impersonal."

"That's the theater. That's the world you're going to be in. It's better if you don't make too much of an emotional investment in your every opportunity. Get used to disappointment, rejection, defeat, and turn your back on it so you can go on."

"You sound so wise sometimes, Chandler."

"I'm just used to disappointments in a different sort of way," he said.

"I hope you'll find what you want out there, Chandler."

"I will," he said. "I've already found it in you."

We kissed and held each other and looked out over the pond. Every once in a while a fish popped up or a frog splashed. The clouds in the distance spread themselves thinner and thinner, revealing more and more blue skies, more and more promise.

"You'll come to New York, won't you?"

"Sure," he said. "When you want me to come."

"I'll always want you to come to see me, Chandler."

He smiled.

"I hope so."

We walked back to the house, holding hands. Mommy invited him to dinner, but he said he had to go to some dinner with his parents. He thanked her.

"Sometimes, I feel so sorry for him," Mommy said afterward. "I hope he'll be happier."

"He will."

"Of course he will," Mommy assured me. "Remember," she whispered, "have faith in the future. Some people are so pessimistic, they miss the wonderful opportunities. They become blinded by their hardships, so blinded they miss their blessings."

"You never did, Mommy."

"The day you were born, I knew I never would," she said.

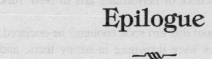

Epilogue

There was a different light on Graduation Day now. Gone was the sense of an end. It was replaced with a wonderful sense of a new beginning.

Uncle Simon brought a truckload of flowers over to decorate the stage, and the people who attended said it was the most beautifully adorned graduation they had ever seen at our high school.

The band teacher asked me to play a solo piece as part of the program, but I asked if I could do a duet with Chandler instead.

"If he'll do it," he said. He had long ago given up on Chandler doing anything at school performances. However, Chandler agreed, and we performed a Beethoven sonata. The applause was deafening.

When the principal handed us our diplomas, he announced what our future plans were to be. I saw how impressed everyone was when they learned I was going to a prestigious school of performing arts in New York City.

"We'll hear about this girl soon enough," he declared.

Mommy's eyes were drowning in happy tears, and Daddy and Uncle Simon looked like twins with their matching smiles of pride.

There were a number of parties afterward, one of the biggest and most elegant at Chandler's home. He and I made an appearance there and then left under the excuse of having to attend a few others. His parents didn't seem to mind. They were enjoying their friends. His mother soaked up her role as hostess.

"I thought I was going to suffocate in there," Chandler declared.

We laughed and drove off, but instead of going to another party, we returned to our favorite place on my farm. Chandler had brought a blanket along and we spread it out and lay beside each other, gazing up at the splash of stars.

"I always found it fascinating that people in the same hemisphere, thousands and thousands of miles apart from each other, could look up at the same stars," Chandler said. "You see that group twinkling there, the Seven Sisters?"

"Yes."

"Let's declare them ours tonight, and every time we can see them let's think of each other, forever and ever, no matter where you are or where I am."

"Okay."

"You're going to be a famous person someday, Honey. You're going to do wonderful things."

"What about you? You're just as talented, if not more so, Chandler."

"I don't know. I don't burn with it the way you do when you play. Not yet at least."

"You will."

"Maybe," he said smiling. He kissed me. "I do love you," he said. "I can't imagine falling in love with anyone else as deeply."

"I hope not," I said. "I didn't think you would want to love me. I thought you would become impatient and angry with me because I wanted to wait until . . . to wait before we . . ."

"I can't help loving you."

"I know it's different for boys. They don't want to be teased, disappointed."

"I'm not feeling teased, but I'm not saying I'm not anxious about it."

He smiled and ran his fingers down my neck and over my breast, bringing his lips to mine.

"There aren't many girls your age who would stop, who would want it to be so special," he whispered.

"Maybe it's because of the way I was brought up. Maybe I've got to break free of so many things first. Maybe I've got to stop seeing Grandad in the darkness, making me feel guilty. I can't help being afraid—not of going to hell, but of becoming like him, spending my life hurting people so I would feel less guilty about myself. Does that make any sense?"

"Yes," he said. "Tomorrow, you will start to leave it all behind. I believe in you, Honey, more than I believe in myself."

He put his arm around me so I could cradle my head against his shoulder and we looked up at the stars again. A cloud drifted along, blocking the Seven Sisters.

"Get off there," Chandler cried. "Go on with you."

The cloud moved away.

And we laughed and held each other and filled our hearts with the faith that we could always do that, always blow away the clouds that threatened our stars.

Visit

V.C. ANDREWS®

At the Simon & Schuster Web site:
www.SimonSays.com/vcandrews

*Read excerpts, find a listing of all titles,
and learn more about the author!*

Pocket Books

2702-01